Happy

J.

RESCUING ANGIE

Guardian Hostage Rescue Specialists: BRAVO Team

ELLIE MASTERS

JEM Publishing

Editor: Erin Toland

Proofreader: Roxane Leblanc

Published in the United States of America

JEM Publishing

ISBN: 978-1-952625-39-8

Dedication

This book is dedicated to my one and only—my amazing and wonderful husband.

Without your care and support, my writing would not have made it this far.

You pushed me when I needed to be pushed.

You supported me when I felt discouraged.

You believed in me when I didn't believe in myself.

If it weren't for you, this book never would have come to life.

Also by Ellie Masters

The LIGHTER SIDE

Ellie Masters is the lighter side of the Jet & Ellie Masters writing duo! You will find Contemporary Romance, Military Romance, Romantic Suspense, Billionaire Romance, and Rock Star Romance in Ellie's Works.

YOU CAN FIND ELLIE'S BOOKS HERE:

ELLIEMASTERS.COM/BOOKS

Military Romance

Guardian Hostage Rescue Specialists

Rescuing Melissa

(Get a FREE copy of Rescuing Melissa

when you join Ellie's Newsletter)

Alpha Team

Rescuing Zoe

Rescuing Moira

Rescuing Eve

Rescuing Lily

Rescuing Jinx

Rescuing Maria

Bravo Team

Rescuing Angie

Rescuing Isabelle

Military Romance

Guardian Personal Protection Specialists

Sybil's Protector

The One I Want Series

(Small Town, Military Heroes)

By Jet & Ellie Masters

EACH BOOK IN THIS SERIES CAN BE READ AS A STANDALONE AND IS ABOUT A DIFFERENT COUPLE WITH AN HEA.

Saving Ariel

Saving Brie

Saving Cate

Saving Dani

Saving Jen

Saving Abby

Rockstar Romance

The Angel Fire Rock Romance Series

EACH BOOK IN THIS SERIES CAN BE READ AS A STANDALONE AND IS ABOUT A DIFFERENT COUPLE WITH AN HEA. IT IS RECOMMENDED THEY ARE READ IN ORDER.

Ashes to New (prequel)

Heart's Insanity (book 1)

Heart's Desire (book 2)

Heart's Collide (book 3)

Hearts Divided (book 4)

Hearts Entwined (book5)

Forest's FALL (book 6)

Hearts The Last Beat (book7)

Contemporary Romance

Firestorm

(Kristy Bromberg's Everyday Heroes World)

Billionaire Romance
Billionaire Boys Club

Hawke

Richard

Brody

Contemporary Romance

Cocky Captain

(Vi Keeland & Penelope Ward's Cocky Hero World)

Romantic Suspense

EACH BOOK IS A STANDALONE NOVEL.

The Starling

~AND~

Science Fiction

Ellie Masters writing as L.A. Warren
Vendel Rising: a Science Fiction Serialized Novel

To My Readers

This book is a work of fiction. It does not exist in the real world and should not be construed as reality. As in most romantic fiction, I've taken liberties. I've compressed the romance into a sliver of time. I've allowed these characters to develop strong bonds of trust over a matter of days.

This does not happen in real life where you, my amazing readers, live. Take more time in your romance and learn who you're giving a piece of your heart to. I urge you to move with caution. Always protect yourself.

ONE

Angie

THREE YEARS AGO

ALL THAT'S LEFT IS AN ACHING EMPTINESS.

The hospital staff line the long hallway leading from my husband's bed in the surgical intensive care unit all the way to the OR, where a team of doctors waits to perform one last operation. The nurses, respiratory technicians, and other medical staff stand shoulder to shoulder, hands clasped, heads bowed.

Even family members of other patients, who somehow know what's happening and want to show their respect, are present. They line the hall, along with the hospital staff, and look at me with somber expressions.

Some shed tears. Not for me. They do so for a man they never knew.

I have to swallow the lump filling my throat. To me, Luke *was* everything.

Without him, I'm nothing.

I know what they see when they look at me.

They wonder if I'm okay.

They praise me for the sacrifice I make.

They secretly give thanks they are not me, that this tragedy befell someone else.

Many don't look me in the eye. Their heads bow, either in prayer, respect, or both. Those with the strength to look at me aren't ashamed of their tears.

This isn't the first time they've lined this hall, and it won't be the last. They stand as witnesses to an ultimate act of heroism as a patient gives their precious gift of life to another.

They honor my husband.

A soft smile touches the corners of my lips. Not enough to lift them, but enough to bring back my last happy moment with Luke.

LESS THAN 24 HOURS AGO, WE HELD HANDS, NERVOUS AND EAGER, AS we drove to our OB for the ultrasound that would tell us if we were having a boy or a girl. We pulled up at a red light and waited patiently for it to turn green as excitement bubbled up between us.

"Are you nervous?" Luke's fingers brush over my wedding band. His feather-light touch means the world to me and says so much with no words.

"Are you?"

"I'm terrified, but excited. Is that weird?" His eyes shimmer with a touch of bronze today.

I love his eyes. So expressive. So exquisite. Perfect in so many ways. I especially love the way he looks at me, like I'm his everything.

"Not at all."

"What are you hoping for?" His bright hazel eyes, nearly the identical shade as mine, spark with joy. "A girl or a boy?"

"I want a healthy girl or boy. The sex doesn't matter."

I see both in my life; a son and a daughter would make our family complete.

"Come on. Are you saying you're not hoping it's a girl like you? A sweet girl who I get to spoil and you get to teach how to rule the world?" His soft chuckle makes my heart turn to mush.

"I don't know about ruling the world, but you don't get to spoil our child. I will not be the bad cop all the time."

"Fine. We'll take turns spoiling her rotten."

"Don't you want a boy? Someone you can wrestle with and teach how to throw a ball? Do all the filthy boy things, like fishing?"

"You think I wouldn't do that with my daughter?"

"I think you're going to be the best daddy in the world to either our daughter or our son."

My fingers curl around his, twining together until we hold hands.

The light turns green, and Luke eases us out into the intersection.

"And you're going to be the best m …"

Tires screech. Something massive slams into our vehicle.

There's a loud *bang* and an explosive *pop*. An acrid smell fills the car.

Smoke billows all around me. Metal groans as it twists and bends.

Blinding pain follows.

The airbags deploy, smashing my face and breaking my nose. The seatbelt saves my life, but cuts the side of my neck, bruises my chest, and injures my pregnant belly.

But that isn't the worst of it.

A shard of steel punctures my midsection.

Luke hits his head when the airbag deploys, and the steering wheel smashes into his chest.

"Luke?" My heart leaps. "Luke!"

He struggles to breathe and doesn't answer.

Luke stretches out his hand. The tips of our fingers barely touch.

He can't speak. He can't breathe, but I feel his words down to the bottom of my soul.

Once the EMTs arrive, everything becomes a blur. Luke's loaded onto a stretcher and into an ambulance while paramedics pump on his chest.

I'm trapped, and they can't get me out until the fire department arrives with the jaws of life. They extricate me as sticky wetness pools in my lap.

I lost a lot of blood. I'm losing more.

And the pain.

The pain brings me to the brink of blacking out, but I desperately claw my way out of that blackness. Maybe it would be easier to let go, but I need to know what's happening to Luke.

As I lay on the stretcher, every jolt, every bump, and every jarring motion brings me to tears.

But I don't care about myself.

I don't remember the next few hours.

They bring me to the emergency department, barely conscious, then take me back for x-rays and other scans. I'm whisked off to the operating suite.

WHEN I WAKE, MY NURSE CALLS THE DOCTOR IN TO SPEAK WITH ME.

"Mrs. Maddox, I'm Dr. Stifle. How do you feel?"

"Groggy." I try to sit, but a sharp pain pulls me up short. "What happened?"

"You were in a car crash."

"Where's my husband?"

"He's still in surgery."

My hand drifts to my stomach and stops at the bandages.

"My baby?"

His brows tug together. "I'm so very sorry. Your son didn't make it."

We were going to have a son. A strangled sound rips out of my throat, but Dr. Stifle continues.

"You were losing a lot of blood." He pauses. "We couldn't control the bleeding. I'm so very sorry, but we had no choice but to remove your uterus."

The hits keep coming. Tears stream down my face as gut-wrenching grief rips me apart from the inside out. I lost not only my unborn son but all the siblings who might have followed.

Dr. Stifle stays with me while I fall apart.

"Where's my husband? Where's Luke?" I need my husband.

He's my rock. My pillar of strength. I can get through anything with him by my side.

"He's still in surgery …"

That's right. I already asked.

"I'll send someone to update you when we know more. In the meantime, you're stable enough to move to the surgical floor."

"Thank you." My reply is wooden, disconnected from my emotions. Those pour through me with ravenous fear.

The staff moves me from the Post Anesthesia Care Unit to the surgical floor, where I wait for news about Luke.

No news comes for a very long time, which leaves me to deal with my grief over our unborn child alone.

———

THERE'S A KNOCK ON THE DOOR. DOCTORS COME IN, AND FROM THE expressions on their faces, they're going to change my life forever.

"Mrs. Maddox, I'm Dr. Pope. Do you mind if we talk?"

"Do you have news about my husband?" My fingers claw at the scratchy hospital sheets and my heart races.

He doesn't need to say a word.

I know.

Dr. Pope clears his throat and tugs at his tie. "I'm very sorry. Your husband went into cardiopulmonary arrest at the scene. The paramedics performed CPR, but they didn't get a heartbeat until well after twenty minutes. His injuries are extensive."

Are—that word means everything. Luke's still alive, but things don't look good.

I'm a doctor myself.

I've delivered bad news like this before. It never gets easier. Dr. Pope is doing his best, but there's no reason for him to explain.

The CPR went on for too long. Starved of oxygen, Luke suffered irreversible brain damage.

"He's on a ventilator. His heart is beating."

"But his brain …" I look at him, not wanting the words to be true, but they are. I see the truth of it in Dr. Pope's expression.

"I'm incredibly sorry. We did the best we could, but …"

"He's brain dead?"

"We can't officially call brain death yet, but yes. I'm so very sorry."

Brain dead.

They don't have to explain what that means. I know about brain death. I know the outcome.

"My husband is an organ donor." Somehow, I force the words out.

I feel nothing.

I can't.

I don't want to *feel* anything.

I pack my emotions into a tight little ball and shove them into a dark corner inside my head. I'll deal with them later. Right now, my rational, scientific brain takes over.

"Luke would want …" A lump forms in my throat, making swallowing difficult.

"We saw on his driver's license that he's an organ donor, but we wanted to confirm …"

"If there's nothing you can do for him, Luke wants to save another person's life."

Tears stream down my cheeks and my throat closes up. My emotions break through the barriers I set up. I try my hardest to hold it together, but I'm moments from falling apart.

"We wanted to confirm with you before we …"

"When?"

"Excuse me?"

"When do you need to harvest his organs? How long …" I fight to swallow. My mouth is dry. "How long will it take to arrange for the …"

Finishing that sentence is impossible.

"Is there anyone you want to call?" Dr. Pope reaches for my hand, but I draw back.

The last person to touch my hand was Luke, and I can't stand for anyone else to touch me lest they erase that memory.

"Mrs. Maddox? Can we call anyone for you? Family?"

I have no family.

My only family was Luke and the unborn child we lost.

"His parents."

I'm not close to his parents. They disapproved of our whirlwind romance and hate that we eloped. His mother blames me for stealing her son. I figured time would heal that wound and it would be something we laughed about years from now. I suppose that will never happen.

"Do you have their number?"

"It's on my phone, but I don't know where any of my personal effects might be. I'm sorry."

"That's okay. If you have their names? Where they live?" He pauses while I try to retrieve the data from my concussed brain. Nothing works like it should.

"I'm sorry, but my memory …"

"Short-term memory loss, and even memory retrieval, are often affected by concussion. It'll come back to you. Would you like to speak to a chaplain?"

I'm not a religious person. Never have been. It's yet another point of contention between me and my in-laws.

"Maybe later." For now, all I want is to grieve.

The doctor says there's no rush, that I can take as long as I need, but that isn't true.

Hours later, the people from Angels of Hope identify a heart recipient who's losing their battle and needs a transplant as soon as possible.

This will be one more thorn that comes between me and Luke's mom. She'll think I gave up and robbed her of seeing her son one last time, but Luke wants this.

"Mrs. Maddox, it's time." My nurse, Paul, comes into my room pushing a wheelchair.

"I'm not ready." I swipe at the tears on my cheek.

"We're never ready for something like this. Let's get you transferred to the wheelchair and over to see your husband."

Paul assists me into the wheelchair.

The surgeons from Angels of Hope are ready. They prepped the recipient for a heart transplant.

Everyone is waiting for me to give the final okay.

When I arrive at the intensive care unit, I don't recognize Luke. Grossly disfigured, his face has so many contusions and lacerations. The swelling obliterates his features.

An endotracheal tube connects him to a ventilator. The EKG leads on his chest transmit to the monitor, showing a slow but steady heartbeat. I grip the arms of my wheelchair and pray.

I pray for strength.

I pray for Luke.

I pray for the nameless stranger who will wake up with my husband's heart beating inside their chest.

Luke was my rock and my number one supporter as I chased my dreams to become a doctor. In so many ways, he is my hero.

Now, he'll make the ultimate sacrifice so that another person can live.

I'd give anything—sell my soul if I could—if only to have one more minute with him.

"We'll give you a few minutes." Paul places my wheelchair as close to the bed as he can. A kind and gentle man, he does his best to make me comfortable.

"But the operation …"

"It can wait. Say goodbye to your husband, Angie. We can wait."

Left alone with my husband, I reach out to touch his hand. My last memory of Luke is of him twisting my wedding band around my finger.

He still has his ring.

I press the back of his hand to my forehead. I pray, and I cry. I curse the driver of the vehicle that ran into ours.

I don't know how long I sit there, sobbing and holding his hand, but at some point, I twist off his wedding band and slip it onto my necklace.

I say my goodbyes.

"I'M SORRY, BUT THE DOCTORS ..." PAUL RETURNS.

"It's okay." I place my hand over my chest, over Luke's wedding band. "I'm ready."

Paul pushes me out of Luke's room while his doctors and nurses complete the final prep. They transfer him from the ventilator at his bedside to a transport vent. They do the same with his monitor leads.

It's hard to let go when his heart still beats, but Luke's no longer with us.

They tuck in his blankets, kick off the brakes on the bed, and push him out of his room, then down the long hall. Paul folds in right behind them, pushing me along.

I follow my husband in a macabre procession down that long hall while hospital personnel stand as witnesses and give their last respects to a hero.

A WEEK LATER, I'M DISCHARGED FROM THE HOSPITAL WITH ONLY HIS ring as a reminder of what happened. They hold his funeral the following day.

To my surprise, Luke's mom doesn't berate me for deciding to proceed with the organ harvest. She hugs me tight and holds on longer than she's ever done before.

"How are you holding up?" Dressed in black with a lacy black veil, she dabs a linen handkerchief to the corner of her eye.

"I'm on autopilot." She gave me a black dress for the funeral. I can't wait to rip it off. "I just want to get this over."

"I understand, sweetie, but this is important. You said goodbye to Luke a week ago, but they did not."

I wanted a small funeral.

Actually, I didn't want one at all, but Luke's mom insisted. The number of RSVPs surprised me, and my small funeral turned into a funeral with full military honors.

I shouldn't be surprised. Luke's military family loved him.

His squadron and the base chaplain's office handled all the arrangements. All I have to do is arrive. Luke's mother makes that happen.

She stands beside me as an honor guard carries Luke's casket draped in an American flag. The chaplain speaks, saying words I don't hear, then a man steps forward to play Taps on a bugle.

A 21-gun salute rings out.

That sound will haunt me.

Tears run down my cheeks as the music plays, then everything goes silent. The chaplain steps forward again as two service members perform the flag folding ceremony. As the honor guard folds the flag, the chaplain explains the significance.

"The flag folds thirteen times, representing the thirteen original colonies. The folded flag symbolizes the tricorn hat worn by the patriots of the American Revolution. When folded, no red or white stripe is visible, leaving only a field of blue stars."

One of the servicemen approaches me for the presentation. I hold back my tears, or try, as he presents the flag and speaks.

"On behalf of the President of the United States, the United States Air Force, and a grateful nation, please accept this flag as a symbol of our appreciation for your loved one's honorable and faithful service." He leans toward me and solemnly presents the flag.

I take it from him and clutch it tight to my chest. Screw holding back my tears. I let them fall, not caring about what others think. Luke's mother was wrong about one thing.

I never said goodbye to Luke. I don't think I ever will.

Two men step forward from the crowd and march up to the casket. The first man places something shiny on the black lacquer, then slams it into the wood with his fist. The other man does the same.

A sob escapes me because I know what that means. To nail their

Navy tridents into Luke's casket is the ultimate sign of respect. The men say nothing, then step back into the crowd.

The rest of the ceremony passes in a blur. People come up and pay their respects. Slowly, the crowd, of well over a hundred, departs except for the two Navy SEALs. They wait until everyone's gone, then approach.

"Mrs. Maddox, we're sorry for your loss." They stand together, shoulder to shoulder, towering over my diminutive height.

"Thank you for coming." I clutch Luke's flag to my chest and wait for them to leave. When they don't, I take a second look. "And thank you for that." I look at the coffin and the two tridents nailed into it.

Luke was the trauma surgeon on one of the Air Force's Special Ops Surgical Teams, so it's likely he ran into men like them.

"Your husband is the only reason we're alive today," the same man speaks.

"Excuse me?"

"He was the SOST surgeon who saved my SEAL team several years ago." The man is about my age, handsome and muscular, like all SEALs. His golden eyes shimmer in the late afternoon sun. "He performed field surgery on my men, saved one's leg from amputation. I owe him a great debt."

"I don't know what I would've done if not for Major Maddox." The other man stands stiffly at attention. "He inserted a chest tube and saved my life. He's a hero."

The man with the golden eyes has a deep, melodious voice that I find comforting. "I wouldn't be here if not for him. He saved two others that day; removed shrapnel from one and stopped a hemorrhage in the other. I don't know how much you know about what your husband did, but to us, he's a hero." The man with the golden eyes pulls out a trident and holds it out to me. "If you ever need anything, just call."

"Thank you, but I can't accept that."

"Not asking if you want it. I'm giving it with a promise. You need anything, you call."

"But I don't even know your name."

"Name's Brady, Brady Malone."

His smile is a thing of beauty. The way it lights up his face is nothing short of brilliant, and those eyes of his are lady-killers.

I'm sure there's a trail of broken hearts littering his past. Some woman, somewhere, is going to be incredibly lucky when she catches this man.

"Thank you." I take the trident and cup it in my hand. "That means the world to me."

"Our deepest condolences, Mrs. Maddox."

The men bow their heads, take one step back, then pivot smartly as one. They march away, leaving me clutching Luke's flag and holding an incredible gift.

As soon as I'm alone, I'll affix the trident to my husband's flag. There may be some tradition I break by doing so, but that's where the honor belongs.

I lost my husband, my unborn child, and any chance for another.

I'm widowed and barren.

But I can proudly say that Luke was a hero.

Now, I begin the tough part: learning to learn to live without him.

TWO

Brady

ONE YEAR AGO

"Bravo One to Overlord. In position." The radio squawks in my ear.

I crouch behind thick vegetation on the outskirts of the bustling port in Cancun. Intel says one of the shipping containers out there contains a dozen girls, young women, who are bound for Colombia and a fate worse than death.

Bravo Team's job is to locate that container and rescue those girls. We're in position and merely hold for Mitzy's technical team to locate the container holding the girls.

They'll do that using *Smaug*, a large drone loaded with specialized tech, like heat sensors. It makes another pass overhead, scanning for the girls.

"Copy that," CJ answers from Command and Control. *"Smaug in position. Scanning."*

"Good copy." I glance back at my team.

Decked out in the best gear on the planet, we're a formidable force. Bravo Two, my best buddy, Booker, squats behind me, while Rafe and Hayes reference a schematic of the shipyard.

Once we know which cargo container holds the girls, they'll determine our path through the maze of containers.

Bravo Five and Six, Alec and Zeb, hold the rear.

"Overlord to Bravo One, target identified," CJ rattles off-grid coordinates that Rafe and Hayes copy down.

"Good copy." I turn around. "Bravo Three, we set?"

"Affirmative." Rafe gives me a thumbs-up.

"Status of patrols?" My comment is for Overlord.

Cancun's port is busy, but they shut down at night, unlike many other ports around the globe. In those places, massive floodlights push back the darkness, turning night into day. Here in Cancun, there are shadows upon shadows.

Dressed in our black tactical gear and equipped with night-vision goggles, we fade into the pervasive darkness.

"None in your vicinity," CJ reports back what I already know, confirming our approach is clear.

During recon, we discovered security at the port is minimal. It's a joke, to be honest. They focus only on the entrances and exits.

We arrived from the water, infiltrating the port after securing our black RIBs to pylons under the docks. We brought three six-man RIBs, splitting our team into pairs, as they will be our transport out.

"It's quiet." Booker taps me on the shoulder.

"You got a concern, Bravo Two?" I rely on my team and always listen to what they have to say.

"Feels off, that's all."

"How?"

"Dunno. Like I said, it's quiet." Booker doesn't explain more than that.

I get his concern. The shipyard should buzz with activity. Tomorrow, they will load all these containers onto a ship and begin their journey to Colombia.

"I need more than that."

Scanning what I see of the shipyard, there are no guards milling about, no dockworkers making last-minute adjustments to the containers, and there's nothing but the wind blowing in my ear.

"That's all I got." Booker glances around.

"It's not enough to call the op."

If we call it, they will load those girls on the cargo container ship.

We have another window to attempt recovery, but sea operations are far more complex than dealing with this on the ground.

"*Status?*" CJ's voice crackles through the comms.

I glance at Rafe, who gives me the thumbs-up.

"We've got a route. Sending now," I report back, and as I do, Rafe uploads the path we'll take to the designated container.

"*Copy that.*" There's a slight pause, then the radio squawks again. "*Received.*"

"Bravo Two says it's too quiet. Any concerns on your end?" Even though Booker can't vocalize what he feels, I respect his instincts. Lord knows they've saved our asses before.

"*Not from our end,*" CJ replies. "*We'll do another sweep to be sure.*"

"Good copy." Hopefully, that will satisfy Booker.

We wait in silence while *Smaug* makes another sweep of the docks.

"*Bravo One, all's quiet on our end. Your call.*"

Booker shrugs.

"We're going in." I glance at Rafe. He gives me a thumbs-up and packs up his gear.

I give the signal to move out.

Falling into line, we move as we train: silent and deadly.

All of us are former US Navy SEALs, recruited out of the military by the organization that is Guardian HRS.

Besides being a SEAL, I operated as a Delta team operative. We did a lot of hostage rescue in Delta.

This feels like old times.

Rafe guides us through the maze. Lifting my fist in the air, I call a halt. The shipping container is right in front of us. We pause, taking in how it sits apart from the other containers.

All around us, containers stack three to five high, but not this one. It's odd, but I can understand. Inside that container, precious cargo waits for delivery. The men in charge will do whatever they can to ensure those women reach their destination alive.

"Bravo One to Overlord, we're in position."

"Copy that." CJ doesn't waste breath on unnecessary chatter. *"Confirmed, ten inside."*

"Ten?"

"Correct."

Two less than expected.

Behind me, Hayes pulls out his bolt cutters. Alec and Zeb climb the nearest container. They'll provide cover if things come down to that.

"The op is yours," CJ tells me all subsequent mission commands are mine to make. *Smaug* will support only.

With a signal to Booker, Rafe, and Hayes, I give the command to move out.

We move as one, four highly trained operatives used to working together as one. Once we reach the door of the container, Booker and I turn toward defense. Meanwhile, Rafe gets the bolt cutters ready.

I scan the area, see nothing, then turn to watch Rafe place the bolt cutters on the lock. That's when I see the wire.

"Freeze!" I shout, but it's too late.

Rafe cuts the lock.

I shoulder him out of the way and shove him behind me.

A bright, fiery flash sears my retinas. Flames engulf me.

As intense heat burns through me, my entire world goes dark.

I HURT ALL OVER WITH NO FREAKIN' IDEA WHAT HAPPENED OR WHERE the hell I am.

"He's conscious." A muffled voice speaks from what seems to be a great distance.

"Push more morphine."

My eyes are open, but I can't see a damn thing. When I try to speak, there's something in my throat, choking me.

My arms don't move. My legs don't either. Panic surges through me then fades away as my body floats on a morphine high and consciousness fades away.

"Will he survive?"

"I don't know. The burns cover the entire left side of his body. With luck … We'll see."

Unrelenting pain consumes me, morning, noon, and night. It's the worst during the debriding sessions when they scrape off dead tissue.

Hydrotherapy is a curse word in my world right about now. It's where they remove all the devitalized tissue. I've taught many of the newer nurses creative and colorful curse words.

Fucking worst pain of my life.

The days blend into one another, but I've got the best burn doctors working on me. At least that's what I remember in my brain fog and morphine-fueled dreams. I float in a morphine fog most days, letting unconsciousness take me when things are their worst.

I've lost count of the number of surgeries. Evidently, early excision and grafting of burns are vital to recovery. They've tortured me through a few too many of those.

"How are you doing today?" Margaret, an old battle-ax, is my nurse, and I meet her cheery smile with a growl and a scowl.

"Fuck you."

"I see." She ignores my mood and goes about her fucking business like she's not about to torture me until I pass out. "Let's look at what we've got."

"How about we not?"

"A comedian today." Margaret begins the laborious process of unwrapping the bandages which cover the burns. "Looking good. No signs of infection."

"Yippee-ki-yay." I'm falling off the sharp cliff of my narcotic high. "How about some juice before my daily dose of torture?"

"I've already given you some."

"What?" I missed her injecting it into my med-line. "Well, fuck me sideways and don't hold back. Can't we up the dose?"

I'm becoming a freaking addict.

"Pain is good."

"Have you ever had your skin sloughed off?"

"No."

"Then don't fucking tell me pain is good." I close my eyes and go to my happy place as pain sinks into every fucking breath.

Debridement.

I hate it, but the docs say it's necessary.

Dermal preservation.

That's the goal. To achieve that goal, they remove the burned tissue layer by layer until reaching viable tissue. Early excision of my burns is supposed to decrease healing time, reduce my discomfort, and prevent infection. It's supposed to improve my overall outcome.

It fucking hurts like a living motherfucker on a skyway to Hell.

"How's he doing today?" The soft voice of Dr. Skye Summers interrupts my living hell.

"He's a ball of warm fuzziness today." Margaret continues her task.

"That bad?"

"Yes. Says the morphine isn't touching him."

"He's already on a high dose."

"Hey, I may be the patient, but I'm right fucking here. Don't talk over me."

"Sorry, Brady." Doc Summers comes to stand closer to the side of my bed. "I spoke with your doctors."

"Thought you were my doc."

"I'm an emergency and trauma doc. I deal with burns on the front end, but this requires a level of expertise far outside my wheelhouse."

"Well, what do the fucking experts have to say?"

"That your vocabulary needs a major overhaul."

"I'm entitled to be grumpy."

"There's grumpy and then there's you."

"So?"

"I know this sucks, Brady. I really do, but you're doing incredibly well. So far, we've avoided infection setting in. The debriding is going well. The grafting looks great. You should recover near full mobility."

"You telling me I'm going to live?"

I remember a dream fog where there was some debate about whether I'd survive.

"Don't lie to me, Doc. When you say functional, what does that mean? Will I be an invalid?"

"Not an invalid. I know things look bad. This is the worst of what you're going to face."

"The worst of it was having that container blow up in my face." I remember nothing of the explosion. Well, not nothing. There was a flash, intense heat, then nothing. I blacked out.

"Touché." Doc Summers covers the irritation in her voice poorly, but she takes my bad attitude in stride. "You will have scarring. There's no way around that, but things look good for rehabilitation."

"Rehabilitation? What kind of rehab are we talking?"

Will I be able to operate? If I can't be a Guardian, life's not worth living.

That is the only question that matters, but I'm not strong enough to ask it. I'm too afraid of the answer.

"Months at least."

"Months?"

"Maybe longer."

"Longer?" My heart can't take that. "So—you're basically telling me I'm screwed? I'm done."

"That's not what I'm saying at all. Look, the road to recovery is going to be long and hard. You're in for the hardest fight of your life. I sugarcoated nothing for you. You'll have scars, but with proper burn care, grafting, and fingers-crossed, no infections to complicate healing, you'll be out of here within a month."

"A month?"

"Two at most?"

"Two?"

"I'm sorry. It is what it is and I …"

"I know. You'll tell me the truth." I grimace as Margaret exposes my burned skin to the air. "You sure I can't have more morphine?"

"I'll up the dose a bit." She turns to Margaret and rattles off another dose of morphine. "You've got this Brady. You're one of the strongest men I know. Tenacious as shit and bull-headed in the extreme, but you've got this."

"But I'm out of the Guardians?" I mean to say it as a statement of fact. I'd rather hear the bad news coming out of my mouth than out of hers. If she says it, I'm done.

"Out of the Guardians? Why would you think that?"

"Why wouldn't I?"

"Because I'm going to do everything in my power to get you back as Bravo One."

A flood of adrenaline? Relief? I don't know what that floaty feeling is, but Doc Summers gives me hope. Or maybe I'm just riding another morphine high.

"You wouldn't shit me, would you?"

"No, Brady. I wouldn't lie about this."

Whatever else she says fades away. My lids grow heavy, and all I want is to disappear.

THREE

Brady

TWO WEEKS AGO

"Hey Brady, how are you doing today?" Doc Summers walks into the exam room and glances at the tablet in her hand. She pulls up my medical record for review. "On a scale of 1 to 10, how's your pain?"

One-fucking-hundred.

"You tell me." I gotta shit-ton of pain and far too many pain pills that do nothing for me.

I grit my teeth and bite back scathing words I know I'll regret. I feel like a fucking five-year-old, stripped and nearly naked, at the doctor's office waiting for my annual exam.

Or worse.

How about the intake physical for the Navy when I was eighteen?

That sucked. Nobody warned me what they were going to do, or where they were going to stick things I didn't want stuck in me. That was the first time I had my nuts fondled, followed by a finger up my butt. I mean, I had the hernia check before, but the butt thing was new. Talk about a surprise.

Welcome to the Navy.

Now? I just roll with it.

Anyhow, I'm not five and I'm not eighteen. I'm thirty-two, but shit if it doesn't feel exactly the same as way back when.

"Don't do that." She gives me a look. It's the same look she's given me for nearly a year, and she waits me out like a saint, saying nothing as I stew about things I can't change.

"Do what?" I snip at the doc.

"Act like a child."

"You calling me a kid?"

"I'm calling it as I see it. You should know by now that sympathy isn't my thing. I will not coddle you, and I'm not taking your shit." She gives me a stern look. "Now, let's start again. How's your pain?"

Unlike when I was five and hated the chilly pediatrician's office, or when I was eighteen getting poked and prodded for my military intake physical, I hate this exam room for similar yet entirely different reasons.

A glance down the left side of my body reveals a twisted mess of post-burn scars, skin grafts, and shrapnel injuries. Even after a year, it makes me sick to my stomach to look at my body.

Thankfully, my hand and most of my arm were spared during the blast. I can still hold a weapon. I can still fight. My chest, abdomen, left buttocks, and left leg took the brunt of that blast in *fucking Cancun*.

The back of my calves and my inner thighs sport grotesque scars. Although, those are not the result of the explosion that nearly took out my entire team and ended my life.

I'd be dead if Booker hadn't dragged my sorry ass out of the flames. Instead of dead, just the left side of my body is a melted mess.

As for the rectangular scars on my calves and inner thighs, that's where the skin grafts came from. They scraped off the top layer of my skin and grafted it over the areas where the original skin sloughed off.

The damaged skin, and grafts, look like a horror show of melted flesh and patchwork skin. I look like Frankenstein's monster. The sensation is shit, and I have ghost pains where third-degree burns took the nerves with them.

I'll never get those back.

"My pain is tolerable." I cringe just saying that. I live in constant pain.

"How are the meds working for you?"

"Dunno."

"What does that mean?"

"Stopped taking them."

"Why?" Her tone tells me she's not pleased.

"Didn't want to get addicted to the narcotics."

"Men are such fools. You need to take those as prescribed. We're tapering the dosage."

"Figured I'd just stop."

"Hate to break it to you, but after months on a fentanyl drip and weeks on oral methadone, your body is tolerant to the opioids. You'll suffer withdrawal."

"Addicted. That's what I don't want."

"Tolerant." She corrects me. "You're not addicted. Your body is tolerant."

"Same fucking shit."

"Totally different game, though." She takes a step back. "You look kind of rough today, and I don't mean that in a good way. I mean it in the worst possible way."

"What the fuck does that mean?"

"You're hyperirritable."

"I'm not …" Shit. I run my fingers through my hair, pissed off that she's right.

I'm mad at the whole fucking world.

"You're sweating like a pig."

"Pigs don't sweat." The sneer I give gets twisted by the scars on my face. It becomes something grotesque.

"And your fingers are trembling." She puts down her tablet and crosses her arms over her chest. "Classic withdrawal. I know you don't want to be on the pills, but we need to be smart weaning you off of them."

"Why can't I just stop?"

It's not like I'm going to pretend she's not one hundred percent right. I know nothing about drugs. Never experimented like practically everyone else out there. My body's what they call opioid naïve. I know even less about withdrawal, but I feel like shit.

"You're in the early stages. It's only going to get worse."

"I don't even know why I'm still here. How long are you going to keep me on the rolls when I'm non-operational?" I blow out a breath and let my shoulders slump. "Just check whatever box you gotta check, release me from the Guardians, and I'll go on my merry-fucking-way."

"We're headed down that road again? I see." She gives me a nice long once over. "I'm not a shrink."

"What's a shrink got to do with anything?"

"You need one."

"I've got my shit locked down tight."

"Is this what you call locked down? We have an excellent psychologist at Guardian HRS."

What *don't* we have at Guardian HRS? We have everything we could ever want and all the things we never knew we needed.

"I don't wanna talk to a shrink."

"So, you're just going to spew your piss-poor attitude on those around you?"

"I'm not …"

"You are, and honestly, I'm not the only one who's tired of it." She places the tablet down and pulls out her stethoscope. I sit straighter when the cold metal hits my chest. "Breathe in."

For the next few minutes, I breathe in and out while Doc Summers listens to my lungs, my heart, and my belly. She grabs her rubber-covered reflex hammer and checks out my reflexes. Then examines my puckered skin.

"How's PT going?" She runs her fingers over my scars.

I feel maybe a tenth of it. I've lost so much sensation. That part of my body doesn't look like me, doesn't feel like me. I don't recognize it as me. Talk about body image problems.

I really need to talk to a shrink. My head is in a fucked-up place, but men like me don't talk to shrinks. Instead, I grumble.

"Piper's a tyrant."

"You're not the first to say that." Doc Summers laughs at that.

"Then you know what I mean."

"Piper is amazing at what she does, and if you give her half a chance, you're going to be surprised at what she can do to help you feel normal again."

"Normal?"

"That's what I said."

"You're a piss-poor liar, Doc." I tug on my jaw. "And Piper is a royal pain in my ass."

"I've heard worse." Doc Summers shakes her head. I can't tell if she's commiserating with me or telling me to shut the fuck up. "Piper is committed. I take it there's friction?"

"Friction? The woman is a fucking beast." If I can call a pint-sized pixie of a woman a beast.

Piper is an obnoxious ball of energy, perpetually positive, perky as shit, and never lets my bad mood ruin her day. The woman's a saint for putting up with my bullshit during my extensive rehab.

What I really hate is how she turns my body into a quivering mess of complete and utter exhaustion after the simplest exercises.

My body is fucking broken, and neither she, nor Doc Summers, can convince me they can fix it.

"You're pretty when you smile." I try to disarm the doc. Maybe I'll get out of this damn checkup faster if I layer on the charm?

If I can knock Doc Summers off her game, I might get her to kick me out. I'm done with all of this recovery and rehabilitation bullshit, and I'm ready to admit what everyone already knows.

I'm no longer fit for duty.

"Ash will kick your ass if …"

"He can try."

She folds her stethoscope and places it back in her coat pocket. Her husband is the lead singer for the mega rock band, Angel Fire. He's lean, tall, and relatively fit, but I can kick his ass using nothing but my little finger.

"Well, let's stop talking about me and my husband and get back to you. How is physical therapy going with Piper?"

Piper belongs to Bent, Angel Fire's bassist. She's also the lead physical therapist for the Guardians. And she doesn't take anyone's shit, least of all mine.

"Why don't you ask her?" I gesture toward the tablet. "Better yet, read what she has to say."

"Oh, I've read what she has to say." Doc Summers's soft laughter turns into a smirk.

"Now I'm curious."

"You tell me first, then I'll let you know what she has to say."

"You're a real ball-buster, you know."

"I know. Now answer the question."

"PT sucks. That's the beginning and end of it. I don't know why we're even trying anymore. Frankly, it's a waste of time."

"That's fair." She places her reflex hammer in the pocket of her white coat then leans back against the counter. "It's the most honest thing you've said since you got here."

"And this is where you share what she said."

"Doesn't seem like you care what she says. You've already decided you're broken and irreparable. You've thrown in the towel and are just looking for a chance to get axed. You're a self-fulfilling prophesy with that piss-poor attitude of yours. Frankly, I find it tiring."

Tiring? What the ever-loving-fuck?

"Isn't that what's going on? Y'all are just fixin' me up so that you feel good about yourselves."

"Is that what you think?"

"Come on, that's what's going on. Any day now, you're going to kick me out of Guardian HRS."

"I see." She gives a nod. "Thank you for sharing that."

"What did Piper say about me?"

She picks up her tablet and taps at the screen a few times, then looks at me. "Sure you want to hear this?"

"It's about me. Damn straight, I want to hear it."

"You asked for it." Doc Summers glances at her tablet. She clears her throat and begins. "Brady Malone is a total douchebag who has convinced himself he's broken and fights me on everything. Every time he comes to see me, I want to kick him in the ass."

"She put that in my medical record?"

"Oh, it goes on from there." Doc Summers arches a brow and a smile tugs on the corner of her eyes. "Let's see …" She clears her throat again. "Brady is the absolute worst out of all his team. I've got the rest of them falling in line, doing the work, making consistent progress, but this douche-canoe is convinced he's broken. The man doesn't have two neurons to rub together, if you ask me. If he could get over himself, leave the damn pity party behind, and put in the work—honest, hard work—then I expect full recovery. He'll always have some mobility restriction because of the scarring, but there's no reason not to return him to operational status, except—of course—that he's a boo-hoo douche-canoe unable to get out of his own damn way. And it's not like the scars make him look like a freak. Yes, they're there. But chicks dig scars. You need to find a shrink to jump into the cesspool of this guy's pity party before I can have a chance of getting him operational again. And good luck with that. His skull is ten inches too thick. That's not man-inches, by the way, but real inches. I'm so over these macho Guardians who whine like little girls."

Doc Summers looks up from the tablet while I pick my jaw up off the floor. Well, fuck me. Talk about having my ass handed to me, and by an overly energetic and perky physical therapist at that.

"You made that up."

"Do you need to read it for yourself?" She turns the tablet around, where I see a thick block of text. I'm too far to read it, but I know Doc Summers recited Piper's note word for word. "There's more, but I think you get the gist."

"I'm not acting like a baby."

"I'm not saying you are, just reading Piper's words."

"And what do you think?"

"You know what I think." She crosses her arms in front of her. "At some point, you're going to have to look in the mirror and make a hard choice."

"And what would that be?"

"You're waiting for us to drop the hammer and kick you out of the Guardians. Yes. You have injuries that are significant, but they're not insurmountable. Your scars …" She makes a vague gesture at my face while I flinch. "Your scars aren't going away, but you're the same man underneath. A shrink isn't such a bad idea. You need to reevaluate the effort you're putting in with Piper and physical therapy. She's a phenomenal physical therapist. Put the same mental energy into that as you did during BUDS, and you'll surprise yourself. You survived one of the world's most brutal training programs to become a SEAL. Are you really telling me PT with Piper is *too hard?*" She uses air quotes to emphasize her point.

"Shit." I run a hand through my hair and grit my teeth. "I feel like such an ass."

"You should." She spins around and marks something on the tablet. "We're done here."

"Done?"

"Yes. You can get dressed."

"What about my checkup?"

"We're restarting your pain meds. There's one more thing."

"What's that?" I narrow my eyes, suspicious of whatever she's going to say next.

"You're off medical hold. I've moved you to training."

"Training? Might as well cut my balls off."

"Sorry, not interested. We'll reevaluate your physical conditioning in a month. Follow through with PT, do the work, and there's no reason you can't be operational when we see each other again. No one's interested in kicking you off the Guardians, but we need to get you back to operational readiness as quickly as possible. Stop whining and do the work. Doctor's orders."

With my jaw once again gaping, I don't have a witty comeback. Not that I could deliver it.

Did she say operational?

I didn't imagine that, did I?

That's all I want after this shitshow of a year. I want to return to what I do best, but I'm scared.

And it says a lot that I admit that to myself.

I'm terrified of what the future holds.

"I'll do it."

"You'll do what?"

"I'll talk to the fucking shrink."

"That's the first smart decision you've made all day. But first …"

"What?"

"First, you're going on vacation."

"What the fuck?"

"Forest's orders. Screw that head back into a good place. Decide what you want out of life."

"Wait a second. You're ordering me to take a vacation?"

"You heard me."

"A vacation?"

"Is there an echo in here?" She twists around, playing it up.

"I thought you wanted me to talk to a shrink?"

"I do, and you will, but after you come back. Bravo team needs you. Your teammates are waiting for you to come back to lead them. Do yourself a favor; take some time to figure out what it is you want. We'll be waiting for you. Until then, mandatory R&R is your prescription for today. Go have fun. Get drunk. Hell, get laid if that's what you need. But go. Get out of here. I'll see you in two weeks." Doc Summers sharply pivots and marches out the door, leaving me speechless.

"What the fuck just happened?" I look around the cold exam room, shaking like a leaf.

FOUR

Angie

PRESENT DAY

THAT CAR CRASH BEGINS A LIVING HELL THAT NEVER ENDS AND A road to recovery that never begins.

Life no longer holds meaning.

My days are listless and robotic. I don't eat. I can't sleep. The house holds too many memories of the man I will never forget.

I miss Luke with every fiber of my soul, but I know I need to move on.

So, I look for something different.

Something worlds away from what is comfortable and safe. I need something to take me away from a life I no longer want to live.

When I finally sit down and ask myself what Luke would want me to do, I sell the house.

I sell our cars.

I give everything we own away.

The only thing of my former life I keep is Luke's wedding band. I wear it around my neck and over my heart. His flag, I give to his mother for safekeeping. I'll come back to it when I can.

It's been three years since his death, and I'm in a totally different world.

I lug a box of surgical supplies somewhere deep within the

jungles of Nicaragua and breathe in the oppressive humidity. Sweat drenches my shirt and drips from my face. For the hundredth time, I wipe my brow to keep the perspiration from stinging my eyes.

We broke camp early yesterday morning, then drove twelve miles deeper into the jungle to the next small village. Arriving after the sunset, we didn't set up our day camp. We barely pitched our personal sleep tents before darkness fell and the jungle came alive.

Monkeys howl into the night. The roars of panthers punctuate what silence there may be. All around us, the jungle fills with screeches, howls, roars, and scuttling noises of its nightly denizens.

I'm too tired to care and fall into a dreamless sleep, completely and utterly exhausted. I'm too tired to think. Too tired to dream. I'm too tired to remember how achingly lonely my life is without Luke by my side.

Two months into a nine-month assignment, it's clear I didn't fully comprehend what it would mean to work for Doctors Without Borders. It's everything they said it would be and more.

The work is hard and is exactly what I need. I'm cut off from the real world. My days begin at dawn and go on well past the setting sun until exhaustion finds me crawling into bed and a dreamless sleep.

It's exactly the escape I'm looking for, and for the next seven months, I'll be serving the people of Nicaragua, victims of ongoing social and political violence.

Doctors Without Borders take the safety of their personnel seriously, limiting our activities and confining us to our camps. We travel with a limited security team and local guides. They keep abreast of the movements of rival cartels, steering us clear of the nearly constant armed engagements between the different groups.

So far, we've encountered no violence, although we've seen evidence of it in passing. I pray that's as close to the action as we get.

Dawn brings a hushed stillness to camp. I scoot out of my sleeping bag and poke my head outside my tent. Smoke curls up from a small fire where Jacob Turner, our lead doctor, brews his morning concoction of coffee and chocolate. It's a caffeine-infused jolt of adrenaline I can definitely use.

Exiting my tent, I stretch, limbering up my body for another day of back-breaking work. Taking a minute for myself, I excuse myself and make use of the field latrine set up some distance from camp. Two steps away from our tiny camp, the jungle folds in around me, swallowing me whole.

I love that feeling. It's just me and the jungle.

The first time I felt brave enough to walk to the latrine alone, an overwhelming sensation of insignificance came over me.

With trees towering far overhead, and thick vegetation soaking in what little light trickles down to the jungle floor, I feel small in comparison.

That sensation calms me.

When I return to camp, Jacob squats beside the fire, holding a cup of coffee close.

"Good morning. Did you leave any to share?" I don't see how Jacob can crouch that close to the fire. What little heat the small fire creates turns sweltering into oppressive.

"Definitely." Jacob sits on the ground. He folds his legs in front of him and takes another sip.

While I hold out a beat-up metal cup, Jacob fills it to the brim with the steaming brew. Not normally a coffee drinker, I'm slowly becoming a convert, especially with Jacob's secret ingredient.

The coffee warms my cup and my hands. I lift the cup and breathe in the rich aroma, closing my eyes with a sigh of contentment.

"This smells wonderful." The subtle aroma of chocolate turns delicious into amazing.

"Tastes even better." Jacob lifts his battered cup and we clink the worn metal.

"You seem to have hit your stride." As our family medicine doc, he leads our little crew.

"Thanks." I take his praise to heart. "I've been working hard."

I knew the work with Doctors Without Borders would challenge me, but I didn't know what I was signing up for. Or rather, I knew our mission would be to bring basic medical care to impoverished villages. I just didn't know how poor the villages would be; how rustic their living really was. Or how backbreaking my work would be.

There is no running water. The roads aren't paved. The people work hard and return home to structures that barely qualify as huts, let alone housing.

Poor and impoverished seem inadequate descriptors of the living conditions we've seen. I'd call it primitive. However, to these people, this is all they've ever known.

"Good morning." Izzy, our pharmacy support, greets us with bleary eyes. "How long have you been up?" She glances at her watch.

"Long enough to make coffee. You want?" Jacob gestures toward the coffee.

She scrunches her nose. "It's a foul brew, but since we have nothing else. Yes, please."

"I will make a convert out of you before we're done." Jacob's deep, throaty laughter brings a smile to my face. He pours for Izzy, then sits back on the dirt. "Have you seen Dan the Dentist yet?"

Izzy snickers at the nickname. Daniel hates when Jacob calls him that, but in his defense, it's funny as shit.

"Heard him snoring all night long." Izzy yawns. "Was quiet as a mouse when I passed his tent this morning."

"Did you look in to check on him?" Jacob wings up a brow.

"No. I did not. Last time I did that … Well, let's just say, that was the last time I'll peek in his tent. He's probably out taking a dump." Izzy glances at the thick jungle hemming us in.

Her mouth is going to get her into trouble someday. She's funny, but her crass humor takes some getting used to.

"Are we really setting up here?" I glance around the tiny clearing.

I didn't get a good look at it last night. With darkness creeping in, I turned my attention to pitching my tent and crawling inside my tiny shelter before too many bloodsucking bugs decided I was their next scrumptious feast.

Noise behind me in the vegetation makes me jump. A man appears out of the thick jungle, followed by another, and another. About a dozen villagers form a loose ring around us.

"Looks like our patients are ready." Jacob stands and brushes the dirt off his khaki pants. He approaches them, speaking fluent Spanish.

My Spanish is poor but getting better. I work with a translator when I see my patients. We're all assigned a translator, even Jacob, who's bilingual, and Stefan, our psychologist, who grew up in Mexico and speaks like a native.

Besides the five of us, each with a translator, about a dozen others join our mission in a support role. It makes for a tight group, but not so tight that we're getting sick of each other.

At least not yet.

I swipe at the perspiration beading my brow and turn toward the trucks still loaded with our gear.

Daniel emerges out of the thick vegetation with Stefan in tow. I give a jerk of my head toward the trucks, and they adjust their course to meet me.

"Good morning, Miss Angie." Stefan's smile is as bright as his eyes. He's the epitome of perpetual happiness.

"Good morning. Looks to be another busy day." I glance back at the villagers. Jacob's translator joins him, and the two of them converse with the locals.

As with every place before this one, the people come early, and all wait patiently while we set up. The younger men pitch in to help. It gives me a chance to practice my broken Spanish.

We unload the heavy medical gear, along with the tents that will become our exam and treatment rooms. Then there's my personal backpack, issued by Doctors Without Borders.

It carries their icon, and my name, on the outside. Inside is my passport, IDs, and emergency currency, in case I get separated from the group.

I sling it over my shoulder and head for my station. It's not long before I lose myself to the backbreaking work.

The work is challenging. With impossible hours that leave me falling into bed too exhausted to think, this is exactly what I need.

A complete and total break from my previous life.

I don't know what my future holds, but for now, I'm content.

"Doc, you need help with that?" Jerald, one of our mechanics and drivers, trots up and picks up the other end of the heavy metal box.

"Thanks."

Together, we carry it from the back of the truck into the tent designated as the Eye Station. Two locals help my translator get the tent ready.

A three-sided tent with an open front is my workspace. It comes with an exam table, two stools—one for me and one for my patient —and the contents of three metal boxes.

That's it.

I spend my days removing cataracts from those who need it, treating ocular infections, and providing basic vision exams. Cataracts are the leading cause of blindness around the world, and I give back the gift of sight to people who otherwise aren't able to receive the medical care they need.

It's seriously cool.

I'm told we normally travel with an optometrist who performs the eye exams and hands out free glasses collected stateside via donation boxes. The optometrist who was supposed to join us, however, had a family emergency which messed with those plans.

Which means, I do double duty.

Over the next few months, with my Doctors Without Borders colleagues, we will stamp out parasitic infections, immunize the community, pull teeth, and I'll give the gift of sight to those suffering from cataracts, ocular infections, and other eye disorders.

I'm going to make the world a better place, one patient at a time.

A distant *popping* of gunfire sounds far off in the distance. I crouch down, then look up at Jerald, feeling foolish. When he shows no reaction, I feel like a fool. He holds out a hand and helps me up.

"Sorry. I'm still not used to that." I give a sheepish grin and pick up my side of the medical gear.

"That was miles away."

"How can you tell?" It's impossible to tell distance in the jungle and even more difficult to say what direction it comes from.

"Experience." He shrugs, and when I expect more of an answer, Jerald says nothing more on the matter.

"Have you ever had people shooting at you?" The danger associated with this job is not insignificant.

Although, I've been told we're safe, or as safe as Doctors Without Borders can make us, I keep my backpack within arm's reach, just in case. Besides my passport and the emergency cash, I carry the rabbit's foot Jerald gave me when he met me at the airport.

"*For good luck during our mission.*" Jerald gave one to me and one to Izzy the moment we touched down in Nicaragua.

Day One of my stint with Doctors Without Borders began with the craziness of getting our gear through customs. They issued our personal packs and gave instructions to keep them with us at all times. Izzy and I each placed our rabbit's feet into our bags. I don't know about her, but I gave that thing a little rub. I needed a bit of luck.

That was over two months ago. Now, I'm an old pro. Practically a veteran. Still have that rabbit's foot, and Jerald's turned into a pretty good friend. He continues to help me with the gear and answers my question.

"Once, but after they realized we were doctors, they let us go. Honestly, it's nothing."

Nothing?

As if trying to provide medical care to a population in the middle of an active firefight is nothing? That's the *one* thing that terrifies me the most.

Our job is to help people at risk around the globe. Some of that work occurs in settings of active conflict or in post-conflict environments.

Nicaragua has plenty of civil unrest, and rival cartels engage in open warfare over territorial disputes. To the south, the *Coralos* cartel controls the populace. To the north, the *Laguta* cartel does the same. We're smack dab in the middle of a hotly disputed border between the two rival cartels.

This job comes with inherent risk, potentially dangerous encounters, and ongoing threats directly related to safety and security.

Specifically, my safety and security.

But I signed on the dotted line.

For nine months, this is my job, one I accepted with all inherent risks.

We follow comprehensive security protocols, but we don't carry guns. I'm not sure how comprehensive those protocols will be if armed men decide not to leave the doctors alone.

There are more *pops* in the distance, further than before, if I trust my ears. The thing is, the thick jungle canopy does weird things with sound.

Our team works for the next two hours setting up our mobile clinics. The distant sound of gunfire fades away.

The eye station stands in the middle of the grouping of tents. First comes Jacob's general medicine tent. Next to him is Izzy's very limited pharmacy. As our family practice doc, Jacob sees the bulk of our patients. Dan the Dentist … I shake my head and reframe my thoughts. Daniel is nearly as busy, but the interventions he provides, much like mine, are limited. His tent is down the line.

Once we leave this area, it can be months, sometimes years, before our patients follow up with anyone with a medical background. This is why Daniel focuses more on tooth extractions than fillings or restorations.

My patients are the elderly, in whom cataracts have stolen their sight, and young children with ocular infections.

We have one psychologist. Stefan provides limited services for those who experience traumatic PTSD from previous exposure to violence. Unfortunately, that's all too common. His patients are mostly the young adults with a preponderance of female rape survivors.

I don't envy him. That's a tough job.

More *pops* sound in the distance. There's more of a back and forth this time, and it's getting closer. Or maybe that's the echoing of gunfire from the hills?

The locals look up, eyes wide. With nervous expressions on their faces, they shift foot to foot. Mothers collect young children, and the elderly slip away.

Our crowd noticeably thins.

Only those desperate to be seen linger, and their expressions turn more anxious as the minutes tick by.

I finish up with one of my patients, a woman in her late sixties. She blinks and sees clearly for the first time in decades. Her expression is the joy I miss in my life. She grabs my hands, thanking me profusely. A younger man, her son or grandson, rips her away and hurries her into the jungle.

"Jacob?" My hands shake as I nervously pack up my gear. "Shouldn't we be leaving?"

Jacob is busy with a patient. He either doesn't hear me or ignores me. I go to Jerald, who mucks about in one of our transports.

"Hey, what are we supposed to be doing?"

"What do you mean?" He looks up from the engine and glances around. His brows tug together.

"The villagers are running away." I make a sweeping gesture showing the few stragglers who still stand in line. Their heads keep popping up as gunfire sounds off in the distance. "Should we do the same?"

"Unfortunately, there's nowhere to run."

"What do you mean?" My gut clenches and goes into freefall with a barrage of gunfire that's most definitely closer than before. The echoes report all around us, making it impossible to pinpoint where it's coming from or how far away it might be.

Whatever is happening, it sounds like a full-scale war in progress.

"Come." Jerald grabs my hand and marches me over to Jacob.

"Dr. Turner, what's your call?"

"Do we know who that is?" Jacob looks up from a young child he's examining for parasitic diseases.

"Hard to say." Jerald rubs the back of his neck. "Could be *Coralos* going after *Laguta*, or the opposite."

"Who do we worry about the most?"

"*Coralos*." Jerald doesn't hesitate. "They've been pushing to expand their territory."

"Pack the camp, but that's it. The last thing we want is to look like we're making a run for it." Jacob breaks the news to the few remaining locals still waiting in line.

"Why is that?" I can't help but ask. I want to *Get out of Dodge,* as the saying goes.

"If it looks like we're running, they'll think we're not who we say we are."

"It's pretty clear who we are." Every one of our trucks and off-road vehicles carries the Doctors Without Borders insignia plastered on the front, side, and rear.

"Unfortunately, others have used our name to smuggle drugs for one side or the other. If they think we're doing the same …" Jacob doesn't finish his sentence, not that he needs to.

I imagine running guns, or drugs, or whatever, for a rival cartel this close to a border dispute does not end well for those who get caught.

"So, what do we do?" I look between Jacob and Jerald. Both are seasoned Doctors Without Borders personnel.

"We pack our stuff and slowly move out. If we get that far."

"And if we don't?"

"Let me do the talking. Do your best not to be seen, and don't draw attention to yourself." He glances at Jerald with a look I can't quite make out. "Remember why you're here. At best, they'll detain us for a few days until they're satisfied we're who we say we are."

"And at worst?" I look between the two men as they exchange grim expressions.

"Let's hope it doesn't come to that." Jacob packs his gear.

I don't like the worried look on his face.

FIVE

Brady

Since I have no choice, and Guardian HRS is paying the tab, I push the limits of what they'll do. I figure it's my only way to get out of forced R&R.

Honestly, I expect my request to be denied. I pick an exclusive resort in Costa Rica on the Papagayo Peninsula. It comes in at a whopping fifteen hundred USD a night. Add food along with activities, and we're looking at three-K a day.

I mean, why not? If this is going to be my last *hurrah* as a Guardian, I'm going out in style.

There's no way it's getting approved.

Twenty minutes later …

"Knock, knock!" Mitzy raps on the half-open door and peeks into my office.

Never had an office until coming to Guardian HRS, but at Guardian HRS, we do things differently.

All team leaders have their own offices. Each team member shares a larger office subdivided into cubicles.

We use it only for training that requires computers, but most of what we do is in the expansive on-site gym, at the range, or in the live-fire mock-ups. Those are basically towns that can be stood up and broken down to replicate future missions.

Guardian HRS is big on prepping for success.

"What brings you to my door?" I glance up from my internet search about Costa Rica.

After putting in my R&R request, the sunny skies and beautiful beaches of Costa Rica caught my eye. That led to diving down the rabbit hole of what I could do if I went.

Is it bad I'm looking forward to getting away?

"I've got your magic ticket." Mitzy reminds me a lot of Piper.

Or maybe it's the other way around and my persistently perky and overly positive physical therapist reminds me of Mitzy?

They're both petite and ferocious.

I guess you have to be when you're that short. Unlike Piper with her red hair, Mitzy's hair is a psychedelic explosion of color. Piper likes to keep her hair in a bob, whereas Mitzy's is a short pixie cut that's as wild and chaotic as her mind.

They both have smart mouths with lots of attitude, giving better than they get, and Mitzy certainly doesn't hold her tongue.

"What magic ticket?" My mother taught me to stand when a woman enters a room, but this is Mitzy.

She's more like what my younger sister would be like if I had a younger sister. All that's to say, instead of standing, I lean back and interlock my fingers behind my head while kicking my heels up on the corner of my desk.

Whipcord smart, beyond brilliant, Mitzy's ability to work on the front lines of emerging technologies is second only to Forest Summers. It makes the tiny thing intimidating, and that's not just me. We're all somewhat scared by the ferocious pixie.

"I believe you put in a request for vacation time." She taps an envelope against the doorframe.

"I did." My focus narrows in on the envelope. "What's that?"

"It's an envelope." She glances at the envelope, then turns her sparkling eyes back on me. "What does it look like?"

"No shit, Sherlock. What are you doing with it, and why would I care?"

"Well, it seems I'm delivering it to your doorstep." She cups her elbow and places her chin on her hand. "Yeah, I think that's exactly what Forest said."

"What the fuck does that mean?"

"Are all Guardians this thick in the head? Nice job, by the way. Give you props for having balls."

"What the fuck?"

"I know what you're doing." She taps her temple with the edge of the envelope. "You pushed and Guardian HRS pushed right back."

"English, please?"

"No one in their right mind would put together an all-expense paid, first-class, vacation to a five-star luxury resort their employer was financing. This reads like a damn honeymoon without the ring, marriage license, or chick."

"I thought they'd shoot it down." I scrunch my mouth into a frown. Evidently, things didn't go as planned.

"You mean, you *hoped* they'd shoot it down, but you don't understand your worth."

"Have you looked at me lately?" I gesture to the scarring over the left side of my face and the scars covered by my clothes.

"Yeah, and the pity party is so last year." Mitzy makes a dramatic show of rolling her eyes. "But the joke's on you."

"How so?"

"Because Forest saw your bet and raised you one."

"He did, what?" That comment gets me on my feet.

"He upgraded your ass to a beachfront bungalow. Skye added in massages, morning and night; you still need that for your scars, and you *will* show up for those. The rest of the day is yours to do whatever the hell it is a Guardian does when he's on R&R."

Massages?

For my scars?

Fucking doctors.

I used to spend my R&R in bed with whatever hot chick I nabbed the night before, but there are few chicks, hot or not, who are interested in a freak with a half-melted face.

It's not that bad.

The scarring is limited to the angle of my jaw and the left side of my neck, but it's something that can't be ignored.

As for my status with the Guardians, there's no way I believe what Doc Summers says about returning to full duty.

"What if I refuse to go?" There's always that option. Maybe belligerence will get me kicked out?

But is that what I want?

There's a very quick, and decisive, answer to that.

I'm a Guardian. A protector and a rescuer, saving other people is in my blood. It's a part of who I am.

It's at the core of my identity.

I don't want to get kicked out of Guardian HRS because of belligerence or failing to get healed up enough to get off medical hold.

I want to stay.

"Oh, it's too late to refuse. Skye tested the waters. You bit and Forest got involved. Are you going to be the one to tell him *Thank you, but fuck off?*"

"I'd never say it like that." The idea did come to me.

"I would." Mitzy shrugs. "But it's not my vacation in paradise. Although, I wish I'd thought of it. Now that the band is back from their last European tour, I need a bit of alone time with Noodles." She taps the envelope on the doorframe and drifts off in thought.

It's easy to forget Mitzy's married. She's also a mom. Which is totally weird. That kid is going to have its head in a blender between Mitzy's crazy brain and Noodles's Zen-esque approach to life. To be a fly on that wall …

"So, what's it going to be?" Her sharp tone pulls my head up.

I flick my gaze to the ceiling and swallow down what I really want to say.

Game.

Set.

Match.

Skye and Forest played me.

"I wish they would lay off, to be honest." I take in a deep breath and blow it all out in a huff. Frustration seems to be my thing these days. I'm mad at the whole goddamn world.

"Why?" Mitzy gives me one of her hard stares. "Because you're beautifully broken? Or because you think those scars make you a monster?"

"Beautifully broken?"

"You heard me." She gives a single shoulder shrug. "Those scars don't define you. They're a testament to your bravery, your heroism."

"They're reminders I led my team into a goddamn trap. I'm lucky none of them were seriously wounded."

Or worse.

"Yeah, that's right. You saved that honor for yourself. Of course, you forget that you yanked Rafe's ass out of the way. By taking the brunt of that explosive charge, you saved his life."

"I …" Shit, I don't know how to respond to that. "I only did what anyone would've done."

"No. You did what Bravo One would do, what a team leader should do. You put your team first, accepting the consequences of your actions. Focus on the life you saved rather than the few burns that only add to your stunning personality."

"You don't get it." She doesn't understand what I've lost.

"Well, according to Skye, your mobility isn't affected. You can still see out of both eyes. You've still got ten fingers and ten toes. Your fine motor control is unaffected. Your PT scores are back at baseline."

"So?"

"It means you can still pull a trigger and hit what you're shooting at." She tilts her head. "Seriously, talking to a Guardian is like speaking to a pile of bricks."

She shakes her head and blows out a breath of frustration. "You're still able to run. I've seen you in the gym with the guys. Yeah, you were hampered at first while the burns healed, and then again after the skin grafts, but your run times are nearly the same now as before the accident. Your proficiency at the range is unchanged. The only thing that's broken is your head."

She makes a point of tapping her head with the tip of the envelope, then continues.

"You look a little different, fiercer, but that only makes you look scarier to the bad guys. For a Guardian, that's probably a plus when it comes to desirable physical attributes."

"Thanks for the rundown, but I don't remember asking for your assessment."

"It's not my assessment."

"Then whose is it?"

"That's an amalgamation of what Skye, Sam, and CJ said."

"What?"

Skye, Sam, and CJ?

Holy fuck. They're talking about me. I run my hand over the front of my face and shake my head.

"You realize the higher-ups have meetings and briefings and status updates and … Well, you get the point. We're always talking about you and your team."

"What about my team? What have you said about my men?"

"Bravo team is all we've talked about this past year. The consensus is unanimous."

"And what is that?"

"It's time to stand Bravo up again."

"I have a hard time believing that."

"What? That it's time to stand Bravo up again, or that you're all we've talked about this past year."

"Yes."

"Yes to which one?"

"Yes to both. Bravo's broken. We're all in some stage of healing and disrepair."

"First off, there may have been one or two other operations mixed in there this past year, but Bravo's on everyone's mind."

"That's the understatement of the year."

Everyone at Guardian HRS knows what Alpha team

accomplished in the past year. Not that they did it alone. It was a concerted Guardian effort, but they took down a major player in the world of human trafficking.

Alpha kicked major ass.

And they did it all while I was on medical hold, sitting out on the sidelines.

Booker, my right-hand man, assisted them on a couple of those missions. The rest of my team basically sat things out as we licked our wounds and tried to heal: body, soul, and mind.

I owe Booker my life. He pulled me out of the fire. If he hadn't, I wouldn't be breathing today.

"Anyway, it's time to stand Bravo up and we can't do that with Bravo One messed up in his goddamn head about shit you have no control over."

Mitzy flings the envelope my way. It sails through my office, hits my chest, and falls to my desk.

I lean down and pick it up.

"Your flight leaves tonight. Pack your bags and have the best goddamn two weeks enjoying the sun and sand and whatever else you do when you're not working."

"I really didn't think they'd bite." My words come out a mumbled mess.

"Well, let's just say there are many people who have a vested interest in seeing you get better. The body is on the mend, but your doc's concerned about the shit in your head. Do us all a favor and sort that out. We need Bravo team whole. It's been too long that Guardian HRS has been operating with one team down."

I open the letter and pour the contents out on my desk. There's an itinerary with all the personal details on it, along with what looks like a dive watch and one of those knotted friendship bracelets.

"Looks like I'm headed to Costa Rica." I grab the watch, scrutinizing it.

"Looks like." Mitzy raps her knuckles on my door. "Do me a favor and try to stay out of trouble. But if you need anything …" She points to the watch. "I know you love to dive, so that's a bit of a gift from me. It has some extra special Mitzy TLC in it as well. Standard stuff, tracker and a sat-comm. And the knotted bracelet is a standard tracker. Wear it."

"Sat-comm?" I ignore her comment about the knotted bracelet but put it on as I examine the watch.

"You spoil me."

"Well, reception is shit down there. I can find you, track you, and talk to you anywhere in the world with that. Although …"

"What?"

"You better not deviate from the plan."

"The plan?"

"Your itinerary. Costa Rica and back. Don't take any detours, or diversions, or other silly things."

"I'd never …" I place a hand over my chest, pretending I'm shocked and wounded by her words.

"I know what Guardians do. We tell you to stay out of trouble and you take it as a challenge to dive right in the middle of it. Consider that watch your phone-a-friend lifeline, but do me a favor and don't. Your stress is showing its ass, and I hope you take all of this to heart in the way it's meant. We really want you better, in body, soul, and mind. I want you better, and I mean it this time."

"Only this time?"

"I wouldn't want you to get sweet on me." She props her hand on her hip. "But you get what I mean?"

"I do, and thanks." I scoop everything up and place it back in the envelope. "I'll do my very best to stay out of trouble."

"Thanks. I appreciate that from the tip of my hair to the bottom of my toes." With that, Mitzy taps the door and departs, leaving me to ponder every word she said.

Mitzy says a lot of crap, but none of it's wasted breath. I'll be replaying this conversation in my head in the days to come.

Until then, I take another look at the resort I picked and glance a look at the amenities they offer.

Maybe they're right? Maybe I need to hit the reset button?

Get my head back in the game?

I send a text off to Booker, telling him I'll be out of pocket for the next two weeks.

Bravo team is his until I return.

But I will return.

I'm a Guardian.

It's who I am.

SIX

Angie

DESPITE THE GUNFIRE, NOT ALL THE LOCALS LEAVE.

For many, we're the only medical care they'll receive in months, if not years. The elderly depart, along with women and small children, but the younger men stay. They're more confident in their ability to evade whatever is coming.

The gunfire closes in.

There's no doubt it's closer.

Figuring out distance in the jungle is difficult, add in the rugged hills and it's near impossible to sort out what direction a sound comes from, but what I know is the sporadic gunfire is most definitely closing in.

My gut tightens, apprehensive about the unknown. We're doctors. Non-combatants. We carry no weapons. We align with no one, except our mission to bring quality healthcare to those without.

We're the good guys.

But will that keep us from harm?

That unsettled feeling in my gut grows. I really hope so.

I get my gear loaded into the back of a truck, then head back to help Izzy with her supplies. Her hands shake as she replaces vials and a wide assortment of pills.

"Gut check. Do we need to be worried?" I snap the lid closed on one of her many pharmacy supply boxes and wait for an answer. This is Izzy's second contract with Doctors Without Borders, which makes her an expert in my eye.

Despite being the only other female in our team, we've failed to connect, meaning we're professionally polite and personally cordial toward one another, but we're not friends.

Jacob and Jerald aren't forthcoming as far as how big of a thing this could be.

"I don't think so." Izzy's response doesn't reassure me, especially with the way her hands shake. "I hope not."

"Has this happened to you before?"

"No." Izzy's head shakes. "But I've heard of it happening to others." Her left hand raises to rub at the rabbit's foot around her neck. I keep mine in my personal pack, whereas she looped a leather thong around hers and wears it around her neck. I often find her rubbing the rabbit's foot when gunfire sounds in the distance.

"And?" It's like pulling teeth to get people to tell me what to expect.

Daniel walks past with a bag tucked up under his arm and two heavy gearboxes in his hands. He overhears our conversation and stops.

"For some, nothing happened. For others, they were detained while they searched their gear. Say goodbye to whatever you have." He lifts the two gearboxes with emphasis. "Most likely, they'll take our gear and supplies, then leave us behind. Don't forget to keep your personal pack on you. If anything happens …"

My heart kicks into high gear, making my pulse hammer in my ears. The expression on Daniel's face does nothing to reassure me.

"Listen." Daniel cocks his head.

The low drone of engines cuts through the air.

"Come." He sets his boxes down on the dirt. "You can leave that." Daniel's dour expression makes my stomach churn.

"What are you doing?"

"Showing them we have nothing to hide. That we're not a threat." He places his hand over Izzy's and gently pulls her from her gear. "Don't look any of them in the eye. Keep your head down. Be meek. Nonthreatening. If they tell you to do something, do it."

"Has this happened to you before?"

"Not me, but one of my buddies."

"What happened to your friend?"

"They took him for ransom."

"Why?"

"Because they can demand exorbitant ransoms for rich American doctors." Daniel gestures for us to follow.

A quick glance around camp reveals everyone does the same. Our small clinic stands in disarray, with half-packed cases all over the place.

We join Jacob and the others near the road as the steady drone of what sounds like several vehicles closes in on our location.

I suck in a deep breath and place my hand over my belly. Like Izzy, my hands shake. Most of my body quivers in fear.

Between the medical personnel, support team, and our local translators, about a score of us face the road as the chugging of the vehicles approaches.

Jacob, Jerald, and Daniel shift to stand in front of me and Izzy. I'm not sure if it's a conscious effort or just happens when they take a step forward to get a better view down the rugged dirt road.

Izzy shifts toward me until our shoulders nearly touch. I grab her hand, and she squeezes mine back as a convoy of five vehicles materializes out of the thick jungle vegetation.

A man stands in the back of each truck, weapon in hand. When they round the bend, they turn those weapons on us.

Izzy gasps while I try to swallow the lump in my throat. The trucks hurtle toward us, moving faster than any vehicle needs to on the rugged roads.

When they slam on their breaks, the tires slide over loose rocks, spitting out gravel behind them. A thick cloud of dust lifts in the air as they come to a sudden halt.

Armed men jump out of the vehicles and yell in Spanish, too fast for my mind to keep up, but I understand what they want.

They point their guns at us and gesture for us to step away from our vehicles. My hands go up. With Izzy and the others, I shuffle to the side.

The rear vehicle comes to a stop, much less dramatic than the previous four vehicles. Men jump out of the back, armed to the teeth.

I scan the men and gulp again.

Daniel says they'll most likely leave, taking all our gear with them. Does that include our vehicles? Not thrilled about having to hike out of here, I can do it if needed. I packed rugged boots for my time in Nicaragua. Not to mention, one benefit of this lifestyle is that I'm in the best shape of my life.

The passenger door of the last vehicle opens. I tense and hold my breath.

The man who exits carries authority as if born with it. His dark gaze takes us in. His slow, methodical assessment makes my knees shake. The malevolence in his gaze makes me shiver. At the last moment, I remember what Daniel said and avert my eyes, but I still feel the vileness of his gaze wash over me.

He shouts and his men leap to obey. I can't make out his Spanish, but his men corral us like animals.

A dozen men encircle us. All train their weapons on our group. I swallow my fear and keep my gaze down.

Jacob steps forward, separating himself from the group. My limited Spanish picks up only one word in three, but enough to know Jacob explains we're unarmed medical personnel on a mission.

He gestures toward the insignia on the trucks. The Doctors Without Borders emblem is emblazoned on every piece of equipment we carry. From the trucks to the tents, to our gearboxes, and our personal gear, there's no mistaking who we are, or what our mission might be.

The man with the dark gaze fires question after question at Jacob, his tone turning darker and more ominous as the questioning proceeds.

Jacob answers each question quickly and succinctly, but the

tension swirling in the air thickens with an escalating threat of violence.

Daniel slowly shifts back to where Izzy and I stand. He speaks, barely moving his lips, and so quiet that I barely hear him.

"Head down. Eyes down. Be humble and meek. Do nothing to draw attention." He said something similar earlier, but I take it to heart now.

"What's going on?" I follow his lead, head down, speaking without moving my lips.

"They think we're running guns for the *Laguta* cartel, using Doctors Without Borders as cover."

The conversation between Jacob and the lead man turns heated. Jacob points frantically at the Doctors Without Borders emblem on the truck closest to him.

I close my eyes, not out of fear, but because it helps to tease apart his Spanish into something I can understand.

I hear *truck* and *search*. Jacob invites the man to search our gear.

With a snap of his fingers, the leader signals his men.

Four guards break away to rifle through our stuff, and they're not gentle about it.

They ransack our supplies, opening our gearboxes and dumping the contents all over the ground. They hop in our vehicles and do the same.

My equipment lands on the dirt, damaging it beyond repair. I bite my lower lip and tell myself it's nothing. We can replace everything.

Not sure how long I stand there, I shift back and forth, fighting dizziness. The humid air makes it hard to concentrate. The pounding in my ears firmly settles behind my eyes as a headache takes over.

Jacob walks with the leader, prodded forward at gunpoint. Those around me, strangers who've become friends over the past two months, shift with nervous energy.

Eventually, all our vehicles are searched. All our gear is strewn across the dirt. More orders are shouted and the men with the guns separate us into two groups.

They move our translators off to the side, line them up, and force them to their knees. My heart leaps into my chest as they're ordered to lace their fingers behind their heads.

My breathing kicks up, turning rough and ragged, verging toward hyperventilation. My head spins, lightheaded and dizzy, as what's happening slowly sinks in.

"*Médico!*" The leader shouts at Jacob, who hangs his head.

I hold my breath as Jacob slowly points out the medical personnel. As he does, men come at us, grabbing and separating us from the rest of our team.

Me, Stefan, Daniel, and Izzy are forced at gunpoint to a spot in front of the lead vehicle, leaving half a dozen of our colleagues remaining.

More is said between Jacob and the leader. Jerald and two of our other drivers join the rest of us by the lead vehicle.

Izzy and I cling to each other. The expression on Jacob's face darkens. Clearly, this is not the outcome he expected.

The men search our vehicles a second time. Their leader saunters over and stops in front of Daniel.

"*¿Hablas español?*" His voice is deep and dark like the rest of him. Barrel-chested, the man is tall, muscular, and clearly leads his men not only by the force of his will but by the power of his body.

My shoulders hunch and I curl in on myself, trying to appear meek and mild.

"*Un poquito.*" Daniel speaks Spanish well, but hedges.

"*Soy fluido.*" Stefan stands a little straighter.

I can't help but think admitting to being fluent in Spanish may not be a good thing.

"*¿Y usted?*" He turns the full force of his presence on Izzy.

"*No hablo español.*" Her words come out in a squeak. Izzy's grip on my hand tightens.

The man turns his heavy gaze on me.

Daniel's Spanish is much better than mine, but I sense any degree of a lie won't go over well.

"*Un poquito. Mi español no es tan bueno.*"

"I see." His malevolent gaze sends icy shivers down my spine. "You're a doctor?"

"Yes."

"What kind?"

"Ophthalmology."

"An eye doctor?" His thick Spanish brogue makes the words sound exotic.

"*Sí.*"

"*Muy bueno.*" The man turns and shouts to his men. "*Tráelos con nosotros.*"

My Spanish is terrible, but I recognize *tráelos* and *nosotros.* They're taking us with them.

My heart races around inside my chest, galloping wildly out of control as my breaths deepen. My headache gets suddenly worse, and the humidity saps the last of my strength.

The man grabs my arm, a solid steely grip that keeps me on my feet.

"*No tengas miedo.*" When I look up at him, he repeats in English. "Don't be afraid."

But I am.

I'm terrified.

Even more so when he drags me to the back of the truck and hoists me up and inside.

"Sit." He barks an order and points at the floor of the flatbed. "Don't run. That will not end well for you. *¿Comprender?*"

"*Sí señor.*" My eyes widen at the genuine threat.

Izzy joins me a few seconds later.

A few minutes pass.

They speak more Spanish I don't understand. One of his men jumps up in the back of the truck and the truck lurches forward as the brake's released.

That's when I look around, realizing they separated Izzy and me from the men. My hand goes to my throat, and I curl my fingers around Luke's wedding band. My eyes close as I pray for Luke to watch over me.

As our truck pulls out and around the others, Jacob and the

other men climb in the back of one of the other trucks. Unlike us, their hands are bound behind their backs.

Daniel stares at me as we rumble by. He says nothing, but I remember every word he said.

Be meek. Stay silent. Lower your gaze.

Our translators remain kneeling on the side of the road, hands clasped behind their heads. The gunman barks a command and they all lean forward until their foreheads touch the dirt.

I silence a scream as the gunman trains his weapon on our people, but I don't see what happens.

Our truck piles on speed, moving much too fast for the deeply rutted road.

We've been taken, and there's no one who will rescue us.

SEVEN

Brady

MY FLIGHT TO COSTA RICA IS BORING AND UNEVENTFUL. I BRING one bag, an oversized backpack, but it's not like I need much. I will spend the next two weeks swimming in the turquoise waters or sunning on the sand.

In between those two activities, I plan on sipping fruity drinks and pounding whiskey until I blackout, only to wake up and do it all over again.

My hotel is a few hours by car from the airport. In addition to the exorbitant price tag of my room, I rent a car and put that on the company tab. I could've taken a bus or flagged a taxi, but I'm not interested in making conversation with anyone.

Besides, I'm up for a drive.

Doc Summers is right. My mind's in a bad headspace.

The woman at the rental counter averts her gaze, refusing to look me in the face. It's a kick in the nuts. There was once a time when I could charm someone like her into my bed.

Now?

The melted flesh across my jaw slides down my neck, which makes charming anyone a thing of the past. Talk about a cock block.

My face used to be my best asset. Now, it stands as a reminder of what I've lost. The new reality of my existence is a face that drives everyone away.

I move out of the hustle and bustle of the city to a more sedate way of living in the rural coastal towns. Blessed with two distinctive coastlines, I'm taking advantage of the Pacific side of the country's magnificent beaches.

Mild in climate, there's no bad time to visit. Warm and not too humid, I look forward to sunny days along pristine beaches lined with palm trees.

The surf's inviting.

The water's warm.

The pristine beaches wait for me.

I could spend my entire time on those beaches, but the dense jungle inland calls to me. Hopefully, the hotel organizes wilderness treks, although my idea of a trek through the dense vegetation is probably a lot different from that of the average tourist.

Still, I'd like to visit the rainforest as a tourist, rather than as an operative with people chasing me.

Bottom line?

Costa Rica has everything and more; a hallmark experience for a man like me.

As I close in on the hotel, my choice in renting a car looks like a stroke of genius. There's nothing for an hour in any direction. Nothing, as in, no restaurants and no bars. Nothing close where I can find company for an evening to scratch that itch.

Without the car, I would be stuck with what's available at the resort. Not that their food isn't phenomenal, but the pickings of young, single women for a bit of nighttime R&R is slim at a resort where couples vacation along with families and their children.

I lower the windows to let the salty air blow into the car. It's beyond gorgeous outside.

White puffy clouds dot the blue skies and hang over an azure sea stretching out to the horizon. The sunsets are going to be amazing, and I look forward to sitting on the beach, drink in hand, while the sun dips below the horizon and turns the sky into magenta flames.

My fingers tap the steering wheel as I take in a long, slow breath. I may already be relaxing. Not that I'll admit it to the doc.

There's something about the air at the beach; a crispness and freshness that feels like coming home. I love the ocean; grew up swimming and surfing in it nearly every day.

I grew up in Newport Beach. Got up early every day to hoof my surfboard to the beach and catch waves while the rest of the world slowly woke up.

I'd get in a couple of hours carving the waves with my board, then I'd head home and make it to school in plenty of time not to be late.

As a teen, I was the epitome of a California surfer with sandy-brown hair bleached out by the salt and sun and a golden tan the chicks loved.

There's just something about water that I love. What I need is a nice long swim in the ocean. That should clear my head.

My love for the ocean is one reason why I joined the Navy and eventually applied for, and became, a Navy SEAL. Water ops are the best ops, although I'm equally at home in the water as I am on land.

My reminiscing of earlier days ends, however, when I drive up to the resort. Tropical flowers spill over and around the lush vegetation. It's a riot of colors and an explosion of tropical scents that makes me want to take in several deep breaths.

The resort drips with money, welcoming its visitors with the knowledge their dollars are well spent. A valet opens my door and waits for me to exit the vehicle.

His face pales when he glimpses my scars, but the dude covers his reaction moderately well. He's upset about the one bag—guess he thinks he'll miss out on a tip—but I shoulder my ruck and tip him extra.

He did, after all, have to swallow down his revulsion of my scars. Dude doesn't know the half of it. My jaw and neck are nothing compared to the left side of my body.

Inside, the check-in process is seamless. The pretty girl at the counter arches a brow at a single guy checking into the honeymoon suite, but her eyes widen when she sees the scars.

More professional than the valet, she fixes a smile to her face and avoids drawing attention to the disfigurement.

After she tells me the honeymoon suite is set on a private cove, I ask for a surfboard to be delivered to my bungalow along with snorkel gear.

With the car taken care of, and my room key in my pocket, I make a leisurely stroll through the main part of the resort, noting entrances and exits and best points to secure the rooms.

I can't help that part of my brain.

It never turns off and only reinforces how ingrained being a Guardian is in my most basic makeup.

There are five restaurants on-site, about the same number of bars, three expansive pools, and a kid favorite—a lazy river with inner tubes. For the adults, there are more than enough Jacuzzis sprinkled about.

Two weeks is a long time to suffer in paradise, but I'm up for the challenge. While I tried to get Doc Summers to kick me out of the Guardians, that's the last thing I want. I'm an operator and happiest when on a mission.

I suppose she understands, and I give a nod to her prescription: two weeks to get my head screwed on straight is probably the best medicine she could dispense.

The rest is up to me. I need to sort through the shit swirling around inside my head and do whatever it takes to get well and back on the active rolls at Guardian HRS.

The honeymoon suite is a bit of a hike from the main buildings. I could use one of the many carts, but I want to stretch my legs.

Set on a private cove, it enjoys a western-facing view that will be fucking amazing once the sun sets. The pristine, white-sand beach is something I'll enjoy soon.

My eagerness to dive into the waters increases. I'll spend the rest of my day unwinding with that long swim and a run.

Once I key myself into the room, I can't help but shake my head at the hilarious upgrade Forest gave me.

There's a spacious living room with an over-the-top bedroom attached. Inside that bedroom is a massive, king-size bed and private sitting area.

Yes, there are rose petals strewn about.

The attached bath has a shower built for two with jets that come out of the wall and a rain shower overhead sure to please a young couple.

Besides the shower, there's a Jacuzzi tub large enough for two. I plan on making use of that later tonight.

I toss my ruck on top of the bed and watch it and the rose petals bounce on the plush covers.

"What to do? What to do?" I pull at my chin as I take in my accommodations for the next two weeks.

Mandatory morning and afternoon massages are part of my itinerary while I'm here. That's Doc Summers's handiwork. The lady at reception handed me a schedule of the massages already booked, but those don't start until the morning.

I peel off my clothes—they're damp from sweat and the ever-present humidity—and pull on my swim trunks.

The tropical waters welcome me with a cool embrace that my body warms up to in no time. I wade in until the water laps just above my knees, then lift both hands overhead and dive into the clear blue waters.

The cove turns the gentle swells of the ocean into a nearly flat, mirror-smooth surface, but beyond the breakwaters, gentle rollers welcome me home. I turn north, keeping the beach to my right, and head out in long, sure strokes.

Once I'm at what I decide is the halfway point, I stop and flip to my back. I stare up into the sky and watch the clouds slowly cruise overhead. Once rested, I begin the three-mile trek back to the resort and my honeymoon suite.

After the six-miler in the open ocean, my body's fatigued by the time I pull myself out of the water. The scarring on my left side pulls, reminding me it's there.

That skin is tighter than the rest of my body but doesn't affect my ability to swim.

It takes a moment for that thought to fully process.

Considered by many to be the hardest part of BUDS, there are several ocean swims required to pass. The one that sucks the most is a timed five-and-a-half-mile event along the California coastline in chilly water, teeming with sharks.

I prefer my sedate six-mile swim. It's a piece of cake compared to that beast of a swim.

The one good thing about hours-long swims is that there's a lot of time to think. And I sat in my head during the entire swim, figuring out what I want in life and where to go from here.

It comes down to two things.

One really.

I'm a Guardian.

That word defines me in more ways than I can count. It's what gets me out of bed each morning.

Few are gifted with the physical attributes to do what it takes to rescue others, putting my life on the line. It requires a certain sense of purpose, strength of will, and sound character. It demands a driving, single-mindedness to persevere no matter the odds.

That stubbornness and obstinate staying power separates those who want from those who can. I've got the boldness and courage to stick with my convictions, even while getting blown apart, literally and figuratively.

I doubt many would take up the torch again, not after what I went through. Maybe that's why I was such a dick to Doc Summers, Piper, Mitzy, and pretty much everyone I work with.

The one thing which can destroy me is fear—fear of not being the man I was.

Fuck.

I drag my hand down my face as that realization kicks in. Talk about a sucker punch to the gut. That's one hell of a wake-up call.

I consider being a Guardian an honor, and I'm past done with the shitty pity party I've engaged in over the past year.

It's time to suck it up and get on with life.

Doc Summers would be so proud of me.

As for the scars?

That voice in the back of my head whispers fear, curling it around the edges of my consciousness. It feeds on my vanity. But it's up to me to suck it up and move the fuck on.

Those scars will not define me.

There's jack shit I can do about them and they're not going anywhere.

Still with restless energy to burn, and a redefined purpose in life, I head for a run around the resort grounds, piling on ten miles before calling it quits.

Back in my room, I have fun with the shower, using the overhead rain shower to wash away the salt from my swim and the sweat from my run. Then I turn on the jets and let the water beat at my exhausted muscles from every angle. Those jets feel amazing over my scars.

Once done, my next decision looms.

Do I order room service and continue to hide out from the hotel guests? Or do I head to the bar and grab a bite to eat while watching whatever's on local TV?

I decide not to drink alone and toss on khaki shorts and a loose-fitting shirt.

Time to be civilized.

No surprise at the prices on the menu at the bar. I settle for a local fish dish and order local beer.

The television is total crap, but I swirl my beer and watch as boredom overcomes me. It's a resort, which means couples and families with kids are the predominant theme. There are no unattached females, which means there's going to be even less here to do than I originally thought.

I could head out. Drive an hour to the last bar I saw on my way here, but I'm too many drinks in to make that the best decision of my night.

It's going to be a long two weeks.

Nevertheless, I'm on local time, which means there's no place for me to be anywhere fast. I sit back and watch the others in the bar, making up stories about what brought the different couples together. I pick my way through my plate, then move on to dessert.

"*¿Más cerveza?*" My bartender takes away the empty bottle and rubs at the sweat ring left on top of the bar.

His Spanish is a surprise, considering most of the resort guests are American, but I'm too caught up in my thoughts to notice. My response slips out in not too shabby Spanish.

"*No, gracias.*"

The bar would be more interesting with a female bartender. Instead, the gruff older man judges me. His eyes keep sliding toward the scars on my face, but he's yet to ask what happened.

I find that's the case with most people. Very few have the balls to ask.

"*¿Qué mas tienes?*" I point at the bar menu.

I'm mostly a beer guy, but I'm feeling a need to branch out. Asking what else he has on the menu is rewarded with him slapping a menu down in front of me. This guy is most definitely *not* a talker, and his service leaves a lot to be desired.

As I peruse the menu, another guest asks for the channel to be changed. Evidently, there's a football match coming on; football meaning soccer for those of us in the US.

Which is perfect. I'd rather sit in a bar watching soccer than stare at the walls of a honeymoon suite with me, myself, and I.

The bartender twists the knob on the television. There's no remote. Static fills the screen, but after two swift smacks to the side of the television, a picture resolves itself.

It's the local news channel reporting on a developing story. From the hurried speech of the reporters, they're excited, which means whatever it is can't be good.

Fucking sharks sniffing out blood.

I sit back and tune out the noise until I hear: *Rehenes tomados por fuerzas rebeldes.*

Hostages taken by rebel forces.

The reporter states how a group affiliated with *Médicos Sin Fronteras* is being held by the *Coralos* cartel. Images of a group of terrified people cower in the background as cartel members claim Doctors Without Borders uses the humanitarian agency to smuggle guns into the neighboring country of Nicaragua.

I swirl the warm bottle of beer on the counter, paying the images half a mind. The footage is bad. Probably taken by one of the rebel's cellphones. It shakes, and the focus goes in and out, but when the footage zooms in on the captive's faces, I can't help but look.

It's a visceral reaction.

I'm a protector. Always have been. Since I was a kid, I was the one standing between the bullies and their victims. Which means I got beat up a lot until I learned how to defend myself.

It's funny how people work. How bullies work. Defending myself did nothing to stop the attacks on my friends. It was only when I learned how to go on the attack, and followed up my promises with action, that the bullies finally stood down.

It's a fundamental truth about humanity, and it takes powerful men like me to protect those weaker than myself.

My attention turns back to the footage, watching the bullies, who call themselves rebels now that they're all grown men.

They kick the hostages and shove them around, screaming at them to admit they're running guns. They cuss and swear, kick and spit, and don't even wait for the hostages to respond.

A response isn't what the rebels want. They want a reaction from the press. They want visibility.

Legitimacy.

They want to instill fear in the local populace, stamping out any resistance before it has time to take root.

And they're doing an amazing job.

At first, the prisoners refuse to look in the camera. They look rough, with dirty faces, matted hair, and gaunt expressions. There's evidence of beatings in swollen eyes, bruised faces, and a caged jumpiness in the way they hold themselves.

The hostages pull back and flinch as the camera closes in. They pan over the faces of four men and two women, grabbing close-ups, no doubt to better the odds of ransom.

When the cameras zoom in, the men pull back. Their eyes dart back and forth as if unsure whether they should look into the lens or avoid it all together.

This is exactly the kind of mission Guardian HRS would take on. We get involved in hostage rescues in one of three instances.

The first is when human trafficking is involved.

Forest Summers dedicates his life to bringing down organizations engaged in the disgusting trade of peddling human flesh.

It's a sad fact, but human trafficking accounts for nearly seventy percent of what we do. The rest of our missions involve off-the-books hostage rescue.

Some financed by the FBI.

They hire us to do the missions they can't, due to whatever political or legal restrictions bind their hands.

Rarely, the CIA will call us. Something like this, if it had political relevance, is right up our alley.

Last, if a private citizen contracts with us to rescue a family member, we'll take on the case if it has merit.

We did that with Zoe Lancaster and Eve Deverough. Both of their fathers contacted Guardian HRS to bring their daughters home.

This hostage situation doesn't scream political interest for the US. Hopefully, Doctors Without Borders has contingency plans in place for something like this.

The reporter explains how the cartel will keep the hostages until their demands are met.

What those demands might be isn't exactly clear. They ask for money and information. Perhaps looking for confirmation Doctors Without Borders is funneling weapons to enemies of the *Coralos* cartel.

Ah, this is a rival cartel engagement. That's a whole other level than dealing with rebels and doesn't bode well for the hostages.

The funny thing is, this kind of mission is exactly the kind of shit I'm trained for. However, this group belongs to the French organization that runs Doctors Without Borders. They draw heavily from the United States for physicians, and other health care individuals, to fill their missions across the globe. I doubt they have the resources to pay ransom for their doctors.

I swirl the last of my beer and swallow the dregs with a grimace when the cameraman zooms in on the hostages again. From the way they shake, they're terrified down to their bones. Probably pissed themselves when they were taken.

The camera focuses in on a woman. She scoots back, head down. Her dirty hair falls in front of her face. The poor thing desperately tries to curl into the fetal position.

The captors aren't having it.

One of them steps into the frame. His arm shoots out, and he grabs her chin, forcing her face up. The woman cowers. Her gaze remains fixed and cast down toward the dirt. Her nostrils flare as her lips press tight together.

When he forces her chin up, her glistening eyes overflow with tears. She tries to make minimal eye contact with the camera, staring anywhere but at the lens, but the man gripping her jaw is determined to force her to face the camera.

She tries to pull back, but he yanks her forward. Blinking rapidly, tears roll down her cheeks, leaving a trail in the dirt coating her face.

Long lashes matted by tears flutter as she tries to hide. Strands of hair stick to her dirty face. Then the most amazing hazel eyes with flecks of gold stare out of the screen.

What is this?

I lean forward, pinching my brows together.

My hand slams on the bar, making the glasses rattle and the bartender jump. He nearly drops the glass he polishes with a questionably clean cloth.

"No fucking way." I grind out the words, not believing my eyes.

The woman is terrified. Her gaze quickly dives back to the dirty floor where it remains.

"It can't be."

"*¿Que es eso?*" The bartender grabs my empty bottle and asks what I said.

"Nothing." But I stare as the feed continues, wishing whoever is filming could swing back to the left—and to the woman I haven't seen in years.

I only met her once.

It can't be.

I rub at my eyes as if scrubbing them clean. My gut tightens, and my pulse pounds.

What are the chances?

But there's no denying the truth.

I know that woman.

What the hell is Doc Maddox's widow doing in the jungles of Nicaragua?

There's not a damn chance she's involved in running guns. The cartel's got it wrong. No one is going to step up and admit blame. Which means they'll continue questing their hostages.

Torturing them.

Terrifying them.

Fuck.

It's not too big of a jump to go from torture to murder.

Talk about a powder keg ready to explode.

Three years ago, that woman stood by her husband's grave. I wouldn't be breathing if not for her husband, Doc Maddox, and I distinctly remember making his widow a promise.

If you ever need anything, just call.

Well, she needs something, and she's living on borrowed time. I'm well aware of how most hostage situations pan out. Too much knuckle-dragging by bureaucrats often leads to a bullet in the head for the hostages.

I owe Doc Maddox a life debt I can never repay, but I can start by rescuing his wife.

Not one to believe in coincidences, this ticks many of the boxes of fate's divine intervention.

What are the chances the universe put me in Costa Rica on the same day *she* needs me?

EIGHT

Brady

THERE'S NO TIME TO THINK BEYOND THE MISSION.

After I leave the bar, I head back to my joke of a honeymoon suite.

What I plan is madness. Going solo on any mission is risky business, but I've got that covered. I may be mad, heading off to rescue Maddox's widow and the others, but I'm not so crazy that I don't reach out for help.

"What the hell are you thinking?" Mitzy's voice screeches in my ear. "You're not equipped for something like that."

"Why do you think I called?" My grip on the phone tightens. "Hook me up. Perform some of that Mitzy Magic."

"And do what, exactly?" Her irritation is a palpable thing. "You think I can just scramble together an entire operation because you called? In what part of your training were you told to head out half-cocked with no backup?"

"That's your job." I use my cajoling voice, trying to sweeten Mitzy up. Unfortunately, she's in full burn mode. "I made a promise to his widow that if she ever needed anything ..."

"I get the whole macho hero mindset, but you'd think for once one of you would try to make my job a little easier. They hired me to plan and execute Guardian HRS sanctioned missions. Not to pander to the random urges of Guardians gone wild."

"Guardians gone wild?" I huff a laugh. "That's a good one."

There's a disturbance on the other end of the call. Mitzy curses, yelling not at me, but someone else. Silence falls for a moment, and I question my motives for requesting the assist.

Mitzy's right about one thing. Rescuing Maddox's widow isn't a sanctioned Guardian event.

While I can't remember her name, I definitely remember her face. Despite the tears of a widow, the woman had grace and a strength of spirit I've never experienced before.

I heard about the accident and what happened. In his final act, Doc Maddox went out as a hero, leaving his wife to grieve his death.

I can't imagine the depth of her loss, but something drew me to her at the funeral.

Doc Maddox deserved the trident. Rafe and I owe our lives to the doc's skills, but as I stood in the crowd, my eyes never once left his widow.

The urge to help, in whatever way possible, grew within me until it became an undeniable force. I made a promise, and I always follow through.

But what were the chances she'd ever call in the debt?

Not that it matters. Something about her grabbed me and drew me.

Doc Summers's voice draws me from my thoughts.

"Brady, this is Skye." The doc is on the phone, which raises my sphincter tone from tense to puckered tight.

It's a big ask—huge—and I risk a lot stepping out on a limb like this.

"I'm going to Nicaragua." I'd rather have the full support of Guardian HRS at my back, but I will go alone. "There's not a damn thing you can do to stop me."

"So I hear." The doc's not happy. "What the hell are you thinking? You can't …"

"I am."

"You're going to get yourself shot."

"Getting shot at is in the job description. Come up with something else to impress me. But don't bother. I'm going, and that's that."

"That's that?" Doc Summers's irritation spills through the phone. "All that brawn and not one lick of brains? You're going to be the death of me. I refuse to let you go."

"You can't refuse." I give a moment for that to sink in. "But you can help."

"Help? You're just lucky Mitzy hasn't figured out a way to teleport me over there because I will throttle you myself."

"But you'll help?" I sense she will and wait.

"That's not up to me."

"No, but you've got sway in high places."

Technically, Doc Summers is an equal partner in Guardian HRS with her brother, Forest Summers. She has the authority to approve this mission. She can also stop it before it begins.

"Look, I know what you're thinking." I try to reason with her. "I can do this."

"We're not discussing your operational readiness. I get you're doing this no matter what any of us here have to say about it, but it's going to cost you."

That's tacit approval to throw the weight of the Guardians behind my rescue attempt.

"Done."

"You haven't heard the price."

"Doesn't matter. I know what I'm going up against. My chances of success are a thousand times better with Guardian HRS. We both know it."

"You remember that when the time comes to repay what you owe me."

"I understand."

"Do you? Because it doesn't seem like you're thinking with all faculties intact. Who is this woman to you? And why do you care so much about her?"

"It's a debt I owe her husband."

"If that's what you want to believe." Her voice gets muted as she covers the phone. "Give the bullheaded asshole what he needs."

Yup, the doc is not happy with me.

"It can't be helped. Hostage situations come with a life of their own: volatile, incendiary, and unpredictable. Bottom line: there's no time to waste."

"Don't lecture me." Her irritation hits an all-time high.

"And thanks." I keep things light-hearted because my *ask* of Guardian HRS is a pretty big thing.

"And don't be a smart ass." Doc Summers isn't falling for my charm.

"Can't help it." A low, throaty chuckle escapes me. "It comes naturally."

"Well, let's skip the shit."

Time to get serious.

She blows out a frustrated breath. "Sam and CJ are joining us in a moment, but you and I need to have a talk."

"About what? The weather?"

"About your …"

"Look, if it's got anything to do with my body not being battleworthy, then shove it in a sock. This is happening, and it doesn't matter what you say, or don't say, about my fitness for duty. Technically, I'm on leave and can do what I want."

I sound like a petulant brat. Gah, I hate myself, but when you dig a hole, might as well go all in.

By now, Mitzy's dug up all pertinent data on the two rival cartels. She's got their entire play list with all the important players and whatever rivalries and border disputes exist between the two groups.

It killed me to see Maddox's widow on the broadcast like that. Knowing what I know about the fate of hostages taken by groups like the *Coralos* cartel, each second she's with them is a second too long.

"Well, if you'd shut up for half a second, and let me get a word in, then you'd know that's not my concern." It takes a moment for Doc Summers's words to sink in.

I forcibly blink as if that helps my hearing.

"It's not?" I give a quick shake of my head, knocking the cobwebs around.

"Your body is healing. Yes, you have months of physical therapy ahead of you, but you're not restricted otherwise."

"Good to know because I'm not turning around. All I need to know is how to cross the border. Can I do it like a normal person, or do I need to get creative?"

"I'm working on that." Mitzy's voice jumps back into the conversation. "Your rental will take you to the border, but you're not allowed to take it into Nicaragua."

"That's a bummer." But it's not my biggest obstacle. My biggest obstacle is knowing where to go.

All I know is Maddox's widow is being held somewhere in the jungles of Nicaragua. That's a lot of territory to cover.

I count on being mobile in Nicaragua. That way, I can cover ground, speak to the locals about the cartel, and somehow ferret out where they might be holding their hostages.

I've gone forward on missions where we had far less to work on. With time, I'm confident I'll figure it out, but that's the rub. I'm working on borrowed time.

"I'll have to find transport somehow, and I'm going to need money. Any way you could send some my way?"

"Working it." Mitzy's reply is tight, which tells me she's multitasking.

"Transport or cash?"

"Both." The sound of keys tapping in the background confirms Mitzy's working some of her magic as we speak. "Do you have any idea where you're going?"

"Not a clue." My reply is flippant, but honest. "I figure once in Nicaragua, I'd ask around."

"Don't bother with that. You'll draw too much attention to yourself. I'm on that now."

The tapping of keys sound lightning fast.

"How?"

"I'm pulling the broadcast up. Was it shot indoors or outside?"

"Outside, not that you can see much. Thick jungle vegetation surrounds a clearing."

Mitzy's ability to perform miracles never ceases to astound me.

When Alpha team rescued Eve, she used nothing other than a photo of Eve standing by a window to track down the location of Tomas Benefield's estate.

That man no longer breathes, and his human-trafficking ring is all but defunct.

I assume she'll do something similar to find Doc Maddox's wife.

It's killing me I don't know her name.

It'll come to me.

"Brady?" CJ's voice comes online. "What's this I hear about you heading to Nicaragua?"

"That I'm going to Nicaragua."

"Don't be an ass." There's a pause on the other end of the phone. "We've got some intel."

"Tell me?"

"First, tell me why this should be a Guardian operation?"

"I know one of the hostages."

"How?"

"She's the wife—er, widow—of Major Luke Maddox, a trauma surgeon with one of the Air Force's SOST teams. He saved my team back in the day. At his funeral, I told his wife if she ever needed anything, I'd be there to help, and it looks like she can use a helping hand."

"Got it." CJ doesn't like it, but he understands. "We're looking into Doctors Without Borders and what they're doing about this."

"I'm still going."

"I hear you, but due diligence never hurts. Tell me your immediate needs?"

Holy shit, CJ's going to support my crazy mission.

"Cash. Weapons. A way across the border. And wheels. A few extra men would be nice."

"We're standing up your team."

My team? Did I hear that right?

"You're what?"

"It's the perfect time for it. You're the last of Bravo to leave MedHold. Might as well spin up Bravo. It's been too long."

Too long? It's been a year of us licking our wounds.

Everyone, except for Booker, landed in medical hold. A thrill of excitement rushes through me, but on its tail, a sliver of doubt worms its way in.

"Thanks. But are we ready?"

Bravo team hasn't operated as a unit since the accident. We've all been involved in various training scenarios, working together as well as apart, but the last time we worked as a team was in Cancun.

I'm thrilled CJ's activating Bravo, but as their team leader it's my job to be with them. Instead, I'll be operating solo until they catch up to me.

"Forest is calling his contacts in the CIA. We'll get you connected and kitted out with appropriate gear." CJ sounds like he's reading off a checklist.

The ability of Guardian HRS to stand up a mission in zero time flat never ceases to amaze me. Their support of my hair-brained rescue should come as a shock, but I'm used to the unexpected.

I'm used to Guardian HRS going above and beyond to rescue those who've been taken and can't rescue themselves. This is what we do.

We're the Guardians: a brotherhood of men who will do whatever it takes. To me, it's more than a creed. It's my purpose.

"Any chatter about meeting the ransom demands?" Can't help it, but I'm curious. There's a lot to be learned from what kind of ransom demands are made and the terms attached to the exchange.

"So far, no ransom's been asked," CJ responds in a flat voice.

"What?" My brows pinch together. "That can't be right."

"We checked." Mitzy is quick to jump back into the conversation. "There's only been the one broadcast accusing Doctors Without Borders of working with the *Laguta* cartel members to destabilize the region."

"That's not good."

"Agreed." The new voice belongs to Guardian HRS's founder.

"We're following that thread and taking precautions." Forest's deep, rumbly voice comes as a surprise.

This mission might start with me, but all of Guardian HRS is jumping on board.

"What about the CIA? Will they intervene?" I can't believe the US will sit back and do nothing while US citizens are being held hostage, especially when political motivations confuse the picture.

"I've got confirmation, and it's not good," Mitzy's voice breaks in.

"What does that mean?" A twisting in my gut and that sour taste in my throat speaks to all kinds of bad news.

"The *Coralos* cartel does, in fact, believe Doctors Without Borders is using their humanitarian aid as a cover for US sanctioned destabilization efforts in the region. But that's not my news."

"What do you mean?"

"There's good evidence to support their claim." Mitzy releases a grenade into the conversation.

"What the fuck? You're saying it's true?"

"I'm saying I believe it might be true. Not that it is. There's a lot of chatter on their internal servers about it."

"You're on their servers?"

"Of course." Her flippant reply astounds me.

I want to ask *how* she does that, but it would be wasted breath. The knowledge she and her team of tech geniuses, and what they accomplish with it, is mind-boggling.

"If you're in their servers, then you know where they're holding the hostages." At least, that's my hope.

"That's a bit fuzzier, but we're pulling apart that video they sent to the press. I'll have a working location in a few hours."

A few hours? That's far better than I expect.

"In a few hours, I hope to be well across the border."

Across the border with no car, maybe a bit more cash, no way to get around other than hoofing it, and no idea where I should look.

Fucking walk in the park.

"What about the CIA? Are they going to sit back and do

nothing while American hostages are in danger?" My question isn't directed at anyone in particular.

It's more rhetorical.

"They're interested in helping, but that's it." Forest's answer comes as no surprise.

"Typical." The CIA likes to dig their fingers into all kinds of shit overseas, but they hate getting their hands dirty.

Or rather, they don't like it when the public finds out about the shit they do.

"Looks like." Forest's deep voice sounds like boulders crashing against each other. "My contact picked up on the first ring. They're aware of the situation. All the medical personnel are American, but as you know, Doctors Without Borders is a French company, which makes the optics muddy."

"Well, shit." I rub a hand down my face and pull at my chin. "What kind of support can I expect?"

"Limited. As Mitz said, they'll equip you with limited firearms - local stuff you can source in country. Your team is spinning up. The soonest we can get them there is eighteen hours."

"Shit. That's longer than I'd like."

"It's longer than anyone likes." Mitzy sounds as disappointed as I feel. "But it's the best we can do for now."

"Understood. From the look of the hostages, my gut says they don't have that much time." Hostage interrogation in a situation like this can quickly escalate to assassination when demands aren't met.

"That's my take as well." Forest isn't normally this chatty.

"I'm worried about Maddox's widow, and the others with her, of course. They won't kill the women, but they can do far worse. I don't have time to wait for Bravo to get in theater."

"That's my assessment." Forest doesn't argue. He understands the Guardian mindset. "Mitz, brief Brady on what you've found."

"On it, boss." Mitzy's perky voice is at odds with the information she delivers. "Where are you?"

"Right now?"

"No, asshole, this morning. Yes, of course. Where are you right now?"

"Waiting for the valet to pull my car around."

"Okay, that's good. I've wired funds. The bank's expecting you. Most of it will be in small bills, so plan accordingly. You'll need the small bills for the border crossing. There are also larger bills for the inevitable bribes. Like I said, we're combing through the feed sent to the news crews. If we're lucky, we'll find the embedded GPS coordinates of where it was shot. If not, I've got some *colleagues* working on that video."

I'm aware of the *colleagues* she mentions. It's a group of dark web enthusiasts, anti-establishment, who take on projects such as this for fun.

"As far as getting into Nicaragua … The border crossing is open. No time to get you different documentation. You'll use your personal passport and cross into Nicaragua as a tourist. Exfil is going to be tricky, but we'll make it work. Easiest is to cross back to Costa Rica, but there are a few snags."

"Such as?"

"Costa Rica requires proof of a plane ticket out of their country when entering from Nicaragua. It needs to be a paper copy."

"How do we get that?"

"I'll work on it. You, of course, have a plane ticket home."

"Not a printed ticket."

"What I'll do is have the bank print out tickets for yourself and the hostages."

"Okay." I listen closely, committing everything to memory.

"You'll cross at the Peñas Blancas border crossing. The good news is you can drive your car to the border, but you can't take it with you."

"How strict is that rule?"

"Strict. Costa Rican rental cars aren't allowed to cross."

"What do I do with it?"

"There's a house at the border. The family who lives there will watch it for you for a nominal cost."

"How do you know this shit?"

"Easy." Mitzy laughs. "Google."

"Gotcha."

"At the border, you'll pay the exit tax. Go inside the Costa Rican exit office. Have your passport and exit receipt handy. They rarely ask too many questions, but you're bound to draw attention."

"And what do I tell them? That I'm going head-to-head with the *Coralos* cartel to rescue American hostages?"

"Ha ha, funny, fuzzball." Mitzy's not amused with my humor. "I'm booking you an amazing Nicaraguan adventure. You want to be a tourist, and now you are. The itinerary is on its way. Use that to answer questions."

"Got it."

"After the Costa Rican exit office, you'll follow the crowds to the Nicaraguan immigration office. They'll check for your Costa Rican exit stamp, so keep it out. There will be an entrance fee and you'll need to show your passport. There may be more questions about your trip. Try to sound excited, but don't draw attention. You're a big, scary guy who doesn't look much like a tourist."

"I can play it up."

"No doubt you can."

"You'll want to grab a taxi to San Juan del Sur."

"I can take a bus. Get the whole in-country experience. Save the Guardians some cash."

"Do not take the bus." Forest jumps back into the conversation.

There's an awkward pause. Right when it drags on long enough to make me jump in, Forest continues.

"Just got confirmation. Look for a taxi with a blue roof. Driver's name will be Antonio."

"Why would I …"

"He's my CIA contact."

I feel like a fool and try to recover.

"Hopefully, by the time you make it through the border crossing, Mitzy will have a location for you. My contact will kit you out and take you as close as possible. The rest is up to you. I recommend waiting for the rest of your team, but you're not going to do that, so I'll save my breath."

"Um—thanks?"

"I sent you the location of the bank. Confirm if received." Mitzy is in no-nonsense mission mode.

A quick check of my phone reveals not only the location of the bank, but plane tickets back for the hostages. I flip through them until I see her name.

Angie.

Angie Maddox.

Hold on, Angie, I'm coming to rescue you.

I scan the rest of the names, committing them to memory, then tuck my phone away.

"There's one more thing." Forest's tone turns serious.

"What's that?"

"Angie is one of our own."

He knows her name? But of course, he does. He's got Mitzy pulling all the data.

"Okay."

"No. You don't get it. Angie is one of our foster rescues. She's family."

"No fucking way."

"Orphaned as a teen after a wreck took out her parents. Got put into the wrong foster home. Spent two years at The Facility getting her high school diploma. Became a doc. Do whatever it takes to bring her home."

"Copy that."

NINE

Brady

CROSSING THE COSTA RICAN BORDER INTO NICARAGUA TAKES longer than it should, but far less time than I fear. The pressure of a clock ticking frustrates me, but I force myself to look like a tourist with nothing but time to kill.

Before I know it, I'm across the border looking for Forest's CIA contact in a taxi with a blue roof.

All the taxis have blue roofs.

Hitching my thumbs under the straps of my rucksack, I readjust my pack and relax my pose. Just a man with time to kill.

I'm totally chill.

Others who crossed the border with me move around me in a stream. Some head to where the buses gather. Others take off on foot. Then, there's those of us waiting for rides.

Keeping an eye out for a man sitting in a taxi not taking fares, it takes a few minutes before I spy a likely subject. I saunter up to the cab. Locals stare at the big man with a backpack and take a few steps back.

I'm used to towering over most people, but in a country where the average height drops a few inches, I'm a fucking giant.

The driver of my intended target looks up from the paper he's reading. The light on top of the taxi claims it's out of service, but I'm guessing he's my guy. I rap on the roof.

"*¿Puedo dar un paseo a San Juan del Sur?*"

He flicks his paper closed and folds it neatly before setting it on the seat beside him. A duffel bag sits in the back seat.

"You sure that's where you want to go?" He responds to my request to go to San Juan del Sur in crisp, unaccented English.

"Unless you've got something else in mind?"

"Get in. We'll chat."

"Antonio?"

"Take it you're Brady?"

I remove my backpack and climb into the back seat.

"Have to say, it's been a long time since Forest came calling." He cranks the engine and slowly pulls out of the taxi queue. Not that it's much of a queue. Things aren't nearly that orderly here. He pulls onto the rutted road, moving slow enough to feel every rut and rock.

"I was told you'd have something for me?"

"I do. Check the bag. Should be everything you need."

I turn to the duffel and open the zipper.

"Nice."

I inventory the contents and shift things over to my ruck. It's standard stuff. A handgun, with enough ammunition to make a difference, a serrated knife, and a machete to match. I dig deeper and find a phone, spotting scope, mirror, and compass. There's none of Mitzy's high-tech gear. It's more standard stuff, beat up, but serviceable.

"Looks great. I appreciate this."

"It's everything you need for where you're going. I'd love to provide an assist, but I'm limited in my movements around these parts, plus Forest said I probably couldn't keep up with you in the jungle." He rifles around the front seat, then passes back a map. "Terrain map for you. Your tech guy located the camp where the video was taken. Not sure if your hostages will still be there, though. These groups travel light and move fast."

Tech guy? Obviously, Antonio hasn't heard of Mitzy. She'd rip his balls off if she knew Antonio assumed she was a dude.

"I hear you." I continue packing away all the gadgets, stuffing them into my bag. "Hopefully, they haven't moved on yet."

It's late, and the sun's already slipped beyond the horizon. That leaves my rescue in total darkness. Which is good and bad.

I can use the darkness to hide my escape with the hostages, but it means I'll be traveling without light to guide me.

In the jungle, that's problematic.

With the map in front of me, I locate the border crossing and a very meticulous X that marks the spot placed on the map for me. The terrain will challenge the best outdoor enthusiast. It's rugged and hilly, crisscrossed by several rivers.

From the terrain markings, many of those come with potentially lethal waterfalls and rapids. I'll have to be careful.

While Antonio fills me in on the arrival of my team, I make quick work out of memorizing the map. It's impossible to get it all down, but I know what's important and what's not.

I trace out three likely escape routes: one by water, one by road, and a hellacious cross-country hike.

"How close can you get me?" A quick scan of the map reveals the camp is located immediately next to a road and near a stream wanting to become a river.

"Unfortunately, not as close as you'd like. Those roads are monitored and the traffic on them relayed down the pipe. I've got two options for you."

I take it he means the road beside the cartel's camp.

"Hit me." I have a feeling both options will suck.

"I can drop you off above. You'll have to traverse a ridge and cross over a valley."

"A valley?"

"It's not as big as it sounds. Bigger than a gulch, smaller than a valley. River at the bottom."

"What's option two?"

"I drop you south of their position. It's basically the same, up a ridge, across a valley."

"I'd rather take the gravity assist. Let's take the high road."

"On it."

I do one more survey of the gear Antonio was able to source for me on such short notice. Besides what I already packed away, there's a first aid kit and a couple of protein bars.

My intention is to get in and get out as fast as possible. Hopefully, with no injuries.

"Did Forest mention where my team is?"

"Only to say they're another twelve hours out."

"Great." While I'd rather have my team, I'm good on my own. No doubt CJ will send updates. "This phone. How good is it in the jungle?"

"You won't have any issues with that. Forest sent that as a thank you gift a few years back. That thing will pick up a signal from underground, underwater, and even in the deepest jungle."

"Underground?"

"Well, a fair distance inside a cave. Don't ask how I know that. Bad memories and all."

"I hear you, and thanks. I damn well appreciate it."

"No problem. This is as close as we get, however."

"How's that?"

"I try to limit my interactions with gringos, and especially those who look like they're in special forces."

"Copy that."

"We've got another hour to go before I drop you. If you've got some larger-sized bills, hand those over. I'll want to go back to my crew and brag about the rich American I picked up at the border."

"You can have it." I pull my wallet out of my front pocket and peel off several bills. I hand those to him and we settle into a comfortable silence. Which means his part of the briefing is over and I have an operation to plan.

I think back at the video of the hostages, trying to gauge their physical conditioning by what little I saw. Getting out of the jungle will be nearly impossible without some degree of physical ability.

I spend the next hour getting acquainted with the terrain. Meanwhile, Antonio drives us deeper into the jungle.

"Amigo, we're here." There's no need for Antonio to say anything. It's pretty clear. He stretches an arm across the back of the passenger seat. "You got what you need?"

"Got what I need." I climb out of his cab and look around. "Couldn't be easy, could it?" I mumble under my breath and shake my head.

With coastal plains on the Caribbean and Western coasts, dense rainforests and rugged terrain occupy the center of the country.

I could be picking my way through cotton and coffee. Instead, I get a hazardous and inhospitable jungle.

I thump the top of the cab and say goodbye to Antonio.

From here on out, I'm on my own.

With a fairly good idea of where I'm going, I begin the perilous trek through mountain and jungle. Running fast, I waste no time.

With darkness approaching, what dim light that makes it through the dense canopy disappears, which leaves me running in shadow.

I slow my run and navigate solely based on stride count and what I remember from the map. From here on out, I run dark.

Water to my left guides me. This stream hooks up with another, and together they join with others to form a slow-moving river. Two klicks along that river is where I'll find the hostages, if the *Coralos* men haven't moved them. I doubt they'd break camp and travel the roads at night. The dirt roads are perilous during daytime hours and deadly at night.

Once I hit the river, I spare some light to reference the map. I'm on the wrong side of the camp, which is both problematic and fortunate.

In the cover of darkness, I slow my pace, making as little sound as possible. This is both to hear my opponents and to hide my presence. Fortunately, the camp is not concerned about quiet. I hear them carousing long before I see any evidence of the camp.

The sun's down. The jungle's in complete darkness. The men kick back, drinking, smoking, and shooting the shit. The glow of their campfires lights up the jungle like a torch, making recon ridiculously easy.

"Like a walk in the park." I wipe sweat from my brow and turn my attention to the camp.

There are about two dozen men in camp. Not my best odds. As for the hostages, my guess is they'll be near the center of the camp. Getting there is going to be a problem, if not damn near impossible.

I certainly can't move in now. The entire camp is up, celebrating. I'll have to sit back and wait for things to die down.

Which I don't like.

TEN

Angie

AFTER TAKING THAT HORRIFYING VIDEO, THE GUNMEN ONCE AGAIN separate the women from the men. They take me and Izzy to a tent near the edge of the camp.

My fear pegs an all-time high. The men keep asking about weapons, yelling at us and accusing us of running guns for the *Laguta* cartel.

Izzy and I shuffle ahead of our guards, prodded forward by the muzzles of their guns. Izzy trips beside me, nearly going down, but I grab her hand and haul her up beside me. She clutches her rabbit's foot and holds it close to her heart.

"Th-thanks." Her breathy voice betrays her fear, and I don't blame her.

I'm terrified too.

We come to a smallish tent, round with a center pole, that stands a few feet above our heads.

"Stay." Our guards flip back the fabric door and toss us into the tent and near-total darkness.

I trip over my feet and fall to the ground. Izzy is two steps behind me. We turn around and scoot backwards, terrified of what the men might do. Except for a small flap at the top, there is no light.

"What are you going to do to us?" Izzy's plea is met with stony silence. "We know nothing. We don't know about these weapons you keep mentioning."

"*Mujeres inútiles.*" Our guard spits on the ground and leaves us.

"What did he say?" I scramble to my feet.

"Useless women." Izzy slowly turns in a circle, taking in the tent's interior. She grips the rabbit's foot around her neck. I hate to say it, but that thing's not bringing her any good luck.

I follow her lead, exploring our surroundings.

Dirt floor. Musty air. Stifling heat. Overwhelming darkness.

The tiniest trickle of water leads from one edge of the tent to the other side.

I wander over to that part of the tent and put my ear to the thick canvas. The muffled sounds from camp reach my ears and tell me nothing.

But the water …

The water tells me much. I'm an outdoor survival enthusiast, or I was whenever Luke was alive. My brain is already churning through how to escape and evade.

I refuse to give in.

I refuse to give up.

"That video …" Izzy makes a circuit of the tent. She appears oblivious to the small trickle of water. "Do you think they'll ask for ransom?"

"Will Doctors Without Borders pay ransom?"

I'm the new kid on the block. The briefings by my new employer were woefully inadequate in situations like this. Mostly, they told us not to worry and to cooperate as much as possible.

"I don't know." Izzy shrugs.

A pile of flea-infested rags is stacked in the tents' corner. No bed. No chairs. Nothing to protect us from the ground. Nothing to protect us from the creepy-crawlies that infest the ground.

"Why do they keep asking about weapons?" Izzy rubs her arms and moves to the center of the tent.

A small flap at the top allows a tiny sliver of diffused light inside. All I see are shadows upon shadows. Everything is indistinct.

But there's one important thing. We're free to move about. Our hands and feet aren't bound. These men don't consider *mujeres inútiles* to be a threat.

"I don't know."

"Why did they separate us from the others?" Izzy stares at the flap that's the only exit from our tent.

"I don't know. But I can guess."

Separation is a form of psychological torture. Separating us makes us weaker.

It's something Luke explained when he returned from SERE training. There are many ways to break a person down. The vast majority of those have nothing to do with physical torture.

It's about destroying hope.

That's what's happening now.

Perhaps our captors think we'll break without the strength of our men to hold us together?

Well, we're not *mujeres inútiles.*

Our men don't make us strong.

"Why?" Izzy's voice shakes.

"To put pressure on the men."

"How does that work? They know nothing."

"It's psychological torture." Exhausted from our capture and terrified by the video, I fold my legs in front of me. "My husband told me about it."

"He did?" Izzy joins me on the ground. "He must be so worried. Maybe they'll ask for ransom from our relatives?"

"My husband passed a few years ago."

"Oh, I'm so sorry." Izzy and I are great work colleagues, but we're far from friends.

It surprises me how much I don't share with my team.

"It's okay." I'm finally at the point where I can talk about Luke without getting choked up. "He was in the special forces."

"Like the SEALs?"

"Air Force, but he often supported the SEALs."

"How?"

"He was a trauma surgeon on the Air Force's special operations trauma team."

"What's that?"

"It's a team that flies into a combat zone to treat the wounded."

"Is that how he died?"

"No. He was home. We were in an accident."

"Oh, Angie …" Izzy places her hand on my arm.

"It's not something I share."

"I didn't mean to bring back bad memories, especially now." Izzy makes a vague gesture.

"Thanks. I appreciate it. For the longest time, I couldn't think about Luke without tears and sobs. This job …" A sigh escapes me. "It's supposed to be about healing and building a new life."

"This wasn't supposed to happen." Izzy takes in a deep breath and folds her knees to her chest. Wrapping her arms around her shins, she props her chin on her knees.

We sit in silence. The minutes slowly creep by, and we jump at every sound outside the tent, then look to each other for support.

There's another reason to separate us from the men. It's something I don't want to acknowledge. Something I won't mention to Izzy.

It helps to have her with me. I don't feel as alone. Which makes me think about Daniel, Jacob, Stefan, and Jerald. They separated us from the men for a reason.

Mujeres inútiles.

The guard's comment repeats in my mind. If they think we're useless, they don't believe we're the ones running the guns. It makes sense, especially after the beating Jacob endured.

Our captors' convictions about the guns make me wonder if there may not be some truth to what they believe, but I've unloaded every piece of gear in our little caravan of trucks. If there were guns, I would've seen them.

"Angie?"

"Yes?"

"If your husband worked with the SEALs, did he do some of the same training? Anything that can help us?"

"He did. After his selection to SOST—"

"SOST?"

"Sorry, that's the acronym for Special Operations Surgical Team. You know how the military loves its acronyms."

"No kidding. Did he do …" Her hand lifts as if grasping for something. "Ugh, I can't remember—a survival school of some sort?"

"SERE."

"That's it."

"Yeah. It prepares military personnel to *survive and return with honor* if they ever find themselves in a survival situation."

"Anything about that which can help us now?"

"His stories about that course were absolutely fascinating. I asked him to teach me many of the survival skills during our own hikes in the wilderness. I know a fair amount about basic survival, but I'm always looking to learn more."

I did a lot of research about Nicaragua before I set foot in the country. My husband's words come back to me. He was such a patient teacher.

Survive. Evade. Resist. Escape.

The mantra keeps me sane in a world that no longer makes sense.

I'm doing my best to survive.

As for SERE … There is no evasion. They already captured me.

I don't resist.

Resistance is futile.

Those words curl around my thoughts, poisoning them. They tell me I'm weak. I'm not worthy. They tell me I don't have the strength to survive.

These whispers … They aren't mine, but the bits and pieces of my deepest fears. They poison my thoughts and make me weak.

Jacob resisted, and they beat him. His face is a bloody mess. What will they do to two women?

A fate worse than death.

I focus on Izzy's question. Is there anything in Luke's stories I can use now? He gave me what I needed. Luke taught me to survive. I dig in deep and remember what he said.

We need to focus and not waste our strength.

"I guess evade is out of the question, seeing as how we're already prisoners." Izzy drags her fingertip in the dirt, drawing little circles. "Survive?" She glances up, capturing my gaze. "How do we do that?"

"I'm going with what Daniel said." It's the easiest way to tell her the truth.

"What was that?"

"*Be meek. Stay silent. Lower your gaze.*" I repeat his words verbatim. There is wisdom in what he says. Some form of hope I grasp.

"That's the opposite of resist."

"We're not resisting, Izzy. We're trying to get through this. See where resisting got Jacob?" My hand presses against my belly, keeping the urge to vomit at bay. Jacob's beating was brutal. "You think surviving is being meek? I say otherwise. It's the strongest thing we can do."

"How does that help?" Izzy curls inward.

I feel her despair. It resonates with the beating of my heart. This fear overwhelms me.

"It buys us time." That's the best answer I can give.

"For what?" Izzy's haunted gaze travels around our prison. "What do they want?"

"Ransom or rescue? They took that video for a reason."

"I suppose they did." She bites her nails and draws circles in the dirt.

"What about Doctors Without Borders? Surely, we're not the first team to get captured by local militia."

I want to believe Izzy holds an answer. I need to believe we're not without hope.

"I don't know what they'll do." She turns a tear-streaked face toward me. It's honest, but empty. There's no hope in her eyes.

But I refuse to accept defeat.

Survive. Evade. Resist. Escape.

Those words are more than they seem. Survive against your doubt. Evade your fear. Resist the fear swimming in your veins. And above all else, escape the bonds that hold you prisoner.

"Let's hope they do something, but between you and me, I don't want to rely on someone else to rescue me. We need to be on the look-out for ways to escape."

"How do we do that when we're under guard? And what about the others?"

"I don't know."

What she says about the others hits me in the gut.

Abandoning them feels selfish, but how are we going to free four men when we're surrounded by armed guards? We'll be lucky to save ourselves.

"I hear you, but I don't have an answer."

"I suppose we see what happens. If we make it, maybe we can get someone to help?"

"One thing Luke mentioned was to keep your eyes down, memorize everything about your surroundings. He said to count your steps. It might be pitch black when an opportunity arises."

"If we do this, though, what about the jungle?"

"Luke and I practiced survival skills on our hikes. The most important thing, if we get separated, is to follow the water."

"The water?"

"Yes. It flows downhill and will eventually drain into the sea."

"What if it drains into a lake?"

"I suppose you follow around the lake and look for water flowing out."

"Makes sense." Izzy pulls her legs in tight and closes her eyes. "Do you pray?"

"I'm not religious."

"Do you mind if I do?"

"Not at all."

"Will you pray with me?"

"I will."

Izzy releases her knees and lets them fall out to the side. I scoot around until I face her. She grabs my hands and bows her head. I follow suit and pray with her.

All the while, I remember the last time I prayed. It was the day I said goodbye to Luke.

The day he became a hero.

We sit in the tent, dozing fitfully, taking turns while watching out for the other. Minutes become hours. My stomach growls. My bladder pinches. Dirt covers me from my head to my toes. Life's basically miserable, but I hold out for hope.

Sometime later, the tent flap opens and a man steps in. He carries a flashlight and shines it at us, blinding me before I remember to lower my gaze.

Be meek. Head bent. Eyes down.

Do nothing to attract unnecessary attention.

"Get up." His heavily accented English makes it difficult to understand, but the gesture is clear.

Izzy and I stand, brushing off the dirt from our pants. We face him together, both keeping our heads down and our eyes on the ground.

The ground crunches beneath his heavy boots as he approaches. The offensive reek of his body odor makes my eyes tear and my nose crinkle.

Izzy's fingers brush against mine. Without thinking, I clasp her hand, needing her strength as much as she needs mine.

He moves to stand in front of Izzy. Aiming the flashlight in her face, he places two fingers under her chin and forces her to look up.

A whimper escapes her as she lifts her chin.

"You are beautiful. No?"

Izzy doesn't answer, but her entire body shakes.

The man swings the flashlight toward me. My eyes squeeze shut against the bright light and stay that way as he places two fingers under my chin.

Like Izzy, I don't fight when he forces my chin up.

"And you. A surprising beauty." Fetid and rank, his breath makes me sway on my feet. "You are a doctor?"

I reply with the slightest nod. It's hard to move, honestly, with his fingers under my chin.

"An eye doctor, according to your colleagues."

"*Sí señor.*" My entire body shakes.

"*¿Tu hablas español?*"

"*Un poquito.*"

"We'll stick with English, then." He releases me and takes a step back.

Arms crossed over a barrel chest, he's a large man. Thick, ropey veins climb up his arms, coiling around the bulging muscles of his biceps.

The flashlight casts his face in shadow. Scruffy beard, bushy brows, his eyes are coal black. His full lips press together as he examines us.

"What do you know about the guns?"

Not sure if the question is for me or Izzy, I shift my feet and focus on the ground beneath his boots.

"We know nothing," Izzy answers in a feeble voice. "Please, we're not involved. All we want is to help your people."

"By giving them drugs and handing out glasses?"

"Immunizations too, and she gives people back their sight."

"Why, you two are saints, then. Should I kneel before you?" His caustic tone makes my gut tense.

I squeeze Izzy's hand, trying to warn her to say as little as possible.

"Is this true?" He flashes the light in my face. "You bring sight back to the blind?"

Knowing where this could lead, I do my best to mitigate the damage Izzy's overshare causes.

"Not blind. Only those with cataracts that make it hard for them to see. I treat infections too that can lead to blindness."

"You are a saint?"

"No, sir. I am no saint. I just want to help."

"So, you come to my country? Help my people? You should stay in your own country."

When I dip my head, my stringy hair falls forward. He reaches out and runs the strands through his fingers.

"This is no place for an American woman."

I say nothing.

"It can be very dangerous." He lifts my hair to his nose and sniffs the dirty strands. Then he flashes the light in my face again. "The girl with the golden eyes. You are a blonde? Yes?"

My response is in the trembling of my body. Inside my chest, my heart is at the races, stampeding like a hundred horses let out of the gates. My pulse roars past my ears and that light-headed feeling is back.

"And you …" His attention shifts back to Izzy. "Blue eyes and dark hair. An unusual combination. Stunning."

He snaps his fingers, and four men come running into the tent.

"Take these two to the river. See that they bathe." His oily gaze rakes us from head to toe. "Then deliver them to my tent."

"*Sí señor.*" The men bend at the waist in deference to the man whom I assume is the leader.

Two come for me. Two grab Izzy.

Neither of us resists as they shuffle us between them, leading us out of the tent.

Like I did before, I gather as much data as I can about the camp. There are a few dozen armed men. Half a dozen tents dot the haphazard layout of the camp. Ours is on the edge of the camp, closest to the water.

About thirty feet across, it's larger than a stream but smaller than a river. Somewhat in-between, the water flows at a nice clip.

I take particular note of that.

There's no particular congregation of guards around any one tent, leaving me guessing where our friends are being held.

There is one tent in the center, larger than the rest. No need to guess who that belongs to. A shudder ripples down my spine, thinking about what will happen to us after we're bathed.

But I'll deal with that when, or if, it comes.

Until then, they're taking us to the water, and water is a potential avenue of escape.

ELEVEN

Brady

Now that I'm here, the urge to rescue the hostages is all I can think about. Although, that's a lie.

I'm here for Angie—to fulfill a debt I owe her husband.

That's not to say I don't care about the others. My goal is to rescue them all. First thought is to wait until the camp quiets down.

There are several half-ton trucks parked alongside the road. If I can disable all but one, find the keys, then it's a perfect vehicle to use as an escape. I've got the roads out of here memorized, and with the other vehicles disabled, I won't have to race down the twists and turns.

That's my best plan. But there are several parts to that plan which require attention. First off, getting on the other side of the river.

Again, I'll need to wait until the men dose off.

Then, I need to find keys to the truck. Hopefully, these men are lazy and keep the keys inside the truck. Won't know until I'm there. Once that's done, I'll need to slit the tires of the other vehicles.

If I haven't alerted the camp to my presence by then, it's a simple matter of finding which tent the hostages are being held inside.

Last step, getting six hostages onto the truck without raising an alarm.

It's a shit plan with lots of places things can go wrong.

Another option is to wait, gather intel, and let my team catch up with me. If the camp breaks up in the morning, I'll have to follow the hostages.

That plan is lowest on my list.

There's no way to ensure I can follow effectively. I could hitch a ride in their trucks, but that's equally problematic. I can still go with slashing the tires, but that alerts them to my presence.

All my options are shit, but I don't expect this to be easy. I scan the camp, counting men, looking for guards, checking out their weapons and the relative positions of their tents. Biggest threat infiltrating the camp is accidentally tripping on ropes securing the tents. I wish the stash Antonio dropped off included night-vision goggles, or a scope, but no such luck.

The sun is finally down, and with it, most of my light.

Movement by the water's edge draws my attention.

Four men surround two women. They prod them with their guns, forcing them down the bank. My gut squeezes and heart rate spikes. Without seeing her face, I know one woman instantly.

It's Angie.

Angie plus another.

Just the women?

Where are the male hostages?

I scan the top of the bank, looking for scouts and lookouts, anyone keeping an eye out, but I see none. This crowd are confident motherfuckers, certain no one will come for them in the jungle.

The four men force Angie and the other woman to the water's edge. The men tell the women to remove their clothes. Then repeat it in heavily accented English.

Angie draws back. Shakes her head. The other woman holds her hand out as if that can protect her. As a student of body language, I know exactly what comes next.

From Angie's fear, she does as well.

It sucks for women. The horror and degradation of capture

includes everything men endure, *plus* the terror of rape. It's an unjust world.

And that's exactly what it looks like is about to happen. Although, why would the men care the women are clean?

That makes no sense, but the bits and pieces of Spanish drifting to my ear make that a certainty.

"Fuck." This is not how I want this to go down.

My many potential plans do not involve a rescue in full view of armed guards.

I'm more of a stealth ops kind of guy.

Slipping in and out of shadows is more my speed, but this requires immediate action on my part. Which means the wheels in my head churn, adapting and overcoming this change in circumstance.

I need to get the women's attention and communicate an exit plan without alerting the guards.

I pull out my weapon and take aim. Four is not a good number. I can easily take down two before the others react. With luck, I can get all four.

The trickier part will be getting Angie and the other girl out of there after I take out the guards.

The only way out—is the river.

Shit. I am not a fan of this plan.

But it's all I have.

The argument at the river continues. The men's voices rise, turning to shouts.

The woman with Angie pleads with the men.

One man grabs at his crotch and makes a vulgar gesture as his comments turn lewd.

I need to act now, before they draw the attention of more men.

I go to a knee and steady my aim. Head shots are preferred, but I can't risk missing a shot. I go for center mass and squeeze the trigger. Speed and accuracy are my friends, but the darkness is my foe.

Pop. Pop. Pop.

I squeeze out three shots.

One. Two. Three.

Three men go down.

Solid shots to the center of their chests. The fourth man looks up.

It's weird, but I can see the whites of his eyes.

He moves behind the woman with the dark hair and shouts to his fellows in the camp.

His wide, terrified eyes scan the far bank.

I should move and hide my position, but I need Angie to see me. The fourth man takes a step back.

It's exactly what I need.

With a fourth shot, I take him down.

Then I'm on my feet, rushing into the water, making way too much sound.

"The water!" I cup my hands over my mouth and call out to the women. "In the water."

Angie's head jerks up at my shout. Her eyes pinch, trying to make out the shadows.

I splash, knowing the risk I take, but the splashing shows against the inky black of the placid little river.

Movement in the camp spells doom.

I point downstream and dive into the water. My long, sure strokes bring me to the center of the slow river.

Angie, bless her soul, grabs the other woman by the wrist and drags her into the water. The woman glances back and forth, scanning the bank and the water, but she allows Angie to draw her deeper into the water.

By now, the camp's fully alerted. Shadows stir at the top of the bank. Men with guns.

"Quickly." I urge Angie to move faster. When she gets mid-thigh, I command her to move. "Dive."

Angie and the woman dive into the river, splashing and coughing while I slice through the water to their side. Gunfire rips through the air, bullets whizzing past our heads.

The men on the bank are light-blind from their campfires making it difficult for them to see through the darkness.

We don't have much time.

Angie makes it to me. She's like a fish in the water. The other woman struggles.

"I c-can't swim." The woman calls out and swallows a mouthful of water. Spitting and sputtering as she fights the mild current.

"Go." I turn to Angie and point downstream. "Don't splash. The river makes a sharp turn to the left a hundred yards ahead. If we're separated, we meet there."

The gunfire intensifies as the men's vision adapts to the darkness. We're running out of time and losing our advantage.

But we are moving.

There's a brisk current.

I grab the other woman.

"I need you to relax. Don't thrash. Grab my arm." I wrap my arm under her armpit and over and around her chest. Supporting her, I roll to my back and kick downstream.

Bullets hiss all around us, diving into the water. The shots are wild and way off. All we have to do is get to that bend in the river. From there, I can regroup and figure a way out of this mess.

This is exactly the kind of rescue I don't want, but I'm a former Navy SEAL and the only easy day was yesterday.

TWELVE

Angie
___

I DON'T KNOW WHY I TRUST THE MAN IN THE DARKNESS.

For a moment—it's the briefest flash of a memory—I see Luke's silhouette.

The voice is different, deeper and huskier than Luke's, but it vibrates with authority and familiarity.

I swear I've heard that voice before.

When the four guards drop, it takes a moment to figure out what's happening.

The gunshots mean nothing.

The camp's been celebrating all night long, shooting their weapons into the air like idiots.

But something is going on. Izzy and I go from near-rape victims to running for our lives.

Or rather—swimming.

Once the man calls out, ordering me to the water, I don't hesitate. I grab Izzy and pull her into the water. The man swims toward us.

Gunfire opens up from the top of the bank. The bullets whiz far too close for comfort and disappear into the surrounding water with a hiss.

Any of those can prove lethal.

Fortunately, none of the men are good shots.

Maybe it's because they're drunk from their celebrations.

Once the man takes Izzy, I head down the river, cutting through the water in sure strokes learned over years of being a kid on the swim team.

I know all about splashing. Splashing wastes energy and slows a swimmer down.

As for the sharp bend in the river, I nearly miss it. Too focused on my strokes and hampered by the near impenetrable darkness of the jungle, I barely make out the far bank coming closer.

In fact, I don't make it out at all.

Instead, tree roots catch and snag on my hands and feet. I stop and pivot, following the curve of the river against the bank with my eyes.

I will not think about what might be in these waters, and facing that fear, I wade back into the middle of the river where it's deepest and head out again. Upstream, I make out the dark form of our savior. He's on his back, supporting Izzy, and moving far faster than seems possible.

Knowing something about special forces, from the stories Luke shared with me, I know what those men are capable of physically.

I assume the man is a special forces soldier, hired by either the United States or Doctors Without Borders, to attempt a rescue of our team.

We leave the men behind.

I clutch at my stomach, feeling sick for escaping while they're still prisoners, but I know better than to turn around.

My strokes are sure and strong, but my boots hamper the fluttering of my feet, making my kick less effective. Fortunately, I have powerful arms.

Navigating the bend in the river is tricky. I hesitate and tread water as I try to pick out a path. To my right, a rocky cliff soars twenty feet in the air. To my left, the jungle crawls all the way to the water's edge.

"You doing okay?" The deep voice of our rescuer gives me a start.

"Y-yes."

He moves to the right, towards the rocks.

"Can you feel the bottom?" His words are for Izzy.

Not me.

"Yes." Izzy's voice is shaky, and she's out of breath.

"Stand. Catch your breath and we'll regroup." He assists Izzy, stabilizing her until she's on her feet. "Go to the rocks." He cocks his ear, listening.

Not sure who that comment's for, I figure it applies to us both.

I swim until I can touch bottom. Then decide I really don't want to step in the soft spongy muck underneath. I head over to the rock, then grab hold of a rocky protrusion and let my feet float with the rest of me.

"Anyone injured?" He looks from me to Izzy, then back again. He keeps his voice to a whisper.

That voice. I've heard it before, but I can't place it.

"Shot?" He turns, looking at both of us. In the darkness, I can't make out his features, but I know this man.

"N-no." Izzy clings to the rock face, standing as high as she can out of the water. It comes to mid-thigh with a small gap between the water and the rock.

"Angie?"

He knows my name?

"I'm good. Not shot. No injuries."

"Good." He runs a hand through his hair, and it's only then that I see the thick rucksack attached to his back.

"You're special forces?"

"Yes, and no." He adjusts the ruck, pulling at the webbing to tighten it after the swim.

"Do I know you?" It's a weird question to ask at a time like this, but there's a really weird feeling in my gut like I know this man.

There's more too—an odd electricity crackling in the air. I attribute that to fear and being amped up on adrenaline.

"Yes."

His one-word answers aren't giving me the info I need. It's frustrating, but then gunfire sounds overhead. Izzy gives a little screech, then covers her mouth, realizing the sound will draw them to us.

"What's our plan?"

"Influx right now. We can't outrun them." He pauses, then crouches down and reaches under the rock's edge. "I've got an idea." He looks at me. "Don't move. Don't make a sound. I'll be back in less than a minute." He shrugs off his rucksack and holds it out to me. "Hold this."

"What are you doing?"

"Seeing if my hunch is correct."

"Your hunch?"

"I think there's a cave under here. See how the water cuts under the rock? If not a cave, we can hide under the rock."

Hide under the rock? He's crazy.

"I do." I take the ruck from him, surprised by how heavy it is. Afraid of dropping it and losing it, I plant my feet in the muck below us and shrug it onto my back.

"We need to hide." He cocks his ear, listening to the dark. "They're sending men our way and we're not going to escape them in the jungle."

And what if there is no cave under there?

He takes a deep breath and dips under the water. His feet brush against my leg as he kicks.

I hold my breath. It's weird, and makes little sense, but he's holding his breath. Why shouldn't I?

I suppose it's my way of knowing when it's time to freak out. If Izzy and I lose him, we're screwed.

And I don't even know his name.

The webbing on the pack makes it hang low on my back. I spread my feet in the muck, establishing a broad base, and lean forward until I'm stable.

Izzy's eyes are wide and frightened. She shivers, although both the air and water are warm. We're in the middle of a tropical jungle where overheating is more of a threat than hypothermia.

That's when I notice the way my hands shake and my teeth chatter.

"We're going to be okay." I try to reassure her, but I don't know what to say. "I didn't know you couldn't swim."

"Drowning seemed a better option than what those men intended." Izzy tries to smile, but the sounds of men crashing through vegetation shuts us both up.

That's when I realize I no longer hold my breath.

"How long has he been under there?" Izzy takes a chance and whispers. Hopefully, none of the men hear us, but I remember something about water and how sound travels.

Not specifically what it means, but enough to know we're better off staying quiet.

The water between us moves. Our rescuer appears like a ghost. I give a little squeak before covering my mouth.

He cocks his head, listening to the sounds of the jungle, then places his finger over his lips. Waving, he urges Izzy and me to lean in close.

His voice is too deep for a real whisper, but he does his best.

"There's a cave three feet back. There's a small pocket of air for a couple of feet, then nothing. Another foot in and it opens to a cave." He cocks his head again. "We can't outrun them, so we'll hide in there."

Izzy's lips press into a flat line of terror. He turns to her and smiles. Desperately, I examine his face, trying to place where I might know him from, but it's too dark and the shadows make it impossible to discern his features.

"We need to go, but first I need to swim my pack inside." He turns to Izzy. "While I take my pack, you and Angie will hide under the edge of the rock. They'll catch you if you're outside. All you need to do is keep your nose and mouth above the waterline. There's about a three-inch gap. You can do this." He turns to me. "Can you …

"We've got this." I grip Izzy's hand. "I'll be with you the whole time."

"When I come back, I'll tap three times on the leg. Like this."

He shows us exactly what he's going to do. "I'll take Izzy first. It's less than fifteen seconds but will seem like forever. You'll need to breathe with me. When I say, we're both going to take a deep breath and go under. I'll pull you to the cave. Don't thrash. Don't resist. Do you understand?"

"I do." Izzy's voice is small, meek.

I feel her terror.

"And what about me? Do you want me to follow?"

"No. I'll get her in, then come back for you. Whatever you do, stay out of sight."

"Okay."

He gestures, and I shrug out of the pack. We pass it between us, then he's gone.

The sounds of the men tromping through the forest grow closer.

"You ready?" I feel the gap between water and stone. "All you need to do is float on your back."

"I don't know how to do that."

"Just lay back. I've got you."

Izzy gives me the eye, but she does what I ask. I point her headfirst into the opening, then lay down beside her. Supporting her head and shoulders, I slowly move us under the cover of the rock.

Seconds feel like minutes and minutes feel like hours. There's no sign of our rescuer and I worry. Izzy grips my hand.

The girl is terrified, but she doesn't balk at any of the things asked of her. That's a sign of great personal strength. My respect for her increases.

With us on our backs, the water laps in our ears, taking away sound. I can't hear the men along the riverbank, or anything else really, but I feel three soft taps on my shoulder. Our rescuer moves my hand from around Izzy's shoulder, taking over supporting her.

He slowly rotates until he's on his back. There's precious little room for the three of us to maneuver.

"On three." He takes in a deep breath and waits for Izzy to follow.

She does, and he blows out. Izzy follows.

"Two." He takes in another breath.

This time, Izzy is quicker and more in synch with him. She squeezes my hand, then lets go.

"One." He takes a deep breath and waits for Izzy to do the same. When she does, he pulls her under and out of sight.

Now, it's just me and men who sound like they're directly overhead. I pull my legs in, worried my feet might poke out from the edge of the rock.

With fear swimming in my veins, I close my eyes and say a brief prayer.

This is *not* what I signed up for when I left my old life behind.

But I couldn't live without Luke. It hurt too much. This is my escape from my old life—the birth of something new.

A 21-gun salute rings through my mind. Memories of Luke's funeral still haunt me.

The bugle plays "Taps." It's a last farewell.

They lifted the flag from his coffin and folded it with great reverence.

Two men I don't know step forward from the crowd.

They pound their tridents into Luke's casket.

The crowd pays their respects, and slowly people leave. It's just me and the two men.

One of them approaches.

He hands me a trident and makes a promise.

"If you ever need anything, just call."

"Thank you, but I can't accept that."

"Not asking if you want it. I'm giving it with a promise. You need anything, you call."

"But I don't even know your name."

"Name's Brady, Brady Malone."

It can't be?

My heart leaps into my throat, then my throat closes up on me.

Grief runs through me, blunted by the years, but still very much present.

Still Raw.

Still hurting.

"Luke?" I whisper his name. "Is this your doing? Did you send this man to me?"

Not one to believe in divine intervention—or fate—I can't help but wonder if Luke didn't bring Brady Malone to help me when I needed him most.

Three soft taps pull me out of my memories. Brady surfaces.

"You ready?" He reaches out and grasps my hand.

When he does, something shifts inside of me. I can't explain what it is, but it's as if a great weight lifts and I can finally breathe.

"Yes."

"On three. One. Two. Three …"

THIRTEEN

Brady
_____

THE WOMEN ARE TOTAL TROOPERS. ANGIE IS SIMPLY PHENOMENAL.

She heads down the river with long, sure strokes. Izzy complicates things, slows me down, but this isn't my first rodeo.

Despite her inability to swim, the young woman doesn't freak out. She lets me carry her down the river and doesn't fight when I pull her under the water to take her to the tiny cave I discovered.

I'd thought to escape through the jungle, but those men move far faster than I expect. Water is our way out of this, but I need to buy time.

With the girls semi-safe for now, I figure it's better to hide than to run.

I rise out of the water into the blackness of the cave. Izzy's right where I left her. She may not know how to swim, but she knows how to follow orders.

Angie is right behind me.

Our cave is cramped and marginally dry. I'm able to get all three of us out of the water.

That's important. We're all completely soaked and muddy, which is going to make the next few hours painful, but I've been in worse situations.

"Everybody doing okay?" I keep my voice low.

"Yes." Izzy shivers beside me.

It's not from hypothermia, but the adrenaline racing through her body.

"I'm good." Angie crawls next to me on the rock and bumps her head against my chest. "Sorry."

"It's okay." The cave is pitch black. I gently guide Angie down to sit beside me.

"Can we spare any light?" Angie's voice is whisper quiet.

"No. Too risky." Any light we use might transmit through the water, alerting the men outside to our presence.

"What now?" Angie finds a comfortable position and settles down.

"Now, we wait." I shift position and bump into Izzy. "Apologies for any accidental touching."

"It's okay," Izzy whispers back. "That was my shoulder."

"Gotcha." I settle back and regroup. "We're going to spend the night here. We should be protected from getting cold, but I suggest we conserve what body heat we can and sleep if you can manage it."

"How?" Izzy is inquisitive.

Angie listens quietly.

"Come here." I'm in a relatively comfortable position. The rock behind my back is smooth, and the ground isn't too bad. "You can lean on me."

We do a bit of readjustment and settle down. I've got both arms wrapped around the women. They curl against me and tremble while the adrenaline slowly leaves their bodies.

It's going to be one long-ass night.

"Are you Brady? Brady Malone?" Angie's soft voice pulls me from my thoughts.

"Yes."

"How did you know? How are you here?"

"What are you talking about?" Izzy shifts against me.

"Brady was at my husband's funeral. He …" Her voice trails off, perhaps confused by how to continue.

"Angie's husband saved my ass, and that of my team, when we were on deployment. I owe him my life. At his funeral, I approached Angie and told her if she needed anything, I'd be there."

"Wow." Izzy's surprise brings a grin to my face. "And here you are."

"And here I am."

"But how did you know what happened, or where we were?" Angie's voice rises and I give a gentle *Shh* to remind her to stay as quiet as possible. "Sorry."

"Honestly, it was pure luck." I lean my head back and close my eyes. Staring into near-total darkness unnerves me.

"How's that?" Angie's voice is whisper-quiet, almost too hard to hear.

"I was on vacation. In Costa Rica."

"But—"

"When I saw the news broadcast about your team being taken, I recognized your face. To say it shocked me is an understatement. Also, knowing a thing or two about hostage situations, I knew speed was of the essence. I crossed the border and came looking."

"You recognized me?" Angie snuggles into my embrace.

"Are you cold?" Maybe I put too much weight on the jungle heat to keep us from freezing.

"No. Sorry, I was just getting more comfortable." When she pulls away, I instantly regret saying anything.

There's something comforting about holding her in my arms.

I grab her shoulder and gently guide her back to me.

"We'll stay warmer if we all huddle together." The moment she pulled away, my entire side felt chilled. Fortunately, Angie settles back down.

"I guess we're going to be cozy." Angie's gentle laughter brings a smile to my face. She's nervous and covering it with a laugh.

"Yeah, I get to spend the night with two beautiful women in my arms, fully clothed, totally drenched, and I can't see either of them. Cozy doesn't describe this."

"You're funny." Angie pokes me in the ribs. "And thanks for letting me get *cozy* with you. First off, you radiate heat, and secondly …" She takes in a deep breath. "It feels good to be held after … Well, after all of that."

"You're a definite trouper." I'm extremely proud of how Angie kept her shit locked down tight. It's sad to say, but that's a rare quality in many men, not to mention women.

"I was terrified."

"But you didn't fight one thing I asked you to do."

"Only because the alternative was worse."

"I can't believe you recognized me on the news feed." Angie brings us back around to our original conversation. "It's been three years. How?"

"I never forget a beautiful face."

"I'm sure I looked anything but beautiful."

"You were traumatized and roughed up a bit, but when I saw your eyes, I knew exactly who you were."

"And you came for me?"

"I did."

"Because of Luke?"

"Because I made a promise to *you*, and I always uphold my promises. For whatever reason, the universe put me close enough to help."

"That's either extraordinarily lucky or the divine intervention of fate." Izzy shifts to a more comfortable position. "The two of you are linked."

"Linked?" Angie asks.

"Bound by fate." Izzy yawns and her body relaxes.

It's an odd thing to say, but it makes me wonder. I'm not a believer in fate, but there's definitely something tying me to Angie.

It makes little sense, but I feel protective of Angie.

Protective? Of a woman you haven't thought about in three years?

My conscience calls bullshit, and I don't have a response.

It's true. In the past three years, I haven't thought once about Angie Maddox.

But when I saw her terrified face on that television screen, there was no doubt I would move heaven and earth to save her.

Heaven and earth may not be involved in this rescue, but I convinced Forest Summers to mobilize the Guardians.

That's nearly the same thing.

"I can't thank you enough," Angie says. "Luck or fate, you couldn't have come at a better time. Those men were going to—"

"I know what they were going to do, and that will never happen."

"You came alone?" Angie leans against me, her head propped on my shoulder.

"Speed is of the essence. I came alone, but my team is on the way. We'll do what we can to rescue the rest of your team. I intended to do only recon work tonight and wait for their arrival in the morning. Getting all six of you out at once would've been best, but when it became clear what those men intended, there was no way I could stand aside and do nothing."

"Thank you. But what happens now?" Angie yawns beside me.

Izzy's nearly asleep.

"Now, we get as much sleep as we can. Tomorrow will be challenging. You're going to need all your energy."

"And what about your team? How will they find us?"

"I'll contact them in the morning and give a debrief. We'll know better then what to do."

"How will they find us?" Angie's smart, always thinking things through. I admire that.

"A tracker."

"Really?"

"Yes. In fact …" I lean forward, trapping Angie in the crook of my arm, as I pull off Mitzy's knotted bracelet with the tracker in it. "Where's your hand?"

Angie hits me in the face, and we laugh in the darkness. Everything we do is by feel. When I find her hand, I slip the knotted bracelet around her wrist and snug it tight.

"There. Now I can always find you."

"But what if we get separated? What about your team?"

"We always work with backups."

"Thank you." She settles back against me with a sigh.

As for my next steps, I reference the terrain map Antonio gave me. Following the rivers and streams is definitely our best bet. If I'm lucky, I'll call him and have him pick us up.

But then what?

It's too risky keeping the girls in Nicaragua. The best thing I can do is get them across the border and into Costa Rica.

The *Coralos* cartel will not send men after them in another country.

Maybe.

It's too much risk for little reward. Fortunately, I have a place, courtesy of Forest, where I can keep Angie and Izzy until I can get them out of this whole mess.

As for my team? We'll figure that out later.

Izzy falls asleep.

"I can't believe you really came to rescue me." Angie's breathy voice does strange things inside my chest, tightening and constricting my breathing.

"A promise is a promise." Playing down the rescue comes naturally, but with Angie, those words carry significant weight.

"I was supposed to call if I needed anything, but I didn't know what I needed. The first year after Luke's death was hard. Harder than hard. I was angry at the world and didn't need any help. I thought it was a really gracious gesture, but I didn't think …"

"I understand. I was a stranger to you."

"A stranger who risked his life to save me. I owe you a debt."

"It doesn't work like that." I shift to a more comfortable position. Izzy doesn't even wake.

"What doesn't?" Angie keeps her voice down; it's breathy.

Sexy.

"Life debts." I try to focus on the mission and keep my mind on task.

"But you saved my life." The soft timbre of her voice makes that nearly impossible.

"Like I said, it doesn't work like that."

"Feels like it should."

"This isn't a tit for tat kind of thing. It's hard to accept help or ask for it when we need it. I'm just glad I was in a position where I could do something."

"Do you believe in fate?"

"I'm not a religious man, but I believe there are forces out there we don't understand." I'm not a believer in fate, but I do believe things happen for a reason.

"I suppose there are."

Silence descends between us for a minute.

"So, Doctors Without Borders? I didn't realize you were a physician."

Unlike Izzy, I'm not ready for sleep. Not that I'd sleep while on duty. Besides, I'm curious about what Angie Maddox has been up to these past three years.

"I am. Luke loved trauma surgery. He paid his way through medical school on a Navy scholarship. That's where we met, actually."

"What kind of medicine do you practice?"

"Ophthalmology."

"An eye doc?"

"Yup."

"And the Doctors Without Borders gig? How did that happen?"

"I grieved for a very long time. Longer than I should've."

"How can anyone place a time limit on grief?"

"Well, there is one according to psychologists, and there are particular stages you're supposed to work through."

"Heard about those."

"I got stuck and I couldn't move on."

"I'm sorry to hear that."

"I'm actually in a good place right now. For the first time in years, I feel as if I can take a breath. I'm not sure how to explain it other than that, but I feel like I have a future. Luke wouldn't want me to live in the past."

"And that got you here?"

"Yeah, sorry. That was your question. I got rid of everything. Sold our house, our cars, all of our stuff. One reason I couldn't move on was because everywhere I looked, there were memories of Luke I couldn't move past. I basically did a hard reset on my life and asked some pretty probing questions about who I was and who I wanted to be."

"And what answers did you find?"

"I want to help people. The money and the fancy office really aren't what I want anymore. I want to honor Luke in a way that makes a difference. He served in the Navy. That road wasn't an option for me. I looked around at a few places and decided Doctors Without Borders was exactly what I needed. It took me out of my life, brought me to an underserved population, and I could make life-changing differences for the people I treated."

"That's an incredible sacrifice. You handled yourself really well out there."

"Thanks." She pauses for a second. "I was terrified."

"Didn't look like it." I squeeze her shoulder and place a kiss on the top of her head before realizing what the fuck I'm doing. "Sorry. I shouldn't have …"

"It's okay." She pushes on my chest and lifts her head from my shoulder. "Intense situations bring people together."

I kissed her?

What the fuck was I thinking?

I definitely need my head examined.

Thank God it was only the top of her head and I didn't dive in to plant one on her lips. Talk about inappropriate.

On a plus note, she's not repulsed. Of course, she hasn't seen my scars yet.

Our conversation winds down, and she eventually falls asleep. Izzy is knocked out cold and doesn't stir when my ass goes numb. I reposition the way I'm sitting.

I get no sleep. Not that I'm not tired, but because someone has to keep watch. Sleep deprivation sucks, but this isn't the first time I've had to stay awake for an ungodly amount of time.

Soon though, the hours pass. From the backlight of my watch, it's early morning, pre-dawn, and time for us to exit the cave.

I want our exit to be in the dark in case someone is still looking for the girls.

My hope is the men looking for them returned to camp. If I'm exceptionally lucky, they'll have broken camp and moved on.

My watch.

Mitzy's words return to me.

It was her present since I love to dive and is packed with all kinds of high-tech wizardry.

I extricate myself from Izzy and Angie, lowering them gently down as I wade into the water. Tapping the screen, I acquaint myself with all the technological goodies. No surprise, there's a text function.

Me: Bravo 1 to Overlord.

Overlord: WTF! Where are U?

I crack a smile. That's definitely Mitzy.

Me: In a dark, dark place.

Mitzy: Not funny... Report.

Whoops, that last bit sounds like CJ.

Me: Have the women. Safe 4 now.

We continue texting back and forth as I explain everything that's happened since the last time I checked in.

My team is on their way. Mitzy sends my coordinates to them while I explain to CJ my plans for getting out of this place.

He agrees with my choice to follow the river.

There've been no new broadcasts or demands from the *Coralos* cartel. The status of the four men is up in the air.

CJ plays things loose.

First things first. He needs the rest of Bravo on the ground. We'll decide later whether they hook up with me or go after the four remaining hostages without me.

Seems to me they should go after the hostages.

As long as we're not being pursued, I should be able to get Angie and Izzy across the border to Costa Rica.

In the end, we decide to remain flexible. My immediate task is to get the women safely out of Nicaragua.

"Wake up." I gently shake Izzy and Angie until they stir.

"It's time to go."

"I'm not looking forward to this." While I can't see Izzy's expression, I imagine she's giving the water a nasty look.

"I'm going out first to make sure it's safe. When I return, we approach it the same as last time. Close your eyes and hold your breath. I'll get you out safely."

"I'll follow." Angie's full of confidence.

"I'd rather you wait until I get back."

"You have Izzy and that pack of yours to deal with. There's no reason to make multiple trips. I'm good."

Thankful for her reminder about my ruck, I shoulder the bag and tighten it down. Not pleased with Angie navigating the short distance by herself, I try to put my foot down.

"And what if you get turned around on the way out?" I inject as much concern into my voice as possible without sounding like I don't think she can handle it on her own.

From what little I've seen of Angie, she's self-sufficient.

"I won't."

I give her a look she can't see but decide I'm not in a mood to argue. If she says she can do it, I'm going to trust she can. I leave the girls to investigate outside.

It's completely quiet outside with no sign of the *Coralos* men. I wait for a few moments, listening hard, and as soon as I confirm we're alone, I remove my ruck, tie it to a nearby branch, then head back inside to the cave.

"I'm back." I announce my arrival, not wanting to scare them.

"Is it clear?" Angie sounds hopeful.

"Yes, we're good." I feel around until my hand brushes against Izzy's thigh. "Grab my hand. Time to get out of here." I lead Izzy into the water. "Now, breathe with me. We go on one."

Izzy is a total trouper. She allows me to guide her outside and makes nearly zero sound as we breach the surface of the water.

Until she looks at me.

She covers her gasp with her hand, but I feel the revulsion down to my core and curl in on myself before I realize what I'm doing.

Turning away, I pretend I didn't hear disgust at my scars in that gasp. I used to draw women to me with nothing more than a wink.

Now, I drive them away.

I'm a freak.

Facing away from Izzy allows me to not only ignore her but to take stock of where we are.

All my senses are on alert, and I reevaluate my plan to travel via the river rather than overland through the jungle. One look at the density of the vegetation and I return to my original plan of river travel.

There are few things we need to worry about. There are crocodiles in Nicaragua, but they infest the larger rivers where there's more food. All we need to worry about is the occasional snake, but those run from larger animals. I'm not worried about those.

There's a stillness in the forest, but it's not quiet. Between bird song and monkeys calling out to their troupes, there's always noise. The chirping of insects and the rustling of leaves as larger animals move through the canopy combine into a background symphony that tells me there aren't any humans nearby.

Men, with their tendency to make tons of noise or obnoxious smells with their tobacco, guns, and unwashed bodies, turn the jungle quiet. It's not quiet, which tells me our pursuers gave up during the night.

Angie joins us and peers across the water to the other side of the bank.

"What now?" She keeps her voice down then turns toward me.

I cringe, waiting for her reaction to my scars, but there's only a smile waiting for me. Her eyes soften as she takes me in, seeing me for the first time since the funeral. "You look different from what I remember."

Curious about what she imagined, I deflect instead of ask. Best to get the whole scar thing out of the way so we can move on.

"The scars?"

"Not those. You look more intense."

"You sure it's not the scars?" Unlike Izzy, she doesn't focus on the disfigurement.

Angie takes in the scars, but only in a cursory scan of my features.

"It's your eyes."

"My eyes?"

"Yes. I saw the change in Luke after one of his deployments. You've seen and survived tragedy. Your eyes are harder. More guarded."

Harder? More guarded?

All she sees are your eyes, lug head. Not the scars.

That realization comes with a punch to my gut. I do not know what to make of it.

Instead of dealing with that shit, I clear my throat and gesture downstream. I've got a job to do, and it's time to focus on the job, not the pretty woman standing in front of me.

"Now, we follow the water."

Izzy's grip on my hand tightens. She's definitely not a fan.

"Don't worry. I'll help you. We're going to make as little sound as possible and float out of here."

With those words, I adjust the pack on my back and lay back in the water. Izzy leans back and I once again wrap my arm around her chest. Then I kick off from the rocks and head to the center of the river where the current is strongest.

I'm eager to leave this place and pray nothing exciting happens along the way.

FOURTEEN

Angie

THE JUNGLE IS SIMPLY—AMAZING.

Wonderful.

Fascinating.

Hundreds of scents lace the air and dance on the breeze. They create an intricate web of sensations that delight and amaze.

There are floral aromas from multi-colored blooms, musky odors from animals I can't see, and there's the overwhelming loamy and musty smell of the vegetation and ground beneath my feet, which anchors everything to the earth.

I love the smell of a freshly mowed lawn—it brings back fond memories from a time before I lost my parents—but this sensation, the scent of the vast jungle, is that and more.

It overpowers the freshness of the river and seeps into every molecule of life. It invigorates and captivates.

As for the river, I ignore what might be in it. Brady doesn't seem concerned about creepy-crawlies, so I decide I won't care about them either, even though I saw no less than three snakes. Two swam near the banks, not interested in the three humans floating in the middle of the river. One was directly overhead, a bright green mass of coils draped over a branch hanging over the river.

I don't think Izzy saw them. If she had, she would've freaked.

There's also something calming about floating in the river; a weightless existence I could lose myself in. I gently flutter my legs, using very little energy, and enjoy the water lapping in my ears and the ever-changing fragrance of the jungle as I pass through it.

Brady brought us out of the cave while it was still dark outside, but the sun's risen since then. I enjoy the sunrise while Izzy learns how to float on her back. Brady grabbed a log for her to use for floatation, and she's trying her hardest not to be a burden.

As for Brady, he's alert and constantly searching the vegetation for any signs of pursuit.

Meanwhile, I live a dream, floating in a small river in the middle of paradise. I've never felt this peaceful. If I close my eyes, it almost seems as if the past twenty-four hours never happened.

Although, every time I look at Brady, reality comes crashing down, yanking me back to where we are and why we're swimming in a river. Every time he catches me looking at him, the most beautiful smile ghosts across his face.

He's a handsome man, although I don't believe he thinks that. The moment he catches himself smiling, his brows pinch together. The smile flees, replaced by a frown.

Then he turns away, leaving my thoughts spinning. Maybe women fawn at him all the time and he's over the attention? Who knows?

I turn my thoughts back to the river and the beauty of nature all around me.

There's a rhythm to the water.

It speeds up in the narrows, where it gets deeper. The smooth surface churns into chaotic ripples and tiny wavelets. Then, it slows down, widening and getting shallow again. The surface smooths out, becoming tranquil and inviting.

When the river slows, Brady kicks with his legs, hurrying us through those sections. I think it's because we're more exposed when the river opens like that. The canopy no longer reaches all the way overhead, making it easier to see three people floating downstream.

Frankly, I prefer the wider areas because that's the only time I glimpse the clouds. In the narrower, faster, more turbulent parts of the river, the canopy closes in around us, turning the bright sunlight into filtered beams of light and dancing shadows.

"How are you doing?" Brady calls out to me.

"I'm good." I cup my hands and scull the water, pulling up alongside him.

"Do you hear that?" He turns his head, listening.

There's something in his eyes that makes my heart skip a beat. They're harder and more guarded than I remember from when I met him at the funeral.

I didn't make that up.

Luke was the same.

He came back from one particular deployment changed. It took time to get him to open up about it. He saw things and did things he could never forget.

That guardedness and hardening became a part of him.

There's a little voice inside my head that wonders if that isn't the same deployment where Luke ran across Brady's team. I know better than to ask or go digging for information like that, but I can't help but wonder.

"Hear, what?"

"We need to get out of the water." Brady angles toward the bank.

"Why?"

"Listen."

I roll my head, pulling my ear totally out of the water. A barely audible, low roar fills my ears.

"What is that?" I shift to follow Brady toward the bank.

"That's the sound of a waterfall, if I'm not mistaken."

"A waterfall?" Izzy shifts suddenly, which rolls her into the water. Brady quickly stabilizes her, but not fast enough to stop her from swallowing water. She coughs and sputters. The poor thing looks like a drowned rat.

"How big?" Her voice shakes with fear.

Depending on the size, we can slip over a small waterfall.

Now wouldn't that be fun?

Sliding down a waterfall in the jungle? It's every kid's secret dream. Or at least, used to be one of mine.

Now, if it's bigger, that's something else. We'll have to figure a way around it.

"That's what we're going to find out." He tows Izzy to the bank, steadies her on her feet near the water's edge, then holds out his hand for support while she climbs up the muddy bank. When I get near, he does the same for me.

The moment our hands touch, it's like holding on to something familiar.

Something real.

I stumble on the way out and fall into his arms.

Brady catches me, holding me solidly against his broad chest. He's tall and towers over me. Broad chest, thick arms, undeniably male, my head barely reaches his shoulders.

I cling to him longer than I should, but there's something comforting about his embrace. It's like coming home.

I let go and take a step back, shaken by the experience.

"Sorry." When I look up at him, the gold in his eyes shimmers in the sunlight.

Like me, his eyes are hazel, flecked with gold. The moment stretches before I realize I'm staring.

Great. I'm a clingy mess.

Not my finest hour, and I don't want to think about what he makes of my clinginess. My heart pounds crazy fast, either from embarrassment or something else, and I press my hand against his chest to stabilize my footing.

"Don't be." His eyes twinkle with that comment. "I'll never complain when a woman throws herself at me."

"I did not *throw* myself at you." I curl my fingers and playfully pop him in the chest. "I fell into you."

"We each have our different versions." His husky laughter forces me to relax.

It's impossible to do otherwise. And while I'm so close, I reach up to touch his scars. His body locks up, and I withdraw my hand as if stung.

"I'm sorry. That was inappropriate." I cock my head and take a good look at him. "You definitely look different from the last time we met."

"Scars will do that." His grimace tells me much about how he feels about those scars.

Brady Malone was a handsome man when I met him three years ago; handsome enough to snag the attention of a widow at her husband's funeral.

He's still ruggedly handsome. If possible, more so than before.

Instead of taking away from his innate beauty, the scars add depth and character, hiding a mystery about the man standing in front of me. I find everything about him fascinating and can't stop staring.

Not because the scars are disfiguring, but because I yearn to know the story behind how he got them.

"It's rude to stare." His eyes pinch, and a scowl turns his expression into a dangerous message that says, *Go away!*

"We all have scars. Yours are on your face. Mine are on the inside. They affect us only as much as we allow, and after losing three years of my life to grief, I no longer allow my scars to define me. I refuse to give them the ability to determine my fate. You shouldn't either."

"Powerful words." His eyes narrow. "You sure you believe them? Because it seems like you're running from yours."

"That's rude and insensitive." My words fill with more spitfire than I'd otherwise like. "I take one day at a time. That's the only way I know how to deal with my grief. You know how I got my scars." I absently clutch at my necklace holding Luke's wedding band. "Maybe someday you'll share the story of how you got yours."

"Someday?" His reply is terse. Gruff. "Try never."

"Whatever." I turn in a huff, needing distance before I say something truly ugly.

His *Try never* sounds like a whole hell of a lot like *fuck off.*

I won't push him, but I'm curious.

Since his reply tells me to back off, I do, but someday I'm going to get him to tell me not only about his scars, but what happened to him and his team on the deployment that brought Luke to their aid.

I don't bet.

Never have.

But I bet the deployment that changed Luke is the one where he met Brady and Brady's team.

"So, waterfall?" I take a step back, making sure I don't trip again, and glance downstream.

The roar of the waterfall is louder up here.

"Yes. Waterfall." Brady's gaze hasn't left me.

"It's rude to stare." I fling his words back at him and turn in a huff.

Brady says nothing. He spins around and heads into the thick vegetation. I'm about to ask why we bothered traveling in the river, rather than on land, when he stops to pull out a machete from his pack. With the vegetation too dense to walk through, he cuts a way through.

Mystery solved.

It's a slow, laborious process, but it lets me watch him move.

The man is something to behold.

All brawn, with broad shoulders tapering down to a trim waist, his ass does a great job of filling out those trousers, and his poor shirt struggles to contain all that musculature. I'm particularly intrigued by the ropey veins crawling up his forearms and how they disappear beneath his shirt.

Izzy slogs behind me.

I thought she was a girly girl, but the woman has chops. Not once does she complain, and she doesn't waste any effort on unnecessary conversation.

She's focused and determined not to be a burden. From her silence, I can tell she's unhappy about not being able to handle herself in the water.

After a few hundred feet, the roar of the waterfall is unmistakable. Brady angles to the right, headed back to the river. Izzy and I follow, three steps behind. The vegetation gradually thins as dirt gives way to rock.

Our gentle river squeezes between two rock faces, rushing and churning as it speeds down a precipitous drop.

Brady steps out onto the rocks and looks down at the mist rising from below. I move to stand beside him and peer over the drop-off.

"Wow." I subconsciously reach for his hand, feeling steadier with our fingers interlaced. Holding his hand, I take a step forward to get a good look at the waterfall. "It's beautiful."

"There's a rainbow." Brady points midway down the falls. His fingers give a little squeeze.

"I see it." I twist to see Izzy and wave for her to join us. "Izzy, come look at the rainbow."

She inches her way out onto the ledge.

"You're not afraid of heights, are you?" I can't help but kid her, but then realize Izzy might be as afraid of heights as she is in the water.

"No." Her smile looks forced. "The rocks look slippery."

A quick glance at her footwear reveals the problem. I wear sturdy boots. She wears an old pair of sneakers with very little tread.

"Well, be careful." I hold out my hand, and she takes it with a nod of thanks.

Clutching me, she peeks over the edge.

"It's gorgeous, and that rainbow …" Her voice drifts off wistfully. "If only we could sit here and admire it."

Her attention shifts to Brady, who practically hangs over the edge. When he wraps a thick vine around his forearm and grips it tight, her eyes widen. I want to tell him to stop, but I resist.

He knows what he's doing.

I hope.

"Do you think they're still after us?" Izzy takes a cautious step toward the edge.

The waterfall is a rare sight.

"How many people, other than us, have stood here over the years?" When I'm in places like this, removed from civilization, that's one of several questions that go through my mind.

"Years?" Izzy takes a step back.

"What about decades?" I can't imagine we're the first humans to stand here, but we are one of a very select few.

Centuries?

"Assume the worst," Brady responds to Izzy while I'm lost in my thoughts.

It takes a moment for me to remember Izzy's question about being followed.

He releases me and turns back to the river. "We move as if they are."

Those piercing eyes of his take in the jungle and his shoulders pull up to his ears.

"What's wrong?" I close the distance between us until our arms brush against each other. Like him, I turn my attention upstream.

"Nothing." Brady's keyed up about something.

"Doesn't look like nothing."

"Just a feeling." The muscles of his jaw clench.

His attention turns down to where the backs of our hands barely brush against each other. His fingers reach out, seeking.

I take his hand. It feels natural holding his hand.

Familiar.

He lifts our clasped hands and stares at the knotted bracelet he put around my wrist last night. "Until this is done, don't remove that. Not for anything."

"Why?"

"Because I can find you with that."

I give a little shake of my head, letting him know I understand.

"You think we're still in danger?"

"As long as you're out here, you're in danger." He kisses the back of my hand. "I won't rest until I have you in a safe place—but if we're separated, I will find you."

"Then I'll stay by your side, so you don't have to." I try smiling at him, but his flat expression gives me pause.

Brady's serious.

He doesn't mention Izzy. That promise isn't for her. My throat closes in and I try to swallow past the lump in my throat. Brady Malone is an unusual man.

FIFTEEN

Angie

A FLOCK OF PARROTS BURSTS OUT OF THE CANOPY ABOUT A HUNDRED yards upstream, squawking and calling out to one another.

They fly toward us, passing overhead.

"Wow, they're beautiful." Green, blue, yellow, and red, the birds are beyond gorgeous. "I've never seen one out of captivity."

"Come." Brady's jaw clenches. "We need to get out of the open."

"I've got mud in places I don't want to mention." Izzy pulls at her clothes. "It's scratchy. Is it just me?"

"No." I feel the same. "Everything's wet and uncomfortable." My feet squish inside my boots. "Brady?"

He stands stock still, watching the area of jungle where the parrots came from.

"We go now." There's an urgency in his voice that wasn't there before.

"How are we going to get around the waterfall?" Izzy peers over the edge, standing some distance back. She doesn't look thrilled about climbing down the twenty to thirty feet to the bottom.

I've never been afraid of heights and have an adventurous spirit.

It's one of the things Luke loved about me. I was his adventure buddy.

Whether it was four-wheeling old forest roads, climbing boulders, or repelling from crazy heights, we loved the outdoors.

I remember his excitement when he came back from SERE, eager to teach me all the survival hacks he learned. He knew I'd think it was something cool to learn and, in teaching me, it cemented the principles he learned in his head.

All that's to say, I'm comfortable outdoors and know what risks are worthwhile and which ones are not.

Climbing down this waterfall is questionable, but doable. No doubt Brady can do it.

I'm comfortable attempting it.

Some places look more slippery than others. With Izzy's footwear, I'm not sure if the risk is worth it.

"We go down, or we go around." Brady comes to the edge to peer down the falls.

When he looks at me, all I see is beauty in his eyes. I remember that from the first time we met. I was grieving my husband's death and shouldn't have had eyes for any other man, but I remember the handsome stranger and the honor he gave my husband.

Whoa!

Eyes for another man?

Am I attracted to Brady?

I do a quick gut check because such a thing is completely unexpected, but I think I might be.

As crazy as it sounds, Brady Malone intrigues me. Yes, there are scars on the side of his face, but that's surface stuff. His eyes draw me in. His confidence is downright sexy. The way he handles himself around me and Izzy shows incredible compassion and respect.

Honor.

The three of us huddled together last night, but not once did it feel wrong.

"You and I have the shoes for it, but Izzy doesn't." I glance at Izzy. She sits on one of the large boulders, taking a break.

"Agreed." His lips press into a flat line. "How are you with climbing?"

"Pretty good."

"Is there anything you're not good at?" The way his eyes twinkle when he looks at me makes my heart skip a beat.

"I love the outdoors."

"Good to know." He winks, and my belly does this *loopy loo* kind of thing. A genuine smile fills my face when he follows that wink with a mischievous grin.

When he turns to Izzy, a twinge of jealousy runs through me. I'm not happy sharing his attention with anyone.

Since Luke died, I haven't looked at another man. It's as if that part of my heart died with my husband. It's the reason I needed a complete reset of my life. I became this hollow shell, waking up each day because that's what I was supposed to do.

I ate because I had to and went to bed when I could no longer keep my eyes open. The world lost its color—its vibrancy—and I became an empty husk, walking through life on autopilot.

That wasn't living.

Doctors Without Borders fills my life with purpose. I'm eager to get up in the morning and willing to work long hours—because it excites me.

Now, for the first time in three years, I'm attracted to a man.

Whoa!

Yeah, that deserves a *Whoa!*

"I'm going to scout for a way down. I agree, this doesn't look like the best option." Brady gestures back to the bank. "The two of you should stay out of sight. I don't think anyone is pursuing us, but there's no reason to make it easy on them."

Damn, for a moment there, I forgot about the men chasing us.

"Come." I gesture to Izzy. "Back in the jungle."

"Are we there yet?" Izzy walks with me back under the cover of the jungle canopy.

"Are you eager to be done with this?" I look all around us and twirl in a slow circle. "It's mysterious and romantic, don't you think?"

"Mysterious, yes." Izzy gives a vigorous nod. "Romantic?" She pauses for a second, then looks back toward the waterfall. "No way. You have a crush on him, don't you?" Her mouth gapes and her eyes widen.

"Shh!" I gesture for her to be quiet. Meanwhile, my cheeks heat like they're on fire.

"You do." Izzy points at me. "You're blushing."

"Will you be quiet?" I grab her hands. "He'll hear."

"So?" Her grin turns into a fit of giggles. "You've got it bad, don't you?"

How do I explain how weird it is I'm attracted to a man at all? It's as weird as it is exhilarating.

Not that it means anything—for all I know Brady's married with two point five kids, a dog, and a white picket fence; the all-American dream—but I think Luke would approve. That gives me a sense of comfort, like I'm not doing anything wrong.

Like cheating—on my dead husband.

I take another gut check.

There's nothing wrong with being attracted to Brady.

Not that guilt ever kept me from exploring the possibility of a relationship. It was never something to think about because I'd have to be attracted to another man to feel guilt. The truth is, I've not looked at any man with any interest since Luke's death.

This is new and terrifying.

I'm not sure I'm ready to go down that road again. I don't know if my heart can handle another loss.

"Cat got your tongue?" Izzy jabs me playfully in the ribs. "He's kind of got that bad boy, rough thing going on." Izzy grows silent. "The scars don't bother you?"

"I barely see them." It's the truth. "Like I told Brady, we all have scars. Some are more visible than others." My hand goes to the chain around my neck and my fingers curl around Luke's wedding band.

I haven't taken it off since the day I removed it from his finger. Thinking about him brings the familiar pangs of grief back to the surface, but it's different now. I remember Luke with fondness, and the grief is no longer the predominant emotion. A smile curves across my lips and fills my breath with hope.

It hurts, but in a good way. I must be crazy because that makes no sense.

"The two of you ready?" Brady's sudden return makes me jump.

"Ready for what?" I try to pretend he didn't just scare the bejesus out of me.

"I found a way down."

"Sounds good to me." Izzy presses on her thighs and stands. "I'm all about being safe."

I flick a small leaf off my sleeve and pretend I'm totally chill with the world.

I'm not.

Not by a long shot.

My heart's off at the races, galloping at breakneck speed. I shouldn't stare, but I can't help falling into the golden depths of Brady's gaze.

His brows pinch together and his hand lifts to cover his jaw.

Where the scars are …

Shit.

I don't mean to draw attention to them, but he's obviously self-conscious about the disfigurement.

"I'm ready." Hopefully, he didn't read too much into my staring, but the pained expression on his face says it all.

Brady heads into the dense underbrush, leaving Izzy and me to follow.

She looks at me, confused.

All I do is shrug. I let Izzy go first and keep my thoughts to myself.

The *safe* way down is a torturous game path—a narrow slice of mud and muck cut into the steep hillside by animals I probably don't want identified.

Brady goes first, stops and holds out a hand for Izzy as she slips and slides her way down.

He offers me no help, but how can he? Only Izzy is within reach and there's no place to adjust our positions while scrambling down the hill.

Izzy falls several times, taking Brady out as they slide until getting stopped by root, rock, or limb.

I laugh the first time they tumble, then fall exactly where they did. The three of us wind up a twisted mess of arms and legs and mud, which goes everywhere and gets into everything.

Brady helps Izzy to her feet, reaches out to help me up, but our muddy hands slip.

The last bit of the trail challenges each of us. Brady slips and slides from one root to the next. He's chaotic perfection, falling, yet staying on his feet. He does that by using the vines overhead, many of which he rips free of their supports.

Izzy tries to walk down the slippery game trail but trips and twists her ankle.

Brady comes to her aid, closing the distance in a flash.

"How are you?"

"I twisted it."

"Here, let's see." He reaches down and hauls her to her feet. "Put some weight on it."

The moment she tries, Izzy cries out in pain.

Brady crouches down to look at her ankle. "Doesn't look broken, just a sprain." He glances up at me, lips pressed into a hard line.

I know what he's thinking. An injury will slow us down. He talks with Izzy, going over how to get her down the slippery trail to the bottom of the falls.

I stay where I am, unwilling to risk slipping and plowing into them. That's the last thing we need, compounding Izzy's injury with another one.

Brady guides Izzy down, taking one step at a time, protecting her ankle as much as possible. Meanwhile, I stay where I am and take in the jungle's beauty.

To my left, the waterfall tumbles down over the rocks. Squeezed through a narrow gap, it shoots out past the rocks a couple of feet.

There's a small cavern behind the water that draws my eye.

When it's my turn to head down, I examine my path and set forth, determined not to make a fool of myself.

Famous last words.

I make it down without breaking my neck only by holding onto root and vine.

The water roars overhead, crashing against the rocks, turning the water into a thick mist. That mist cools the air, providing some relief from the relentless jungle heat.

It's not a huge waterfall as waterfalls go, maybe only twenty or thirty feet, but the amount of water coming over the edge is nothing short of breathtaking.

We're all caked in mud and look ridiculous.

"How's your ankle?" I turn to Izzy.

"Tweaked." Izzy gently bears weight. Her eyes pinch with pain. "I'll be fine."

"Can we fashion a splint?" I look at Brady. "She can walk between us."

"We'll rest here for a minute." Brady scans our surroundings. "I'll see about that splint."

"Do either of you smell as bad as me?" I make a show of smelling my shirt. "Did we slide down mud, muck, or excrement?"

"You mean shit." Izzy's eyes twinkle with mischief.

"I was trying not to swear."

"This smells like *Yes, to all three.*" She turns toward the waterfall. "And that looks like exactly what we need. Brady, do you think we could wash some of this off?"

The place she points to is an outcropping of rock ten feet from the base of the falls. Some of the water gets diverted. It's not too much flow to knock us off our feet and collects in a small pool before sending it downstream. It's the perfect place to rinse off the muck.

"Be quick about it." His attention shifts to the top of the waterfall. Brady never forgets his job. He remains alert and hypervigilant. "I'll be right back."

SIXTEEN

Brady

"Aren't you going to wash off?" Izzy calls out to me as I head back into the forest to look for something to splint her ankle.

That injury is going to slow us down.

"Maybe when I return." The jungle is quiet, too quiet, which makes me nervous.

If we're being followed, whoever's tracking us is phenomenal at their job.

I'd feel better with the strength of Bravo team around me, but until they join up with me, it's a one-man show.

"You can take your shirt off—show us those muscles." Izzy teases me, then turns to Angie. The expression on Izzy's face turns downright impish. That girl is up to no good. "Right, Angie?"

Angie's face turns the prettiest shade of pink and a ghost of a smile fills mine. She's even prettier when she blushes.

But then my smile fades.

No one wants to see me with my shirt off.

Not anymore.

I turn around, giving the girls privacy.

"Someone's gotta keep watch." I glance up at the top of the

waterfall and examine the banks on either side. "Besides, I need to find something to help you walk with that ankle."

In addition, I need to scout ahead. This waterfall is the first of many. There's a second waterfall beyond this one and more beyond that. Our journey in the river is nearing an end.

Which sucks.

With Izzy's injury, it makes sense to stick with the river, as it keeps her off her foot, but with a cascade of waterfalls in front of us, that's no longer an option.

This waterfall empties into a broad basin before tumbling down another twenty feet into a series of small pools. Those gather, joining for a few hundred feet, then there's another series of drops after that.

"It's feeling better." Izzy winces when she attempts to place weight on her ankle.

That's definitely going to slow us down.

My attention shifts to Angie. "Can you make sure she doesn't slip again and make it worse?"

"I will."

"Good."

Unlike Izzy, Angie's reliable. I feel as if I can lean on her to help with this rescue.

Izzy is simply a hot mess.

As for this rescue, complacency is a genuine threat.

Just because I don't hear, or see, signs of pursuit, doesn't mean we're in the clear.

Those parrots give me pause. A passing predator probably disturbed the flock, but I'm not willing to assume when it comes to the girls' safety.

By now, my team should be in the country. While I look for something to brace Izzy's ankle, it's time for a check-in with Command.

The assets they've put together determine my next steps.

Me: Bravo One to Overlord.

Overlord: Received Bravo One. SitRep.

It takes a moment to brief my status. Command listens to my report, holding their comments for the end.

The electronics Antonio gave me are toast, destroyed by immersion, but Mitzy's gear works like a charm.

Overlord: Bravo inbound via chopper.

Me: To?

I'm curious where they're going to deploy Bravo. By now, especially with the escape of the girls, I'm pretty certain they broke camp and moved on.

Overlord: You.

Me: Me?

Overlord: Affirmative. There's a clearing...

CJ gives me coordinates for a small clearing where the helicopter can land and get the girls out of this disaster. It'll be nice to have real backup. The clearing, fortunately, is not that far from us.

I'd never have found it on my own.

The dense jungle can open up twenty feet from where a person stands and they'd be oblivious to it. The vegetation is that dense.

I'll have to clear a path with my machete, but it's less than a hundred yards. That's the length of a football field.

Totally doable.

And Angie can help Izzy walk the distance.

A tremendous burden lifts from my shoulders.

Me: ETA?

Overlord: Forty minutes.

That's about how long walking a hundred yards through dense jungle will take. I take in a deep breath and blow it out nice and slow.

Me: Understood. Good Copy.

Command asks a few more questions, which I answer until they're satisfied. We keep things short and to the point. In less than an hour, Angie will be safe.

Once we secure the girls, Bravo and I will return to extricate the four hostages I left behind.

While I talk with Command, I search the underbrush for something to brace Izzy's ankle.

An itching sensation between my shoulder blades keeps me on edge. After I find what I need, I return to the waterfall at the precise moment Angie removes her shirt. Her eyes widen and she clutches the shirt to her chest, looking mortified.

"Sorry." I perform the most perfect, most pristine, about-face known to mankind.

The flash of a rifle scope catches my eye

I twist around and rush the women, grabbing each by the waist, and hauling them through the falling water. A bullet strikes the rocks, ricocheting wildly in the air.

Behind the waterfall, Angie turns wide, terrified eyes at me.

"Brady?" Her hands shake. "What do we do?"

There's not much room behind the waterfall. Angie gives me her back while she pulls her shirt back down over her head and covers her breasts. I wish I hadn't seen her breasts.

My body is hypersensitive around her, waking up when it should stay silent, and by *it*, I mean my dick.

I tap a status update to Command, letting them know we're under attack. Unfortunately, Bravo is still forty minutes out.

Fuck.

I pull my weapon from where it sits at the small of my back and check my ammo.

"Is that even going to work?" Izzy eyes my weapon. "It's been under water."

"It depends on the quality of ammunition." Angie steps in, answering before I can open my mouth. "I'm sure it works."

I love her faith, but I don't share it. Depending on what Antonio gave me, the next few minutes are going to be a shit show or a freakin' miracle.

If the primers still work after our swim.

If the powder didn't get wet.

The weapons Guardian HRS use still fire after complete immersion, but this?

I have my doubts.

"How many shots do you have?" Angie's curiosity interests me. Her questions are on point.

"One in the pipe and fifteen in the magazine." I slide out the magazine and confirm the count.

"Look, time is running away, allowing whoever is out there to reposition himself. He knows where we are. All he has to do is flush us out." I explain, knowing Izzy may not get it, but Angie will.

My girl is smart and knows her stuff.

"Flush us out?" Izzy attempts to put weight on her injured ankle. "I can't run." She pulls out the leather thong with the rabbit's foot. Squeezing the poor thing, she gives me a look. "I think it's broken."

"Maybe. Maybe not." I believe we make our own luck, but I won't say that to Izzy. "Or maybe your good luck charm is overwhelmed?"

"How so?" Izzy gives me a look.

"Maybe it was luck that brought me to the river last night. Maybe it helped us find that cave to hide inside?"

"Didn't help with my ankle." She glances down at her injured leg.

"Maybe it gave you a sprain instead of a break." The poor rabbit's foot has seen better days. It's a soggy, muddy mess.

"Maybe." Her trembling hand stills and that look of despair in her gaze fades.

I may not believe in good luck charms, but that kind of belief in something greater than ourselves helps those who do. I'd never try to squash something like that, and as far as luck goes, I'm more than willing to borrow a bit of Izzy's luck.

"Don't worry. He'll keep us safe." Angie throws an arm around Izzy's shoulder.

I love her faith in me, but I'm not sure how much of it I share. My plan is to leave the girls behind the waterfall and take out the man tracking us.

A man who's most likely moved from where he took that shot and is closing in on our position.

"Look, I have to go out there." My gaze captures Angie, conveying much of what I can't speak out loud.

Izzy's too freaked out as it is, without telling her what a shit show this is.

But Angie …

She gets it.

"What can I do to help?" Fire sparks in her eyes and her lips set into a grim line of determination.

"Stay with Izzy."

What else is there for her to do?

It would be awesome if I had my Bowie knife, or machete, in addition to my weapon. Unlike the ammunition, which may or may not fire, the knife's edge is sharp and the machete can cut through bone.

What I need is my ruck.

It's on the other side of the waterfall, sitting pretty on top of one of the rocks.

"I'm going to slip out and circle around. Try to find who's out there and take care of them. The two of you stay here until I come back for you.

"Brady …" Angie releases Izzy and flings herself at me. Her arms go around my neck. "Please be careful."

Every molecule in my body takes notice of Angie. Every freakin' cell wakes up. My dick is awake and interested, standing tall and proud.

Fucker.

I try to ignore how wonderful her wet body feels plastered against mine, but when she lifts on tiptoe to place a kiss on my lips, it's like an explosion goes off in my head.

The kiss is short, barely a kiss, but damn if it doesn't make the foundations of my world shake.

"For luck." She takes a step back and looks down, but the flushing of her cheeks tells me I'm not the only one affected by that kiss. "Please be safe.'"

Safe?

I'm going out blind, hunting a man with a rifle with nothing but a handgun and questionable ammunition. If I'm lucky, I'll be able to get to my knife.

"I'll try."

And since she gave me a kiss …

My hand wraps around her waist, and I yank her against me. My head tilts down until my lips press against hers.

My kiss is longer than hers, hotter than hers, more aggressive—than hers.

And I don't give a damn.

When I release her, Angie's hand flies to her chest. She takes a shaky step back and grasps Izzy's hand. Her fingers brush against her swollen lips, and she looks at me with simmering passion in her gaze.

Or maybe what I feel is merely reflected in her eyes? With a shake of my head, I clear my thoughts. This isn't the time.

It's time to leave.

With the taste of Angie on my tongue, I duck out from behind the waterfall and clear the ten feet of open space in record time.

The report of a rifle sounds and a bullet whizzes overhead, flying wide. The man behind that rifle has horrible aim—and he's cocky.

He didn't shift his position.

I know exactly where he is, but it's going to take time to get to him.

And while I thread my way through the thick vegetation, remaining as silent as possible, he has time to move in on the girls.

For the next however long—it feels like hours but is probably less than a few minutes—we play a game of cat and mouse.

He knows I'm outside, moving in on him. Used to stealth, I know how to minimize the sound of my passing, even in vegetation as thick as this.

I scoop up a handful of mud to smear over my face. It'll make it harder for him to see me. I crouch and listen.

The man stomps through the vegetation. I follow his progress on the other side of the water based on the birds he scares out of the canopy. He closes in on the girls as my heart rate spikes.

Then I see him.

Peering out of the vegetation, his attention is on the waterfall and his quarry on the other side.

I lift my weapon. Take aim.

Finger on the trigger, I slowly squeeze until …

Nothing.

The hammer falls, but the primer fails.

That answers that question.

Fuck.

Time for an alternate plan.

But how am I going to get to him before he grabs the girls?

Once he has his hands on them …

Stop that.

There's no time to waste on errant thoughts.

How am I going to take him down?

The man stands at the edge of the second waterfall, gun trained on the girls. He looks nervously to the side, trying to peer through the vegetation.

Trying to find me.

And, like me, he scans the bank opposite him. That's when an idea strikes. With his attention focused on the ground, I need to come at him from a different direction.

And fortunately for me, nature provides exactly what I need.

A quick glance overhead brings a grin to my face. Then I'm up, headed away from the water.

Back up to the top of the waterfall.

And up—into the canopy.

It doesn't take long before I find what I need.

The guy knows I'm somewhere out here. He's bold and stupid.

I've got one shot at this and pray the vine I select for my daredevil attempt doesn't snap and drop me like a load of bricks.

I intend to disarm the man, then take him down by brute force.

One deep breath and I kick off from the thick tree limb.

Hurtling through the air, I'm like fucking Tarzan swinging on a vine. My movement draws the man's attention. The muzzle of his weapon rises. He turns toward me.

Aims.

When he squeezes the trigger, everything slows down.

My ears ring with the report from the rifle. Smoke billows out of the end of the barrel. The concussive force slams into my chest. I tense, waiting for the shot to bite into my flesh.

But the man's aim is shit and I'm unstoppable.

I raise my feet and plow into his chest.

He staggers back. One step. Two steps.

The rifle swings wide. His grip fails.

Spinning in the air, the rifle flies into one of the smaller pools by his feet, plunging out of sight in the murky water.

Unarmed, the man's arms windmill as he struggles to remain upright. He glances down at the second waterfall, fear filling his face.

Momentum carries me forward. Boots pressed against his chest; my goal is to push him over the edge.

At the last moment, he grabs my legs. As I swing back, I save him from a deadly fall.

He lets go while I drop into the water.

It's me and him now.

No weapons.

Just us.

I lean forward, placing the balance of my weight on my toes, and anticipate the man's attack.

He rushes, head down, like a bull. As he comes at me, I step to the side and wrap my arm around his neck. Using his momentum to yank him off his feet and force him down. He hits the rocks, then slides into a small pool.

He's back on his feet before I blink.

Standing in thigh-deep water, he shakes his head. I extend my hand and give a little flick of my fingers, telling him to come and get me.

He charges again.

I step to the side and try again to push him over the edge of the waterfall. He stares at me with murderous intent.

Which is totally fine.

I feel the same way.

He comes at me again.

There's no time to move. He hits me head on, barreling into me and knocking me off my feet.

I go down hard and fall into the water. He's on top of me and takes advantage, wrapping his hands around my neck, holding me down—underwater.

I tense, preventing him from crushing my windpipe, but I still can't breathe. Not with him holding my head under the water.

The next few seconds are tense.

He's solidly built and uses his weight to keep me under. I grapple with the man, getting nowhere.

With my air giving out, I thread my hands through his arms. Pushing out sharply, I force his elbows to bend.

The pressure on my throat eases.

His grip loosens.

I knee him in the groin.

Hard.

His hands release and I surge out of the water, gulping for air.

The look on his face is priceless, but despite any injury to his nuts, he doesn't go down easy.

He straightens and takes two steps back. Fury fills his face as he rushes me again.

I duck under his arm, spinning as best I can, and kick him behind the knees. His leg buckles, taking him down.

But the man doesn't stay down.

Fucker.

He's back on his feet. Attacking again.

I land a brutal series of blows to his gut, his solar plexus, and give a sharp uppercut to his jaw. Each strike forces him back, but he doesn't go down.

He staggers, getting tired and losing steam, but the man's not done.

I square off against him, shaking out my fingers and stretching my neck. All my attention focuses on my opponent.

"Pagarás por esto, gringo." He spits the words out and curls his fingers into fists.

He's the one who's going to pay for this. Not me.

The water doesn't slow him down.

It doesn't slow me either.

He launches forward, and we trade a series of punches and kicks. Neither one of us gains the upper hand.

This has become a war of attrition.

The man who fatigues first will fail, and from the looks of it, pay the ultimate price.

My body handles the fight better than I expect. The scarred left side is tight, but the muscles underneath are ripped and toned. My reflexes are better than ever and I'm furious.

I move in a blur, deflecting his blows as I slowly tire him out.

I'm not the fastest man on Bravo team.

I'm not the strongest.

I'm not the most agile.

But I am the one who lasts the longest in a fight.

Endurance is my strength, and I rely on that to win this.

I deflect a series of kicks and thrusts aimed at my groin. His technique is rough, most likely learned on the streets. I honed mine over years of intense conditioning and practice.

I take the offensive, launching at my enemy with a flurry of cuts and stabs. My arms are my weapons. I spin and kick. Each attack connects solidly.

The man grunts. He staggers.

We trade punches for a time. I lead. He defends. We step around the other, dancing a deadly game.

My opponent is good.

Weariness creeps in.

I don't know about him, but I train to never quit.

I'll quit when I'm dead.

I dodge a blow and launch a fierce counterattack. Each attack pushes him back setting him up to end this fight.

The scowl on my enemy's face deepens.

His balance falters.

I come at him with another round of punches and kicks, the last aimed square in his chest.

He steps back, then slips at the edge of the falls. The whites of his eyes show as his body continues moving backward. The man reaches out, trying to grab me, but I pull away.

He clutches nothing but air as he drops.

It's only ten feet down to the second waterfall. Normally, he might survive such a fall, but a pile of boulders breaks his fall and his back.

His body goes still.

I watch for signs of life, but when there are none, I race back to the waterfall where I left Angie and Izzy.

SEVENTEEN

Angie

"What do you think is going on out there?" Izzy squeezes my hand. She leans forward, trying to make out anything happening outside.

The noise from the waterfall makes it impossible to know what's happening.

"I don't know." Right there with her, I don't like being in the dark. "Let me see if I can see anything."

"No." Izzy clutches at me. "It's not safe."

"I know, but Brady is out there all by himself." He has no backup. I feel like I need to be out there—helping him. "I'll be careful. I'm just going to peek."

"Don't leave me." Fear threads through her voice.

I feel the same terror, but I'd rather face my fear than hide from it.

"I'm not leaving you. I'm just going to see what's happening."

A low moan escapes Izzy. She folds her arms around her legs and rocks herself.

I inch around the edge of the falling water and peek outside.

There's nothing to see.

Nothing.

I don't know what's worse. Seeing nothing? Or that crippling dread knowing Brady's out there alone?

Fighting for us.

I return to Izzy's side.

The one thing I know is we can't stay here. One of two things is going to happen. If Brady returns, we'll have to run.

Now that we know people are after us, we can't stay in one place. If Brady doesn't come back—I take in a deep breath—if he doesn't, then our captor will force us to move.

"How bad is your ankle?"

"I can hop." Izzy grimaces. "But not far."

I have to help Izzy.

Beside one of the smaller pools are the branches Brady brought back to splint Izzy's ankle. I assume, inside that pack, there's something to bind the branches in place.

An idea comes to me.

"What size shoe do you wear?"

"Why?" Her brows pinch.

"My boots will stabilize your ankle."

"Oh."

Fortunately, we're the same size. We pull off our shoes, Izzy moving much more gingerly than me.

"Let me put yours on first, then I'll help you put my boots on."

I'm worried the swelling around her ankle will make it impossible to put my boots on. After we make the swap, I help her.

"Let me loosen the laces. We'll tighten everything down after we get it on."

Izzy winces as we slowly insert her foot into my boot, but it fits. I blow out a relieved breath and tighten down the laces.

In addition to stabilizing her ankle, the boot should keep some of the swelling down using compression.

"I'm tired." Izzy blows out a breath. "And scared. What if …" Her eyes flick to the left, toward the direction Brady went.

"Let's deal with the things we know. Nothing else." I finish with the boot. "How does that feel?"

"Snug."

"Too tight?"

"I don't think so."

"Okay." My attention shifts to the waterfall. "If I could just get to those sticks."

"Don't go." Izzy's hand shoots out again, tighter now, gripping my arm hard enough to leave a bruise.

Her fear is a palpable thing. It reaches out to me, trying to ensnare me, but I beat it back with the force of my will.

"Okay." Eventually, we have to go out. This isn't a safe place to hide, and it's not like we're even hiding. Whoever is out there saw Brady push us behind the waterfall.

We're sitting ducks.

Brady gave specific instructions, and while I'd love to be out there, helping him, I know I'll be a distraction he doesn't need.

A distraction that could cost him his life.

For that reason, I stay put, even if it goes against everything I believe.

He's going up against an armed man, without backup, and without knowing if there aren't more men out there.

Waiting with Izzy isn't my choice. I'd rather be out with Brady, doing something.

As long as that *something* doesn't distract him.

Minutes pass.

Izzy gets increasingly jumpy. My nerves are frazzled and frayed. I close my eyes and say a silent prayer for Brady's safety.

I touch my lips, remembering the kiss he returned.

Mine was a cautious thing. Without knowing whether he's married with a kid or two, I took a chance. I figured his wife wouldn't mind a stranger giving her husband a kiss for good luck.

But there is no wife.

Not with the kiss he returned.

And, oh boy, the riot of sensation that ripped through me was incredible. Warmth bloomed in my chest and rippled outward, making my fingers and toes tingle. When he let me go, my entire body shook with sensation.

Is it too much to hope he might be attracted to me?

But this is a rescue.

My emotions are unreliable. Heightened by our current circumstance, will those feelings still be there after this is over?

Who knows and who cares? All I can do is live in the moment and dream.

A shot rings out.

Izzy jumps and I scream. I clamp a hand over my mouth while my heart beats wildly beneath my ribcage.

We're both jumpy. Fear does that to a person, and that jumpiness leads to mistakes.

For that reason alone, I have no business being outside.

My only question is, who fired that shot?

Was it Brady? Or the shooter?

Is he all right?

There's no way to know.

Sudden movement on the other side of the waterfall brings a gasp to my lips. Two shapes collide out there, spinning and twisting, punching and kicking.

Fighting hand to hand.

"What's going on?" Izzy props her chin on her knees. She feels gingerly at her ankle, probing the swollen tissue.

I need to stabilize that ankle.

There's no way to know if we'll have to run.

"I don't know." I push off the rock and head for the edge of the waterfall.

"Angie—what are you doing?" Izzy keeps her voice down, although there's no need. The water covers all sound.

"I'm just going to peek."

"Don't let them see you."

"I won't."

"Be safe." Her voice drops to a whisper.

Them?

She thinks there's more than one man. It's a logical guess.

Why do I envision only one?

This is the problem with assumptions. Why wouldn't there be more than one man hunting us? But why would our kidnappers care about two women? We're not worth the effort they're putting in to tracking us down.

"Izzy?"

"Yes?"

I go over to her and sit beside her on the rock.

"Is there any reason to think the cartel is right?"

"About what?"

"Running guns …" I stretch my feet out in front of me and run my hands up and down my thighs.

"No. Why would you say that?"

"Because they think we are, or someone in our group is. Have you seen anything?"

"Nothing." She presses her head against the smooth rock behind her. "I've thought about it a lot, but I've emptied every truck since we started. If there was something, wouldn't I have seen it?"

"That's what I was thinking, too." I reach for her hand and gather it in mine. "I feel like we would've seen something."

"Me too."

"Then why are they after us?"

The backside of the waterfall is beautiful. It's no different from the front side, but there's something magical about the backside of a waterfall.

It sparks memories from childhood; happy memories before the car crash took my parents from me. After that came darkness as I entered foster care as a teen.

Not the best experience. Brutal comes to mind. But then, strangers saved me. If not for The Facility, I would never be where I am now. They gave me a safe place to learn, far from the physical abuse of my foster parents. I finished high school there, then left to make the best of my life.

My thoughts turn back to the cartel. I don't like things I can't understand. Why chase two women through the jungle? It makes my stomach churn, especially when I remember that foul man who entered our tent.

Not that I'm being sexist about it—I'm all for women's rights— but there are some truths that exist to this day. Nicaragua is a country where progressive women's rights are not the norm. Men are in charge.

It's a country where women do what they're told by the men in their lives. What women don't do is run guns. That's men's work. So, back to my question.

Why did they send someone chasing us through the jungle?

Is it *machismo?*

That rotten man couldn't stand the fact two women escaped his grasp? He has to track us down and drag us back to camp to save face?

It's possible.

The way all the others deferred to him made my skin crawl. The things he said to Izzy, and me, still make me shudder.

He wanted us showered for one particular purpose, but is that enough reason to send a man—or men—after us?

I don't know, but I've come to learn not to believe in the inherent goodness of men. I've seen the ravages of civil unrest in the people I've treated over these past months.

These people live with the threat of ceaseless violence. There's no escape for them.

There may be no escape for us.

Blurry movement rushes toward where we hide. I catch my breath and stumble backward.

"What's going on?" Izzy unfolds her legs and pulls on my arm.

Wobbling on one good leg, she stands with me to face this new threat.

Brady barrels through the water and catches my eye. "Time to move out." He barks an order, then heads back outside.

"Come on, Izzy. Wrap your arm over my shoulder. I'll help you walk."

She does as I say, placing her injured ankle closest to me. Together, we hobble our way out into the open.

Brady dives into one of the pools and pulls out a rifle from the water, then he shoulders his ruck. He checks the weapon, then slings it over his shoulder. His turbulent gaze turns to me.

The grim expression on his face grows darker. His brows knit together as he scans the top of the waterfall.

"How many men?" I move with Izzy as she gingerly tests her weight on her ankle.

"Just the one."

Only one?

I breathe out a sigh of relief.

"I have to splint her ankle." I stabilize Izzy, helping her to sit on an exposed rock.

"You switched shoes." He gives me a look. It's filled with respect.

"Yes."

"Good idea."

His praise brings a smile to my face.

"Um, do you have any bandages in your pack to wrap this?"

"I do." He unslings the rifle and removes his pack. "Give me a moment." He opens his ruck and rummages around inside while I look around the collecting pools.

"Where did …" I search the pools at the base of the waterfall, looking for a body.

"You don't want to know." His expression is flat, emotionless. His eyes are cold.

I know what that means.

Brady killed that man.

Curiosity pushes me to ask the obvious, but Brady would have shared if that's what he wanted. Since he says nothing, I decide not to push.

"Here." He retrieves a small roll of gauze. "It'll go faster with two."

"Thank you." I hold the sticks on either side of Izzy's ankle while he wraps them in place.

"It's the best we can do." He stands and stretches his back. "Come. We need to move."

"Brady …"

"What?"

"I can help Izzy, but we might move faster if you help her instead of me. I can carry your ruck."

"I've got it."

"I know you've got it, but it makes no sense to burden you with helping Izzy *and* carrying that pack."

"You're something else, you know that?" He gives me a long, hard look.

"I don't know how to respond to that."

But there's no reason to respond. Brady removes his ruck and hands it to me. We shift Izzy between us. As I expect, he wraps an arm around her waist, supporting her far better than I ever could.

"I'm ready." The pack is heavy, but I settle it on my back. Brady is much larger than me, which means I have to cinch the straps down tight.

"Good." Brady grabs the rifle and points to the far bank. "We can't follow the river anymore. It's a series of falls from here on out. We head back into the jungle, to a clearing near here."

His attention shifts to the sky as he explains about his team. I follow the direction of his gaze, wondering what he's looking for, but then he heads out, half carrying Izzy over the rocks as he makes his way to the far side of the bank.

I follow behind them, slipping over the slick surface of the rocks. Izzy's shoes are not sturdy like my boots. If I'm not careful, we'll both have twisted ankles.

I slow my pace, taking better care of where I place my feet. I won't slip on the rocks. I won't get tripped by the roots of trees. I refuse to add another injury to our three-man crew.

Brady makes it to the far side of the bank. He shades his eyes with his hand, then waits patiently for me to catch up. He's about to say something when I slip on a rock.

Lips pressed into a thin line, the muscles of his jaw bunch. He says nothing as I scramble back to my feet and close the distance between us. Before I get to him, he takes Izzy into the underbrush.

"Where are we going?" I rush behind him, trying to keep up.

I could never help Izzy the way Brady does. With her injured ankle closest to him, he supports her as she runs, taking almost her full weight.

On a sprained ankle.

I struggle to keep up, but not enough that I don't look where I'm going. I place each foot with purpose and scan ahead. Brady's on the move, not slowing with Izzy clinging to his side. Every now and then, he looks back. Each time, a surge of adrenaline lights a fire in my veins and I close the distance.

But it's too fast.

Too far.

I slowly fall farther behind.

He's done this before and it hits me suddenly. In his past, he rescued a teammate from a firefight, running just like he is now, supporting his injured teammate the same way he supports Izzy.

I run after him.

Ahead of us, the vegetation thins. Brady races into a clearing, half carrying Izzy. Overhead, the steady *chop-chop-chop* of an incoming helicopter cuts through the air. Brady covers his eyes and looks up. Izzy balances precariously beside him on one good leg.

Meanwhile, I rush through the last bit of jungle, pushing the dense leaves and vines away from my face.

My lungs burn.

My heart pounds.

The muscles in my legs scream in pain, forcing me to stop. Hands on thighs, I double over and gasp, sucking wind.

In the clearing, Brady takes a knee, pulling Izzy to his side as a helicopter rushes in, skimming over the jungle canopy. It flies low and touches down. Three armed men, decked out in tactical gear, jump out and point their weapons toward the jungle.

The rotors kick up a strong wind that flattens the grass and bends the lush vegetation.

Brady and Izzy cover their eyes and turn away. He scans the edge of the clearing, brows pinched together, looking for me.

I lope into a run, not worried about running at breakneck speed, and pick an easy pace. Our eyes meet, and I slow my mad dash. There's no reason to trip over a root, or stumble over a rock, not when rescue is this close.

Brady gives a sharp nod and helps Izzy to her feet. He rushes her toward the helicopter. One of his men meets him halfway. They shift Izzy between them and the other man carries her into the helicopter.

Meanwhile, Brady turns back toward me.

A smile fills my face and my feet pick up the pace. I can't wait to run into his arms and be done with this nightmare.

An arm stretches across the path in front of me. It hooks my waist and yanks me off my feet.

Gunfire rings out all around me.

The men with the helicopter take a knee and return fire.

I open my mouth to scream, but a rag presses against my nose and mouth. The aromatic fumes make me gag and burn my eyes.

I can't cry out. I can't shout.

Everything around me fades to black.

EIGHTEEN

Brady

LORD, I HOPE IT'S JUST THE ONE MAN, BUT ASSUMPTIONS ARE A beast. They rear their heads at the worst time, teaching painful lessons.

It's why I don't waste time.

The helicopter's inbound, and we have some distance to cover. My greatest concern is the jungle slowing us down, but the vegetation thins, allowing us to sprint toward the clearing.

Locking Izzy to my side, I show her how to run with me. We three-leg it through the jungle, with me supporting most of her weight.

Fortune definitely smiles down on us as a game trail reveals itself and heads in the direction of the clearing. Hope fills my heart that we'll make it.

There's little reason to think otherwise.

If there were other men, they would've revealed themselves by their movements. Other than shocking the jungle to silence, as we crash through the underbrush, there's no sound of pursuit. Honestly, the creatures make it easy on me.

Their silence is a godsend.

Izzy and I break through the vegetation and race into the

clearing. I take a knee, bringing Izzy gently down beside me. A quick check behind me doesn't reveal Angie, but her movement through the jungle tells me everything I need to know. She's strong and fast. Angie can do anything.

I take a breather and close my eyes to listen for her, tracing her path as she catches up to us.

We're almost there.

I can barely believe this crazy jungle rescue is at an end.

The helicopter closes in on my position as we catch our breath. Izzy gulps air beside me while I measure each breath, bringing my heart rate down.

I pushed Izzy hard. Angie too. I do another quick check on Angie's progress. She's closing in.

My girl is a fighter, and she ran right on my heels. The ruck slows her down, but she doesn't stop. The woman is fucking amazing.

Strong and resilient, nothing stops Angie. Most women would cave under the stress, but not her. She takes to the whole thing as if we're caught in some romantic adventure. Which, if I'm to be honest, I wish was the case.

The idea of spending my days with Angie as we explore the wonders of this jungle sounds amazing. She's not afraid of getting her hands dirty, nor does she balk at hard work. I've never met a woman like her.

Most of the chicks I've been with cry if they chip a nail. Their beauty isn't even skin deep. It's far shallower than that. Angie is layers and layers of beautiful, beginning with what's on the outside and delving all the way inside to what really matters.

She's perfect.

Izzy is a different story. She's got a bit of spitfire in her—I'll give her that. She conquered her fear of water by necessity, but she's a girly girl.

Too soft for my tastes, but I give her a nod of respect. She did what needed to be done. That's a quality I respect in anyone, man or woman.

Hell, that's what got me through BUDS. It's an inner fire that never goes out, a determination to win, no matter the cost.

I couldn't ask for two better women to rescue in the jungles of Nicaragua. They worked with me, never against me, making my job easy. It never ceases to amaze me how much those we rescue make things harder on themselves and hinder our efforts to save them.

Once I get Angie and Izzy safely aboard the helicopter, it'll be time to regroup with my team and plan the next phase of this mission. There are still four of their colleagues held captive somewhere in the jungle.

That job is something I don't look forward to, mainly because it means leaving Angie behind. There's a definite spark supercharging the air between us.

"I hope those are your friends." Izzy huffs beside me, trying to catch her breath. Her gaze cuts to the sky and her ear cocks toward the sound of the helicopter.

Our ride out of here is coming in low and fast.

The helicopter appears like a hellion, skimming dangerously close to the forest canopy as it races to the clearing.

The pilot comes in hot—a tactical move perfected by helicopter pilots during the Vietnam War and passed down to successive generations of hotshot pilots.

The downdraft from the rotors sends dirt and debris flying toward us. My heart swells with joy when Booker, Hayes, and Zeb jump out. Despite their tactical gear, which covers their faces, I recognize my teammates by the way they move.

Booker, my second in command, is our team's medic. He's saved my life too many times to count.

Hayes is solid. Tree trunk legs, stocky build, he's packed with muscles and moves like a tank. The man's nearly indestructible.

Zeb is a man of rigid routine and values perfection in everything he does. His moves are precise. He doesn't waste effort on extraneous movement, and he's got one hell of an eye. The man's precision with a rifle makes him the perfect sniper for the team.

Rafe stays in the helicopter. Our sniper, his skill with a rifle is unparalleled.

Alec faces the other way, protecting the other side of the helicopter from unknown threats.

The moment my men jump out of the helicopter, I pull Izzy to her feet. Half carrying her, we do the same three-legged run toward the helicopter.

Weapons up, the men of Bravo team scan the edge of the jungle, looking for threats.

Booker breaks away from Hayes and Zeb, jogging toward me. He shoulders his weapon and takes Izzy off my hands. He gets her inside the helicopter while I turn back toward the jungle.

I run a hand through my hair and stare at the narrow game trail, certain my eyes deceive me. I can't hear shit now that the helicopter is here.

Brows pinched in confusion, I jog back the way I came, then duck and cover when gunfire sounds all around us. Bullets bite into the dirt as I dive to the ground.

Every shot misses by a mile.

Hayes and Zeb return fire, shooting into the jungle where our unseen opponents reveal their location by the flashes of light from their muzzles.

I pop my head up and scan the area. Spread out in a semi-circle, active fire pins my guys down. They're vulnerable out in the open.

"Brady, we've got to go," Booker shouts over the gunfire.

The only thing saving my guys is whoever's out there in the jungle are horrible shots. One or two bullets ping against the metal frame of the helicopter, but none pierce the armor plating. None of my men are injured, and I need to keep it that way.

I take one more look out at the jungle, desperately seeking Angie.

A figure appears from the shadows. He grips Angie's limp form and holds a rag over her nose and mouth.

No need to wonder what's on the rag. Chloroform is a noxious chemical and fast-acting. Angie's out like a light.

The bottom of the world drops out from under me, and into that endless pit, my heart tumbles. A queasy, shaky, gonna-get-sick sensation grabs a hold of my guts and twists hard.

This can't be happening.

Whoever that man is, he's a bastard, revealing himself only to show what he's taken from me. Our gazes lock in a visceral battle. The corner of the bastard's mouth crooks up in a feral grin as fury boils in my blood.

He didn't just take Angie. The bastard's rubbing it in my face.

I have half a mind to charge the man, but Booker calls out once again. We're surrounded by well over a dozen men. Their aim might be shit, but one of them is bound to get lucky.

I won't risk that with my team.

With a clenching of my jaw, I swallow the horrible tang of defeat and make the hardest decision of my life.

"Fall back." I push to my feet and sprint toward the helicopter— away from Angie.

NINETEEN

Brady

THE MOMENT I'M UP AND RUNNING, BULLETS WHIZ THROUGH THE air, missing me and burying themselves into the ground with a puff of dirt.

My men hop onto the helicopter as the pilot lifts off. By the time I close the distance, it's already a few feet off the ground. Booker and Hayes reach down, hooking under my arms as I leap up. They haul me into the helicopter as it rises into the air.

An expert under fire, our pilot's seen plenty of action. She spins in the air, giving the shooters the smallest target she can, then the nose of the helicopter dips down as she races out and away.

Before I know it, we skim twenty feet over the jungle canopy, banking to the south.

"What the fuck was that?" Booker shouts to be heard over the noise of the helicopter. "No one said anything about it being a hot zone." His tone isn't meant to be accusatory, but each word rips into me, flaying me from the inside out.

"Fuck if I know." I feel like a failure, committing the ultimate sin in hostage rescue.

Instead of bringing Angie to safety, I left her behind.

I failed her.

I rap the side of my head with my knuckles. All I see is Angie hanging in that man's grip. Her arms are limp. The tips of her toes brushing the ground. Head hanging to the side.

The way that man's searing gaze reached out to me was like a punch in the gut. His taunting gaze was victorious and turned my stomach.

That's his first mistake. There was no reason to reveal himself, but he wants me to know he has what's mine.

The fucker makes it personal.

"We have to go back." I shift to a more comfortable position and stare out over the vast expanse of the rainforest.

The clearing is no longer visible. It's as if the jungle swallowed it up. Somewhere out there, in enemy hands, my girl is at their mercy.

"Go back?" Booker looks at me like I've grown a second head. "We're outnumbered. Are you out of your mind?"

"They've got Angie." I cup my hands over my mouth and shout back.

"Do you even know who *they* are?" Booker tries to get me to see reason.

"The *Coralos* cartel, obviously."

I don't know that for a fact, but it's the only thing that makes sense. But why? Why go to all that effort?

"We had to leave." Booker grasps my forearm and grips tight. "You made the right call. You had no other choice."

It doesn't help that Booker's right and does nothing to relieve the overwhelming panic thrumming through my veins. I fucked up.

I fucked up big time.

I rub my palms on my trousers and take in a slow, deep breath.

Going off half-cocked is the best way to wind up dead. The rational side of my brain knows Booker's right, but all I want is to go back to that clearing and rescue Angie from the brute who took her.

Memories of Angie and Izzy being forced down to the riverbank at gunpoint surge through my mind. The way they were ordered to strip brings an animalistic growl to my lips. That's who has my girl —a monster and a rapist.

That's her fate if I don't get to her soon.

I press the knuckles of my fist to my forehead and squeeze my eyes shut as anger fuels my need to hunt down that man and destroy him.

Booker grips the back of my neck and pulls us together until our foreheads touch. "We'll get your girl back, but now is not the time." He releases me and leans back. "Please tell me you marked her." Booker holds me in a fierce stare.

"I marked her." I bite the words as they leave my mouth. At least, I did that part right. It's the only saving grace to this whole damn fucked up mission.

As long as Angie doesn't remove the knotted bracelet, we can track her anywhere in the world. It's the only thing keeping me from jumping out of the helicopter to save her.

I know what needs to be done, and that requires planning and preparation. It means time—time she doesn't have.

Mitzy will track Angie's location. We'll set the full force of Guardian resources to take her back.

I suck in a breath and scan the interior of the helicopter. Izzy shakes and rubs that mangled rabbit's foot. Booker wraps his arms around her shoulder, providing what comfort he can. Tears roll freely down her cheeks. I'd go to her and tell her we'll get Angie back, but I'm not in the right mental place to do that right now.

It's a miracle I'm holding my shit together as well as I am.

The only good thing about this disaster is that it's nice to have the team back in action.

The last time all six of us were together, we walked into that shit storm in Cancun. Burns scarred the left side of my face and body, then wasted the better part of my year as I tried to recover. Others were injured. Broken bones, contusions, burns, and smoke inhalation were the least of our worries.

To be honest, I'm surprised we're here at all.

We were lucky that day.

Nobody died.

But our first mission out since then is not going well.

Not because of my team.

No. This disaster is all mine.

It takes an hour before we land. I don't know if we're still in Nicaragua, or if we crossed over into Costa Rica. I'm certain the governments of both nations might have something to say about that.

Transporting armed men across borders must break a million local laws.

But I don't care.

I don't care about any of it.

We land in an open area near the coast. All around us, white canvas tents pop up out of the ground. Armed men wander around, weapons slung over their shoulders. Their uniforms are sloppy. Their demeanor is far too relaxed, but when the six of us pass, those men stand a little straighter. They eye us, perhaps wondering who we are. More likely, they're measuring themselves against what it means to be a Guardian.

Booker stays beside Izzy, guarding her from the stares of the surrounding men. When we pass by the medical tent, he snaps his fingers, then points to Rafe and Hayes. "Take her to medical."

Is it my imagination, or does Booker look like he doesn't want to let Izzy go?

"Come with us, Miss." Rafe holds out his hand. "We're going to take you to medical."

Izzy takes Rafe's hand under Booker's harsh glare. Rafe and Hayes peel away from our group, protective of their charge, and head toward a larger grouping of tents while I eye the armed men all around us. Booker watches them until they disappear inside the tent while I survey the camp.

As for the men, none are on patrol. They wander aimlessly as if they're on a casual Sunday stroll.

"Who are they?" When I give them the eye, Booker fills me in.

"Local military assisting the Taskforce." He turns to Alec and Zeb, snaps his fingers, and sends them running. "They're more useful than they look."

"That's good because they look …" I know better than to finish that sentence, but there's no need. Booker knows exactly what I was going to say.

We're elite operatives with extensive training. It's hard to remember not all those in our line of work can say the same.

"Where are they going?" I follow Alec and Zeb as they head toward the centermost, and largest, tent.

"They're going to run a bit of interference for you." Booker flashes his pearly white teeth at me.

"Interference?" I tug on my shirt.

It's caked in dried mud and things I don't want to think about. I must smell like a dead animal. Booker's giving me a wider berth than normal.

"Figure you need a moment before debriefing." He gives me a once over and scrunches his nose. "And a shower. You, my friend, reek."

He's not wrong about that, the debrief or how I smell.

The last thing I need is command breathing down my neck, debriefing me before I have a chance to sort out what the fuck happened back there. My gut clenches and a sharp stabbing pain pricks at my heart.

I've never left anyone behind.

Never.

The rest of what Booker says finally makes it between my ears.

"Taskforce?" My forehead furrows with that.

"Doctors Without Borders did what they could. They drummed up international attention, and the local government doesn't want to look like they're not in control."

"Are they?"

"Hell no. Sam and CJ are running the show."

"Forest?"

"He didn't come." Booker shakes his head.

"That's odd."

"Above my pay grade." Booker nudges my elbow. "You ready to face the wrath of Mitzy?"

"Wrath my ass. What's she got to be pissed about?"

"You were supposed to do recon only, keeping a low profile until we arrived."

"Oh, right." I rub at the muck and mud coating my face.

The expression on Booker's face says he wants to know why I went off-script.

He has an idea. I called it in, but he wants the details. I catch the words he uses. He calls Angie *my girl*.

Not much gets past him.

Not that I care one bit what he thinks. He's my brother from another mother. I don't keep secrets from him.

He knows it's personal for me, and he knows what that means.

I'm going for blood.

"Where's the team's barracks?" My tone is harsh, biting, but I don't give a damn.

"Over there." Booker points to a smaller grouping of tents.

"Any chance there's a shower?"

"There is, but Mitzy …"

"Mitzy can wait. First, I'm going to wash this jungle off of me. I've got mud in places I didn't know could get dirty. Then I'm walking over to medical and getting a shot of whatever parasitic meds they'll give me."

The river looked clean, but all kinds of creatures swim in it. I would've taken Angie and Izzy overland if the jungle had cooperated. It was too thick, and I needed to get them as far from that camp as fast as possible.

My plan worked until it didn't.

"It's your funeral when she finds out you made her wait." Booker lifts his hands up and out. A cheeky grin fills his face.

"I just need a minute." Surrounded by the force that is the Guardians, I feel like a failure. Losing a hostage during a rescue is the very definition of mission failure. I did that and more.

I should never have pulled ahead of Angie the way I did. Lord knows, I know better. But Angie excelled at everything before that. She was unstoppable, and I *assumed* … And that's the beginning and end of that colossal fuckup.

Assumptions are a bitch and I walked right into that.

Angie is not one of my teammates. I never should've relied on her the way I did. All that accomplished was putting her in danger.

But those men?

A tiny voice inside of me argues against beating myself up.

Where did those men come from?

Not that I want to make assumptions, but the man who caught us at the waterfall must have called in our position. Unfamiliar with the roads around that area, my assumption is those men came to take back the girls.

But why?

I press my hands to my temples and squeeze. This kind of thinking is a sure way to bring on a monster headache.

"Did you bring any of my gear?" I check out the command center, looking for movement, but there's no psychedelic pixie running toward me. Mitzy's amazing, but she can be a little *too much to handle.*

"Of course." Booker punches me playfully in the arm. "Wouldn't leave you hanging."

"Great. I just need you to cover for me." The hours of no sleep are piling up on me. Fatigue pulls at me like a monster. My eyes droop and I stagger like a drunkard, weaving this way and that.

Booker says nothing, so maybe it's all in my head, but I need the four S's—shit, shower, shave and sleep—plus tons of caffeine.

Sleep won't be happening—not until Angie's safely back in my arms—but I can do the other bits.

I'm thankful for Alec and Zeb running interference with Mitzy. I hope they send her on a wild goose chase.

They deflect her long enough for me to get cleaned up and change into something that isn't full of jungle juice. I figure if my boss, CJ, isn't looking for me, I'm good. He understands what a shower can do for a man's state of mind and the wonders a hot meal will do for his soul.

He also knows I need a moment to decompress after the colossal failure that mission was. It's something I respect about CJ. He knows because he's an operator like the rest of us. We breathe the same air and have been through the same shit.

Mitzy doesn't understand that. She thinks we can switch on and off like her computers.

While Alec and Zeb keep her running, Booker hangs out with me while I clean up and change into a fresh set of clothes and a dry set of boots. While my stomach protests, demanding food, I decide to check in with CJ and see what we can make of the mess I created.

When I enter the command tent, Mitzy is out looking for me.

CJ and Sam sit behind a pair of metal desks, feet propped up, hands laced behind their heads. They look totally chill, but I know that's not the case. They were briefed during our flight in. No doubt they're lobbing potential scenarios back and forth.

CJ takes one look at me and shakes his head.

"Come on, Sam." He gives a jerk of his chin to Sam, the man Forest Summers appointed to lead the Guardians. "Let's get this guy some food." CJ spins his finger in the air and points toward the opening of the tent. "Turn around. The food here's not that bad, and we can kill two birds with one stone."

"Meaning what?" I stand at a modified parade rest.

If I was still in the military, this is where my commanding officer would dress me down for my epic failure and read me the riot act. I might lose a stripe, or two, then I'd be sent on my merry way, left to stew about what a failure I'd become.

That's not the Guardian way.

"You can debrief while you eat." CJ shoves Sam's boots off the desk. "Let's go."

My stomach chooses that moment to growl, reminding me it's been well over a day since I've eaten anything. My shoulders slump. The thought of having something warm to eat while Angie is still out there guts me, but I never refuse a meal when operating. A guy never knows when his next meal's coming.

"How are you holding up?" CJ clamps his hand down on my shoulder. "Rafe debriefed us. I'm sorry about Angie Maddox." He says something else, but then clamps his jaw shut. CJ knows I don't need him blowing sunshine up my ass.

"I fucked up." My head hangs and my feet drag.

"Not necessarily." CJ shoves me toward the chow hall.

"Huh?" I pull up short, confused as shit. "What the fuck does that mean?"

"It means there's a bit of sunshine coming our way."

"Sunshine? What the fuck you talking about *sunshine*?" My neck heats as my anger rages. "I lost her. I fucking ran ahead, leaving Angie behind to get captured all over again."

"Yes, that's true, but you did something else that's going to lead us right to them."

"What's that?" Then it hits me like a load of bricks. "You're tracking her." I look between Sam and CJ, mouth agape. "If you're tracking Angie, why are we standing around with our thumbs up our butts?"

We need to get going. My fingers twitch as CJ talks me down.

"Think about it, Einstein." A very perky, perpetual ball of energy interrupts our conversation.

Mitzy is several sizes too short, but when she glances between Sam and CJ, she somehow appears as if she's looking down her nose at them.

"She's leading us right to their camp," she says. "While you've been on your nature walk, we've been having one hell of a time locating where the *Coralos* cartel is holding the other hostages. If we go guns blazing after your girlfriend now, we may never know where their main camp is."

"Your fuckup is going to bring all of them home." CJ grins like a goddamn Cheshire cat who caught the canary.

I don't care what they say. All I want is to get my girl back. It's a miracle I make it to the chow line.

"It's Chili Mac today." Mitzy pushes in front of me and grabs a tray. "I'm going to load up on brain food." She pokes at my side. "You should probably fill up too."

"You mothering me now?"

"No, but we're sending your team out the moment we've acquired the intel we need. I see you showered." She gives Booker the evil eye. "Time to eat and sleep if you can."

"As if."

Mitzy's the first to finish her plate. She picks up her tray and gives our half-eaten trays a dirty look. "I don't know about you, but I've got work to do. If you boys are done, why don't you go do whatever pre-mission prep you normally do, and Brady …" She gives me the once over.

"What?"

"You look like shit. Not that you will, but try to get some sleep. I need you at your peak, not looking like a zombie. We're launching as soon as we get a location."

"How long will that take?"

"Now, if I knew how long that would take, then I'd know where the cartel is holding the prisoners. If I knew that, we wouldn't be having this conversation now, would we?" With another dramatic flick of her eyes, Mitzy lets out a long sigh. "I swear, working with Guardians is painful."

She grabs her tray and disappears.

The moment she's gone, CJ and Booker crack up.

"That woman …" Booker doesn't finish his sentence.

There's no need.

We're all smiling.

"Come on, Bravo One." Booker stands and taps my shoulder. "Let's get you some shuteye. As much as I hate to say it, I agree with Mitzy. Let her team do their thing. The moment they know something, we'll be back in the muck. Until then …"

"Yeah, yeah." We say our goodbyes, which I yawn my way through. Keeping my eyes open as Booker walks me back to our temporary barracks proves difficult. Not proud to say it, but I'm asleep before my head hits the pillow.

That's okay though. My dreams fill with holy hellfire raining down on the asshole who took my girl.

I will get Angie back.

No matter what it takes, I'll rescue my girl.

TWENTY

Angie

BONE-JARRING BUMPS RATTLE ME BACK TO THE LAND OF THE LIVING. Hands tied in front of me, feet duct-taped together, someone threw me into the back of a beat-up rust bucket of a truck. The metallic tang of oxidized metal floods my nostrils.

Another bounce lifts me into the air, not even an inch, but the thud when I land on my shoulder is excruciating. A moan slips out of my mouth as I try to find a more comfortable position.

Try being the operative word. I don't succeed.

When I crack open an eye, a disheveled, unshaven man peers down at me with a grimace and a scowl. His bushy brows send his dark eyes into a pit of shadows. Those eyes pinch when he realizes I'm awake. He hefts his gun.

There must be a point where fear and our survival instinct flee us. I should be terrified, but that queasy, shaky sense of dread abandons me. I'm oddly calm.

It's weird—and into that surreal sense of quietude, my brain focuses on how dappled sunlight filters down through the canopy. It watches dust motes floating in those ethereal columns of light.

But then, those bright flashes of light flicker at the right frequency to give me one hell of a headache. I curl inward and close my eyes.

That's when the fear strikes.

Spasms make my body jerk as terror courses through me. My stomach revolts, but I fight the urge to vomit with everything I have left. This isn't the time to be weak. It's the wrong place to come apart. I need to focus and concentrate on being resilient.

Whatever comes next, I need to meet it head-on; not simpering like a fool.

Despite subjecting my bruised shoulder to more abuse, as we rattle down the rutted road, I remain on my side. It's a better choice than turning to my back or lying on my belly.

This way, I can watch Mr. Scowly-Pants and his gun.

He frightens me too much to keep my eyes closed. He says nothing to me, and I say nothing to him. Other than me and him, we're the only two people in the back of the truck. I suppose my kidnappers feel I warrant only one guard.

But there are trucks behind us.

Several.

The chugging of diesel engines follows us through the jungle. We're in the lead truck but only because we kick up a cloud of dust that clogs the air behind us. If we were in the middle of the caravan, or the rear, I'd be coughing up dust.

With no idea how long I was out, there's no way to know where I might be now. North, South, East, West? I don't know.

How is Brady ever going to find me?

I barely know the man, but there's one truth I latch on to. He'll find me because he's a Guardian, and that's what a Guardian does.

At least I have that.

But Brady will find me for another reason. He'll find me because something is growing between us; a connection that goes beyond simple attraction that ties us together.

It binds our fate.

It's a feeling that delves deep and takes root within me.

All I have to do is make it easy for him to find me.

But how do I make that happen?

The man across from me shifts in his seat. He lifts a butt cheek to let out a loud and wet-sounding fart. When he looks back at me, he belches. There's no apology for the social faux pas. This guy doesn't give a shit about such things.

Repulsive comes to mind.

Slowly, the surrounding vegetation thins. Trees, which once soared upward to form a canopy over a hundred feet high, grow shorter. The thick boughs, which interwove to support the jungle canopy, thin and stretch through open space.

Instead of a perpetual twilight, more light filters through to reach the ground. We continue on our bumpy journey for what seems like forever. Local farms crop up here and there, telltale signs of civilization in this poor place.

Down more dirt roads, we continue our journey, but they aren't as steep, not as curvy, and not nearly as rutted. The ride eases and my shoulder gives thanks.

For a spell, a deep sense of weariness comes over me, and despite struggling to stay awake, my lids bounce closed until that's where they stay.

My sleep is rudely interrupted sometime later when I'm jostled awake. The man with the gun leans over the side of the truck, lowering his weapon. Dirt cakes his pants, dust covers his boots, and the stench of his unwashed body makes me gag when he turns around to manhandle me into the air.

I scream when he lifts me in his arms and wriggle like a worm. He lowers me over the side of the truck and I cry out. I struggle when I'm set on my feet, then cry again when a different man slings me over his shoulder like a sack of potatoes.

That man marches through what appears to be a well-established camp. I say camp only because most of the structures are tents, and the few permanent buildings are a mixture of mud and metal siding.

He angles toward one of those. It's a building—sort of. Mud and muck form the walls. A piece of ratty cloth acts as a door. A slight breeze makes it flutter in the air. Overhead, sticks and aluminum siding weave together to form a patchwork roof.

The man carries me inside, marches to the far end of the building, where another man sits on a rickety wooden stool. That man lumbers to his feet and draws out a ring of metal keys from his pocket. He turns to what looks to be a metal cage and opens the lock. The metal door squeals in protest as he pulls it open.

The man carrying me approaches the door, then sets me down on my feet with as much care and attention as he did when slinging me over his shoulder. With my feet bound, I can't find my balance. Not that it matters.

The man who brought me shoves me, pushing me back where I fall on my ass and barely avoid striking my head on the dirt floor.

The cell door closes. The first man disappears, and our guard picks up the magazine he was reading, completely ignoring me.

"Angie?" A voice calls out from the dimly lit cell. "Is that you?"

I know that voice. It belongs to Stefan Carmine, our psychologist.

"Stefan?" I roll until I can manage a sitting position. With my hands in front of me, I work on ripping through the duct tape wrapped around my ankles. "Is that you?"

"Yes."

He crawls forward, practically dragging himself over the dirt floor. He looks like a train ran him over. His face is barely recognizable, swollen and bruised, with dried, cracked blood and dirt everywhere.

"Where's Izzy?" He glances behind me, but there's nothing to see.

"I don't know." Well aware of the guard listening in on our conversation, I speak nothing but the truth. However, I keep things vague.

"What happened to you?" He grips my hands, pulling them away from my effort to free myself from the duct tape.

I can't get the damn stuff to rip.

"Let me." Stefan works on the tape, using his teeth to help.

While he does that, I bring my wrists to my mouth, and with an eye on the guard, I use my teeth to rip through the nearly indestructible tape. I'm free moments later and rub at the chafing on my wrists.

"Where are the others?" I glance around me, peering into the dark corner where Stefan appeared from.

"Daniel is …" Stefan looks over his shoulder. "They just brought him back. He'll be out of things for a bit."

"What have they done to you?" From the injuries to Stefan's face, my question is rhetorical. "What do they want?"

"They think we're running guns for the *Laguta* cartel. They claim the southern regions of Nicaragua as their territory and are in a territory war with the *Coralos* cartel."

"If we were running guns, they would've found them at our camp. What did they say when you told them?"

"They don't believe us." He swings around and crosses his legs in front of me.

"Where's Jacob?" Our lead physician, Jacob, is also our leader for this mission.

"They took him when they brought Daniel back."

"So, they're …"

"Rotating between us."

"Where's Jerald?"

I like Jerald. He's young, energetic, and always looking for ways to pitch in.

"I don't know. They took him that first night and we haven't seen him since."

"Do you think they …"

"Honestly, I don't know. That's what we feared when they took you and Izzy. It's been well over a day. What happened to you?"

I bite my lower lip, not sure how much to share. The guard appears to read his magazine, but it's been several long seconds since he turned a page. No doubt they gave him orders to watch over the prisoners and report back anything we may say.

But what do I have to hide?

It doesn't feel right to resist and withholding information may only make these men more suspicious rather than less.

"After they separated us, they took us to the river."

"The river? Why?" Stefan's brows tent together, cracking open a cut on his forehead. The wound weeps.

"Your …" I point to my forehead, showing the place his cut bleeds.

He swipes at his forehead with the back of his hand, staring at the blood only moments before turning back to me.

"It's nothing."

"You should let me look at you."

"Other than my eyes being swollen, angry, and bruised …"

"I may be an ophthalmologist, but I know basic medicine."

Unlike Stefan, who's a psychologist, I went to medical school. I trained as an intern on medical and surgical wards before my residency, where we focused on the eyes. But most eye diseases result from systemic illnesses.

"I trained in basic first aid and basic trauma support. I appreciate it, Angie, I really do, but we have nothing to slap on a cut, let alone treat the infections that will set in after another day of this."

"I'm so sorry."

He places a hand under my chin and lifts it until I have no choice but to look at him. It's an intimate gesture but means nothing. Stefan is happily married, with three young boys at home. He's a healer like me, attuned to emotional distress and injury to the mind.

"What happened to you? Was Izzy with you?"

My eyes dart to the guard. He's on the same page he was before, confirming my suspicions, but I have nothing to hide.

"When they took us to the river, there was this man …"

"A man?"

"An American."

"Really?"

"Yes, and he took out our guards."

"How?"

"He shot them, and then he shouted at us to get in the water. We ran …" I shake my head. "I'm so sorry. We never meant to leave you behind."

"Angie, there is nothing you could've done to change things. I'm glad you escaped. Only, I'm sorry—I'm sorry you didn't make it."

"Izzy did."

"She did?" His eyes brighten, then close as his lips move in silent prayer.

"Yes, and I almost did too, but …" I blow out a breath and feel tears pricking at my eyes.

The emotional toll of the night we spent in that cave, and the day following on the river, is about to break through my carefully shored-up defenses.

"It's okay." He touches my arm this time. The physical contact pushes back the tide of my emotions. Stefan gives me a moment to collect myself, then continues. "Do you know who he was?"

"I don't." With the guard listening, this is where I skim the truth, telling as little as possible. "It's not like we had a lot of time, and I was scared the whole time. We didn't exactly speak. It's like I was on autopilot. Not thinking. Only reacting."

"Extreme stress can do that to a person. I'm not surprised."

"They hurt you." I take another long look at Stefan, scanning him from head to toe.

They didn't go easy on him. His face is battered and bruised. From the way he splints his breaths, my concern for a rib fracture goes up. That kind of pain keeps people from taking deep breaths, which can lead to pneumonia setting in.

He's right about infection.

This is about the time we'll see it take hold, and infections in this kind of environment can be a death sentence.

"They hurt all of us, but we know nothing about what they want to hear."

"Izzy and I talked about that."

"You did?"

"A little." I shrug and flick my hair back over my shoulders. It moves as one mass, caked in stuff I don't want to think about.

Disgusting doesn't begin to describe my personal state. I'm covered in mud, sweat, and river water. "Honestly, we've unloaded nearly every box, every crate, every canvas bag. If there were guns, don't you think we would know?"

"That's what I tried to tell them, but they say we're liars."

"I'm sorry they did this to you."

"All we have to do is stay strong. If that man came for you, maybe he's working with the CIA?"

Stefan looks at me, but I give another shrug. There's no way I'll mention the Guardians. Not that it would help.

I still don't understand who the Guardians work for or what they were doing in the jungle. They may very well work for the CIA, or the FBI, or the Nicaraguan government. Or it could be some other organization Doctors Without Borders contracted to rescue us.

"At least, Izzy's safe." I hate to say it, or even admit it to myself, but I'm angry she's free when I'm not. Not a second later, I berate myself for wishing that our roles were reversed.

I'm a horrible human being.

I draw up my knees and wrap my arms around my shins. Propping my chin on my kneecaps, I peer into the shadowy corner where Daniel lies in an unmoving lump.

"How is he?" I force myself to go to him.

"Roughed up like the rest of us, knocked unconscious, but he's breathing."

"I'm going to check on him."

"Please do." Stefan comes with me as I move deeper into the cell.

"Have they fed you? Given you water?"

"Not much. Don't drink the water." He lowers his voice. "I think they take a piss in it before bringing it in."

"Point taken."

Daniel doesn't budge when I gently shake his shoulder, but he's breathing and responds to pain. Those are two good things.

It takes a moment because I have to dig deep into my days as an intern when I did a rotation in the emergency department, but I knock out the cobwebs.

First, I perform a basic assessment. Called the ABCs, it covers the very basics of emergency medicine with establishing a stable airway, ensuring breathing is adequate, and there's appropriate circulation.

The secondary survey takes that further, focusing on things like shock and bleeding issues. Like Stefan, Daniel is beaten and bruised. Dried and cracked blood cover the minor cuts on his face. So far, there's no sign of infection.

It's hard in the dim light, but the skin around the cuts doesn't look any redder than the surrounding area. I peel up his shirt and gasp at the dark bruising covering both his sides.

The beating was excessive.

"Stefan?"

"Yes?"

"How many times have they taken you for questioning?"

It's hard to remember how much time's passed since the cartel kidnapped us. On one hand, it feels fleeting, as if only minutes passed. Other times, it feels as if it's been weeks.

The truth is, Izzy and I spent a little over a day in the jungle with Brady. Weird how it feels as if I've known Brady all my life. Thinking about him brings my hand floating up to rest over my heart. It's an unconscious movement, and when I realize what I've done, that knotted bracelet catches my eye.

I can find you anywhere in the world with that.

My heart skips a beat. Maybe two.

And I suck in a breath.

The dirty, knotted bracelet will bring Brady back to me.

It's as if a fog lifts.

Our situation is not desperate. There is hope.

Movement behind me spins me around. Immediately on the defensive, I brace for the unknown.

Two men drag Jacob into the building. Like Daniel, he's unconscious. His toes drag over the bare earth and his head lists to the side. I can't tell if he's breathing.

The men shout at us to move back from the door. Knowing this is not our moment to escape, I scrabble backward with Stefan as the men open the door and bodily toss Jacob inside with no regard for his safety.

I rush toward him, arms out, trying to protect his fall, but Jacob slams into the ground as I gasp for breath. As I scoot closer, a third man I didn't see initially steps around the two guards.

He reaches out with a thick, meaty paw of a hand to grab me by my hair. He hauls me up and off my feet as my hands fly to his hand. Pain pulls at my scalp as I scream in pain.

"Fucking *puta*. *¿Cómo estuvo tu nado?*" He alternates between English and Spanish, asking me how my swim was.

I dangle in the air, my toes barely scraping the ground, as I grip his wrist. He leans toward me, dark eyes, fetid breath, yellow teeth, and a look that would make the devil scream.

"*Eres mio ahora.*" He suddenly releases me, but before I collapse, he stoops down and tosses me over his shoulder.

I push against the small of his back, eyes wide, too terrified to scream.

Jacob wasn't breathing when he landed on the dirt floor.

My gaze shifts to Stefan.

His expression is one of deepest regret. He reaches out and grasps nothing but air as the two guards slam the cell door shut on him.

Without a backward glance at my colleagues, the leader of the cartel stomps outside and heads to a tent somewhat set apart from the rest. Halfway there, he shouts something at the two men following us.

With my poor knowledge of Spanish, all I comprehend is one word in ten, but I understand when he tells them to leave him alone.

Alone?

With me.

Something withers and dies inside of me because there's no way Brady and his Guardian brothers can get to me in time.

The two men peel off as if bitten by a viper, and I have no doubt this man's bite stings like death itself.

Last time, this monster ordered the guard to make sure Izzy and I cleaned up in the river. This time, he no longer cares.

He marches me inside his tent and drops me on a mattress.

His mattress.

The only bed in the room.
I scoot back, but there's nowhere to go.
He reaches for his belt …

TWENTY-ONE

Brady

"GET UP, BOSS." BOOKER SHAKES ME AWAKE, PULLING ME FROM DEEP slumber.

After years at this job, I'm instantly alert. I blink to clear the sleep from my eyes and run my hand down my face.

"What's going on?"

"Mitzy found them. We're loading up in ten."

"No mission brief?"

"No time. We do it on the fly."

It takes less than a minute to get dressed and pull on my gear. Decked out in black tactical gear, we meld into the shadows.

Armed with the best weaponry on the planet and technical gear nations would be envious of, we operate in all the spectrums. From infrared, through the visual range, our optics push our capabilities into the ultraviolet.

It's what we use to mark our targets. Instead of a red dot the enemy can see, we send out a laser shining in the invisible ultraviolet spectrum of light. Our goal is for the enemy to never see us coming.

"Clue me in." As I strap on my armor and ammo, I wait for Booker to brief me on what Mitzy's team learned while I was catching Z's.

"They've got Angie Maddox, put her in a vehicle, and drove for several hours."

"Why didn't we stop them en route?"

Booker pauses for a second, allowing me to catch up and refocus. He's a smart man and knows there's more than a hostage rescue going on between me and Angie.

If we ambush the trucks while they're still moving, we won't know where they're holding the other four hostages. I remind myself there's more than Angie's life at stake.

My mind's back on track.

"Never mind that." I gesture for him to continue. "Go on."

"Mitzy fired up her drone and tracked the caravan. She's got intel on their camp, their men, and is tracking enemy movements as we speak."

"You've done a lot while I got my beauty sleep."

My body's accustomed to getting very little sleep, but I know when I've had more than a catnap. I slept deep, hitting REM several times, where my dreams centered on Angie and all the things a man does with a woman he loves.

"How long?" I ask.

"Less than forty minutes by chopper. We're loading up now, with Infil a few klicks out. No jungle to slow us."

"What are we looking at?"

"Farmer's fields. No electricity. No lights. The camp is guarded, but there's no perimeter fence. It's primitive, with a mixture of tents and mud and brick structures."

"Do we know where Angie is?"

"I assume so. Mitzy sent me to wake you the moment the convoy stopped, and she confirmed they were staying."

"And the rest of the team?"

"Waiting on you, sleepyhead."

Once again, I blink away the sleep and double-check my gear. Booker's fully kitted out and armed to the teeth.

"Check me." I hold my arms out while Booker approaches and checks my gear. The one thing we never skimp on is preparation. The buddy system is excellent for many things. Double-checking each other is the best way to make sure none of us goes on a mission missing vital things, such as ammunition or a knife, or any of several other things.

Booker slaps my chest, telling me to turn around. Once he's finished checking out my setup from the back, he taps me on the shoulder.

"Team's at the helipad—waiting." He turns toward the door.

I'm right on his heels.

Less than five minutes after Booker wakes me from the dead, my feet hang out of the helicopter as we skim over the tops of the canopy.

Wind beats at my face. The deep vibrations of the helicopter's rotors spinning overhead feed the adrenaline surge flowing through my veins.

My teeth grind as Mitzy briefs my team on the way to our Infil.

I'm coming, Angie. I'm coming for you.

We repeat back information Mitzy's team feeds us, closing the loop on our communication, which ensures nothing vital is missed or misunderstood. The operation is simple, as far as operations go. There are six of us and scores of the enemy on the ground.

Exfil will be two klicks down the road, in the middle of a fallow field Mizty's drone found.

"They have taken her to a building on the east side of the camp. From infrared signatures, I make four individuals inside. One is female." Mitzy calls out information her drone feeds her in real-time. "One is inactive or incapacitated. No movement noted. One other is stationary."

She describes the movements of the people in the building with Angie. The optics on *Smaug*, her high-altitude drone, rival those on satellites.

"That's three and a guard, as I make it. Not four and a guard."

"Hard to say, but I agree."

"So we're still missing two out of the four male hostages."

"Looks like." Mitzy isn't happy. "I have no way of distinguishing them from the others."

"Understood." The muscles of my jaw ache from gritting my teeth.

Turning toward my team, I switch to a private channel.

"I need ideas."

We either figure out where the other two hostages are being held, or we leave two men behind. I don't like the last scenario. Our mission is to bring everyone home, and that's exactly what we're going to do.

A quick check of my watch shows we're closing in on our insertion point.

"Infil in two minutes." I alert my team to allow them to prep.

We're coming in hot. The helicopter isn't stopping to land. We're fast-roping it, which means we'll descend a thick rope without a harness. It's a technique used to deploy troops from a helicopter in places where it's impossible, or unwanted, for the helicopter to touch down and allow quick response in a crisis. All that's to say, it allows us to conduct our operations with as much stealth as possible.

It's fun as shit, but technically, complicated and risky. Basically, we jump for a big, thick rope and slide down using gloves only, no harness. We can't bring a full rucksack with us, but we don't need a ruck for this operation.

Our pilot zooms in toward the landing zone. My men do one last buddy check, securing our gear, then we're off and down the rope. As the commander of this mission, I'll go last, ensuring my entire team makes it down.

Booker, my second, goes first. He grabs for the rope and slips out of sight. Rafe follows. Then it's Hayes, Alec, Zeb, and finally me. The rope whizzes through my grip, heating my gloves while the draft from the rotors beats at me.

I land, light on my feet, and release the rope. Jogging away, I signal the pilot that we're all safely down. The pilot banks to the right and disappears into the night.

"All good?" I call out to my team, making sure we're good to go.

All of them return thumbs up.

"Overlord, we're on the ground."

"*Copy that, Bravo One,*" CJ confirms our progress. "*Two klicks to the North. Mitzy's sending coordinates.*"

"Good copy." The screen on my right forearm flickers to life. More gear from the tech team, the integrated display embedded in our sleeves, is like having a fully functional tablet at our fingertips.

A 3D terrain map pops up with a suggested route to the *Coralos* cartel's encampment. Booker and I look it over and approve the suggestion.

"Head out." I take the lead, loping into a fast jog that will take us the two klicks in the least amount of time without winding us unnecessarily when we arrive.

The ground disappears beneath me as I run through the fields and leap over irrigation ditches. The farmers' fields are ripe with cotton, a major crop for the country, and easy to cross. We make stellar time.

"*A hundred meters out,*" CJ's voice crackles over the comms.

I bring Bravo to a stop. We take another look at the map. The building Angie and the two other men are in is on the near side of our approach. Between us, a line of canvas tents presents a barrier we need to cross.

Kitted out all in black, we're well hidden from the casual observer, but any lookouts will spot our motion. Whether we take out the camp guards first, or attempt to bypass them and sneak inside, is my call.

Taking them out risks other members in the camp finding their bodies. That will set up a full-scale alarm. Not taking them out means they'll be an obstacle we'll have to cross with our three rescued hostages, one of whom appears to be injured.

"*Overlord, to Bravo One,*" Mitzy's voice crackles in my ear.

"Go on."

"*We note activity approaching the hostages. Four men. Two bracketing what appears to be an injured man. The last follows behind.*"

The benefit of *Smaug's* eyes and ears far above us is invaluable. We have two injured hostages to recover.

"Copy that." I exchange a look with Booker.

He gives a slow nod, confirming what we're all thinking.

"The third hostage?"

Mitzy hates assumptions, but sometimes there's no way around them. We're still missing the fourth hostage.

"Agreed." There's a pause on the other end.

Bravo closes in on the camp. We pause for last-minute updates from command.

There are none.

"Boss?" Booker looks to the left, where a guard kicks back, smoking a cigarette. The tip glows red as he sucks in, then gray smoke billows out, coiling in the air as he exhales. His rifle sits to the side, propped up against a tree. It's out of reach.

Sloppy.

But that's not all he carries. Twin pistols sit in his bandoleer. Several cartridges fill the small pockets on the belt crisscrossing his chest.

The man takes another slow drag of his cigarette, then flicks the spent butt to the ground. He presses his hands to his lower back and groans as he stretches.

Rafe reaches around to his back, pulling out his pistol. He grabs for the silencer, screwing it on as he looks at me, waiting for my command.

We lie on the upward bank of an irrigation ditch. The scruff and weeds growing next to the field obscure our presence.

I signal Alec to move into position while Rafe uses that eagle vision of his to take out the guard.

With the knowledge of a second injured man, whether to take out the guards first or try to move past them twice, once on infiltrating the camp then again on exiting, becomes moot.

Injured hostages always slow things down.

Alec crawls up the bank, then waits for the guard to turn his back before jogging into position. As he closes in, Rafe takes the shot.

It's eerie how silent it is, taking that life. Rafe hits the man in the back of the head, and as the guard's body slumps, Alec catches it and drags the body into the ditch. He's up a second time to grab the man's rifle. With that task accomplished, we move to the guard to our right and repeat the process.

"Bravo One to Overlord, we're in position, ready to move."

"Copy that, Bravo One. There's been a development."

"Go on."

The pause from command tells me whatever comes next is something I won't like.

"Those men deposited the third hostage, but they …"

The long pause on the other end makes my blood turn icy cold.

"They took Angie. She's on the move."

While I appreciate the succinct message, it's the worst possible news.

Booker turns toward me. After years of operating with him by my side, we seldom need words to communicate what's going on in our heads.

Which means we pivot fast.

No wasted conversation.

I gather my men. "Rafe, you and the others proceed to the tent. You've got two known injured. Assume the third is the same."

"Copy that, boss." Rafe secures his pistol and silencer.

"We meet at the hedgerow."

Half a klick back, we came across an obnoxious hedgerow that hindered our progress. It's the perfect place to shelter behind while waiting for the rest of the team to gather.

"If we're not there in ten, move out."

"Copy that." Rafe signals to the rest of Bravo to move out.

While they slip away into the night, I sit with Booker and try not to lose my ever-loving mind.

I say nothing. He knows exactly what's going on in my head.

As for the fourth man, we'll have to deal with that later.

"Mitzy …"

"Yes, Bravo One."

"Guide us in."

"Copy that.."

The rest of the team knows exactly where they're headed. We

mapped the entire spread of the camp and it's visible on our HUD displays. We, literally, have an X marks the spot.

Booker and I, however, need Mitzy to guide us.

"Lead us to her." I silence my comms, then rise from the bank with only one objective in mind.

Rescuing Angie.

Hold on, Angie. I'm coming for you.

TWENTY-TWO

Angie

"Please …" I hold out my hand, as if that can stop this man from raping me.

"I like it when they beg, *puta.*" He sneers at me. "Go on, beg for me." That sinister sneer morphs into a vicious grin. His breathing deepens. His arousal grows. "Make me hard for you."

My gut clenches and my heart races at breakneck speed. Fear courses through me in a maddening frenzy to get the hell out of here.

The thick, humid air makes it hard to breathe, and as for escape? There's nowhere to go and no place to hide.

The tent flap pops as a passing breeze blows through the camp. The snapping fabric draws my attention. It's completely dark out there, but I envision myself pushing past this despicable man and escaping into the night.

The darkness will shield me.

With his belt unbuckled, the man reaches to undo his fly. "You're a pretty thing, and pretty American girls fetch nice prices at auction." Despite his thick accent, the man's English is perfect.

There's not a word there I don't understand, but my brain trips over what he says, certain I didn't hear what I think I did.

"What?" My hand flies to my stomach as his words sink in.

"With the right training, you will make me a fortune."

Whatever bit of hope that remained within me shrivels up and dies. It's like watching a flame go out. Only I'm the flame and it's my life I'm going to lose.

Not in death, but to something far worse.

Think!

Not all resistance abandons me. There's still the tiniest spark desperately flickering within me. It's not willing to give up.

Somewhere—out there—Brady and his team of Guardians will not forsake me. He will come for me.

All I have to do is bide my time—survive and endure.

That must be my motto.

Don't give up.

I'm not!

"Only weak men enjoy raping defenseless women." The longer I get him to talk, the more time I give Brady and his men to find me.

My biting tone only brings a grin to his dirty face. He leans in close, breathing on me. When I pull back, his eye catches on the necklace around my throat. I can't help it. My hand flies to the necklace and the gold wedding band that belonged to Luke.

"Now that's a pretty thing. Gold?" The rank odor of his breath is nearly enough to make me pass out.

My hand trembles, clutching Luke's wedding band in a death grip. When the man reaches for the gold band, I retreat until my back brushes against the wall of the tent.

His dark eyes grow impossibly darker as he grabs my wrist. Fingers digging into the sensitive skin of my inner wrist, I cry out as my fingers release. The moment they do, he grabs Luke's wedding ring and rips it off my neck.

"No ..." I leap after him, grabbing at his forearm as he lifts the band to his face to better inspect it.

He doesn't even look at me as he tears my fingers from around his forearm and slams me back down on the filthy bed. He bites down on the gold, then gives a satisfied nod.

"This will do."

"It's mine. Give it back." I know better than to sit up, or challenge him, but there's no way in hell he's taking Luke's ring.

My attention snags on the knotted bracelet Brady gave me. It will allow him to find me anywhere in the world, but how long does that take?

"I like women who fight." My captor reaches inside his pants while my throat dries up. "Especially pretty girls like you. You won't fight me after I'm done with you. Once you've been fucked by a real man, you'll beg me to keep you."

I'll beg, but not for the reason he thinks.

Come on. Think!

"You're the one who's weak."

"Do I look weak to you?" He gestures toward the tent flap and what's out there. "I am the leader of the *Coralos* cartel. My men worship me. They live for me, and they die for me." He lifts the wedding ring, examining it before slipping it around his pinky finger. The gold flashes in the light as my desire to kill increases to a boiling point.

He's a man who values his strength, and that is how I will distract him.

"But you don't keep the women you take. You're going to rape me, then you're going to give me away. You may be the head of the *Coralos* cartel, but you work for another. You bow to another."

I try to inject as much conviction into my voice as I can manage. The truth is—I'm falling apart inside. There is no bravado, false or otherwise. I'm two heartbeats from falling apart.

His brows tug together, and he pulls his hand out of his pants. That scowl of his returns, but this time, it's not aimed at me. From the way his forehead bunches, and the muscles of his jaw tick, I struck a nerve.

How do I use that to my advantage?

Think!

"Such a shame." Curled up at the head of the bed, it takes everything I have left to unclasp my hands and relax my posture.

"What do you mean?" His tone turns ominous.

"You may have captured me, but I'm not yours to do with as you please. Another pulls your strings. That's not strength. That's submission."

My words are a stretch, and I take a tremendous risk insulting this man.

I have nothing to lose.

He's going to rape me.

That's the beginning and end of this. I won't take it lying down, literally or figuratively.

I will fight to the bitter end.

I'll endure, but only because I have value on the other side of this. He never said there was someone over him, someone who forced him to hand over the women he takes.

That assumption is wholly mine, and it may be a massive stretch.

For a second, I nearly crack a smile in victory. It bounces at the corners of my lips, but I silence the twitch before it costs me.

I assume I'm *all that,* and this monstrous man would never willingly give me to another. As if I have *that* sort of value. I've never been this cocky in my life. That kind of self-confidence has never been mine, but I claim it now.

I claim it with every fiber of my soul.

I'm pretty, some would say attractive, but I'm not model gorgeous.

There's no reason to believe this man would desire me in that way—that he would want to keep me for himself.

But I have to believe he wants me if I'm going to survive. I need to manifest that desire within him to covet and claim me as his own.

All he wants is a quick fuck and the thrill that comes from hurting a woman who can't fight back. He's a cretin, the lowest of the low, and I'm insane to think he *wants* to keep me.

I'm even crazier trying to turn that into reality.

Once he's had his fun, what do I mean to him? Why not sell me to the highest bidder? I'm worth that much to him. It's something.

But my survival instincts kick in and they create the conditions that may save me in the end.

Why?

Because that small voice in my head tells me if this man hands me over to whoever runs this auction, my life really is over.

I *need* him to want me.

To covet me.

And, boy, does that turn my stomach.

"I never said that."

That?

I struggle to remember what he refers to. What was it I said?

"You're mine tonight." His shoulders twitch, denying my words. "What happens after is none of my concern." If I wasn't looking for a reaction, I would've missed the tell.

"I suppose you have no choice but to settle for just the one night." I arch a brow, challenging him. "I'm surprised he gives you that much. How very generous of him to give you measly scraps, especially when he profits from the sale. I bet he doesn't share those profits with you. What do you get? A finder's fee? Is that how it works? You scour the local villages for pretty girls. Maybe you kidnap an American tourist here and there? You do the work, and get what? A night to do as you please?"

I roll my eyes and sigh as if commiserating with him.

"Enough! I have a better use for that mouth of yours." His hand goes to his crotch, gripping his swollen member.

"Put that diseased thing anywhere near me, and I swear, I will bite it off."

"You can try." His head tilts back and laughter roars out of him, engaging his entire body.

I spring off the bed and race for the door, but only make it two steps before his meaty arm hooks around my waist. He lifts me off my feet and body slams me back on the bed, knocking the wind out of me.

I bounce on the stiff mattress and struggle to breathe. No matter how hard I try, *I can't breathe!*

He comes at me with rope. Flipping me onto my stomach, he roughly yanks my arms behind my back and ties my wrists together. Then he leans on my legs, wrapping a thick rope around my ankles. He forces my legs to bend and grasps my wrists. Placing his knee to my lower back, he forces me to arch my back as he ties my ankles and wrists together.

His rough handling is less consideration than an animal might receive and I suddenly understand how tenuous my existence must be.

Tears pour out of my eyes and roll down my cheeks. My shoulders ache with the strain of the unnatural body position.

He flips me to my side, lifting me by my wrists and ankles. As I struggle on the bed, trussed up and helpless, he opens a wooden box and pulls out what looks like a medieval torture device.

Black leather straps wrap around a thick metal ring the size of my fist. Buckles dangle at the other end. He comes at me, lifting the disgusting thing to my face.

"Do you know what this is, *puta?*"

I close my eyes, defeated, and bite back a mewling cry.

No. No. No. This is not how I want my life to end.

Only, my life is not at an end.

It's far worse than that.

This is the beginning of something new.

Something horrendously evil.

Something I won't survive.

He bends over me. The stench of his unwashed body infests the air. It coats my tongue and floods my nasal passages as I take in a shaky breath. The urge to hurl overwhelms me, and as I gag and wretch, I do exactly what he needs.

I open my mouth.

The moment I do, he shoves that metal ring into my mouth, scraping it against my teeth as he pushes in behind them. With the metal ring forcibly opening my mouth, he leans over me, bringing his crotch to my mouth and nose.

I gag and try to hold my breath, but the biological need to breathe forces me to inhale his stench.

He's hard. Swollen. Grossly aroused.

Tears stream down my cheeks. Saliva pools in my mouth. I cough and wretch. Then, suddenly, he collapses on top of me. One moment, he stands over me. The next, his body loses all muscle tone.

His weight pins me to the mattress, but he doesn't move.

Panic swirls inside of me, a rabid fear clawing at the darkest corners of my mind. Forced open, something primal erupts from my throat, mewling into the chaos of this moment.

I jerk beneath him, but he doesn't budge.

He's unnaturally still.

The weight of him presses down on me, making it hard to breathe, and that's when I notice the silence. Not only is he not moving, the man isn't breathing.

He's still because …

"Angie?" A voice calls out my name. "Angie, are you okay?"

Two black shapes materialize inside the tent, emerging from the shadows. Men carrying weapons. Black helmets sit atop even blacker goggles. Black on black on black, the men are like wraiths, silent and deadly.

It can't be …

I try to answer, but with the ring gag in place, my words are unintelligible.

The weight of my attacker suddenly lifts. A man peers down at me. He sweeps matted and tear-streaked hair out of my eyes. Sheathed all in black, I stare into the visage of death incarnate.

The man reaches behind my head.

I fight him. I fight with all I've got, but I'm too weak. He's too strong, and my hands are tied behind my back.

"Christ, Angie, stop fighting. It's me. Brady." The man lifts the dark goggles off his face. His skin is painted black, but those hazel eyes, flecked in gold and copper, are eyes I know very well.

"Brady?" I lose it and completely fall apart.

"Your safe, luv, it's me. Now, are you going to stop fighting and let me rescue you?"

Brady eases the ring gag out of my mouth, especially careful not to crack my teeth. The moment the foul metal is gone, I close my lips and try to get rid of the metallic tang coating my tongue.

Someone works on the ties binding my wrists and ankles. The

incredible pressure on my shoulders suddenly eases and I cry out as pain shoots through my shoulders and arms.

"Sorry." The unknown voice is comical in his apology, enough to bring a smile to my face.

I realize what's happening. They're here to rescue me. The joy flooding my senses is too much to contain. A crazy grin fills my face. I'm like a loon with a smile I can't contain.

"Are you okay?" Brady buries his face in my neck, and for a moment, it feels almost as if he sheds tears too. "Did they hurt you?" The growl in the back of Brady's throat promises retribution.

My gaze shifts to the dead man who sprawls on the ground beside me. My would-be rapist is dead. Shot through the back of his head.

"He was going to rape me, then give me to someone to auction off to the highest bidder."

Brady tenses. The man beside him sucks in a breath.

I can't describe the emotions flowing through me. They're too complicated to process. Overwhelming joy follows on the footsteps of terror so deep it crushes the soul. Next to that is relief. Relief that I'm free. That I won't suffer the degradation of rape.

Relief for my friends …

"Brady? What about the others?"

My body is confused, not sure whether to weep for joy or wallow in the injustice of it all, but it remembers the others: Daniel, Jacob, Stefan, and Jerald.

"You have the others?" I grip Brady's arm. "They're being rescued as well?"

"Yes, luv." His thumb sweeps along my cheek and our gazes interlock, colliding in a fission of need, want, and something beyond comprehension.

My soul fuses with his, confused and insecure. There's danger in entrusting a piece of yourself to someone else, and I may trust too soon and too far.

"Brady, we have to move." The other man calls out, unfamiliar and pressured to act.

"I'll carry her." Brady tugs me tight to his chest.

"We need her mobile. I need your gun." Insistent and demanding, the other man makes no secret he's not happy. "Mrs. Maddox, can you stand? Are you mobile?"

Mrs. Maddox.

I haven't been called that since before Luke died. Since selling everything I owned and reinventing myself, I left that name in my past. It pulls at me, and in my fear-state, Luke reaches out. His voice calls to me.

Angie, get up. Run. I'm here, babe. I'm with you. Run, babe. Get up and run!

My gaze sweeps to the dead man and latches onto Luke's ring squeezed onto the man's pinky finger. With an animalistic growl, I pull at the ring.

But it doesn't move.

I cry out, getting frantic, twisting and yanking on the ring. Brady comes to stand beside me.

"Move aside." The tone of his voice fills with compassion.

"He took Luke's ring." He snapped the chain holding it around my neck.

Brady places his hand on my shoulder and pushes me back. "Let me get it for you."

"It's stuck." I desperately claw at the ring, but it's not budging.

That's when I see the steel glint of the hunter's knife. Brady pushes me behind him, then he chops the man's finger free of the hand it once belonged to.

I bite down on my knuckles while a million emotions flow through me.

Brady's gloves drip blood, but he shows me the ring he cut off the man.

"Your necklace?" He scans the ground.

"He ripped it free."

"Okay." Brady wipes the ring on the dirty bedsheets, then opens up a pocket on his chest. "I'll keep it safe for you."

I want the ring, but it's too big for my fingers. It'll slide off and I have no pockets to keep it safe. While I don't like it, I give a nod. If there's one person on this planet that I trust, it's Brady.

I swipe at my cheeks. His golden-hazel eyes captivate me. Nearly identical in color to mine, we share that unusual trait. With Luke's words sounding in my ears, I find strength I never knew I had.

I turn to the other man. Like Brady, he's cloaked in blackness and death, but I don't fear him. I recognize him as the savior he is, and I answer his question.

"I can run."

With Luke to guide me, and Brady to stand by my side, I can do anything.

Luke's words fill me with a strength I've never known. I place my hand against Brady's chest, feeling the steady beating of his heart.

"I'm good."

Brady sets me down, then tugs those dark goggles over his face.

"Let's move out."

TWENTY-THREE

Brady

I take the shot the moment we enter the tent. That monster stood over my girl, doing God knows what. Only years of intensive training keep me focused and prevent me from losing my shit and ever-loving mind.

The urge to tear that man limb from limb takes a great deal of self-control to tamp down. I do what I'm trained to do and put a bullet in the back of his head, but rage burns through me.

If we were a moment too late …

I refuse to think about what that asshole intended. Not that it matters now.

He's dead, and I've got Angie.

She's safe.

Now, to get out of here without raising an alarm. Hopefully, Rafe and the others secured their targets. Fortunately, it's late. Most of the camp is asleep or drunk. Their security is a joke.

Angie stays right behind me, hovering in my shadow. Fear rolls off her in waves. She's in shock, trembling and processing slowly. I don't think it's hit her what just happened.

I signal Booker to head out, back the way we came, then reach behind me and physically place Angie's hand on my belt. I exaggerate the movement. It's not unusual for rescued hostages to act against their interests at this point during a rescue.

"Don't let go." With her hooked to me, I take off after Booker.

We weave in and around the tents, sticking to the shadows until we reach the edge of the camp. The replacements for the two guards we took out have yet to appear. The moment they do, a general alarm will go out.

Our goal is to get out before that happens. We pause for a moment, ensuring the way is clear. This is the riskiest part of the rescue, as we have an open area to cross before heading into the fields where we can once again disappear.

Like back in the jungle, Angie impresses me with her resilience. The shock fades and she keeps up with us, not once slowing or complaining.

Once we hit the fields, we slow our pace, then arrive at the hedgerow to wait. Rafe and the others aren't here, although I expect them to be slower, considering two of their rescues are incapacitated.

We're still missing the one hostage.

"Angie, who was with you in the first tent?"

Her brows pinch together, thinking through my question. "Stefan was there. Daniel too. He's injured. I mean, they both are. Daniel more than Stefan. Daniel wasn't moving. When they brought Jacob back, he was unconscious."

"What about Jerald?"

"I don't know." She wrings her hands and bites at her lower lip. "I was there for such a short time. Daniel said they're convinced we're running guns for the *Laguta* cartel, but there's no way that's true."

"Sounds like they're confused about a lot of things." Something about this whole thing doesn't make sense.

We sit in silence, waiting for Rafe and the others to return. A few minutes later, the alarm finally sounds in the camp.

Gunshots ring out as the idiots shoot into the sky, yelling at the top of their lungs and making a shit-ton of noise.

Maybe they discovered their dead leader. Or maybe the rest of

Bravo team is in trouble. Booker and I hold firm, waiting in complete silence as the seconds tick by.

The camp lights up. The idiots are either burning their tents or stoking their bonfires.

Sound to my left grabs my attention. In the infrared on my goggles, I make out several men closing in on our position. A quick look behind them reveals no sign of pursuit.

Two of my men shoulder the wounded hostages, carrying them in a modified fireman's carry. One man limps along. I mark him as the third hostage, most likely Stefan. Oddly, he carries several backpacks on his back and slung over his shoulder.

We leave one man behind.

I tap my comms, patching into command.

"Bravo One to Overlord."

"Read you loud and clear, Bravo One. Report."

"We have four hostages, one female, three males. We're short one. Please advise."

"We have no further intel. Suggest you call it."

"Copy that." My lips press together. I hate leaving anyone behind, but I can't sacrifice the welfare of four for the one.

Would I walk away if it was Angie I left behind?

Best I don't answer that question.

Rafe jogs up to me and reports.

"Got just the three. None knew where the fourth is being held. They haven't seen him since they arrived."

"What's that?" I jerk my chin toward the one rescue carrying the bags.

"Their personal packs." Rafe shrugs. "They were in the tent. Had been rifled through, saw passports and other ID. Retrieved them."

"Copy that, and no word on the last hostage?"

"None."

That doesn't bode well for Jerald.

As soon as the others arrive, Angie rushes toward the men. I hold back my irritation while she hugs Stefan and checks the other two. She sheds more tears. Asks about Jerald.

Silence falls over the group.

I think they understand.

Stefan hands the backpacks to Angie. She takes them without a word, then hugs each man again before returning to me.

"What's in those?" I gesture to the backpacks.

"Personal gear. We had them when they took us. We're supposed to carry them at all times."

"Why?"

"Our IDs and passports are inside, plus a bit of emergency cash. We're supposed to have it in case we get separated from the main group." Her gaze flicks back toward the camp.

I take note how she doesn't mention kidnapping as a way one of them might find themselves *separated* from the rest of camp.

"They took them from us."

And evidently kept them close to the hostages.

"Okay, we move out." I turn toward Angie and reach for her hand.

It's something I wouldn't normally do with any other rescue, but I don't give a damn. Booker catches me holding her hand. He huffs a laugh and shakes his head.

"Not a word." I head out, taking Angie with me.

Rafe and the others fall in line while Booker takes up the rear. As for the men in the camp, they're too busy shooting bullets into the air and building their bonfires. Meaning, none of them are out looking for their missing hostages.

My initial thought of Exfil was to use the cartel's own vehicles, but with the abundance of farmer's fields, we decided on using the helicopter to both bring us in and take us out.

With two injured hostages, we're slower than expected, but make good time. We're used to this kind of shit.

We cross the field without incident. Since there's no sign of pursuit, we shift to the road, making it easier to travel and increase the pace.

My team double-times it for two miles. Normally, I'd worry about a female rescue keeping up, but I know what Angie's capable of. My girl is fierce.

Before long, we close in on the field where our pilot waits.

It's weird that no one's out looking for the missing hostages. Maybe losing their leader caused complete and utter breakdown in their chain of command.

It wouldn't be such a bad thing.

I settle Angie on one of the bench seats and sit down next to her while the rest of my team secures the other hostages. Once we're set, I give the signal for the pilot to take off.

The rotors spin up, whirring as they cut through the air. We rise into the night and head back to our base camp.

Angie clutches my hand the entire time and places her head on my shoulder as we fly off into the night.

I turn to catch Booker's eye. With my goggles still adjusted to infrared, I see him clear as day. We exchange a look with one another. Our extraction went a little too smooth, a little too perfect. Not that I'm complaining about a well-executed operation, but something feels off about the whole thing.

TWENTY-FOUR

Brady

___

When we land at our base camp, Angie clings to me. She gazes out at the camp with wide eyes and looks completely overwhelmed. However—and I hate this—but my desire to stay by her side comes second to my duty as a Guardian.

That mission needs to be debriefed, and I can't do that with Angie. I feel bad about it, but fortunately, Izzy comes shrieking toward us.

"Angie!" Izzy can be heard by nearly half the camp. She limps toward us, freshly showered and wearing borrowed clothes dug up from somewhere.

"Izzy?" Angie releases me, then takes my hand in hers again. "Brady, do you mind?"

"No, luv. You go with Izzy. She can show you where you can get cleaned up. I have to debrief anyway." I pull her to me, not caring who sees what, and plant a fat kiss on her lips.

The kiss surprises me almost as much as everyone around us. It's not the kiss I want to give, but it'll do for now. With a squeeze to her hand, I release her into her friend's custody.

"I'll find you once I'm done." I lick my lips, loving the taste of Angie left behind on my tongue.

Her fingers brush over her lips, and a dreamy expression fills her face. It's the most beautiful thing I've ever seen in my life.

Which makes the next two hours of debriefs nearly intolerable. All I want is a moment alone with Angie, a moment away from escaping through the jungle and rescuing her from monstrous men. I want to hold her in my arms and do nothing but watch the sun go down over the ocean.

Which reminds me …

"Hey, CJ, you got a moment?" I head over to where CJ and Sam sit around a computer screen. They're reviewing data from our operation.

"Sure, what's up?" CJ leans back and stretches his neck.

"I was just thinking …" Now that I stand in front of my boss, and his boss, I feel a little foolish.

"Spit it out." Sam cracks a grin. His eyes twinkle as he elbows CJ in the ribs.

"What's that for?" I glance at Sam with suspicion.

"Nothing." Sam folds his arms over his chest. "Ask whatever it is you want to ask."

"Um, okay?" I rub at the back of my neck. "I was just thinking about Angie and Izzy."

Sam's brows lift. "Both of them?"

He damn well knows I don't mean both. The thing is, I can't ask for what I want without including Izzy.

"What are you thinking?" CJ gives Sam an irritated look. He almost rolls his eyes.

"It's just with what they've been through. I was thinking they'd do better unwinding away from here."

"What's wrong with here?" Sam continues to question me, but he's having fun. I hear it in the way his voice lifts.

"It looks like the camp we rescued them from."

"Which camp?" Sam continues asking questions with the smirk on his face getting bigger and bigger. "The one you rescued Angie from, or the one you rescued them both from?"

"Does it matter?" The muscles of my jaw bunch.

"Stop messing with him." CJ pokes Sam in the gut this time. "The answer is yes."

"You don't even know what my question is."

"You want to know if you can take the girls back to the resort in Costa Rica, and my answer is yes."

"Excuse me?" I didn't even have time to work my way around to that, but CJ somehow hit it on the head.

"Looks like you're gonna have to spell it out for him." Sam cracks a genuine smile this time, but he doesn't let CJ finish. "Look, you spent all of one day on leave. We owe you two weeks."

"I'm not …"

"You never would." CJ leans back. "I swear it's impossible to get any of my Guardians to take leave, but this mission is a wrap. For what it's worth, it was great seeing Bravo in action again. I'd say the team is back, stronger than ever. I'm impressed with how well this operation went off."

"We're still missing one hostage."

"True, but Mitzy's team is on that. She deployed her swarm and those little drones are doing what they do best."

"And that is?"

"Collecting data and snooping where we can't. I have no doubt we'll know where the mechanic is being held by morning."

"Then we'll head out again?"

"I suppose that's up to you."

"Meaning?"

"Are you going to take your woman to that honeymoon suite? Or are you going to lead the mission once we have the green light?"

"You seriously have to ask?"

As much as I want to be with Angie, and have a moment to simply be with her without all the stress of escape, there's no question where I'm needed most.

"No. I know your answer, but we guessed you'd want to take Angie to the resort." He thumps Sam and snaps his fingers. "Pay up."

"You made a bet?" I look between them, not sure whether to be pissed or amused.

"Yeah, Sam said you'd jump at the chance to take your woman to that resort. I said you'd finish the mission."

"Well, of course I'll finish the mission, but I think it's a good idea to move Angie and Izzy if we can. Lord knows they need some pampering, and they shouldn't go unescorted. Booker and I can take them, then turn around and return here."

"Funny how you don't offer the same for the men." Sam gives me a look.

"All three of them are in medical, getting treated by the doc." I bite my tongue, refraining from telling Sam off.

"Speaking of …" CJ tucks away the five-dollar bill Sam gave him. "Skye wants you to stop by."

"Why?"

"She wants to look at you." CJ shrugs. "See how things went."

He's not as nonchalant as he looks. CJ, along with Sam, and many others, remain concerned about my operational readiness after the accident. My body and mind took significant damage following that fiasco.

CJ was okay for me to lead Bravo on our first operation back as a team, but concern over my readiness remains. It's a not so gentle reminder how much everything I do is being scrutinized by the higher-ups.

Thankfully, things went well. Except for leaving one hostage behind, it was a picture-perfect rescue. I'm not the only one breathing a sigh of relief.

"I don't need the doc poking and prodding me. There were no issues during the op. My mobility is a little restricted on the left side of my body, but not enough to prevent me from doing my job." I feel a need to defend myself, not to mention I took care of that shooter pretty damn well at the waterfall. No disability there.

"Not disagreeing with you." CJ doesn't mince his words or sugarcoat them. "But that doesn't excuse you from having her look."

"Fine." I press my lips into a firm line. "And Angie?"

"I see no reason not to let her and Izzy take advantage of what Guardian HRS is already paying for." He flashes me a grin. "And no reason you can't finish out your two weeks of R&R with her ... er, them." CJ's having fun busting my chops.

It's difficult keeping a straight face and remaining professional. As for me joining Angie once my role here is done?

Abso-fucking-lutely.

"After we take care of Jerald."

"Of course." CJ stands and clamps his hand on my shoulder. "The team did great tonight. I'm impressed but not surprised. You always give us a thousand percent. Tell that to your team."

"I will."

CJ isn't one to hand out compliments freely. I take his words for what they are and barely keep a massive grin from filling my face. CJ never would've sent Bravo out if he had any concerns about our ability to accomplish the mission.

None of us stopped training after the explosion. Once each of us was released from medical hold, we went right back to training alongside the other Guardian teams. Booker assisted on a few missions, filling in holes on the other teams when one of their members was sidelined by injury.

None of us stopped.

All of us worked toward one common goal. We wanted to see Bravo operational again. My chest swells with pride. It's a good day when a mission goes well and I impress the boss.

"As for the girls ..." CJ stops me. "You sure you want to escort them?"

"Absolutely."

"Good. Plan on leaving within the hour."

"That's quick."

"They're taking the chopper. I want it there and back before we need to spin up again."

"I'm not comfortable with them traveling alone. If you need us to stay ..."

"It's less than an hour's flight. I can spare you for that. Mitzy's team has nothing actionable yet. Go. Come back. And after we find the last man, you can join her in Costa Rica."

"Thanks."

My preference is to escort them myself, so I'm happy CJ's willing to cut us loose for the two hours it'll take to fly there and back. I'm not so happy about leaving her and Izzy alone at the resort, but the danger against them is over, and the resort has plenty of security to keep their guests safe.

After everything she's been through, she needs breathing space to process what happened.

"We'll get it set up then. There's no knowing when Mitzy's drones will find the mechanic, or what condition he'll be in. After tonight, I wouldn't be surprised if they pack up and leave or disband altogether. You dealt quite the blow, taking out their leader."

"I was wondering about that." I scratch my head. The mission left me smelling rank, but I cleaned up before going after her. "I'm surprised the *Coralos capo* would've been there. Are we sure he was in charge? There's not someone else?"

"We're not sure of anything, but you'll be one of the first to know if things change. Meanwhile, get yourself cleaned up, and take care of your girl."

"Yes, sir."

CJ knows how I feel about Angie.

Something similar happened to him when he met his wife, Melissa. He rescued her from a tornado, then a serial killer, and fell in love with her the moment he set eyes on her.

I've never been a believer of love at first sight, but it's like getting struck by lightning. Everything changes in an instant.

Knowing that Angie will be taken care of, I leave CJ and Sam to plan the next operation. Mitzy's nowhere to be seen, but all that means is that she and her tech team are hard at work.

Before heading to the showers, I detour to the medical tent, where I check in with Skye and the men we rescued.

"How are they doing?" I pull Doc Summers to the side and ask about the men.

"They were worked over pretty hard. I'm flying them out."

"Really?"

"There's internal bleeding, cracked ribs, and infection is setting in. They're pumped full of painkillers right now, and I'm flooding their bodies with antibiotics, but they need more definitive care. Not this." She makes a vague gesture around the interior of her mobile hospital.

Her words are comical, considering Doc Summers trained with the Air Force's Special Ops Surgical Team, learning all about how they bring cutting-edge medicine to the front lines. And when I say cutting-edge medicine, I'm talking about major surgeries in a hot zone. It's incredible what her team can do.

"How do you feel?" She turns her attention from her other patients to me. "Any problems? Limitations?"

"None."

"None?"

"Well, the scars are tight."

"That's why you need to focus on therapy." Doc Summers shakes her head. "The best thing you can do for full recovery is to focus on physical therapy in addition to scar therapy."

Scar therapy.

It feels like a joke. Evidently, I'm supposed to massage the scars. It has something to do with limiting contracture and increasing mobility, especially around joints. I think it's a crock of shit, but Doc Summers believes otherwise.

"I will, Doc. I will." For the first time, I mean it.

I don't want to be half the man I can be for Angie. She deserves the best of me.

"Well, from my standpoint, you're good to go. I'm going to insist on another six months of PT with Piper …"

A groan slips out of me. "She's the worst."

"She's the best physical therapist on the planet."

"Then I'll follow doctor's orders, and once this mission is done, I'll put in the time."

"After you get back from leave."

"After the mission …"

"No, Brady, I mean after you get back from leave. We pulled you early for this mission. Or rather, I should say, you did that all on your own, but you need time away from the work. It probably feels good right now, back doing what you love, but you've got endorphins screaming through your body, numbing the pain. You say that side of your body was a bit tight. In the morning, you're going to realize how much of an understatement that is. Trust me in this."

"I will."

"You won't. I'd be surprised if you did. At least, I got a chance to do my due diligence and tell you to take time off. Body and mind, Brady. It's all connected, and they're both important."

But I'm not doing it for myself. There may, or may not, be a future between me and Angie. Intense situations often elicit feelings that fade once that intensity is gone.

There's no way to know if that will happen between us, but I'm going to do everything in my power to discover if what's growing between us is real or the result of what we went through.

My greatest fear is that I might have to face the fact things aren't what they seem. Angie may not be into me at all, and I've made it all up in my head.

I don't know how I'll survive rejection like that.

Doc Summers is right about my head. I still have a lot of issues to deal with, least of all is how others see me.

Or how I see myself.

TWENTY-FIVE

Angie

"WELL, ANGIE, YOU LOOK GOOD." SKYE SUMMERS PUTS AWAY HER stethoscope and turns back around to me. "I'll prescribe a few things." She rattles off anti-parasitic medicines alongside a general antibiotic regimen to combat anything the jungle may have given me.

Izzy bounces by my side. She completed her medical exam when she came in with the helicopter that was supposed to take me out of the jungle with her.

"You sure she's alright?" Izzy hasn't left my side since Brady handed me off to her. She's doing more than hovering. The girl is smothering me.

"Physically, you're in great shape." Skye cocks her head. "We have trauma specialists if you want to talk about what happened."

By trauma specialists, she's not talking about surgeons, but psychologists who will dig in my head about how I feel after my abduction.

I'm a bit confused about how to characterize my kidnapping.

Was it one event? Separated by the time I spent with Brady in the jungle?

Or is it two separate events?

The first kidnapping where we were all taken as a team, and Izzy and I escaped? And the second kidnapping with the botched rescue?

"Angie?" Skye leans toward me. "Did you hear me?"

"Yes." The faintest smile fills my face. "And thank you, but I think I'm okay."

"Think?"

"I'm still processing, I suppose. It's too soon." I tell her the truth and punctuate my words with a shrug.

"I talked to Dr. Meadows." Izzy pipes in with something that's meant to be reassuring. "He's a great listener."

Evidently, Dr. Meadows is the onsite shrink.

"Yeah, but I don't think I need to talk to a stranger." I place my hand on Izzy's arm. "I'm not there yet."

The only person I want to talk to about the last couple of days is currently debriefing his mission with leadership.

"I completely understand." Skye's got a great bedside manner. "If you change your mind, you know where to find me."

"Thanks." I button up my shirt and make sure the rest of my clothes are back in order. "Can we see the guys?"

"Of course." Skye finishes her note on her tablet, then places it down on the sparkling clean stainless steel table.

"How are they?" I fidget, brushing the tips of my fingers against my thumb.

"Well …" Skye hesitates. "I suppose patient-doctor confidentiality can be bent here. I won't tell you anything you don't already suspect. Both have suffered significant trauma during their questioning."

"You mean torture." I can't help but interrupt.

"I was trying to avoid that word. But yes, they each suffered extensive trauma. I've stabilized them for transport."

"Transport?"

"Yes. We'll fly them back to Guardian HQ. We have a fully staffed hospital there."

"You do?" Izzy's eyes about bug out of her head.

"Unfortunately, with our line of work, we have to provide comprehensive care."

"Comprehensive?" Izzy still looks stunned.

I know what Skye's talking about, but only now put all the pieces together. I've run into Guardians before, only I was just a kid. A teenager grieving the loss of her parents and surviving an abusive foster home.

This is the group that rescued me all those years ago.

"From trauma care to annual checkups. We provide our Guardians with free medical care, as well as those we rescue. It's an unfortunate reality, but many of our rescues come to us in rough shape."

"It's incredible that you offer that to those you rescue." Izzy's eyes shine with respect.

"Most of them have nothing. We provide everything they need to reintegrate back into the world. From medical care to psychiatric trauma care, we also offer education, self-defense, and more. In fact, we have a whole residential facility where many of our rescues pick up the pieces of their lives."

I know that place. I lived there for two years. How did I never put the two together before now?

"Wow, that's impressive. What's it called?" Izzy continues with her questions.

"The Facility." Skye gives me a flat look, then smiles. "My brother named it. He's not very original with stuff like that. In fact, he's incredibly practical."

"I'd love to see The Facility sometime." Izzy looks at me. "Don't you?"

"Excuse me?"

"Don't you want to see it, too?"

"Um …" How do I explain this to Izzy?

"You can come whenever you want," Skye says. "In fact …" She turns to me. "We have an ophthalmologist on staff, but are always looking to expand, and we're always short pharmacists. I don't know what either of your plans are after this debacle, but if you're interested in a change of employers, I'd love to show you our hospital and the many other services we offer."

Return to The Facility?

No, she means working for Guardian HRS.

"Wow. That's incredibly generous. Thank you. The last thing I expected after all of this was a potential job interview." I reach for Izzy's hand and give it a little squeeze.

"Agreed." Izzy presses her palm to her temple and squeezes her eyes shut. "I guess we need to get a hold of Doctors Without Borders and let them know we're okay."

"We've already contacted them." Skye clears her workstation.

"You did? When?" I ask.

"The moment Bravo One ..." A smile brightens her face. "I mean, the moment Brady called in from the field. Forest doesn't waste any time."

"Yeah, sounds like it." I turn to Izzy and give another squeeze of her hand. "I guess we'll have to talk with Doctors Without Borders and see where we stand with our contract. I don't know about Izzy, but I'm not tied down. I'd love to speak to whoever runs your Ophtho department."

"Count me in." Izzy releases my hand and presses her fingers to her temples, rubbing circles. "Silly question, since I know you do, but can I get something for this headache?"

"Certainly." Skye's eyes pinch as she takes Izzy in. "You mentioned nothing about head trauma during your exam."

"I didn't, and I don't. Have head trauma, but I suffer from migraines. They're normally well-controlled with prophylactic medicine, but stress and a day or two of missed meds are a sure-fire way to bring on a nasty migraine."

"Sure. What do you take for prophylaxis, and do you have a preferred abortive med that you take?"

While Skye and Izzy talk about Izzy's migraines, I take a moment to do nothing more than breathe.

Everything feels surreal. As if someone else is living this moment other than me. The only thing that feels real, and this is terrifying, is the time I spent in the jungle with Izzy and Brady.

All the rest of it is like a dream.

Goosebumps break out on my skin, and I run my hands up and down my arms as a chill runs down my spine.

There's a knock on the door and a man speaks from behind the curtain.

"Can we come in?" His deep baritone holds a bit of a Texas twang. It's a sexy voice, created to drive women crazy.

"Sure, CJ," Skye calls out over her shoulder. "We're done in here."

"Great." CJ enters and scans the room. When he sees me, his face breaks out in a grin. "You must be Angie."

"In the flesh."

CJ crosses the room to shake my hand.

"I'm here to apologize, grovel, and buy my way back into your good graces."

"Excuse me?"

"Well, we botched your rescue, and for that, I'm eternally sorry. Not our finest Guardian hour."

"There was nothing you could do. There was at least the one man after us. After Brady …" I clear my throat and alter what I was going to say. "After he took care of him, there was no way to know if there were any more. Izzy's ankle …"

"It was my fault." Izzy hobbles over to me. "If I hadn't sprained my ankle, then we all could've moved so much faster. Brady practically had to carry me to the helicopter."

"And he can run pretty damn fast." Thoughts of Brady brighten my expression. "He did everything he could, and once the helicopter landed, chaos broke out. If he'd come back for me, one of your men, your pilot, or Izzy would've been shot. That's not something I could live with. I don't fault the Guardians for what happened."

"Well, it wasn't our finest hour, and you have my apologies."

"The second rescue went off fabulously. I should thank you instead of you apologizing to me. This organization is incredible. The vision behind it is staggering, and your resources are mind-blowing."

"I'll let Forest know you approve." His wink is devastating. "Speaking of, I was wondering if our amazing doc released the two of you."

"They're released." Skye props a hand on her hip. "Why?"

"Sam and I had a thought about what we could offer them."

"Offer?" Skye's left brow wings up. "What's that mean?"

"We were just thinking this camp isn't the best place to recuperate after everything they've been through and thought we could make use of ..." CJ hesitates and alters whatever he was initially going to say. "You know—that place in Costa Rica."

The expression on Skye's face is almost comical to watch. There's surprise, then joy. That's followed by that look when someone's just been let in on a secret.

A secret neither Izzy nor I are a part of.

"That sounds perfect." She turns to us. "What do the two of you say to that?"

"I'm not sure what we're supposed to say anything about." I look at Izzy, needing support.

She returns the same no-idea-what-they're-talking-about look to me and shrugs.

"CJ was just reminding me about accommodations we have for one of our Guardians in Costa Rica. It's a resort with almost two weeks left on the reservation. It might be the perfect place for the two of you to de-stress after your abduction. The best way to get over the trauma of something like that is to talk about it, and who better to talk to than someone who shares the same experience?"

"They took everything from us at the first camp we escaped from. I saw our backpacks. They're supposed to hold our IDs, personal medications, a small amount of local currency. Basically, all the things we'd need if separated from our group, but I don't know if any of that is left. It looked like they dumped them and went through everything."

"They probably took the money and left the rest. Maybe your passports and IDs are still with them."

"I hope so because I don't think we can cross into Costa Rica until we get our passports reissued."

"You'd be surprised what we can accomplish." CJ rocks back on his heels.

"Do you know where they are?" I glance at Izzy. "Maybe your meds are still in your bag?"

"Maybe." She nods. "Can we go look?"

"Absolutely." CJ swings his arm wide, gesturing for us to go ahead of him.

"Thank you so much for taking care of us and the guys." I turn to Skye and grip her hands. "I can't tell you what it means to us. Can I poke my head in and see how they're doing?"

"Absolutely. In fact, I'll go with you. We'll see if we can't sort out the bag issue and get all the passports and other IDs sorted."

"Great." I exit the room first, followed by Izzy and the others. CJ directs me through the modified field hospital while I rubberneck my way through it.

With Luke's experience with the Air Force's Special Ops Surgical Team, I'm familiar with both field hospitals and trauma teams. Everything feels familiar. Luke would've loved working with the Guardians after he retired from the Air Force. Unfortunately, that wasn't in the cards for him.

CJ takes us to an equipment room where several medical go-bags fill the shelves. Off in the corner sit five navy blue backpacks with the iconic Doctors Without Borders logo emblazoned on the front.

"Wow." Izzy hobbles ahead of me, kneeling down on the canvas floor. She pulls out each backpack, setting them up in a row.

I bend down to help and wind up sitting back on my ass. In addition to the logo, our bags have our names embroidered on the outside. I pull up Daniel's bag and look inside.

The bags were thoroughly searched. Ransacked comes to mind. But they left bits and pieces inside. I find a picture of Daniel's family, his wife and two sons, at the bottom of his bag.

"Jackpot." Izzy peers inside a bag, then dumps out the contents. "Angie, help me go through this."

We spend the next few minutes sorting through the stuff left behind. All of our passports are present and accounted for, as well as personal photos and other identification. All the money is gone, as well as Izzy's migraine medicine, but my rabbit's foot is there.

"See." She lifts the lucky charm.

"See what?"

"It is good luck. They took everything but that. It's a sign."

"A sign?"

"Of good luck. My rabbit's foot protected us in the jungle, and yours is the only thing left of your stuff."

"If you say so." Her superstitions aren't mine, but I'm not going to argue. We made it out of the jungle, and even if I was left behind the first time, getting captured again let the Guardians save our entire team. Maybe there is something lucky with the rabbit's feet.

I sort everything into six piles. Jerald isn't here, but we have his bag.

After we have the piles sorted, I put each person's small pile back into their packs. With our passports in hand, we can go to Costa Rica. A resort sounds just about right after what we endured.

"I'm going to take this," Izzy says. "Hold it for Jerald until he's rescued." She folds his backpack and stuffs it inside her bag."

We'll have to check with Doctors Without Borders. We still have a signed contract with them, although I don't see how they'll say no. There's no way to recover this current mission.

"Looks like we're going to Costa Rica." I turn to Izzy and we hug.

Looks like we finally broke the ice and became friends.

TWENTY-SIX

Angie

"THEY TOOK MY MEDS." IZZY BLOWS OUT A FRUSTRATED BREATH. That headache of hers is growing despite the abortive meds Skye gave her earlier.

My head hurts as well. It's the stress of the whole situation; another reason a few days relaxing at a resort sounds perfect.

Now, add in a spa with invigorating massages and I'm all in.

"Let me show you where the others are." Skye points to the door. "Air Evac will be here within the hour."

"Thanks—and while I know you've reported in with Doctors Without Borders, Izzy and I still have a contract we need to figure out."

"I may have that info for you." CJ's drawl is something else.

From the glint of gold around his ring finger, the man is taken. Not that I have eyes for anyone but Brady, but the man definitely has a voice on him.

"You do?"

"Yes. They know we're evacuating the others and that there's still one of you missing. We told them about you and Izzy."

"We've got another seven months with them."

When I investigated working with the well-known relief agency, it surprised me they worked with renewable nine-month contracts. Although, I suppose it makes sense.

A busy doctor can take nine months off to provide humanitarian aid but needs to return to their practice after that to remain current with new advances.

It's something I considered before signing on the dotted line. Although, I quit my previous practice when I did the whole fire sale on my previous life.

Skye's offer to work for the Guardians couldn't come at a better time. If there's one thing I've decided, it's that this is my first and last stint with the global relief agency.

One kidnapping is enough for one lifetime, and I've suffered two back-to-back.

I'm ready for stability. Not to mention, if I work for the Guardians, the chances of staying close to Brady go up a thousand-fold.

There's more than a spark between us, and I feel somehow at peace with the thought of moving on. It's as if Luke looked down on me and gave approval for me to live my life to the fullest.

I sling my bag with my passport inside and carry Daniel's and Jacob's bags. Izzy slings Stefan's over her shoulder and carries hers. We follow Skye to the room where our friends and colleagues are waiting.

Only Stefan is awake.

"We heavily sedated Jacob and Daniel," Skye says. "I had to perform surgery to stabilize Jacob's internal bleeding. You can talk to them, but they won't be able to answer."

"Izzy? Angie?" Stefan rises from the cot he rests on. With a groan, he pushes himself to the sitting position and swings his legs around. He looks exhausted. "You're a sight for sore eyes. Come here." He holds out his arms.

Izzy and I don't hesitate.

We run into his embrace, eyes tearful and at a loss for words. We hug him as hard as he holds us. At some point, I sob. Or maybe Izzy cries first.

All I know is our sobs turn into happier things. There's laughter and smiles.

Skye hands us tissues. All three of us dab at our eyes.

"I'm so glad the two of you are safe. When they separated us, we thought …" Stefan gestures toward the recumbent forms of Jacob and Daniel. "What a shit show."

"You can say that again." I wipe at my tears.

He shakes his head. "When they dragged you out of that tent, I've never felt so helpless. Then the shadows came alive, and next I knew, they were there to rescue us. I kept telling them they needed to get you." Stefan gives me another hard squeeze. "It's really good to see you."

"It's good to be seen." More tears trickle down my cheek. "How are you?"

"Not as bad as them." He looks over at Jacob and Daniel. "Doc Summers and her team are freakin' amazing. Because of them, Daniel will live."

"And how are your injuries?"

"Doc's worried about my spleen. Head trauma." He points to his head. "Her team wakes me up on the hour, every hour."

"Sorry, but we don't have the imaging capability. I need to rule out a bleed." Skye props her hands on her hips. "But you're looking better and better."

Stefan turns to Izzy. "It's great to see you both. Angie gave me the Cliffs Notes of your jungle adventure. Someday, you'll have to share the complete story with me."

Izzy sits beside Stefan on the cot. She takes his hand in hers. "We're just happy you're going to be okay."

"Same." He turns to CJ. "Any word on Jerald?"

"None, but we're working it." CJ's response is short, clipped, and devoid of pesky things such as details.

Which worries me.

From everything I've seen of the Guardians to date, they've got excellent intel. I close my eyes and say a prayer for Jerald's sake and quick return.

"I'm just going to …" I point toward Daniel and Jacob.

Skye says they're sedated, but that doesn't mean they can't hear me.

I hold each of their hands and tell them how strong they are, how they're going to pull through, and how I can't wait to see them when we're back in the States. I tell them how our reunions will be filled with stories that grow longer by the year as we recount what happened here.

When I'm done, I turn around, well aware Skye and CJ haven't left us alone.

"Um, do you mind if we have a moment?"

"Sure. No problem." CJ holds the flap that acts as a door while Skye ducks out of the room.

The moment they're gone, I turn to Stefan.

"Now, tell me how you're really doing? A headache? Is she worried about bleeding? How serious is it?"

"Slow your roll. I'm beat up and feel like shit, but otherwise, I'm okay. She said they have to observe me for twenty-four hours."

"And Daniel? Jacob?"

"Thanks to the doc, they're stable. She says they're flying us out soon."

"Skye said within the hour." Izzy bumps her shoulder against Stefan's. "We asked to come see you before you go."

"You're not coming with us?" Stefan's brows tug together.

"I don't think so." Izzy turns toward me. "I guess we should talk about it?"

"What does that mean?" He shifts his attention between us.

"The Guardians offered us a place to recover." I don't share with Stefan that the place is a resort. Somehow, that doesn't feel right.

"Sounds like a plan. I take it you don't need medical? That nobody …" He can't ask outright, not that I blame him.

"Izzy and I escaped before anyone could do anything. Other than picking up any of many parasitic passengers from that river, we're okay."

"I sprained my ankle." Izzy points to the brace on her ankle.

"But it's not bad. I can gimp along and don't need crutches. After a few days of resting, ice, compression, and elevation, I should be good to go."

"And I'm good. Nobody touched me." Well, that one bastard touched me, but he didn't have time to rape me.

Brady was there to rescue me—for the second time.

"Well, if this group is offering you someplace to de-stress, take it. And it'll be good for the two of you to be together to talk through things when … You know. When you need to …"

"That's kind of what I was thinking." I look at Izzy, asking silently if that's what she wants as well.

Honestly, the idea of spending days in a resort sounds like the best therapy on the planet.

There's a knock on the door and a man pops his head inside. "Sorry, but we need to get them ready for transport."

"Looks like that's my ride." Stefan spreads his arms out wide again. Izzy and I fold into his embrace. "Take care of each other, okay?"

"And you take care of them."

"You bet." He cups my cheek. "We'll catch up later."

"We will." I press my palm to the back of his hand.

"Be strong girls. I'll see you on the flip side." He repeats the same gesture with Izzy.

"Got it." Izzy and I lean down and each give him a kiss on the cheek.

I'm going to miss Stefan, but I bet he's eager to get home to his family. Hopefully, he won't have to spend too much time in the hospital under observation.

Izzy and I leave Stefan and the others with Skye's medical team to prep for transport. Outside the medical tent, Izzy turns to me.

"I didn't want to speak for you, and I know you probably want to stay here to be with Brady, but I really could use a few days at that resort. I'm not ready to rejoin civilization."

"I know exactly what you mean. I was hoping you'd want to go."

"But Brady? Don't you …"

"He's busy with Guardian duties. They're going to head out as soon as possible once they know what happened to Jerald."

"I feel bad he's still in that mess." Izzy presses her hand against her sternum. "I feel guilty that we're free while he's still …"

"Let's send out prayers for a swift rescue and take advantage of what the Guardians offer. We can rest, relax, and talk when we're ready." I shake my head. "What a crazy few days."

"Crazy." Izzy wraps me in a hug. "If I ever need another abduction buddy, I hope I get you. Not that I want you to get abducted again …"

"You're silly." I can't help but laugh. "If I'm ever abducted again, I'd want you as my abduction buddy, too."

We laugh at the silliness of it all, but we mean every word. There's no way I would've had the strength to endure what we endured alone.

Izzy and I catch CJ exiting the medical tent and tell him we want to take him up on his offer.

And if I wasn't impressed enough with the speed and efficiency of the Guardians before, they continue to amaze me. Before Stefan and the others are loaded onto their medical evacuation helicopter, Izzy and I are flying to Costa Rica in the back of a different helicopter.

With Brady and Booker as escorts.

It's a tense flight because neither Brady, nor I, can tell the other what we're thinking.

My biggest fear is this thing between us may not be real. That my feelings are overblown because of the situation.

While we don't speak during the forty-minute flight, he holds my hand the entire time. Izzy sits beside Booker, looking small and uncomfortable next to the imposing Guardian. But I don't watch them.

I pay attention to every touch and every caress Brady gives me during that flight.

After going through customs, we're met with a car and driver.

It's time for our escorts to say goodbye, and I'm terrified this really is our last goodbye.

"Be good. Don't get all crazy, and please don't leave the resort." Brady folds me into his arms. Those warm, hazel eyes of his shimmer with gold and coppery flecks.

Izzy gives a little flap of her hand to Booker, standing awkwardly while Brady and I say our goodbyes.

Instead of a kiss on the lips, Brady presses his lips to my forehead. It's one of the most tender kisses I've ever received.

"I promise to be good." After he releases me, I hold up my left hand, swearing to behave.

"Well, not that good." Izzy takes my hand. "There will be drink involved. Heavy drinking."

The glare Brady gives her stops Izzy in her tracks, but it's the look Booker throws her way that makes her gasp.

Here I thought the electricity sparking in the air was only between me and Brady.

Unfortunately, Brady and Booker can't stay. They're needed back at the temporary base Guardian HRS set up with the Nicaraguan government.

I say my goodbyes and try to keep a smile on my face as Brady and Booker turn about-face and march off without us.

"Damn, but that's a mighty fine ass." Izzy props her chin on her knuckles. "Mighty fine."

"I agree, although I have a feeling you're not talking about the same ass."

"They both have mighty fine asses, but I didn't want you thinking I was perving on your man."

"My man?"

"Shit yeah, girl. You and Brady are fated to be together. You're the poster couple of love at first sight; struck by lightning."

"We are not."

"Are too." Izzy lifts her nose in the air, teasing me.

Together, we giggle.

We laugh.

We pile into the vehicle and get ready to spend the next however many days pampering ourselves silly at the Guardian's expense.

As for Brady, he said he'd come when he could, but his duty is elsewhere at the moment. I can't fault him for that.

Jerald is still out there, missing, while we're kicking up our heels.

TWENTY-SEVEN

Angie

Izzy squeezes my hand and squeals when the resort comes into view.

"Oh my God! It's beyond gorgeous."

I lean my head against the window and take in the lush resort with a bit of bittersweet regret. I'm happy to be here, glad Izzy's with me, but I wish someone else was here with me.

I miss Brady.

"Big difference from that jungle." I place my palm on the window and let my fingers drag down the glass.

"You wish Brady was here instead of me?"

"I don't."

"You're not a good liar." Izzy wraps her arm around me and gives me a hug. "Maybe he'll join us once they find Jerald."

"I feel so bad for Jerald. Lord only knows what's happening to him. Do you feel guilty about all of this …?"

I make a sweeping gesture at the meticulously manicured grounds. Blooms of all colors and varieties complement the dark green foliage. We've entered paradise.

"They'll find Jerald, and there's absolutely nothing we can do to help them. I'm ready to lie on the beach all day, drink fruity drinks, and enjoy actual food."

"Me too." As much as Izzy and I have bonded and grown closer because of what happened, she's right. I wish Brady were here instead of her. "I'm looking forward to real food and alcohol. Lots and lots of alcohol."

When we pull up to the resort's check-in, our lack of luggage surprises the bellhops. We literally carry nothing but the clothes on our backs and two nearly empty backpacks. Brady and Booker gave us some cash, but it's not enough for a full wardrobe.

"Come on, sleepyhead." Izzy spins around when she realizes I'm not by her side.

"My head's in the clouds and …" I gesture down at the clothes I borrowed from a woman I don't even know.

Once I got out of that shower, my jungle clothes were gone and these were in their place. "What are we going to do about clothes?"

"I don't know, but we can ask when we check in." Izzy practically skips to the check-in counter.

I let her take care of business while I admire the rich decor, a mixture of highly polished wood, marble, and Spanish architecture. The entire resort is open and airy with incredible views of the turquoise waters.

I can't wait to explore.

Izzy finishes check-in then rushes over to me.

"You're never going to believe it."

"What?"

"We're in the *honeymoon* suite."

"No way."

"Yes way, and it gets better."

"How can it be any better than that?"

"They have a string of boutique shops and we get to charge it all to the room."

"I don't know about making the Guardians pay …"

"It was on a note the receptionist handed me, and it's not like we're going to go crazy. I say we get something to swim in, something to wear around the resort, and a dress or two for the swanky restaurants they have."

"You don't think that'll be too much?"

"I don't, and the best part is they'll deliver whatever we buy directly to the bungalow."

"Well then, I guess we're going shopping." I shift my backpack on my shoulder. "Unless you want to go to the room first?"

"She said it's a bit isolated from the rest of the resort, so I figure we buy some string bikinis and spend the rest of the day poolside. I'm starving. She said they serve food and drinks at the pool."

"That sounds like a brilliant plan."

Over the next hour, Izzy and I pop our heads into the boutique stores at the resort. The prices are what I'd expect, way over-inflated, but we need something to wear.

Initially, I thought Izzy would go overboard, spending money that's not hers, but she's an incredibly frugal shopper.

We each make it out of the store with two light dresses, a bikini, one pair of shorts, a couple of shirts, sandals for the beach, a large-brimmed hat, and enough sunscreen and bug spray to keep us from burning in the sun and getting carried away by mosquitoes.

All of it gets delivered to our room, except for the bikinis and the shorts. We change into them in the dressing room and head out to the pool, where we spend the rest of the day drinking, sunning, swimming, and relaxing.

It's a beautiful day with a sunset that turns the sky to ochre with sheets of golden flames. After a quick dinner, and more time at the bar, Izzy can no longer keep her yawning at bay.

"I'm spent." She lifts her arms overhead and stretches while another yawn escapes her.

"Come on, let's check out this *honeymoon* suite." Her yawn has me yawning. Weird how that happens.

Set within a private cove, bungalow is a loose term to describe the heavenly accommodation. We barely explore the suite. It has one bedroom with a massive king-sized bed and an incredible bathroom, with a shower built for two, along with a Jacuzzi tub. There's a main sitting area, a small bar, and even a tiny kitchen.

I suppose, if the lovebirds want, they never have to leave this place.

We share the massive bed, falling asleep almost instantly, and wake with the chirping of tropical birds outside the windows along with a gentle breeze blowing in off the ocean.

I rise first, grab my bikini, and head outside to check out our private cove. An outer reef protects the water from rollers coming in off the ocean. The light breeze sweeps across nearly mirror-smooth water, causing fetches that disturb the stillness of the ocean.

After grabbing a set of fins and mask, I head out. I'm a strong swimmer with a love of the water. I'd give anything to head out into the ocean and go for a mile swim, but I've only ever done that during a triathlon. We had spotters and people watching over us.

I'm not brave enough to go beyond the outer reef alone, but I'm perfectly comfortable snorkeling within the beautiful cove.

Our days begin and end much the same. I'm up early for a morning swim by myself. Izzy's a late riser. Once she gets up, we head to the main resort where we spend the rest of our day sitting poolside, talking about everything and anything except for our kidnapping.

Neither of us is ready to dive into that.

We try out each of the restaurants onsite and hang out at the bar until our yawns drag us back to the bungalow long after the sun has set.

The Guardians send us cellphones, which lets us reconnect with those we left behind. Or rather, allow Izzy to reconnect with her family.

I'm an orphan.

Like me, she's single and unattached. Unlike me, she's the youngest of five siblings who all want her to come home.

There's no one for me to call. No siblings. No parents. I was orphaned as a teen, then did my time in foster care.

The first home social services placed me in was a nightmare. My foster parents were abusive. I ran away and found a shelter. The next day, strangers came and took me to The Facility.

It was great.

I graduated high school, then set out on my own, going to college, then applying for medical school.

Who knew the people who took me to The Facility would be the ones to rescue me again?

It feels—right. As if I've come full circle.

"I feel terrible." Izzy clutches the phone to her chest.

"Why would you feel bad?"

"Because I'm leaving you."

"Right." I gesture around the luxurious resort. "You're leaving me in paradise."

"Leaving you alone. Are you sure you don't want to go with me?"

"I'm sure your family's fantastic, but I don't think I'm in a place where I'll make a good houseguest. I don't want to ruin your homecoming."

"I understand, but it's sad you don't have a family."

Her words hit hard. She knows about Luke, but not the baby we lost, or that I can never have children. Those are things I don't share with others. Her comment is innocent, but it stings.

I rub at my breastbone, trying to ease an ache that will never fully leave me.

"It's not sad. I'm used to it."

"Well, you can still come with me. My family is pretty awesome, and they'd love to meet you."

"Maybe later. I wouldn't want to intrude. They're going to be thrilled you're home and are going to be all over you, wanting to make sure you're okay after the *trauma*." I use air quotes for emphasis.

"Well, we have one night left, so let's make it count." She's quiet for a bit. "We haven't really talked about what happened. Do you want to talk about it?"

"I'm actually in a great headspace right now. I've been thinking about what Skye said, and I'm going to see if there's an opportunity to work for the Guardians. If they'll have me."

"I have a feeling Skye handed both of us those jobs, if we want them."

"Have you thought about it?"

"I have, and I have nothing set up. If you go, I'm definitely going to check it out."

"I don't have any other place to go, but I want to make sure it's a good fit for me before I commit. There's another week on the reservation here, and I'm going to take full advantage of the break."

"That sounds wise, and if you want me to stay …"

"Girl, your family's been asking you to come home since you got that phone, and I see the look in your eyes. Don't worry about me. I'm good." I stare at her and playfully shove her. "Really."

"Okay. I'm going to believe you and not feel guilty about leaving you alone."

"Trust me. I'm okay. Now, how about dinner? The steak and seafood place, or bar food?"

"Definitely steak." Izzy gives a girly squeal.

We set our reservation then head to the bungalow to put on the dresses we bought at the boutique. Made of light cotton gauze, the fabric cinches at the bust and waist, but then floats in a cloud around our legs.

Neither of us felt buying makeup made sense, especially on Guardian HRS's dime, but we don't need it. After a few days in paradise, we're both sun-kissed and our skin glows. Besides, we're not looking to hook up with strangers. Not to mention the resort is full of couples, not singles.

We're fish out of water.

The hostess seats us at a table for four. There are plenty of tables for couples, but she's smart and gets that we're just friends. We're not here for the romantic vibe.

The table faces out toward the ocean. A light breeze blows in over the sand. Outside, tiki torches light the many walkways meandering through the resort. We order fruity drinks with umbrellas and sit back, enjoying another sultry night.

"This is a far cry from Nicaragua." I take a sip and stare out over the ocean.

The sun set a few minutes ago, treating us to another amazing sunset. Now, the sky deepens to dark blue, purple, and black as the first stars poke out of the night sky.

"This is true. No sweltering humidity, there are few mosquitoes. No ants." Izzy lifts a finger, punctuating that point.

"I've heard about the ant colonies in the jungle, but I never believed until—"

"Oh, that was so funny when they took over your tent." She covers her laugh with her hand.

"Well, none of you told me not to keep food in my tent."

"We assumed." Izzy's laughter lightens the mood.

We trade stories of our time together on our mission. The work was tough, but I really enjoyed the opportunity to give back to those who weren't born with the privileges I enjoyed.

"Do you think you'll ever sign up for another mission?" Izzy sips her drink, finishing it, and calls the waitress over to order a second round.

"I think I got what I needed out of the experience."

They let our entire team out of our nine-month contract with the relief organization, which means Izzy and I are both technically out of work.

But I gained clarity about my life.

Debilitating grief no longer defines me.

I learned what I needed.

I can still have fun.

I can laugh. I can dream about the present and the future. Most of all, even if things don't work out with Brady, I feel as if Luke reached out and gave his blessing for me to live a full life.

Since my rescue, I wake up every day eager for what the day will bring, rather than dreading how long it will be before I can crawl back under the covers.

I feel good about myself and my future. All the madness of the jungle is behind me.

TWENTY-EIGHT

Angie

Izzy's leaving me.

Her family wants her home, and as the youngest sibling, her brothers demand she come home.

This is our last night together, and I'm not afraid to say I'm going to miss her. We've definitely bonded, and I'll go as far as to say she's officially my best friend.

Our waitress brings the next round of drinks and we place our orders. Nothing happens fast in this place. There's no rushing through dinner. No hustling to get to the next activity.

"So, what are you going to do here without me?" Izzy leans back, enjoying the light breeze that lifts tiny wisps of her dark hair.

"I'm going to go parasailing."

She cringes when I say that. For the past few days, I've tried to get her to sign up for a tandem ride, but her fear of heights trumps my enthusiasm.

"Have fun. That's a never proposition for me."

"I thought I might try one of their horseback rides."

"Get on the back of an animal that's ten times my size? No way." She shudders while I grin.

For a woman brave enough to sign up to work with Doctors Without Borders, she comes with a lot of phobias.

"Read a book while hanging in the hammock?"

There's a two-person hammock in our private cove. After we got the phones delivered, the first thing we each did was download an e-reader app and load up a bunch of books.

We spent several lazy afternoons there reading romance novels and spy thrillers. Our taste in books is rather similar.

"You've got my number, right?" Izzy squirms in her seat. She keeps checking the entrance.

Our waiter delivers a bread basket, and she grabs a roll.

"I've got your number, the number of your parents, and all four of your brothers' cellphone numbers," I say. "We're definitely keeping in touch."

"You know, if things don't work out with you and Brady, all my brothers are single." She lowers her voice to a whisper. "And they're smoking hot."

"I'm not looking for love."

"You sure about that?" Izzy glances over my shoulder and her lids flicker with surprise.

"Yeah." I blow out a breath. "I'm open to the possibility, which is a big step all on its own." My hand lifts to my neck.

To where my necklace should be, but it isn't there, and Luke's ring is gone.

Not gone.

It's in good hands. Brady's keeping it safe for me—I hope.

"How open?" Izzy squirms in her seat and her smile gets bigger with each passing second.

"Huh?"

"How open to the possibility of love are you?"

"I don't know. It's not something you ever see coming. If something falls in my lap, I …"

"You mean someone?"

"Well yeah, that's what I mean."

The hairs on my nape stand on end as a current of electricity supercharges the air. That little tingle gathers at the base of my neck and dances down my spine, bringing on a full-body shiver.

"What about me?" I know that sexy voice and practically leap out of my chair.

My knees knock the table, making the water slosh out of the glasses.

That voice belongs to Brady, and he's as arresting as I remember, strong and powerful, commanding and overwhelming.

He draws the eye of every woman and the glares of all of the men. The harsh lines of his face soften with his signature smirk, and the scars only add to his beauty.

Brady pulls back my chair before I upturn the table. I spin around and stare into the most beautiful eyes I've ever seen on the most handsome man on the planet.

"Brady!" My hands go around his neck and I lift on tiptoe to hug him, only Brady doesn't go for the hug.

He angles his head to capture my mouth in a kiss that sweeps through me like a firestorm.

My entire body lights up as his lips crash against mine. All my nerves take notice, thrumming and humming along as the tenderness of the kiss sweeps me off my feet.

But then, he delivers a wicked sweep of his tongue, demanding entrance to my mouth. Oblivious to the others in the restaurant, he sucks and nips as my insides tighten and pull—and twist.

And spark.

Mindful of the other guests, he doesn't totally devour me. His arm wraps around my waist. The kiss ends as he bends down to press his lips against the bare skin of my shoulder.

A shudder ripples down my spine—it's a wave of sensation that warns of far more than a simple kiss. Breathing in the rugged scent of him, my lungs fill. I can't get enough of Brady Malone.

"Izzy? I thought you were going to pee your pants. You were squirming so much." His deep voice turns teasing and light.

"Wait a second." I turn back to Izzy. "You knew?"

"He called this morning." Her cheeks turn bright pink. "Wanted to know what kind of headspace you were in."

"But, you *just* decided to go home today." She's leaving because of Brady, not because her family wants her home.

"That's not true. I've been talking to my brothers since we got the phone. I was just dragging my feet, but when Brady called …"

I slug Brady in the chest. It's nothing more than a light tap and does nothing to budge the powerful Guardian. "I can't believe the two of you set this up."

"That's not all." Brady reaches around and grabs my napkin. "Take a seat."

After he seats me back at the table, he gives Izzy a brotherly hug, kissing the top of her head.

"Nice to see you, Iz."

"You have a nickname? When did that happen?"

"I'm sensing a bit of jealousy?" The corner of his brow wings up. He's amused.

"I'm not jealous, just overwhelmed."

Brady takes the chair next to me, then scans the room. His face brightens. "Just in time."

"What?" When I twist around, our waitress brings over a bottle of champagne and three champagne flutes. "I can't believe you set this up."

He reaches out and takes my hand in his. "I've missed you."

Then it hits.

"If you're here, does that mean …" I'm hesitant to ask about Jerald, but hopeful.

Out of everyone in our team, Jerald was the most friendly toward me, always helping. Because of him, I survived near-crippling homesickness my first week with the team.

Which was ironic, considering I no longer had a home.

"We found him, and he's safe. Bruised and shaken but didn't suffer nearly the same injuries as the others."

"What happened to him? Why wasn't he with the others?"

"I don't know. CJ and the rest are likely asking those questions. It might be because he's not medical."

"How would that matter?" Izzy's eyes are wide, watching our waitress open the champagne.

The loud *pop* brings a moment of silence to the room, then the soft conversation around us rises again. Once the champagne is poured, Izzy lifts her glass.

"To the Guardians, and Brady in particular, for saving me once, and Angie twice. I hate heights, and I'm not a fan of rivers, but you made it easy to be strong. I couldn't have done it without you."

"Hear, hear." I lift my glass, toasting Brady.

He looks different in casual wear. Linen pants, with a matching shirt with long sleeves, he looks like a tourist out to have fun. His relaxed posture belies the strength of the Guardian underneath.

"To two amazing women. You're stronger than you know." He lifts his glass a little higher.

I still can't believe he's here and want to pinch myself because this surely must be a dream.

Dinner is relaxed and fun. It's a far cry from the jungle where we were terrified and fearful for our lives. I love this version of Brady even more than the Guardian I know.

He smiles easily. Tells tall tales. Laughs at Izzy's jokes. Through it all, he never once stops touching me. Whether holding my hand or pressing his leg against mine, he shows me with each touch what I mean to him.

In no hurry to do anything, we stretch dinner out to a three-hour event, dining on steak and lobster until we can't eat another bite. The bottle of champagne disappears, and we order more drinks, which we take to the beach.

While I want to spend time alone with Brady, somehow this feels right. The three of us started this adventure together, and it's as if we're putting that nightmare behind us by making new, more enjoyable, memories now.

There's only a light dusting of clouds, which means the stars show off. We lie down on the sand, not worried about our clothes or getting sand in our hair.

We trade off pointing out the constellations, making it a contest. Then sit quietly as meteors shoot overhead.

When we're all fighting yawns, it's time to call it a night. Brady gets up first. He helps Izzy up, then folds her into a hug.

"I'm glad I got to know you. Safe travels tomorrow."

"Wait, where are you staying tonight?" I look up at him, suddenly upset.

His broad back flexes, showing off his muscles. Bulging ridges and deep valleys define his arms, and his corded neck reminds me of hardened steel. The man oozes masculinity right alongside a danger sign I shouldn't ignore.

This man has the power to wreck me.

"I was going to get a room." The smirk on his face isn't there by chance.

If Brady was going to get a room, he would've done it before now. He's gaming the system, and I'm perfectly fine with that.

"Nonsense." Izzy looks between us and props her hands on her hips. "How about I take the couch and the two of you ..."

Brady yanks me up and tugs me tight to his body. He's definitely interested in exploring things between us, but I sense a bit of hesitation.

He's very good at reading people, and he's reading me now.

"Izzy's right, stay with us." I step in, pretending to offer something he already assumed was his. My heart beats a mile a minute.

I want him near, but I'm not ready to share a bed, or do any of the things that come after that.

Izzy is the perfect buffer. She'll keep us from rushing into something I may, or may not, be ready for, and the last thing I want is to rush things with Brady.

He cocks his head, watching the play of expressions march across my face, then huffs a laugh.

"That sounds perfect, but I'll take the couch." His deep voice makes the very air shiver and sends tendrils of sensation snaking out to me. The fine hairs on my arms stand up and delicious heat coils between my legs.

"Oh, you can't ..." Izzy's about to ruin everything.

"Izzy ..." I interrupt. "He's fine on the couch." I need time to figure out what I want with the man standing in front of me. His eyes simmer with desire and fill with lust.

I hope she figures out the subtext. I'm thrilled Brady's here but overwhelmed at the same time. Meaning, I need a moment to process and decide where I want things to go between us.

She looks at us, then rolls her eyes.

"Fine. But we all know where he'll be sleeping tomorrow night." She spins around and stomps off toward the path leading to our secluded cove. When I turn to follow, Brady grabs my hand and holds me back.

"Are you okay with this?"

My heart beats wildly, and my entire body is on high alert. There's a fluttering in my belly that's one hundred percent nerves.

I feel like a schoolgirl getting ready for Prom night with the boy who may, or may not, pop her cherry, depending on how the night goes.

"Honestly, I'm nervous."

"Because of me? I can get another room."

"No. That's not what I meant. It's the good nervous, but I'm not ready to rush in ..."

"Hey, luv ..." He grips my chin and stares deeply into my eyes. "We've got all the time in the world. There's no reason to rush anything. I have no problem sleeping on the couch after Izzy leaves if that's what makes the most sense."

It's funny how he leaves the door open for more without forcing the issue. That's simply one more thing to love about him.

As for tomorrow night ...

TWENTY-NINE

Brady

AFTER WALKING THE WOMEN TO THE HONEYMOON SUITE, AKA *THE bungalow*, it's not long before we all settle in to sleep for the night. It's barely past eleven, but Angie and Izzy are tired, evidenced by nearly nonstop yawns.

They settle in on the massive, king-sized bed while I grab a set of extra blankets and a pillow from the closet. I don't remember lying down, but bright sunshine wakes me early.

It shines through the eastern-facing window directly into my eyes. A quick glance at my watch reveals it's barely past six.

There's no sound from the bedroom, and a quick peek reveals the girls are still fast asleep.

Not wanting to wake them, I dig through my belongings and pull out a pair of board shorts. My body's itchy, filled with too much extra energy, and I know exactly how to fix that.

The day I arrived, I went for a six-mile swim and followed it with a run. A long swim sounds like exactly what I need.

It's just me and my body, pushing the limits of what I can endure. Once I hit that *wall*, my mind kicks in with the mantra *Never stop*. Then it becomes a battle between mind and body.

For a moment, I consider wearing a wetsuit. It keeps some of the chafing down during a multi-miler swim, but I'm just going outside the breakwaters for a mile or two. I should be able to go out and come back before the girls wake.

My mouth twists. If anything happens between me and Angie, those scars will demand a conversation.

Grabbing one of the oversized beach towels, I take a snorkel, mask, and fins. As for the scars, Angie will either run like all the others, or she'll accept me, scars and all.

Beneath a bright, blue sky, the sun just barely begins its morning journey overhead. There are no clouds except for fine wispy tendrils far overhead.

The ocean is still.

The sun's yet to heat the air.

The wind's yet to kick the ocean into a froth.

I slip on my fins, then head out.

Beyond the breakwater, I set out with a freestyle stroke, cutting through the water. One mile becomes two and two becomes three.

I stop at the same place I turned around last time. Spinning around, I head back toward the resort.

Once the cove comes into view, I cut in toward land. I pull off my fins once the water's shallow enough to stand, then pull off the mask and snorkel, shaking the water off my face and out of my eyes.

Head down, I drag my feet through the sand, back where I left my towel above the waterline, loving the way the grains of sand feel against the soles of my feet.

I don't look up, and that's a mistake.

"Oh my God!" Angie's cry has me snapping my head up. Dread coils in my guts and heat rushes outward in a wave of shame and self-loathing.

So much for easing her into the disfiguring scars. I pull to a stop and stand with my feet spread apart as her horrified gaze takes me in from head to toe.

Slowly, I bend down and retrieve the towel. I hold it at chest level as my entire body shakes.

"Why didn't you tell me?"

"Tell you what?"

That I'm a monster? Too horrific for public consumption? That I don't deserve love because I'm a disfigured freak?

But do I blame her? It's hard enough for me to live with the side-eyes and horrified looks, but to have her stand beside me and endure the same?

Not going to happen.

My head hangs as that spark inside of me sputters and goes out.

By now, I should be used to the way others see me. But I'm not. I know what I looked like before the accident, and this new body doesn't match my perceptions of how I look.

I suppose it's good that we're getting this out of the way. Soon Angie will decide she needs to leave, and I'll be alone again.

"Does it still hurt?" Angie's eyes shimmer. Her brows tug together, concerned, but interested.

Curious, but cautious.

She's not running away.

Fine tremors make my entire body tremble. I hold the towel to my chest, trying to cover as much of the disfiguring scars as possible. I hate that she sees them because they make me feel like less of a man.

Doc Summers would say that kind of thinking is exactly why I need to sit with a shrink and talk about my *feelings* and *body image* issues.

I don't need a shrink digging around in my head to know the scars don't change who I am.

But here's the thing—It matters to me.

My entire body stills when her soft gaze sweeps across the grotesque tapestry of puckered flesh and pale, shiny skin.

"Sometimes." I spread the towel out, covering as much of my chest and side as possible. "The sensation is—off."

Confused is a better word.

"Can I ..." Her hand lifts, then snaps back when a low growl vibrates in the back of my throat.

The sound comes out of nowhere, surprising me nearly as much, or more, than her. I'd apologize, but that would mean acknowledging that feral sound came from me.

Her brows tug together. She does that when she thinks. It's cute and sexy.

Damn sexy.

I'd give anything to dive into her head and find out what she's thinking, but I also fear what I might find.

Does she see a disfigured monster? Does my ravaged body disgust her? Am I a freak she can't tear her gaze away from? Does she think less of me now that she knows I'm broken?

My gaze hardens, and my eyes glint. I fade back half a step, using the towel as a shield.

THIRTY

Brady

"I'm sorry. I didn't mean ..." Her voice catches and trips over itself. "I can't have ... I can't have children." She blurts out that last bit.

"Excuse me?"

Where the fuck did that come from?

"I can't have children." She repeats herself, then gestures toward my scars. As she does that, her other hand rises to sit over her belly. "Your scars are on the outside. Mine are inside. Or maybe you have scars inside of you as well? If we can't share the worst of ourselves, how can we share the best?"

"Is that what you think is happening here?" I can't help the sting of my words. They're meant to push her away and end the pain that comes after rejection by a woman. "We're not sharing anything."

"You're wrong."

Angie doesn't look horrified. Her face doesn't twist with disgust like so many women's faces have in the past. Instead, she looks at me with an expression far too dangerous. There's compassion and something else.

Something treacherous.

I hold the towel tight against my body, knowing all I wear are a pair of swim trunks behind it. The scars cover me from my jaw, down my neck, to the tip of my left shoulder, and down to my hip. From there, they wrap around to my ass and extend further down my thigh.

They're not only visible. They're unavoidable.

Others, women, who saw the scarring, ran from the disturbing sight. Hands covered their mouths, and they couldn't flee fast enough.

It's different with Angie.

When she looks at me, I don't feel like a freak.

Correction.

When she looks at my face, I don't feel like a freak. The scars covering my body are far worse than those on my face.

I don't want her to see them.

"You're in my way." I gesture toward the folding doors leading into the beach bungalow. When I try to shoulder past her, she reaches out and touches my arm.

My entire body jerks from her touch as if I've been stung.

"Don't." A scowl fixes itself on my face.

"Don't, what?"

"Don't touch me."

"Why?" Her eyes widen in shock. "What if I want to touch you?"

"You don't want any of this." I want to tell her why she doesn't want a damaged man, but she beats me to it.

"I want all of it." She gives a little shake of her head. "Isn't this what you want? Us? Together?" There go her brows again, tugging tight.

She's confused but committed to continue this wretched conversation.

This is when sane women normally walk out on me. If they don't, I invariably push them away. I don't want to be the freak they fucked, and I refuse to be a sideshow at a circus.

"Maybe we want different things?" It's a lie, but my insecurity is a vicious beast. It rears its head and makes me say things to hurt Angie.

To push her away like I did the others.

I'd rather hurt her than face her rejection. That's not something I'll survive. The truth is, I want a happily ever after with this incredible woman.

I want it all.

"I don't believe that." Angie takes a step toward me. Her hand lifts again.

Seeking.

Demanding.

I stumble back and swallow a curse.

Why did I wear swim trunks instead of a wetsuit for my swim? A wetsuit would've covered everything up and we wouldn't be having this conversation at all.

Her hand falls back. Angie cocks her head and looks at me for the longest time.

I say nothing, wishing this moment would pass as quickly as possible. She needs to move out of my way so I can take a shower in peace.

But no.

Angie doesn't move.

"It's not going to work." She firms her stance, digging in.

"Huh?" I'm not against playing dumb.

"I know what you're doing."

"I'm trying to take a shower after my swim, and you're in my way."

"You're trying to push me away."

"Am not."

That's exactly what's going on here.

I sound like a petulant child.

"You don't get to push me away after that kiss in the jungle. Or did you forget what happened at the waterfall?"

"Kissing you was a mistake."

No sooner are the words out of my mouth than there's a gasp on her lips and tears in her eyes.

"If you're trying to hurt me, Brady, it's working, but I'm not backing down. I'm not going anywhere."

"Sorry, but it's the truth. You were a job, and it was unprofessional of me to touch you."

"A job?" Her lids pull back, making her eyes look huge. "You're seriously standing in front of me, telling me I'm nothing more than a job? That the kiss was nothing?" She folds her arms across her chest. "You're full of shit."

"It was wrong to kiss you, and this is why. You need to accept the truth."

"You're a liar, Brady Malone, and a bad one at that." She takes a step toward me. Using her eyes as weapons, she dares me to fall back and give ground.

"It's not a lie, and the sooner you realize it, the better." My voice deepens to a growl, but I don't back down.

I hold my ground, while clutching that towel, terrified it might accidentally slip and reveal the grotesqueness of my broken body.

What I hate the most right now is that my body has a mind of its own. It doesn't give a shit about hiding my disfigurement.

All it wants is Angie—and it's rising to the occasion.

Blood races to my cock, leaving me light-headed and making me sway. Each beat of my heart sends more blood to engorge my cock; less blood to think.

My body doesn't know it's ugly. It doesn't know it's broken.

All it does is hunger for Angie.

Lord, but she's the most beautiful thing I've ever seen. My gaze travels over the expanse of her body.

Probing.

Demanding.

Flaring.

Desire tunnels within me and wakes up parts of my body I gave up after the accident.

"The man who kissed me didn't kiss me because I'm a job." Her fingers curl into cute little fists. "You kissed me because when we're together, the air becomes supercharged. Electricity crackles around us. It draws us together. I didn't think I'd ever be attracted to another man after Luke died. I didn't *want* to be."

"Why?"

"Because …" Her gaze drops to her feet and her voice softens. "It felt as if I was betraying him. Yet, you don't see me turning away from this. I'm not the one hiding behind a goddamn towel. I'm not the one saying mean things to hurt me. If you think that's going to push me away, you couldn't be more wrong. I'm not whole. I can never have kids. That's a huge, aching hole I have to carry with me for the rest of my life. I know what it feels like to have something taken away, and while my scars aren't on the outside, they're still very real." Anger infuses every word, turning them into weapons that lash out at me. "What are you afraid of?"

"Nothing."

"Bullshit." She calls me out. "Try again."

"I don't know what you want to hear, but that's the truth. Sometimes emotions intensify in situations like this. You were vulnerable and I …"

"If you tell me I made it all up in my mind, I'm going to come over there and rip you a new one." Her neck flushes and her cheeks turn the prettiest shade of pink.

"Angie …"

"Don't you dare *Angie me* anything. Tell me you don't feel the air crackling around us?" Her fingers curl, tightening into fists. "If you stand there and deny there's something happening between us, I'll never forgive you." She takes in a shaky breath. "So, tell me, Brady Malone, what's it going to be?"

"Angie, don't." My fingers dig into the plush cotton of the towel.

"Don't, what?" She lifts a finger. "Don't you dare tell me what I feel isn't real. Don't you dare tell me that kiss didn't move the earth. Don't stand there and lie to me. Man up and admit you feel everything I'm feeling. Don't hide your emotions. I deserve far better than that. I deserve your respect."

Fuuuck!

"It's just …" My grip tightens. "You deserve more than a broken man."

"More?" Her brows practically climb up her forehead. "Broken?"

"That's what I said." I tug on my ear. This conversation isn't going the way I think it should. "You deserve better than me."

"And how …" She lifts a finger. "No, let me start over. Why?" Her shoulders lift to her ears. The next words out of her mouth are barely a whisper. "There's no one better than you. Why would you say that? Why would you hurt me like that?"

"Because I'm broken. You deserve a man who isn't …"

"Isn't what?" Her hands shift to her hips and she cocks one leg forward, demanding an answer.

"You deserve a man who isn't a monster." I drop the towel and close my eyes.

I won't survive Angie's rejection. It'll gut me and very well may be the last straw that truly breaks me. I brace for the inevitable.

For some time, she says nothing. Her soft breaths are the only sound other than the pounding in my chest and the ragged pull of my own breaths.

"Is that what you think?"

I crack open one eye. Nothing but love radiates from her face.

"It's the truth. Far too many people, men and women, have turned away in horror when they see my scars."

"You couldn't be more wrong." She shakes her head, then lifts her chin to stare directly into my eyes. "When I look at you, all I see is a man I hope feels the same about me as I feel about him. I have scars too. I'm no longer whole. All I have to offer is myself. No children. No family. I have debilitating deficiencies. I'll never get it back."

"Angie …"

"No. Let me finish. You're not a monster. You're perfectly imperfect and breathtakingly beautiful. Those scars speak of heroism and bravery. They tell the story of a man who put the lives of his men above his own. Who put his life on the line to rescue me, countless others before me, and many more who will come after me. That's not broken. It's far from it."

She closes the distance while my entire body shakes. Angie cups the side of my face, the side with the scars, and I can't help but flinch.

There's no revulsion or disgust in her eyes. There's nothing but adoration and acceptance. It's almost as if she doesn't see the scars at all.

But that can't be true.

It can't.

"You're uniquely gorgeous and perfect in every way." Her eyes shimmer with unshed tears. "And if you let me, I want to figure out where things are going with us."

Angie brushes the pad of her thumb over the scars on my face. Her feather-light touch trails down my neck, skimming up and over the rubbery ridges and bumps of melted skin, which will never fully heal. Her fingers flutter across my collarbone and stop at the tip of my shoulder.

"I wish you could see what I see when I look at you." Her hand sweeps back toward my throat while the muscles of my jaw clench.

My entire body wakes up beneath her touch, sensations shoot through me, and a desire unlike anything I've ever known rises within me.

When she places her palm over the center of my chest, I find the courage to look at her, but Angie isn't looking at my face. Her gaze focuses on her hand and the damaged flesh beneath it, which covers half of my chest.

"I can't imagine how this must have felt." Her palm glides over my skin, and her fingers flit over the ugliness. "The pain must have been unbearable. Tell me how this happened."

"I …" My voice catches, and I have to clear my throat before continuing. "I don't remember much about it. Everything happened so fast."

Her fingers continue their dance over my skin.

With the damage to the nerves, and the extensive skin grafts, the sensation over the burned tissue isn't quite right.

The fluttering of her fingers doesn't track with the movement of her hand sweeping over the scars. Ghost pains and phantom sensations make it impossible to follow her touch.

"Someday …" Her chin lifts and her gaze ensnares mine. "Someday, I hope you feel comfortable sharing what happened with me." Her lips press together. "Isn't it funny how a single moment can alter the trajectory of your life?"

Her exploration of my damaged skin moves down to my abdomen. Most of the scarring lies along the side of my body, over my hip, and down the outer side of my thigh. She examines nearly every inch; some is hidden beneath my shorts.

"Things happened fast for me as well. In the blink of an eye, I lost my husband, my unborn son, and my ability to ever have children of my own. I thought my life was over, and for years, it was. But I pushed through my grief and battled crippling depression. I finally realized Luke wouldn't want me to wallow in misery. He'd want me to live, to smile, and to find love again. He'd want me to be happy. I can't help but think you deserve the same."

"My father used to tell me chicks dig scars." I huff out a pathetic laugh. "But he didn't mean scars like these. I've never seen chicks run as fast as they do once they get a look at what's under the hood."

"Their loss." She places her palm over my sternum and closes her eyes. "My gain. You've got the heart of a hero. The compassion of a saint. You're brave enough to fight demons and monsters in the flesh. You're all of that and more, and your scars are nothing more than a tiny piece of who you are. Don't push me away because you think I can't handle the surface-level stuff. I'm here for what's inside."

She lays her cheek against my chest. "I'm here for your heart and your soul, and if you try to push me away, you haven't seen me fight for what I want. Rather than running away, I am running to you. I'm not here to see whether there's a future between us, but *what* that future will look like." Angie pushes on my chest and leans back. Her face tilts up to look at me. "Now, about that kiss at the waterfall …"

THIRTY-ONE

Brady

ABOUT THAT KISS …

I'm taken back to that moment when we first kissed. When Angie kissed me. It was so short, it barely qualified as a kiss, but it shook me down to my core.

That never happened before, and I've kissed a lot of women. Compared to Angie, those kisses were empty things, driven only by the need to move on to the next step and fulfil a mutual need to fuck.

Angie's kiss was something else. She gave it '*For luck,*' and asked me to be safe while I took care of the man sent out after her and Izzy.

Then I kissed her back.

Again, it wasn't just a kiss.

I took possession claiming Angie with aggression and need—*need* being the operative word. The need to make her mine burned through me with a ferocity I've never experienced.

Passion surged between us. Her swollen lips and the look she gave me hinted at something deep and powerful growing between us.

"Brady?" Angie looks at me, concerned.

I clear my thoughts and focus on the present.

"Yes?"

"Where did you go just now?"

I touch the pads of my fingers to the curve of her jaw. Memories of that kiss thunder through me, forcing me to face an uncomfortable truth. Angie's already a part of me.

"After the accident, I tried going to the bars for casual hookups. There was once a time when all I had to do was crook a finger and women would come running, but that all changed. The rare times I could get a woman to look beyond the scarring on my face, those on my body sent her running. I'm no catch."

"You're thick in the head as well." Angie once again runs her fingers over the scars. "Those women didn't deserve you. They didn't see you. You're beautiful."

"I'm a monster."

"That's what Belle thought when she first saw her Beast, but you're far more than what's on the outside. I see you." Angie cups my jaw and lifts on tiptoe. "I see all of you, and I'm not running away."

"That's the second time you've said that."

"It feels like you need to hear it more than once."

"Well, aren't we a pair?" For the first time since she intercepted me after my swim, a genuine smile ghosts across my lips. "How about I take a shower and we head to the buffet? The resort has tons of activities for couples. We could get a massage, go horseback riding on the beach? A hike through the jungles where someone isn't hunting us?" A smirk tugs on the corner of my mouth.

"All of those sound wonderful, but now that Izzy's gone, we could do something else." Angie's gaze drops below my waist.

Without the towel, there's no hiding my arousal. I had hoped she wouldn't notice, but Angie seems to notice everything about me. I'm not used to such forwardness in the women I date. It's sexy as fuck and terrifying as well.

She skims her palm down from where it presses against my chest to the waistband of my swim trunks. She stops there, then glances up at me. All I see is the fluttering of her lashes and the way she nibbles on her lower lip.

My girl isn't afraid to express herself, but there is some timidity. This is what I love about her; she's a wonderful mix of contradictions. She's strong, yet weak. Aggressive, yet timid.

She's fucking incredible and irresistible.

Shoving down any hesitation that remains, my focus turns from pushing Angie away to claiming her the way she deserves.

"*You* are an incredible woman." I wrap an arm around her shoulders and pull her toward me.

"And you're an incredible man." Her fingers dig at the waistband of my trunks. "Now, about that shower …"

Angie twists out of my embrace and heads to the shower built for two. Her hands go to the bottom of her shirt.

While I gape, she pulls it over her head. She tugs on the strings of her bikini top, and the bright red cloth falls to the ground.

A groan escapes me as I look down. My cock is eager and ready. It's always two steps ahead of me, but this time, we're on the same page.

Angie is mine.

She was mine from the moment we met.

While her beauty is striking, it's the strength of her soul that shines the brightest. Trauma touched her. It took from her. It scarred her. Yet, she faces the future with hope.

Somewhere along my journey, I lost that ability.

While I don't believe in fate, it's hard to deny how it touches my life. Our lives. My injury has defined my life for too long. It's a part of me, but it doesn't own me. Just like Angie's trauma doesn't own her. We were brought together for a reason; two broken souls finding strength in the other.

While I stare at the doorway leading into the bathroom, where Angie waits for me, I take a moment to wrap my head around what all of this means. Sex with Angie won't be like any of the meaningless sex I've had before.

It's not about scratching an itch or satisfying a physical urge.

It's about two damaged souls becoming one.

A beam of light shines into the room. It warms my cheek while making my nape tingle with anticipation. A grin curves my lips into a deliciously freeing smile. Joy sparks in my chest and shoots outward from there, invigorating me and infusing my body with delight and pleasure. I feel lighter, floating on a cloud of happiness so profound it's indescribable.

On the heels of the joy surging within me comes something else. Something I'm well acquainted with but have missed since before the explosion, which changed my life. It's an eagerness to torment and delight my girl until she's thoroughly ravished and floating in a sea of bliss, euphoria, and ecstasy.

"Brady …" Angie calls out from the bathroom. The shower turns on and I hear her moving inside. "Don't make me come out there."

"Hardly." I drop the towel and yank at the swim trunks.

Following Angie into the bathroom, I come to a sudden halt when I see her naked backside and the water streaming down her skin. She glances over her shoulder and gives me a look of satisfaction mixed with relief.

I love her confidence because of her insecurities. She's bold, not afraid to step outside of her comfort zone, willing to risk rejection, and completely fearless.

It's the sexiest thing on the planet.

"Damn." Angie twists to get a better look at me.

I stand before her, completely naked, with my scars standing front and center. As before, there's no revulsion on her face, no disgust in her eyes. Instead, she takes in my damaged body with desire sparking in her eyes.

"I didn't think it was possible." Her words whisper over my skin, making the fine hairs on my arms stand on end.

"What's that?"

"You're a handsome man, Brady Malone, but you're even more without the clothes."

"I doubt that." But her words definitely stroke my ego, among other things. When her gaze dips below my waist, her admiration rises.

"Well, you don't see what I do." She turns fully around and I get my first glimpse of her naked flesh.

My breath catches, and my dick bobs, giving a nod of encouragement.

"I could say the same. In fact ..." I close the distance between us.

The time for hesitation and deep thoughts is behind me. Now is the time to take what belongs to me. The need to touch her, kiss her, and claim her rushes through me.

I'm not here to physically take her, although I will. I'm here to indelibly mark her as mine, to brand myself onto her soul in a way that can never be removed or forgotten.

I intend to make her mine.

She stares at me, breath caught in her throat, with an intimacy that wasn't there moments ago. We both know what's about to happen, and we're dragging out the moment, turning it into a memory neither of us will ever forget.

That sparking chemistry between us returns. It's been there from the very beginning, growing, building, turning into an irresistible force. The air shimmers with electricity. It sparks in our eyes as the disruptive charge builds, setting us in motion.

I move toward her, prowling with lethal intent. Her lips part. A gasp escapes her as she takes one step back, and then another. She backs up against the tiled wall, chest heaving, tits bouncing.

Damn, but she's got the most perfect tits I've ever seen. Not too large. Not too small. They'll fit perfectly in my hands, and her nipples beg to be tested and tormented as well.

Which I'll do, but not now.

I want to take things slow for our first time, but her heaving chest and panting breaths make that nearly impossible.

Closing the distance, we collide in a violent collision of grappling arms and clashing mouths. When our lips touch, heat shoots through me. Her breasts press against my chest as my cock pushes against her belly. The burning demands of my body overwhelm me, but damn if I care.

"Condom?" My voice cracks with the sudden realization this may be as far as we go. I didn't plan for this. I'm not prepared.

"On the soap dish." Angie's lilting voice carries a hint of laughter. "I planned ahead."

I can't help but laugh. "I suppose that's one thing I won't live down."

With protection no longer an issue, we return to the kiss. Our lips fuse as our mouths and jaws collide with the passion freely running through us. Unbridled and uninhibited, we maul each other like we're both horny teenagers and this is the first time we've had sex.

We're too eager. Too anxious.

We grind our bodies together, rubbing and humping, completely out of control.

It's perfect.

With Angie laying claim to my mouth, and refusing to let go, I let my fingers explore. I take first one breast, and then the other, in my hand, pinching her nipples until her soft cries turn to delicious mewls of pleasure. My hand drops into the soft cleft between her legs.

Angie rises on her toes as my fingers find her slit and my thumb strokes her clit. With our mouths embroiled in that kiss, I bring her to orgasm with a tactical set of moves that makes her squirm and cry out as she comes on my hand.

"Brady …" She pants through the vestiges of her orgasm, then looks at me. "I need you. Now." Her demand isn't something I can refuse, but our bodies don't align the way I need them to.

I hitch her leg around my hip, then lift her up and off the shower floor. With both her legs wrapped around my hips, the broad tip of my cock notches at her entrance. Water falls all around us, but she's slippery and wet down there.

I hold her in my gaze and slowly push past her opening, making sure it's not too fast or too deep. I'm a big man and have accidentally hurt other women before. I've learned to go slow and take my cues from my partner.

The moment I push past her opening, sensation explodes through me.

So wet.

So warm.

Pleasure unfurls, shooting out with tiny flickers of electricity. My entire body shakes with the effort to slow things down and give her body a chance to adjust to my size.

Angie trembles in my arms, squirming and moaning.

"More, Brady. Deeper. I need more." Her fingers dig into the skin of my shoulders as her head tilts back until it rests against the tiled wall.

I tremble with her, overloaded with sensation, and terrified I'll come too soon. Angie's body fits me like a glove. I feel her *everywhere*.

Fuck, but I'm going to come, and I'm not yet seated inside of her. Just one thrust and I'll be done. The exquisite grip of her body, wrapped around mine, is simply too much.

I choke back a groan and bite my lower lip, needing the distraction of pain to keep me in the game.

"I don't want to hurt you."

"You won't." Her breathy moan is a total turn-on. "You can't."

With me holding Angie, I'm fully in control, which means I decide how deep and how fast. She's tougher than I think, which means …

I grab her hips and force her down on my cock while I thrust up. Her body grips me, all wet and warm, absolutely perfect. All around me, her sweet smell floods my senses. I taste her on my tongue and go back for more.

The moment our lips meet, her sexy cries set my hips in motion. She's fucking incredible, hotter than hell, and my equal match in everything. Her little moans and the sexy way she whimpers urge me on.

I free one hand from gripping her ass and supporting her in the air. I skim my hand up her wet skin, across her shoulder, and up her neck. Twining my fingers in her hair, I take control of her head. Placing my hand between her skull and the hard-tiled wall, I protect her as my thrusts intensify.

She screams as I thrust upward. Her fingers dig into my shoulders. Her legs tighten around my waist. I grow painfully hard as I drive viciously in and out. While I fuck her, I ram my tongue down her throat. It's brutally aggressive, but she meets me thrust for thrust.

It's the most aggressive kiss I've ever taken; brutal, raw, animalistic, and she meets me stroke for stroke. She's fucking amazing.

"Harder, Brady." She pulls away from my kiss and buries her face between my neck and shoulder. Her panting breath loses its rhythm and her soft, mewling cries escalate. "I'm almost there … More."

Harder?

I can definitely do that.

I release the last of my restraint and plow into her with everything I've got. My balls tighten as tiny jolts of electricity set my skin on fire. Pressure builds at the base of my spine, coiling and tightening, until it releases violently and suddenly.

My orgasm is brutal, an aggressive force I can't contain. Unable to slow down, I jerk and groan, thrusting like an animal, rutting and fucking, until my cock practically explodes.

She climaxes with a moan. Her fingers dig into the flesh of my arms, scraping and drawing blood as her entire body convulses and jerks.

I spiral into that abyss, falling with her, as pleasure courses through us both.

Together.

Joined as one.

That should be enough, but I'll never get enough of my girl. After I catch my breath, I turn her around and fuck her from behind. Then I go to my knees and taste her for the very first time as she comes violently on my face.

For the rest of the day, I use her mercilessly, experiencing the most passionate sex of my life. Not to be outdone, Angie treats me to the best blowjob in my life—twice.

I take her back to the shower to clean up but wind up bending her over the sink and taking her from behind again.

We fall into bed where I take her again. In every position, I pull orgasm after orgasm out of her sweet body, and when I feel I can do no more, she coaxes me on with a seductive bite to her lips and an evil glint in her eyes.

She's a beautiful temptress, and she's all mine.

My cock loves it, rising each time, until we're both spent. Utterly exhausted and incredibly satiated, Angie falls into bed with me in a tangle of limbs where we drift off, blissfully content.

We don't wake until noon the next day, and when I do, the first thing I do is stare at her sleeping form, completely enraptured by the woman I hold in my arms.

Inside my chest, the piece of her heart she tenderly gave to me, melds with mine, where I'll carry it with me for the rest of my life.

THIRTY-TWO

Angie

WE SPEND OUR DAYS ON ADVENTURES.

Horseback riding along the beach.

Tandem parasailing.

Long hikes in the jungle—without the fear of pursuit.

We swim every morning and watch the sun fade below the horizon every night.

I try to hang glide and fail. We swim in the cove, looking at the reef. Brady convinces me to learn how to scuba dive, and fortunately, there's a course at the resort. It takes two days, but I swim far beneath the surface of the water, a traveler from a different world.

At night, we make love beneath the stars. We try, once, in the water of the cove, but sex on the beach, or in the water, is not something I recommend. Getting sand out of those spots is challenging, to say the least.

At the end of what seems like endless days, we fall into bed, where we give in to carnal desire until we're spent, exhausted, and happy.

He tugs me tight, and I curl up against his chest. When I wake, he's already up, watching me.

I finally work up the nerve to go beyond the breakwater. We take our snorkels, masks, and fins and head north along the coast. After a mile, Brady turns us around.

The thrill of swimming in the open ocean is as exciting as it is scary. As long as I don't think about sharks, I'm good; and one morning a pod of dolphins joins us for a bit.

Each day, I need to pinch myself, because this can't be real.

"How are you holding up?" Brady marks our progress along the shore.

We tread water beyond the breakwater, catching our breath before making the journey back to the cove. This is actually the easiest part of the swim because we get to ride the swells as they roll in.

"I'm good." I lie on my back and float. "I've never been this relaxed."

"I have a surprise for you." Brady's husky voice never fails to set off the butterflies in my stomach.

I'll never get enough of this man.

"A surprise?" I spin around to look at him.

He's a fish in the water, almost as if he was born to it. I'm a strong swimmer, but nothing like the way he attacks the water.

"Yes, but it means I have to leave you alone for a bit."

"Okay …" I draw out the end of the word, suspicious, but knowing whatever the surprise is, it's important. "So, you're going to leave me unsupervised for how long?"

I will admit, I'm selfish about my time with him.

That will need to change once we're back in the real world. We'll both have jobs that demand our attention, and his job will take him from me for days, or weeks, at a time.

Fortunately, I'm used to handling myself during a deployment. Lord knows, Luke and I spent far too much time separated because of his job.

Things are different when I think about Luke.

Instead of a sharp stabbing pain in my chest, there's warmth and the remembrance of love. I'll always miss him, and he'll always have a piece of my heart, but I'm open to the possibility of sharing what's left with another.

I hope that turns out to be Brady.

"Not long. Less than an hour." He keeps his answer vague.

"How about I come with you?"

That way, we won't be apart.

I'm *very* selfish of my time with him.

"That would ruin the surprise." He moves toward shore, turning to his back and finning in while staring at the sky overhead.

I follow suit, and it's not long before we're standing waist-deep and taking off our gear.

"An hour?"

"I promise." He kisses my cheek and flashes one of his devastating winks.

Those things make my tummy flip and other parts of my body heat.

"How about a shower first?" I arch a brow, knowing he won't let that opportunity go to waste.

We settled the whole protection during sex issue after a frank and open conversation. Since I haven't been with a man since Luke died, I'm clean, and Brady gets tested regularly. His last tests were negative, and he hasn't been with anyone since. Then there's the baby issue, but since I lack essential baby-making capabilities, that's a non-issue.

We haven't talked much about the future, although I can't imagine a future without Brady in it. The one thing we need to discuss is his desire for children.

Obviously, I can't give him that.

But we'll get there when it's the right time.

"You promise not to follow me?" He gives me the eye while holding out his hand.

Honestly, I thought about it, but my words are true. It's impossible to sneak up on Brady. I've tried and failed several times.

Unlike me, his sneaking skills are Ninja level Expert.

"If I did, you would know." We walk across the sand, hand in hand.

This feels right.

With a toe-curling kiss, Brady leaves me with a glint in his eye and a secret mission he did not divulge despite the pretty damn epic blowjob I treated him to in the shower.

I decide to lounge in the bungalow and read another of my books.

Izzy and I are reading a spy thriller together. We read five chapters a day, then get on the phone to talk about what we read and what we think will happen next. The two of us are definitely close.

I'm on chapter three when there's a knock on the door.

"Odd."

We have summarily dismissed room service for the rest of our stay. Brady did that on account of the weapons distributed around the bungalow. There's one under his pillow and another shoved between the cushion and arm of the couch.

Those aren't things maids need to randomly come across while cleaning the room; besides, we're both neat freaks.

"Who is it?" I cautiously approach the door. There's no peephole for me to look through, which surprises me.

"Angie?" A male's voice calls out. It's a voice I know well.

"Jerald?" I rush to open the door and my friend is there. "Oh my God, it's you." I fling my arms around his neck and pull him in for a hug. "You look horrible."

He looks like he's seen the inside of a meat grinder. Both of his eyes are swollen; the left is nearly shut completely. Cuts, abrasions, and bruises mar his face. There's swelling over his cheeks. His lips are split. And his nose looks to be broken in too many places.

"What did they do to you?" I release him and gesture for him to come inside. "Can I get you anything? Water? Soda? Alcohol?"

"Is it that bad?" He huffs a laugh, then limps inside, guarding his ribs. "I haven't looked in a mirror."

"Don't." I try to keep the mood light, not focusing on our abduction. "What happened to you? When the Guardians couldn't find you, I feared for the worst. And the guys didn't know what happened to you either."

"Trust me, it's good to be seen." He hobbles over to the bar and takes a seat on a stool. "Something strong to numb the pain sounds just about right. Do you have any whiskey?"

"We do."

He looks around the room, taking everything in. Not that there's much to take in. The room looks uninhabited. It's a part of the whole neat freak thing.

"This is an odd choice of rooms. Is Izzy with you?"

"No. She left about a week ago."

"This is a pretty swanky room. I guess ophthalmology pays well?" There's a harshness in his tone that rubs me wrong. I choose to ignore it, considering what he's been through.

"The room is a gift from the Guardians."

"The people who rescued you?"

"Well, they rescued you too, but yeah."

"I was hoping Izzy was here with you."

"Sorry, but we talk every afternoon. You can talk to her then. Or we can call her now?" I pull my phone from the back pocket of my shorts. "She'd love to know you're okay."

"No, that's okay. I'm just really glad to see you. Were you hurt? Did they …"

"Neither of us were hurt. There were a few scrapes and bruises during our escape, and Izzy sprained her ankle, but that was it. You and the others took the brunt of it."

"Yeah."

"They kept asking about guns and such, but we all unloaded gear at some point. I'd think if there were guns, we would've noticed."

"You'd be surprised what people can hide." He sips the whiskey and grimaces when the alcohol burns the cut in his lip.

"How did you know we were here?"

"I, ummm …" He pauses for another sip. His brows tug together, almost touching, as if he's thinking hard. "I must've heard the Guardians talking and had to make sure for myself that the two of you were okay."

"Thank you. That's incredibly kind of you. We're actually doing very well. What are your plans? Are you staying here? Did you get a room?"

"Yeah." His reply is distracted, almost dismissive.

I can't help but ramble at the mouth. Now that Jerald is safe and sound, it feels like I can take a deep breath. The whole monstrous ordeal is finally over. Jerald scans the room again.

"I've lived in some pretty spartan conditions, but this is the first time I've been reduced to the clothes on my back." He downs the last of the whiskey and places the highball glass on the bar. "Did they recover any of our gear?"

"I'm afraid not. The cartel took everything."

"That's not …"

"Not what?"

"Nothing." He looks around again. "The only thing I care about is in my backpack." He tries to laugh, but that turns into a coughing fit. He splints his ribs and tries to breathe. "Fuckers broke a rib or two."

"I'm surprised Skye let you go."

"Skye?"

How can he *not* know the pretty doctor?

Jerald appreciates a pretty face. He tried hitting on me the first week of our mission, but back pedaled hard when he realized I was still a grieving widow. He became like a big brother, looking out for me, helping me with my gear.

"You can't have missed her. She's the Guardian's doctor."

"Oh …" He runs his hand through his hair. "My memory is a bit of a shit show right now."

"With everything you went through, I'm surprised she let you leave."

"I'm not the best patient." He takes another sip. "To be honest, I just wanted to check in on you and Izzy. They flew the others out the day before I arrived."

"How did you get here without your passport?"

"Huh?"

"They recovered our personal packs. Izzy and I went through them. Yours was there, too. They took everything. I don't remember seeing a rabbit's foot, but everyone's passports were there. How did you cross the border without a passport?"

When he runs his hand through his hair, it trembles.

"If Izzy's not here, does that mean you're alone?"

"Brady, the Guardian who rescued us, is here."

"Oh. Will he be back soon?"

"He's off on a *secret* mission, but he should be back within the hour."

"Um, do you mind if I use the restroom?" Jerald squirms on the stool.

"Sure. It's just in there." I gesture toward the bedroom. "I can't wait for you to meet Brady."

"I look forward to it, but I don't have a lot of time. I have somewhere to be."

"Oh …" I thought he was staying at the resort, but I keep my question to myself. I may have misunderstood.

While Jerald heads to the bathroom, I clean the counter.

It's almost noon, and I'm hoping he'll stay long enough to have lunch. I want him to meet Brady and give his blessing.

The seconds tick by and Jerald doesn't return. Not to be weird about it, but I go to check on him. He didn't seem very steady on his feet.

When I tiptoe to the door of the bedroom, scuffling noises come from the other side of the door. I push it open a crack, then tug my brows tight together.

All I see is Jerald's back, but it's what he's doing to my backpack that brings a gasp to my lips. He spins at the sound. I take a step back, and then another.

"I really wish you hadn't done that." Jerald rises to his full height. He towers over me, but that's not what makes me gasp the second time.

That gasp is for the wicked-looking Bowie knife he pulls on me.

"What are you doing?" I take another step, not sure what's happening.

"Retrieving what's mine." His expression turns dark; murderous comes to mind.

"I don't understand." I glance at my backpack, confused.

"Where are they?"

"Where are what?"

"The diamonds, silly. What did you do with the diamonds?"

"I don't know what you're talking about. There was nothing in my bag."

"Don't lie to me, Angie. I am not in the mood."

I hold out my hand, like that will protect me, and take another step back. Perspiration beads on my brow as my heart lurches into overdrive. Filled with panic, my heart practically rips itself out of my chest, trying to run.

From Jerald.

My dear friend, Jerald.

"Put the knife down and talk to me." I shift my trajectory, angling toward the couch and the gun Brady hid there.

That gun is for intruders coming in from the front door and windows. The one under his pillow is a weapon of last resort.

"I want to know where the fucking diamonds went."

"I know nothing about any diamonds." My voice turns shrill, panic-stricken, and my entire body trembles. I nearly trip over the coffee table.

For every step I take, he takes two, closing the distance between us. I'm a fast runner, but not fast enough to get to the door, and open it, before he can catch me. I also can't escape out of the windows. Brady locked them to keep intruders from getting in, never suspecting I might invite the intruder inside.

I'm effectively trapped.

Tears shimmer in my eyes, blurring my vision, as dread wraps its cold tendrils around my heart. My lungs seize into an icy cold block of breathless terror.

But if I can get to the gun …

A gun trumps a knife.

I back up against the couch, moving to the cushion where Brady hid the gun. In my head, I rehearse what I need to do and how much time I'll have before Jerald is on me. It's going to be close. I need to stall him.

"Why do you keep mentioning diamonds? The cartel was interested in guns."

"No, they weren't." He makes a rude noise. "They were interested in you."

"Me?" I point to my chest.

The last two steps, he doesn't close the distance. Instead, his grip on the knife tightens. He lifts my backpack, shaking it in front of me.

"You and Izzy, two pretty Americans ripe for the plucking."

"You're not making any sense."

"What's so hard to figure out?"

"All of it."

"Then I'll spell it out for you." His sneer forces me back a step. The back of my knees hit the couch and I tumble into it. Jerald lifts my backpack, shaking the hell out of it. "I bring them two pretty females. They give me diamonds."

"But the guns?"

"There were no fucking guns." He shouts at the top of his lungs. "Those fucking Guardians ruined everything. When you escaped, they came at me."

"The Guardians?"

"No, you stupid bitch. The fucking cartel. I put the diamonds in your bags, but when you escaped, they came after me."

"How could you do that to us? And Jacob? Stefan? Daniel? They tortured them." Surely, they wouldn't …

What Jerald intended for Izzy and me suddenly hits me like a sledgehammer. A sour taste builds in the back of my throat. I gag, struggling not to lose my shit.

My hand falls to the seam between the cushion and the couch. My heart's in full berserk mode, beating wildly and out of control, as adrenaline kicks in and my flight or fight instinct fully engages.

I lunge, moving as fast as I can to grasp the pistol grip of Brady's gun. He showed me how to use it, how to rack the slide, and turn off the safety.

But I'm too slow.

Jerald crashes into me. He's heavy and so much bigger than me. Jerald knocks the gun out of my grip and straddles me on the couch.

I can't breathe.

I can't move.

I can scream, but no one will hear.

We're all alone.

I wriggle beneath his weight, but there's no way I'm moving him. He brings that wicked blade up to my throat and all my thrashing stills, except for the heaving of my chest.

"Jerald, this isn't you. You're my friend. Why are you doing this?"

"I'm not your friend. Never was. Now, what the fuck did you do with the diamonds?"

"I don't know what you're talking about." I scream back at him, feeling my cheeks heat with fury. "When we found the backpacks, they were empty. Only the passports were there."

I'm trying to put two and two together, but it's as if Jerald speaks a whole other language.

Think!

How am I going to get out of this?

With a guttural cry, I do the only thing I can think of to get free. I jab upward with my knees, hitting him right in the nuts.

He howls in pain, and the knife drags against the skin of my neck.

Burning.

Cutting.

But when he hunches over and grabs at his balls, I slip out from underneath him and vault over the back of the couch. Frantically searching, I locate the gun.

There.

I leap for it, spinning to my back as my fingers wrap around the handgrip. Remembering what Brady taught me, I rack the slide and pull the trigger.

The gun fires with an ear-splitting report so loud it deafens me.

Cotton puffs out of the couch as Jerald leaps back, uninjured.

I scoot back and take aim again. The primal instinct to eliminate a lethal threat brings everything into focus.

It's as if time stands still.

I line up the sights and squeeze the trigger.

Sharp pain in my ears follows the sudden report.

The bullet punches its way through Jerald's chest, leaving a gaping hole that quickly fills with blood. Jerald staggers back as surprise fills his expression. He looks confused and falls to one knee.

Blood pulses out of the bullet wound, soaking into his shirt as he coughs and spits up blood.

I think we're done and breathe out a sigh.

Only he climbs back to his feet and stares down at me with murderous intent. I scramble back, but he crashes into me, landing in an uncoordinated pile of arms and legs.

That knife glints in his hand as he slashes down, aiming for my throat.

THIRTY-THREE

Brady

SOMETHING DOESN'T SIT WELL WITH ME AS I LEAVE THE PRIVACY OF our cove. I can't say what it is, but it's as if I feel someone's eyes on me.

Shrugging off the odd sensation, I continue down the path, eager to get the necklace from the on-site jeweler. It's a special piece, something I hope Angie loves.

The moment I round the bend, which separates our private retreat from the rest of the resort, that itching sensation between my shoulder blades returns.

It pulls me to a halt and forces me to stop and observe my surroundings. I would've missed it if I wasn't keyed up, but there's another set of footprints heading toward the bungalow.

A man's footprints.

That's all it takes for fear to grip my stomach.

Between one second and the next, I go from happy and relaxed to on point. All my training kicks in, and while I want to run back to Angie, I know that's the worst thing I can do.

I move off the walkway and thread my way through the dense foliage. I'll work my way around our bungalow and come in through the back window.

Except, you locked all the windows.

Fuck.

Not that it matters. The windows aren't made of glass but are louvered slats of wood that will break with a single kick.

It takes far longer than I want, but I make my way around the bungalow. I stop at the windows of the main room and listen. Sure as shit, there's a man inside with Angie. From the sound of it, things are turning from bad to worse.

Despite the urge to see what's going on, I remain out of sight. The last thing I need is for whoever's in there with Angie to see me and escalate this into a hostage situation. Bent double, I crouch around the bungalow until I'm at the window leading into the bedroom.

The voices rise inside. Angie's pleading. The man threatens.

I check the lock on the window and curse at my paranoia. Not once did I think a serious threat would come from inside. But I catch a break. One louver rots from water damage. I pull on the wood, trying not to make too much noise.

The wood pulls free without a sound, which lets me snake my arm inside and unlock the window.

Angie shouts in the other room. There's a scuffle. A gun goes off, deafening in the close quarters. I shake my head and leap through the window. Not wasting any time, I go to my pillow and grab the weapon I placed beneath it.

More sounds of a scuffle. A second shot rings out. My ears ring from the overpressure inside a closed space, but I don't stop.

I move out.

Leading with my weapon, safety off, finger on the trigger guard, I round the corner and see a crazy man on top of my girl, slashing down with a knife.

I take aim and fire.

His body crashes on top of Angie in a heavy, uncoordinated heap. Bastard's fucking dead.

I rush over. Kick the man's knife away. He's not dead until I say he's dead.

"Are you okay?" I spare a quick glance at Angie, but my focus is on the dead man. There's blood on her shirt, but I expect that from my shot.

Not dead until you say he's dead.

It's something they drilled into us at BUDS and is where the double tap came into being. One shot to the chest and one to the head. When our victims fall, they fall dead.

But I place my fingers over his neck. The bastard's dead eyes stare up at the ceiling. There's no pulse. Not that I'm expecting any.

Beside me, Angie scoots back and hugs her knees. When I turn back to her, my eyes go wide. On my feet, I scoop her into my arms and rush over to the kitchen island.

"You're hurt."

"I'm okay."

"I'll be the judge of that."

Angie's so pumped up on adrenaline she doesn't feel the wicked gash along her throat. I grab paper towels, wet them, then wipe at the blood. It covers her entire throat. Some of it is his, but far too much of it is hers.

When I clean her up enough to see the wound, I bite back a curse and yank out my phone.

"Call HQ."

I put the phone on speaker and toss it on the counter.

"Overlord to Bravo One, what's your status?"

Everyone at Guardian HQ knows I'm on leave. There's zero reason for me to call the hotline. Well, except the one.

"I need medical and a crew."

"Medical and a crew, copy that. Explain."

"Knife wound to Angie's neck, and I've got a dead guy on the floor."

"Copy that."

The connection goes silent for a moment, then CJ's voice comes online.

"What the hell are you up to?"

"Nice to hear your voice, boss."

"Can't say the same." CJ pauses for a second. There's muffled conversation on his end of the line. "Medical is inbound. I'll put

Skye on in a moment to talk you through initial care. Tell me about the body?"

"Male. Late 20s."

"It's Jerald." Angie puts her hand over mine, where I keep pressure to the wound on her neck. "He was crazy …" Each time she speaks, the gash on her neck opens and more blood trickles out.

It's not lethal.

I know enough first aid to check that, but the bleeding concerns me.

"Shh, don't talk. I've got you." I readjust how hard I push on her neck. There's a fine line between keeping enough pressure to stem the bleeding and closing off her airway. "CJ, did you copy that?"

"Good copy. She said Jerald?"

"Affirmative."

"Well, shit." More silence is on the line. "He went MIA."

"And you didn't think to tell me?"

"Cool your jets. There was no reason to suspect."

"Sorry." I can't help but snap. I need somewhere to direct my anger.

While waiting for them to figure out my next steps, I glare at the still form of Jerald.

The bruising on his face tells the story of torture. It's what we assumed when we rescued him, but that can be faked. I wish I hadn't killed him because I'd love to add a few more bruises to that busted-up face of his.

"Brady …" Angie reaches for me.

"Shh, luv. Don't talk. It makes the bleeding worse." No way in hell am I losing her.

"Diamonds …" Her voice grows weaker. "He kept asking about diamonds."

THIRTY-FOUR

Angie

ALL THE ADRENALINE THAT KICKED IN WHEN JERALD ATTACKED ME fades, leaving me overwhelmingly exhausted. Brady keeps wanting me to be still and not talk because of a cut along my neck, but I need to tell him what Jerald said.

However, that exhaustion pulls at me. At some point, I drifted off because I wake in a small medical room.

"Hey, luv …" Brady's husky voice is like a warm embrace.

"Hey." I lift a hand to cup the left side of his face. It's the side with the scars. "Where am I?" Something tugs on my neck.

"You're in the clinic at the resort. He cut you pretty bad on your neck."

"I don't remember getting cut."

"I'm not surprised."

"Why?"

"It's something that happens amped up on adrenaline in a survival situation. All I'll say is it's well known that soldiers will keep fighting after getting shot, remembering nothing but a sudden impact that knocked them down. The body does what it does to survive, and whining about a minor cut when you're trying to stay alive makes little sense."

"Um, okay? I'll take your word for it."

I don't believe him. If I'd been cut …

My hand drifts down to the pulling at my neck and finds a thick bandage covering over half my throat.

"Brady …" My voice shakes, as does my hand. "What happened?"

"I was hoping you could tell me. Something didn't sit right with me, and I circled back around. Heard you and Jerald arguing. I came in through the back window, and I'm fucking glad I did." He leans down to kiss my forehead. "You're something else. You know that, don't you?"

"I'm nothing special."

"And that is one thing I love the most about you." Brady takes my hand. "You're not like any woman I've ever known."

"That's because you were looking in the wrong places. Frog hogs are not soulmate material."

"I'm going to regret sharing my sexual history with you, aren't I?"

A laugh escapes me. When we had the sex talk, my sexual history paled in comparison to his *frog hogs*—obsessive women who basically do anything to be associated with a US Navy SEAL, and by *associate*, I mean fuck.

"I have enough material to last a lifetime."

"A lifetime?" His eyes glint with mischief. "Is that on the table?"

"You said the L-word first."

"I did not." His face breaks into a grin.

"Did too."

Our easy banter is what I love the most about us, and there definitely is an *us*. I feel it where it counts, deep down, inside of me.

"Excuse me?" A man knocks on the doorjamb and pokes his head inside.

"Hey, Doc, she's up."

"I see." A man with a white coat steps into the room.

"Angie, this gentleman is Dr. Diego González. He stitched you up."

"Dr. González, it's nice to meet you."

"I see you're awake." He holds a tablet in his hand. "I have Dr. Summers who wants to listen in. Is that okay?"

"Of course."

Dr. González hands the tablet to Brady, who jumps off the table and gives the doctor room to examine me.

"I just want to check on the stitches and make sure the bleeding's under control."

Brady makes faces at me, while I try to keep a straight face during the doctor's examination. He confers a few times with Skye, and the two of them discuss antibiotics.

I give a little wave to Skye and notice several other faces in the camera's view. One of them is Izzy.

"Hey, I thought you were going home to your brothers?"

Izzy ducks out of the field of view, looking guilty as shit. I don't get to finish my question because Dr. González and Skye have a conversation about my wound.

My takeaway is there's a gash about as long as my hand is wide along the right side of my neck. It's deep, but superficial. I don't know how something can be both deep and superficial, except they seem to think that's a good thing.

Before long, I'm released by the doctor, but then face interrogation by local officials. No one from Guardian HRS can get to us quickly, but we put that tablet to good use. There's attorney representation on the line, as well as an FBI liaison.

The Spanish flying back and forth is too fast for my limited skills. I'm lost quickly and sit with Brady, holding hands, while they come to some arrangement.

There's some back and forth about Brady's weapons. They get confiscated by the police, but they finally release us.

Or rather, we're placed under police escort.

They take us back to the bungalow, where we're allowed to retrieve our personal effects, minus the guns. I don't have much, and since everything I have was purchased onsite, I have no suitcase to bring any of it back with me.

Except for …

"Brady, do you see my backpack?"

As silly as it sounds, that backpack means a lot to me, for many reasons. It represents new beginnings. Not that I'm leaving Luke behind. He'll always be a part of me, but that backpack is a testament to one of the most courageous things I've ever done.

My time with Doctors Without Borders, despite what happened, will always be one of the happier times in my life. I won't be signing another contract with them, but I found a new purpose in life.

And, of course, I found Brady.

"It's not in here." He calls out from the master bedroom, where he packs his gear.

"You sure?" My memory appears to have holes in it.

Closing my eyes tight, I try walking through what happened with Jerald.

I found him digging through my backpack in the bedroom. Then he came out … It all comes back in a flood of memories, crashing into me. I stagger and grab the arm of the police official watching over me.

"*Señorita, ¿estás bien?*"

It's kind of him to ask if I'm okay. To him, I probably look like I'm going to fall over any second.

"*Si, estoy bièn.*" I tell him I'm okay.

Despite my near faint, I look around the room, stepping clear of the blood. Which is a major feat considering there's a lot of it everywhere. Some of which belongs to me. Jerald's body's already been removed, but signs of our scuffle are everywhere.

There, under the couch, the strap of my backpack pokes out.

"*Eso es mio.*" I point to the bag. "*Tiene mi pasaporte adentro.*"

I tell him the bag is mine, and my passport is inside of it, but I'm sure I botch the Spanish.

We're not allowed to touch our effects until the local police search them.

There's an *investigation* underway, but it's pretty clear it's all for show. Whatever went down between our attorney, the FBI liaison, and local officials, our departure from Costa Rica appears to be a top priority.

The officer retrieves my backpack, looks inside, then pulls out my passport and the rabbit's foot Jerald gave me months ago. I'd forgotten about it. The officer, however, seems satisfied. The passport and rabbit's foot go back inside and he hands over my backpack. I take a quick peek, but there's nothing else inside.

Knowing better than to say anything about diamonds, I won't mention it until we're back on US soil. We enjoy a police escort from the resort to the airport. They walk us all the way to the gate and wait for us to board before leaving.

"That was—something." I snuggle against Brady as the plane gets ready to depart the gate. Costa Rica was certainly an *interesting* place to visit. "They couldn't get rid of us fast enough."

"Guardian HRS pulls some heavy strings." Brady holds my hand the entire flight. "There's not much they can't do."

"I'm beginning to see that."

I lean back to watch takeoff, then snuggle against Brady again. We sit in first class, which means we only had to endure the stares of *all* the passengers as they boarded after us.

"I hope it leaves a scar." I press my palm against the bandage at my throat.

He looks at me weirdly. "Why would you say that?"

"We'd be a matched pair."

"That's … You can't …" He shakes his head. "I don't …"

"Did I leave you speechless?" I cup his cheek, the left one, and let my finger trace the scarring there. I want him to know I accept him, scars and all.

"It's just …" He tries again, and fails, while I sit back and laugh.

Overhead, my backpack and his go-bag lie side by side, snuggled together just like we are in our seats.

The sum total of my worldly possessions sits inside that raggedy backpack.

"I don't want you to be scarred." Brady isn't letting my comment go. "Not there. Not where anyone can see it."

"It wouldn't bother me." I don't think he realizes I was teasing.

"It would bother me." From the tone in his voice, he speaks the truth.

"Why? It's just a scar."

"Trust me, it's more than that."

We settle in and our conversation drifts to other topics. He asks about Izzy and how everything that happened brought us close together. I get him to open up about the Guardians and love the way he talks about them like they're family.

Which makes sense.

Intense situations often form tight bonds, which brings me back to what's happening between us.

"Skye offered me a job."

We fall silent for a time; therefore, my comment catches him by surprise.

"You're taking it, aren't you?"

"Well, I thought maybe we should talk first."

"About what?"

"Us?" I clasp my hands and press them against the nervous butterflies dancing in my belly. "What do you think about us?"

"I think we're wonderful."

"Just wonderful?"

"More than wonderful." He grabs my hand and threads his fingers with mine. "I know you're still processing your grief, but I hope there's some room for me in your life."

"There is."

"Is it too soon to ask you to move in with me?"

"Maybe?" I nibble on my lower lip while he plays with my ring finger.

"Too soon to put something here?"

"Brady ..."

"It's what I want—can't lie about that, but I'm in no rush. If you need time, you need time. I know what I want, and I'm not going anywhere."

"Honestly, I don't know what I need, time or otherwise. Things between us happened really fast and that worries me."

"Why?"

"What if it doesn't last?"

"We'll last."

"How can you be so sure?"

"Because I feel you in here." He points to his chest. "We share a connection few ever get to experience."

"I feel you too."

"You said Doc Summers offered you a job?"

"I did. She offered Izzy one too. I guess they're looking to expand."

"Is Izzy interested?"

"I think so."

"Then how about we do this …"

"What?"

"Well, let me finish." The right side of his face tics up in a grin. "I was *thinking* we get the two of you a place to live together. It'll be good for both of you."

"But what about you?"

"I've got a place to live."

"That's not what I mean." I shove him playfully. "I *thought* you wanted me to move in?"

"I want far more than that. I want you for the rest of my life, but I thought, maybe we slow things down a bit. Take the time to get to know each other when people aren't trying to kidnap or kill you."

There's his grin again. It's pretty damn sexy.

"That would be nice, but you may decide I'm an incredibly boring person."

"Luv, you didn't bat an eye when I took you to the open ocean to swim. You jumped at the opportunity to learn to scuba dive. You even tried, but failed, to learn how to hang glide. If there was ever a woman hand-picked to be mine, it's you, and who knows? I may even dig that totally cool scar on your neck." His tone turns teasing, but he's serious about every word.

"You're incorrigible."

"You love it."

"That's true. I do." I lean back to look him in the eyes. "And for the record, I'm totally in love with you, too."

"Hey, pump the brakes and slow down." His expression turns comical. "Don't get all crazy with the I love you, you love me, we're a happy family …" He sings Barney, the Purple Dinosaur's most beloved and most hated song.

"If you don't stop, I swear I'll make you pay."

"Pay? How?" He challenges me.

"Remember what I did in the shower?"

His eyes get wide.

"Yeah, no more of that."

He wraps his arm around me and pulls me in for a hug.

"No more then, but come on, Barney's song's in your head now, isn't it?"

It stays there for the rest of the flight, during the debriefing by the Guardian team, and for the rest of the week as I settle into what's becoming my new life.

After Luke's death, my world crumbled.

My desire to continue living without him disappeared.

I never reached the point of taking my own life. I was fortunate to recognize the danger signals and do something radical to alter the trajectory of my life.

Selling our home, our cars, and all our things gave me the perfect blank slate on which to rebuild.

But here's the thing. That slate wasn't entirely blank. Luke steered me through every decision. I truly believe he looks over me, and I know I make him proud.

I have a new job. I live with my best friend. And I somehow stumbled upon a man who loves me as fiercely as I love him.

I have an entire community of people eager to welcome me into the fold, and with the Guardians, I have a new purpose in life: helping others who can't help themselves.

I found closure.

I found peace.

Most of all, I found love.

Someone once told me that when you love someone, you give them a piece of your soul and they give you a little piece of theirs. When they die, they take that piece of you with them.

That's why losing them hurts so much.

You can drown in that grief, or you can remember a little bit of them is still within you. You can choose to live for them, and carry that little piece of them with you for the rest of your life, or you can choose otherwise.

I chose to live. For the first time in three years, I'm excited about what the day will bring, and look forward to what comes next.

But there's one thing that still bothers me.

It's in what Jerald said before he died, and as I look at the diamond solitaire Brady put on my ring finger, I can't help but wonder what he meant about the diamonds.

BRAVO TEAM; A WHOLE NEW SERIES OF PROTECTOR ROMANCES showcasing the Guardian Hostage Rescue Specialists. Rescuing Isabelle (aka Izzy) is the next book in the exhilarating new BRAVO TEAM series.

Read Izzy and Booker's story, grab your copy of Rescuing Isabelle HERE.

These former Navy SEALs, DELTA Operatives, and Special Ops soldiers turned **_Guardians & Protectors_** are guaranteed to capture your heart and leave you breathless.

Turn the page for a sneak peek at the explosive combination of Izzy and Booker.

THIRTY-FIVE

Rescuing Isabelle

FIRST CHAPTER

Book Two in the Guardian Hostage Rescue Specialists: BRAVO
Team series.

———

SOMEDAYS, I WANT TO PINCH MYSELF, BECAUSE THIS KIND OF LIFE
never happens to a girl like me.

Now, if I could only get my four, overprotective, overbearing,
and overly paternalistic brothers to back off, this could be the
perfect life.

Perfect except for the whole abduction-in-the-jungles-of-
Nicaragua bit and the subsequent running for-my-life thing.

Except my brothers will *not* get off my case about it. They
demand I *go home*.

Where it's *safe*.

Safe feels a whole hell of a lot like oppressively smothering. I
love my brothers, but they can be way over the top when it comes to
their baby sister.

However, I've successfully put them off.

At least for a bit.

That trip home needs to happen, but I'm going to stonewall them for a little bit more.

I'm not ready to step away, especially when it comes to days like today.

And my view?

It's one in a million.

"Whatcha thinking, Izzy?" My best friend in the whole wide world, my abduction-and-running-for-my-life-buddy, Angie, gives me the eye.

She knows exactly what I'm thinking.

Hell, every female within sight of the spectacle in front of us is thinking the same damn thing.

That's due to the six mighty fine Guardians flexing their muscles in a virile display of jaw-dropping, fantasy-inducing, testosterone-infused masculinity.

And my dirty mind is overflowing with all kinds of wicked fantasies.

"I'm not thinking anything you're not." I cross my arms and give her a look. "Your mouth is open, and you're drooling." I call her out for calling me out.

Angie likes to think, since she's got a ring on her finger, that she's above ogling the drool-worthy display, but she's totally guilty of checking out not just her beau, Brady, but all the men of Bravo team.

Just.

Like.

Me.

Her heart may belong to Brady Malone, but she watches them all.

"Oh yes, you are." She reaches over and pinches me. "And if I'm drooling, you're foaming at the mouth. You so want a piece of Booker Holloway." She pinches me.

"Hey, stop that." I yank away and rub at my skin. "That hurt."

"Not until you admit you've got an eye for Bravo Two." Her light hazel eyes twinkle with amusement. Yeah, she's having fun with me.

"I won't."

But the thing is…she's totally right. I've got a major lady boner for Booker Holloway, especially after what the women of Alpha team told me about how he made ends meet before he became a Guardian.

Before he became a US Navy SEAL.

It's deliciously naughty.

My man is an ex-exotic dancer—was an exotic dancer. Evidently he doesn't do that anymore.

Bummer.

Although, he supposedly taught the men of Alpha team how to bump and grind on their women.

In Vegas, no less.

But that's a different story.

"You don't have to say it because it's scrawled all over your face." Angie makes a circle in front of my face, then preens in victory because she knows she's right.

Booker used to star in an all male review on the strip in Vegas. He's got the moves and the body for it. I don't doubt it for a second. Not that I didn't due my due diligence and confirm for myself.

I've got the pictures and the proof; after a little detective work and an assist from Mitzy, the technical lead for Guardian HRS. I call her a wizard, because that woman is amazing. She makes me feel like an underachiever.

Which I'm totally not.

Straight A's in high school were followed by straight A's in undergrad, and those continued in Pharmacy school, where I graduated…with honors.

I'm a valedictorian three times over. I thought that was pretty bad ass until I met Mitzy. I've come to realize, I'm merely ordinary; at least when I try to measure myself up against the talent hired on at Guardian HRS.

"I hate you." I tighten my arms and hunch inward.

I hate that Angie's right, but there's no denying the truth. The scariest thing is I think he may like me too.

"Want me to ask Brady if Booker's into you?"

"No!" That makes me cringe.

Isn't it funny how no matter how old we get, we never leave the schoolyard? Here I am, pining over a boy, thinking he might like me, but too chickenshit to get off my ass and find out.

"Hey, lunch break is almost over." Angie starts packing up the remnants of her meal. "We've have to get back to orientation."

Our new employer definitely offered us one sweet deal. Two actually. One for each of us. They hired me on as a pharmacist. I'll be working at Guardian HQ's onsite hospital during my initial onboarding, but then I'll shift to the pharmacy at the Facility where Guardian HRS is looking to expand.

Angie got the same offer...to work for Guardian HRS, that is. She's not a pharmacist, but rather an ophthalmologist. She'll remain at the onsite hospital, joining their current Ophtho team.

"What if we fake tummy aches? Tell them we need fresh air to recover?" My gaze turns back to the men scaling the sixty-foot wall in front of us. Bravo team is a little over two thirds of the way to their objective.

"I think that'll go over like a ton of bricks. Come on. You can watch them tomorrow too."

Bravo team is in between assignments, which means they fill their days working various scenarios and honing their skills. As for Bravo team, my bestie is currently engaged to Brady; the man who single-handedly rescued us from the *Coralos* cartel after they abducted our entire medical team.

He's the lead for Bravo team. They call him Bravo One.

Booker's Bravo Two. Then there's the rest of the team: Rafe, Hayes, Alec, and Jeb.

The whole team looks like they're carved out of granite; all hard lines and rough edges, perfect specimens of the male form.

"*Le sigh.*" I lean back and press the back of my hand over my forehead in a dramatic gesture. "They're all stinking hot."

"But you have the hots for one." Angie giggles. "And from the looks he gives you, the feeling has to be reciprocated. I could ask Brady to look into it."

"No! Don't you dare. And I'm not into Booker. He's an overprotective, over-bearing ass." My lips twist, turning my smile into a frown. "That man is flawed, with a capital F, as in over-bearing, over-protective, and over-everything. He's just like my brothers, and you see how I react to their demands."

"I do, and you love that about Booker." She continues to tidy up our picnic spot. "It's what draws you to him."

"Does not."

"You can't lie to me." She turns her attention back to the rock wall the men scale as a part of one of their training exercises. "The air sizzles when the two of you get close."

"Don't know what you're talking about, and as far as sizzle, look who's talking? You and Brady are like lightning with the way you make the air crackle." I lean back and tilt my head, getting a really fabulous look at the way Booker's ass fills out his pants. He traverses an overhead reverse incline with a full ruck on his back.

The man reaches out with those powerful arms. Those deft fingers feel around for a blind grip. Once he's set, his body swings out into open space. I can't help but gasp, worried he might fall the fifty feet between him and the ground.

But he doesn't.

Booker uses the momentum of his body to his advantage. He hooks a boot on a rock overhead, then hand over hand, pulls himself up the rock face. That gives me plenty of time to admire the way he fills out those black tactical pants of his.

The man has a mighty fine ass, and from what little I've seen of the front package, there are delights there to be had as well.

Yep, my mind is totally in the gutter. As for the gutter, Angie leads me into a trap.

"I bet you'd kill for Booker to get bossy with you."

"Shut up." I smack her in the arm, but the heat in my cheeks tells the truth.

Can't help it. I love a man who knows what he wants. When he goes after it with single-minded determination, I turn into a swoony puddle of goo.

It's true. I like a man who knows how to take charge, but only in the bedroom, and only when I'm in the mood. Meaning, that overprotective shit better not flow into any other part of my life.

The problem with Booker is he's not the kind of man who knows how to turn off his natural protectiveness. His take charge attitude is a 24/7 kind of thing as well.

And I don't respond well to that; except the bedroom.

With my cheeks aflame, I gather my trash and pack up the rest of my lunch.

"I really hate you."

"You love me far too much to hate me."

"I do." I tilt my head back, wanting one last view of the spectacle that is Bravo team.

They're near the top of the sixty-foot artificial rock wall. Not aware of the specific objective of this training exercise, I don't know if they did well or failed. Knowing the way Brady leads his team, and how Booker backs him up, I bet they busted expectations.

Angie and I stand, then police our picnic spot, making sure we leave nothing behind. As we do, my phone rings. I pull out my cellphone and glance at the screen.

"Ugh! Will they ever stop?"

"Your brothers?" Angie's eyes flash with mirth. "Which one?"

"Elder Dingleberry." That's what I call my oldest brother.

He's a decade older than me and likes to think that gives him parental privilege over my life, and my life choices.

He was the loudest when it came to expressing concern when I first joined up with Doctors Without Borders.

I loved that job.

Absolutely *loved* it.

My first nine-month contract found me in the Caribbean where I worked with my team to stamp out parasitic infection, provide live-saving immunizations, and dole out anti-malarials and antibiotics like they were going out of style.

Talk about a dream job.

My life's been blessed. I've never wanted for anything. To give something back to those less fortunate than myself is the golden goose of selfless acts.

My second contract brought me to Nicaragua, and while the first two months were amazing, the abduction thing was less than stellar.

Elder Dingleberry feels that proves his point about how dangerous my work with Doctors Without Borders was. He wants me close to home where he, and the other Dingleberries, can watch over me.

I'm one of those people who believe every cloud has a silver lining. As horrific, and terrifying as that might have been, it brought Angie and me together. Before that event, we were cordial colleagues. We worked side-by-side, but never connected. Now, we're practically inseparable.

We'll still be together when we're old and gray. It's one of those *life-ships*. That's what my mother calls a lifetime friendship. Angie's definitely my life-ship.

Even when she's being a pain in the ass when it comes to Booker.

The hissing of rope running through carabiners snaps my head up in time to see the six Guardians rappelling down that sixty-foot rock face. I don't know how they do it, but they all kick off the wall at the same time, swing out, then gently arc back inward. Their feet touch the wall one time, then they kick off and drop to the ground.

It's like watching water ballet. They're so in synch with each other, it's like they're a living, breathing, machine working in unison.

Since I'm currently holding my breath, I'm going to call it breathtaking, because I'm certainly amazed, impressed, overwhelmed, and a little bit tingly down there. More so when Booker looks my direction and gives one of his devastating winks.

Dear lord, just shoot me now. Because now he knows I've been watching him.

Angie clutches the ring tied around her neckless. Like me, she's breathless and overtaken by these strange emotions.

The ring on that necklace belongs to her late husband. On her finger, however, the diamond engagement ring Brady gave her glitters in the light.

I envy my best friend. She found, not just one, but two soulmates to love. Whereas I've never dated. Never experienced young love—thank you Dingleberries.

No man stands a chance against my brothers.

My phone rings…again.

"Aren't you going to answer?" Angie looks down at my phone.

I swipe away the incoming call with a growl forming in the back of my throat.

"No."

"They'll just keep calling."

Angie's not wrong about that. After our Nicaraguan jungle adventure, we both moved to California. We share a small two bedroom townhouse while we figure out our lives.

In this case, *figure out* means however long Angie's going to make Brady wait to tie the knot for real.

He's always at our place, and where Brady goes, Booker follows. Those two are tight.

All that's to say, Angie hears my phone go off day and night. My brothers are persistent bastards.

"You know…" she gives me a sideways glance. "If you don't talk to them, one of them, if not all four, are going to come out here and drag you home."

"They'd like to think they could." I shove the phone deep into my back pocket.

"All I'm saying is what they've told me."

I forget my brothers text Angie as well. It's a two pronged attack. Annoy me, and my bestie, and one of us will cave.

"You're not answering those texts, are you?" I narrow my eyes with suspicion.

"I wouldn't do that to you." She gives me a look, almost offended, but smoothes it out with a smile. "But I will tell you the texts are getting more and more insistent."

"I'll go home when I go home, and not a minute sooner."

"Hey, I'm on your side. Just telling you what they're saying to me."

I stop and pivot. Grasping her hands, I give them a little squeeze. "And that's what I love about you."

"What?"

"That you put up with my family drama. I regret ever giving them your number. You're a saint for putting up with them."

"It's not that hard to ignore a text."

She gives me a look like I'm over reacting and am overly grateful, but Angie doesn't know my brothers. They're not ones to stop at a text.

"Well, how about we get through the rest of the afternoon. I'll text them when we get home."

"Um, Izzy…" She gives me a look. "You didn't forget, did you?"

"Forget about what?"

"Brady and…"

"Oh shit." I cover my mouth. "I did."

It's Friday night, which means Brady and Booker are coming over for dinner. Since Angie can't cook worth a damn, I volunteered to whip up one of my amazing dishes.

"But that's perfect." My step lightens. "I can talk while I'm cooking. It's a natural kicking them off the phone stopping point."

"Okay, but please no drama with Booker tonight. Will you promise to behave?"

"I always behave." With a shake of my head, I skip a step or two ahead of her. "He's the one who's always putting his foot in his mouth."

"Great…" Angie rolls her eyes. She almost looks disappointed, but she loves me. "You're not going to behave."

"I will if he does."

"Just shoot me now."

There it is. Angie's eyes do a double flip and triple twist with that eye roll.

"What do you care? The moment the food's done, you and Brady are going to get all lovey-dovey, leaving Booker and me to…"

"You could get cozy with him."

"Not happening."

"I'm telling you. The two of you make a nice couple."

"I don't want *nice.*" Nope. That's not what I want at all.

And I'm not wrong about Booker. He's over the top, moving from tolerable to unbearable Alpha asshole in a split second.

Unfortunately, he's exactly the kind of man I'm attracted to.

"THE GUARDIAN HOSTAGE RESCUE SERIES GETS MORE INTENSE with every book." ~ Susan from Goodreads.

"MEET BRAVO TEAM, FORMER MILITARY SPECIAL OPS SOLDIERS turned hostage rescue specialists. With dangerous missions, heroic rescues, nail-biting suspense, and sizzling romance, the entire series is an addictive adrenaline rush from the first page to the last. Fierce protectors, the Guardians are a band of brothers who'll face any danger to rescue those who've been taken."

Get your copy of Rescuing Isabelle HERE.

Please consider leaving a review

I HOPE YOU ENJOYED THIS BOOK AS MUCH AS I ENJOYED WRITING IT. If you like this book, please leave a review. I love reviews. I love reading your reviews, and they help other readers decide if this book is worth their time and money. I hope you think it is and decide to share this story with others. A sentence is all it takes. Thank you in advance!

ELLZ BELLZ

ELLIE'S FACEBOOK READER GROUP

If you are interested in joining the ELLZ BELLZ, Ellie's Facebook reader group, we'd love to have you.

Join Ellie's ELLZ BELLZ.
The ELLZ BELLZ Facebook Reader Group

Sign up for Ellie's Newsletter.
Elliemasters.com/newslettersignup

Also by Ellie Masters

The LIGHTER SIDE

Ellie Masters is the lighter side of the Jet & Ellie Masters writing duo! You will find Contemporary Romance, Military Romance, Romantic Suspense, Billionaire Romance, and Rock Star Romance in Ellie's Works.

YOU CAN FIND ELLIE'S BOOKS HERE:
ELLIEMASTERS.COM/BOOKS

Military Romance
Guardian Hostage Rescue Specialists

Rescuing Melissa

(Get a FREE copy of Rescuing Melissa

when you join Ellie's Newsletter)

Alpha Team

Rescuing Zoe

Rescuing Moira

Rescuing Eve

Rescuing Lily

Rescuing Jinx

Rescuing Maria

Bravo Team

Rescuing Angie

Rescuing Isabelle

Military Romance

Guardian Personal Protection Specialists

Sybil's Protector

The One I Want Series

(Small Town, Military Heroes)

By Jet & Ellie Masters

EACH BOOK IN THIS SERIES CAN BE READ AS A STANDALONE AND IS ABOUT A DIFFERENT COUPLE WITH AN HEA.

Saving Ariel

Saving Brie

Saving Cate

Saving Dani

Saving Jen

Saving Abby

Rockstar Romance

The Angel Fire Rock Romance Series

EACH BOOK IN THIS SERIES CAN BE READ AS A STANDALONE AND IS ABOUT A DIFFERENT COUPLE WITH AN HEA. IT IS RECOMMENDED THEY ARE READ IN ORDER.

Ashes to New (prequel)

Heart's Insanity (book 1)

Heart's Desire (book 2)

Heart's Collide (book 3)

Hearts Divided (book 4)

Hearts Entwined (book5)

Forest's FALL (book 6)

Hearts The Last Beat (book7)

Contemporary Romance

Firestorm

About the Author

Ellie Masters is a USA Today Bestselling author and Amazon Top 15 Author who writes Angsty, Steamy, Heart-Stopping, Pulse-Pounding, Can't-Stop-Reading Romantic Suspense. In addition, she's a wife, military mom, doctor, and retired Colonel. She writes romantic suspense filled with all your sexy, swoon-worthy alpha men. Her writing will tug at your heartstrings and leave your heart racing.

Born in the South, raised under the Hawaiian sun, Ellie has traveled the globe while in service to her country. The love of her life, her amazing husband, is her number one fan and biggest supporter. And yes! He's read every word she's written.

She has lived all over the United States—east, west, north, south and central—but grew up under the Hawaiian sun. She's also been privileged to have lived overseas, experiencing other cultures and making lifelong friends. Now, Ellie is proud to call herself a Southern transplant, learning to say y'all and "bless her heart" with the best of them. She lives with her beloved husband, two children who refuse to flee the nest, and four fur-babies; three cats who rule the household, and a dog who wants nothing other than for the cats to be his best friends. The cats have a different opinion regarding this matter.

Ellie's favorite way to spend an evening is curled up on a couch, laptop in place, watching a fire, drinking a good wine, and bringing forth all the characters from her mind to the page and hopefully into the hearts of her readers.

FOR MORE INFORMATION

elliemasters.com

facebook.com/elliemastersromance

twitter.com/Ellie__Masters

instagram.com/ellie_masters

bookbub.com/authors/ellie-masters

goodreads.com/Ellie_Masters

Connect with Ellie Masters

Website:
elliemasters.com
Amazon Author Page:
elliemasters.com/amazon
Facebook:
elliemasters.com/Facebook
Goodreads:
elliemasters.com/Goodreads
Instagram:
elliemasters.com/Instagram

Final Thoughts

I hope you enjoyed this book as much as I enjoyed writing it. If you enjoyed reading this story, please consider leaving a review on Amazon and Goodreads, and please let other people know. A sentence is all it takes. Friend recommendations are the strongest catalyst for readers' purchase decisions! And I'd love to be able to continue bringing the characters and stories from My-Mind-to-the-Page.

Second, call or e-mail a friend and tell them about this book. If you really want them to read it, gift it to them. If you prefer digital friends, please use the "Recommend" feature of Goodreads to spread the word.

Or visit my blog https://elliemasters.com, where you can find out more about my writing process and personal life.

Come visit The EDGE: Dark Discussions where we'll have a chance to talk about my works, their creation, and maybe what the future has in store for my writing.

Facebook Reader Group: Ellz Bellz

Thank you so much for your support!

Love,

Ellie

Dedication

This book is dedicated to you, my reader. Thank you for spending a few hours of your time with me. I wouldn't be able to write without you to cheer me on. Your wonderful words, your support, and your willingness to join me on this journey is a gift beyond measure.

Whether this is the first book of mine you've read, or if you've been with me since the very beginning, thank you for believing in me as I bring these characters 'from my mind to the page and into your hearts.'

Love,
Ellie

THE END

Printed in Great Britain
by Amazon

45297935R00192